Daniel C. Colesworthy

The Old Bureau

and other tales

Daniel C. Colesworthy

The Old Bureau
and other tales

ISBN/EAN: 9783337345150

Printed in Europe, USA, Canada, Australia, Japan

Cover: Foto ©Andreas Hilbeck / pixelio.de

More available books at **www.hansebooks.com**

AND OTHER TALES.

BY D. C. COLESWORTHY.
||

> Professions are nothing — behavior and actions everything. Acts of obedience, love and mercy are wanted; and nothing else will satisfy the understandings of men, or the purposes of God.
>
> JOHN NEAL.

BOSTON:

ANTIQUE BOOK STORE,

No. 66, CORNHILL.

MDCCCLXI.

STEREOTYPED BY COWLES & COMPANY,
17 WASHINGTON ST., BOSTON.

CONTENTS.

———◆———

THE OLD BUREAU.

CHAPTER I.

Where'er a single human breast
Is crushed by pain or grief,
There I would ever be a guest,
And sweetly give relief.

As I was passing down Exchange Street several years ago, I stopped in front of an auction-room, to examine the various articles that were exposed to be sold under the hammer. I had been there but a few moments, when I heard a female voice inquiring, "Is this old bureau to be sold to-day?" On looking up I perceived the question had been addressed to me by a young lady with a sad but pleasant countenance. I replied that all the articles spread on the sidewalk would be disposed of to the highest bidder.

"I should like this bureau, if it goes low enough," she said, pointing to an old-fashioned article that was standing among the other furniture, "but I never bought any thing at auction in my life, and as I see no woman here, I don't know as it would be proper for me to bid."

"It would be perfectly proper," I remarked; "but if you wish it, I will bid off the bureau."

"If you will, sir, I shall be greatly obliged to you."

"How high are you willing I should go?"

"I don't know exactly how much it is worth, but if it sells for three or four dollars, you may buy it."

"Shall I speak to a handcartman to leave it at your house?"

"No, sir; I will call at noon and settle for it, and have it taken away. I am very much obliged to you for your kindness."

So saying, the young lady went away, leaving me to wonder who she was, and of what use the old piece of furniture could be to her. I examined it, took out the drawers, but saw nothing remarkable about it. At eleven o'clock, when the auction commenced, I was present, and, after waiting nearly an hour, the auctioneer remarked, "We will now sell the bureau, what will you give, gentlemen?" One man offered two dollars, another three, and I bid a half-dollar more. Four dollars were bid — four and a half, and five dollars. I was astonished that the old thing should bring so high a price. What could I do? See it sold, and disappoint the lady? The thought struck me that it might have belonged to some friend, and she wished to purchase it on that account, and, rather than disappoint her, I resolved to bid again. Six dollars were offered, by another, to my utter astonishment; but when our hand is in, and we wish for an article, we seldom let another outbid us; and so I offered, until the old bureau was run up to ten dollars, and I purchased it for half a dollar more. Certainly, I would not have given four dollars for it to use myself. However, I bought it, and had it sent to my room, telling the auctioneer, if a lady should call for it to inform her where it might be found. I examined it again and again, and began to regret my purchase, feeling almost certain that the young woman would not thank me for what I had done; but I never mourn over a bad bargain; my philosophy will not permit me to do so.

A little after dusk, as I was sitting in my sanctum, the young lady came in with an apology for intruding, and remarked, "You bought the bureau, so the auctioneer informs me."

"Yes, I bought it, but at an extravagant price, I assure you."

"What did you give?"

"Ten dollars and a half."

"You astonish me. What can I do? I had no idea that it would bring over three or four dollars, and am not prepared to pay for it to-night."

"I suppose it was foolish in me to give so much for it, but I presumed you wanted it very much."

"I did, sir, and would not value paying double the amount for the bureau, if I were able, rather than not to have it."

"So I apprehended. Perhaps it may have belonged to some friend of yours?"

"Yes, sir; that bureau was once my mother's"—and I noticed a tear come in her eye which she endeavored to conceal—"but she is dead now, and I wished to keep it in remembrance of her."

Thinking the lady might be poor, I told her she might take the bureau that night if she wished, and pay me for it when she found it convenient.

"I am greatly obliged to you for your kindness; but would rather that you should keep it until it is paid for."

I urged her to take it, but she refused, saying—"I will see what I can do, and call upon you in a day or two," and bidding us good-evening, she left us.

There is something very mysterious about this woman, thought I. It may be that she is poor, and in
very destitute circumstances. But she shows an excellent heart, and the warmest attachment to a deceased
mother. Her education must have been good, and she
has evidently seen better days. And I thought the
next time she should call upon me, I would ascertain
something more of her character and circumstances—
perhaps her name—which I felt deeply anxious to
learn.

In a day or two the young woman called upon me again,
and with tears in her eyes, remarked, "I don't know
what you will think of me, but all the money I have in
the world is five dollars; this I have brought you towards the bureau you were so kind as to purchase for
me." So saying, she placed the money before me in
silver.

"I shall not take the money at present," I remarked,
"I can do without it, you may take the bureau, if you
want it, and when you are able, at some future time,
you may pay me."

She expressed a great deal of gratitude, and said, "I
should rather you would take what I have." And nothing I could say would induce her to receive the money
again.

"You appear to have seen some affliction?" I remarked, as I saw the tears in her eyes.

"Not much, sir; I must confess that I have not always been as poor as I am at present; for I have seen
better days. When my parents were living, I never
knew what it was to want for any thing; now I cannot say so."

"How long have your parents been dead?"

"About six years since, my father died; and it was four years ago last Saturday when my mother was buried."

At the mention of her mother's name, the tears came fast to her eyes — a tender chord was touched; I saw it, and made no more inquiries, and she took her leave.

It was nearly six weeks before I saw the young lady again. She then called upon me with the remainder of the money that I had paid for the bureau.

I protested against receiving it at that time, thinking it might have been inconvenient for her to pay it; but she insisted that I should have it, saying, "I am under great obligations to you for your kindness. Had it not been for you, I should have lost the bureau, the only relic of my mother; for it was then impossible for me to raise the amount you so generously paid. I shall never forget your kindness."

"Do you wish to take the bureau away?"

"I have spoken to a cartman, who will call here in a short time, and have it removed out of your way; for I suppose you will be glad to get rid of it."

"Not at all. I am pleased that I was instrumental in doing you a little service, and if ever you need assistance, I shall always be as ready to render it."

"I thank you, sir, with all my heart."

At this moment, the man came for the bureau, and, bidding me good-evening, the young lady left my room.

CHAPTER II.

I ask a lowly cot,
  With sweet content within,
  Where Envy shall molest me not,
  Nor Pride shall tempt to sin.

" Going, going — will you give but two dollars for this excellent bureau ? " — exclaimed Mr. Bailey, the auctioneer, a year or two since, as I was passing down Exchange Street. " Here, Mr. C." he said, turning to me, " buy this bureau ; it is cheap enough ; it is worth more for kindling-wood than it is going for — just look at it — going, going — say quick, or you lose it."

Two dollars and fifty cents, I bid, as I saw that it was the very same bureau that I had bought several years before for ten and a half dollars, and the bureau was knocked off to me.

This is singular enough, thought I, as I had the article carried to my room. Where is the young woman who formerly owned it? Who was she ?

I made several inquiries, but could not ascertain who she was or what had become of her. The bureau had been carried to the auction-room by an individual whom Mr. Bailey never saw before, and all my inquiries to ascertain what became of the young lady seemed fruitless.

Several months passed by, and still I heard nothing of the young lady, when one day, not knowing but I might get some clue to the former owner, I took out all the drawers separately, and examined them. I saw no writing whatever. In the back of the under drawer, I noticed that a small piece of pine had been

inserted. It looked as if it had been done to stop a
defect. Prying it with a knife, it came out, when to
my astonishment I found several gold pieces, to the
value of about fifty dollars, besides a note for twenty-
five hundred dollars, with interest, value received, made
payable to Sarah —— when she should become of age ;
it was a witnessed note, and had been running about
a dozen years, signed by a very wealthy man, whose
reputation for honesty was not exceedingly good. Without mentioning to a single individual what I had discovered, I immediately renewed my efforts to ascertain who Sarah —— was, and where she could be found.
I learned that a girl of this name formerly lived with
a Capt. P——, and did the work of the kitchen. Of
him I could obtain but little information. His wife
recollected the girl, and spoke of her in the highest
terms. She believed she had married a mechanic, and
retired from the city, but his name she could not remember. By repeated inquiries, I ascertained that
Sarah, with her husband, lived on a small farm on the
road that leads from Portland to Saco. Taking an
early opportunity, I started for the residence of the
young woman. After several inquiries upon the road,
I was directed to the house. It was a pleasant situation, a little in from the road, and every thing looked
neat about the dwelling. As I drove up to the cottage who should come to the door but the very woman
I had been so long anxious to find. She recognized me
at once.

" Why Mr. C——, how glad I am to see you ! Where
in the world did you come from ? Walk in and take
a seat."

Her husband was present—an intelligent looking man—to whom she presented me.

"I have often thought of you," she remarked, "and when in Portland have been tempted to call and see you; but although I have not called, be assured I have not forgotten your kindness, and I never shall forget it."

"But you seem happier than when I last saw you."

"Be assured, sir, I am. My husband has hired this little farm, where we have resided for the last two years, and we make a comfortable living, and are as happy as we could wish. In the course of a few years, if we have our health and prosper, we are in hopes to purchase the farm."

"What does the owner value it at?"

"He values it at about fifteen hundred dollars. We have had to purchase a great many farming things, or we should have made a payment towards it."

"But what has become of your bureau?"

"I fear I shall never see it again," she replied, and after a pause said—"I believe I have never told you how I have been situated?"

"You never did."

"When my mother died, it was thought she left some property in the hands of an uncle of mine, that would come to me when I became of age; but he said it was not the case. With him I resided a short time."

"Was your uncle's name ——," said I, mentioning the individual who had signed the note in my possession.

"Yes, sir—that was his name. He was very unkind to me—made me work so hard, and was so cross, that I was obliged to leave him, and earn my living by doing the work of a kitchen girl. One day I learned that he was about to dispose of what little property my mother had left, to pay an old debt of hers. As soon as I found it was correct, I immediately went to the auction-room, and found it too true. You know about the bureau, the only article of my mother's property I could purchase — and had it not been for your kindness, it would have gone with the rest. The money I paid you was earned in the kitchen. As I found it inconvenient to carry the bureau with me, I asked my aunt's permission to put it in her garret, which permission she granted. On calling for it when I was married, I learned that my uncle had disposed of it with some other things at auction. I would rather have lost a hundred dollars; not that the piece of furniture possessed any real value, but it belonged to my beloved mother" (a tear came in the poor woman's eye), "and on that account I did not wish to part with it. But it was gone, and it was useless to speak to my uncle about it; he was entirely indifferent about me and whatever concerned me."

"Suppose I shall tell you that I have now that bureau in my office."

"Is it possible! You astonish me, Mr. C——. Have you, indeed, the old bureau?"

"I have, and what is better, I have something for you here" — taking out my pocket-book, and placing the gold and note on the table — "these are yours."

"Why, sir, you more and more astonish me."

"They are yours. After I became the owner of the bureau, I found this gold and this note concealed in one of the drawers. There are nearly fifty dollars, and the note is good against your uncle, for nearly three thou-

2

sand dollars — every cent of which you can recover, as he is abundantly able to pay."

The astonished young lady could not speak for some moments; but when she recovered from her surprise, she only expressed her gratitude in tears; nay, more, she urged me to take half the amount; but I utterly refused, telling her that it pleased me more to have justice done to her, and be instrumental in adding to the happiness of those I considered so worthy as herself and husband, than to be the possessor of millions.

When I left, I promised to call on her soon again, and, in the mean time, to make arrangements for her to receive her just dues from her unworthy uncle.

When I called upon Mr. ——, the uncle of Sarah, and made known to him the object of my interview, he was disposed to treat the matter with indifference; but when I told him of the consequences of his refusal to do justice to a poor relative, when his course and conduct should be made known, he at once acceded to my proposals and immediately made arrangements for the payment of the note and interest — begging me not to expose him to the world — which I have never done — believing as I sincerely do, that he has heartily repented of his course, and is now a better and a wiser man!

Sarah's husband purchased the farm on which he resided, stocked it well, and is now an independent farmer. It is difficult to find two happier souls than Sarah and her companion. May prosperity attend them to the close of life.

I often call at the farmhouse of my friends, and spend there many a happy hour. It was but a week or two since that I saw them, and they were cheerful, and seemed perfectly contented and happy.

JUDGING FROM APPEARANCES.

It is not those who make a boast
  Of generous deeds which they perform,
Who for the needy do the most,
  And find them shelter in the storm.
In humble life meek virtues spring, —
  To glad the heart, to bless and cheer, —
That never fly on eagle's wing,
  Or on the printed page appear.

" THERE goes old Jacobs, the mean man!" exclaimed a young person to his companion, as he was standing in the door of a shop.

" Who is old Jacobs?" inquired his friend.

" Have you lived in town six months, and never heard of the fellow before? He is one of the meanest fellows in the place. He saves every cent he gets, and hoards it up, but for what purpose no one can tell, as he has but two children and they are well enough off. And his dress shows what the man is. He buys the meanest cloth, and looks like a lumper."

" What's the fellow worth?"

" That's more than I can tell. Some rate him at a hundred and fifty thousand dollars, some less. But there's no telling what the man is worth. But his meanness makes him notorious, no one respects him. Why, he was never known to give a cent to any charitable institution, and the poor might starve, for aught he would care."

Mr. Jacobs was a man of some seventy years of age. He commenced life a poor boy, but had contrived to rake together quite a fortune. By those who had been less successful in business, he was accused of all sorts of trickery and deception. It was said that but little of his property was accumulated by strict honesty. At the time of which we speak, his wife had been dead several years, and both of his children were settled in life. Mr. Jacobs attracted some attention — being somewhat singular in his own dress and appearance. There was nothing like pride about him ; he purchased for his own use that kind of clothing which he thought would wear the longest, without regard to the prevailing fashions of the day. Whenever a subscription was raised for a benevolent object, Mr. Jacobs was the last person called upon. It was currently reported that he never gave a cent for any benevolent object whatever.

During one severe winter, a fire broke out in town, and consumed the dwellings of many of the poorer class. The charitable portion of the community raised a subscription for their relief, and many dollars were contributed by the wealthy, and by men in moderate circumstances. At this time, a gentleman called upon Mr. Jacobs, and requested a few dollars from him. After hearing what the man had to say, he remarked,

"I cannot put my name down, you know I never do."

"Isn't it your duty to give something to aid the suffering, Mr. Jacobs?" said the gentleman.

"Perhaps it may be; but suppose I don't choose to give any thing?"

"Put down a couple of dollars, you will be none the poorer for it."

"No, sir; I will not put my name down for a single cent."

The gentleman left him, remarking to himself, "Old Jacobs is the meanest man I ever came across. He is not worthy to live in civilized society."

And he didn't fail to express his opinion wherever he went. Stepping into the store of a merchant, he received a dollar from him, and then he related his interview with Mr. Jacobs.

"He is a wretched mean man, I know," said the merchant, "you can't tell me any thing about him. I never knew him to give away a cent in my life; and I have known him full five and thirty years. The children may beg at his door — the poor widow may entreat, and the suffering may beseech him, but in vain. They get nothing for their pains. I'm glad there are some men with souls in our community. But for them there would be a world of suffering."

"Did I show you the letter that I received this morning — the letter that contained the money?"

"No. What money?"

"I received a letter through the post-office that contained one hundred dollars for the relief of the sufferers."

"Indeed! from whom did it come?"

"I cannot imagine; the only signature was S——. He is a benevolent man, whoever he may be."

"What a contrast to old Jacobs!"

"The writer of the letter has a whole soul, but as for Jacobs', it would dance on the point of a needle."

"True, he is a mean wretch."

The gentleman, after going the rounds of his district to obtain funds for the sufferers, found that he had

2*

collected several hundred dollars, which were equally
distributed among the unfortunate.

A poor widow was called upon, and several dollars
given to her. She expressed her gratitude in tears, saying—

"I have not a stick of wood to burn, and scarcely
any thing to eat in the house, and but for your kindness, I should have suffered.   I always find that the
Lord raises up friends and will not let me suffer.
About three years ago, I lived in one of old Jacobs'
houses, and you know how particular he is to have the
rent paid on the day it is due.   My quarter's rent was
due; the money was ready, but I had nothing to eat in
the house.   I was out of meat and potatoes, and had
but a dozen sticks of wood.   Mr. Jacobs called for his
rent.   I told him my situation, and asked him to take
one-half, and loan me the balance for a few days.   He
refused, saying he must have all that was due to him.
I gave him every cent I had; but the unfeeling man
only gave me a receipt, and left me.   I never felt worse
in my life; I had scarcely any thing to eat in the house,
and nothing to buy bread with.   But the Lord was
good to me then, as he has been ever since.   Just before
nine o'clock, somebody knocked at the door.   It was a
cartman.   He said he was directed to leave the articles
in his cart at my house.   I thought it was a mistake.
But he had particular directions, he said, and would
not carry them away.   I asked him who sent him, but
he said he did not know nor care, since he had got the
job, and was paid for it.   There was a half-barrel of
flour, a leg of bacon, a bushel of potatoes, some sugar
and tea; and I assure you, sir, no person was ever more
grateful.   Who the benevolent man was that remem-

bored me, I never knew, and probably never shall.
The present you have given me reminds me of the past.
A thousand thanks for your kindness ; Heaven will re-
ward you."

From every source the character of the old miser Jacobs received a.severe handling. Rich men and poor,
the widow and the orphan, were of opinion alike in
this respect. He had but few friends, and seldom associated with his neighbors. There were a few individuals who were as mean as Jacobs — but they were not
as wealthy — with whom he appeared to be on intimate
terms. From the earliest recollections of those who
had lived by his side a half-century, he was always considered close and penurious. Whenever he was owing
an individual, however, it was always noticed that he
paid promptly ; but this was no virtue. He had the
means of settling every demand. His town tax and
his pew tax were paid on presentation of the bill, but
when there was a contribution in the society to which
he belonged, the deacons always noticed that he never
put into the box more than a half-dime, and this
amount he never failed to give, whatever might be the
object of the contribution.

In the neighborhood where Mr. Jacobs resided, there
lived a young man by the name of Edward Mason.
His parents were poor ; but, when quite a lad, he devoted much of his time to reading and study. The old
miser appeared to feel some interest in young Edward,
and repeatedly remarked that he would make a smart
man. Although the young man was in humble circumstances, Mr. Jacobs never offered to give him a dollar, or otherwise assist him.

One morning as Mason was passing along the street,

a gentleman with whom he was slightly acquainted,
stopped him and inquired if he would not like to enter
college.

"I should," said the boy, "but my parents are not
able to give me an education."

"I think, as you take to learning, that a classical education will be of great advantage to you. For some
days I have thought on the subject, and now I'll tell
you what I propose to do. If you will continue diligent in your studies, I will procure the necessary funds
and have you enter college."

Edward thanked his friend, at the same time remarking: —

"I did hope Mr. Jacobs would render me some little
assistance; but now I have no hopes of him. He is almost too mean to live, as every one knows."

Young Mason continued his studies, and when prepared, he entered college — his friend furnishing the
necessary means. His vacations were spent at home
with his parents, and occasionally he called upon his
old friend Jacobs, whom he found to be as sociable as
ever to him. But gradually he became weaned from
the miser, and took occasion to speak disrespectfully of
him. During one of the vacations, he called upon the
old gentleman, and contrived to pin a piece of paper to
his back, on which was written, "I am a miser!" As
Mr. Jacobs passed along the streets he heard much
laughter, but did not suspect the cause till he called
into a merchant's counting-room, who, seeing the paper,
pointed it out to him.

"This is some of Mason's doings," said the old gentleman. "He should have more respect for me, and
feel that I am too far advanced in life to be trifled with."

Ever after this circumstance, Edward was shy of the old gentleman, but he was free to condemn his niggardly course and miserly disposition. When he was with his associates, and Mr. Jacobs happened to pass along, he would fling out some improper remark, that caused a laugh at the old man's expense. Finally, Mason graduated, studied law, and commenced practice in his native town. He had brass enough to be a good lawyer, and impudence sufficient to succeed. Edward had not been in practice but a year or two, before he was engaged in a case in which Mr. Jacobs was an interested party. Mason was opposed to him. In his plea he was very severe upon the old gentleman. He touched upon his mean and niggardly behavior, which had become notorious for a long series of years, and accused him of being any thing but an upright man. He had never been known to be generous in a single instance; just like a sponge, he was constantly drawing in, but letting nothing out.

"Everybody," he continued, "in this vicinity, has heard of his disposition; even the children shun him. If I should repeat one-half the follies and meannesses that are laid to his door, most of which are true, I have no doubt you, gentleman of the jury, would be astonished beyond measure. But I will not rake up the past. In the present case you have heard the evidence on both sides, and, if you have an iota of common sense, you cannot hesitate in whose favor to decide."

Notwithstanding the plea of Esquire Mason, the jury decided in favor of Mr. Jacobs.

Having the name of being a hard character, no one seemed to put any confidence in him, and his enemies often resorted to the entanglements of the law, depending mostly upon his unpopularity for their success; but they were often defeated.

The name of Jacobs became so notorious on account of his reputation for meanness, that no one pretended to call upon him for charitable purposes. He was known as the rich miser, and likened unto Dives of old.

He had lived to the common age of man and longer, and the period drew nigh when he must give up the ghost. The old gentleman was taken sick, but he was calm and collected. His minister called upon him often, and from the tenor of his conversation, appeared to feel a deep interest in him.

"I have not long to live," said Mr. Jacobs to his pastor, "and I know not but I am willing to go. I have spent many years, and I hope I have not spent them in vain. I trust I have done some little good, and I hope I may do some more."

The minister was struck with astonishment at his language. "He must be wandering," said he to himself. "Everybody knows that he has been oppressive to the poor, and saved every mill that came into his hands."

"This is a wearisome life," continued the sick man, "and we are not rightly judged. Our motives few can understand. They are deceived in us."

" True," replied the pastor, "man cannot look into the heart of his neighbor."

"Thus far I have endeavored to live a useful life, and I hope to be at rest in heaven; not on account of my own righteousness, but I trust in the mercy of God."

Just as the pastor was about to reply, Mr. Jacobs said, —

"As I do not expect to continue long in the world, I wish to entrust to your care several papers, which you will find in a small trunk in my desk. The keys are lying on the window."

The minister assured him he would do as requested, and took the trunk from the desk.

In a day or two after, the old gentleman died and was buried. It was singular to hear the remarks that were made after his decease. "He was no benefit to any one while he lived," one remarked, "and I am not sorry he is dead." "He was an old reprobate," said another, "and the Devil has got him at last." "His whole life was worse than a blank," remarked a third, "and no one regrets that the old fellow is dead."

Mr. Jacobs had been dead but a few days when the minister of the parish called some of his friends together to examine the contents of the trunk, for there, they were led to suppose, his will was deposited, and other important documents.

Judge of the surprise of the gentlemen when, on opening the papers, they found that, for the last fifteen years of his life, Mr. Jacobs had distributed annually from fifteen hundred to two thousand dollars among the poor of his native place! There were the documents and receipts to show this fact. He had gone through the city unknown and in disguise, and distributed his money where he found want and poverty. It was he who sent the money in a letter to the gentleman who solicited charity of him, with such apparent ill-success, when so many became homeless on account of a disastrous fire. It was he who sent the poor widow the flour, tea, etc., after she had paid her rent. It

was he who had repeatedly sent to benevolent societies
hundreds of dollars through the post-office ; and it was
he, too, who furnished the means of educating Edward
Mason, the lawyer, who treated him so unhandsomely.
He spent many hundred dollars for his benefit. After
leaving a few thousand dollars apiece to his sons, in his
will, the remainder of his property, amounting to about
one hundred thousand dollars, was to be kept as a per-
manent fund, the interest of which was to be distributed yearly among the poor of his native city.

When these facts were announced, the current of
public opinion changed. He whom they looked upon as
a mean wretch, now appeared little less than an angel,
and no language was too exalted to speak of the public
benefactor.

On a further examination of his papers, they found
hundreds of little slips of various dates for more than
two score years back, for cash received of A, B, C, etc.,
for various sums of from five to a hundred dollars
each. Thus had this gentleman gone about, and in secret distributed his money, helping the sad and de-
sponding — while hundreds were denouncing him —
pointing the finger of scorn and calling him every bad
name they could think of. He suffered the reproach and
contumely of his fellow-citizens without a murmuring
word, and from those, too, who had received countless
favors from his hand.

After his death, everybody was anxious to do justice to the man, who, when living, all pretended to despise ; and no one exerted himself more than young Mason, the lawyer. A large monument was erected over
his sleeping body, on which was inscribed his name and

age, and the day of his death, with the following line beneath : —

"JUDGE NOT FROM APPEARANCES."

Since the death of Mr. Jacobs, the inhabitants of the town in which he lived have been extremely careful how they judge their fellow-creatures. If a man has the appearance of being mean and miserly, and a word is lisped to his discredit, a dozen voices will exclaim, "Don't judge him till he is dead — remember old Jacobs." The old are respected and revered. No young man, for many a year, has been known to speak a disrespectful word to the gray-headed and infirm. The singular life of Mr. Jacobs has exerted a happy influence throughout the place, and hundreds every year, who receive comforts from the interest of the property he left, speak of him with tears of affection. His memory will never die.

3

THE WAY OF THE WORLD.

'Tis not true wisdom to subdue
A foe beneath our feet;
To cause the heart where virtue grew
To practise base deceit;
To plant within the happy breast
A thought to give it pain;
Or enter circles pure and blest
An impious end to gain.

In the thrifty town of N——, resided a gentleman
by the name of Jones. He was a trader, and, through
a series of prosperous years, had accumulated a large
amount of property. When a young man, he was seriously disposed, and became a professor of religion.
As his piety had never been questioned by his brethren
of the church, he always continued a communicant.
In the common acceptation of the term, he was a Christian. Within a stone's throw of Mr. Jones' residence,
in a neat but humble dwelling, resided a gentleman by
the name of Watson. He, also, was a trader, and did
business in the same street with his neighbor. This man
made no pretensions to goodness; was not a professor
of religion, but attended meeting at the same church
with Mr. Jones. His circumstances were humble, and,
though he attended well to his business, he did not prosper as his neighbor. Mr. Watson belonged to that class
of men who are called sinners — the world's people — in

distinction from those who have united themselves with some Christian church

We have said Mr. Jones prospered in his business. Those who were professors with him — of the like faith — always purchased their articles at his store — and when their friends from the country were in want of goods, Mr. Jones was invariably recommended as a safe man to deal with, and one who kept articles of a superior quality — "For," said they, "he is a member of our church." The minister also patronized him.

Thus Mr. Jones prospered and made money fast. He usually charged a heavy price and made a large profit on his articles. Very few were disposed to ask a reduction from his prices. The trader was stern, and to request him to take less than he asked was equal to saying that he charged too high for his goods. It was generally sufficient to know that he was a professor, to place implicit confidence in all that he did. If it were whispered, by any one, that Jones did not deal fairly, and that he took advantage of his customers, the church silenced the suspicions by their creed, which took none to its bosom, who were not perfectly honest and trustworthy.

The professor was never absent from his pew on the sabbath, and at evening lectures he was a constant attendant. Here he was very active. Seldom would he attend a conference meeting where he was not called upon to read a portion of Scripture, give an exhortation, make a prayer, or select a hymn to be sung. Having unlimited confidence in his own abilities, Jones seldom excused himself. He would beseech sinners to give their hearts to God, not to love the world, nor the things of the world, but, by a consistent Christian life, pursue the path to heaven. His voice was clear and distinct, and, with perfect command of himself, whatever he said gave perfect satisfaction to the whole church.

Morning and night he assembled his family, read a chapter from the Bible, and then offered prayer. He was very punctual in attending to his religious duties, and never on any occasion, neglected to perform them.

Jones was a selfish man, however, and seemed to dislike those who were in the same business with himself, and used his strongest endeavors to prevent purchasers from trading with them. But no man did he seem to dislike more than his good neighbor. If a member of his church was known to buy of Watson he would mention the circumstance to two or three of the brethren, that they might look into it — " For," said Jones, " we are like children of one family — we should strive to promote each other's temporal as well as spiritual welfare. I patronize the brethren, and it is but just that I should be patronized by them.

No one disputed his argument, and the offender was persuaded to do right the next time, and strive to pursue that course which would be likely to give the least offence to a brother.

It was with difficulty that Watson, by strict attention to his business and economy in his family, could succeed. The church and society threw all their patronage in the hands of their wealthy brother, while he had to depend almost entirely on transient custom. But he did not murmur, and always treated his neighbor with respect. When a purchaser could not be suited at his store, he would invariably send him to Mr. Jones.

Watson was modest and unassuming in his conduct. His pew was in a humble place in the church, his family were neat but not extravagant in their attire, he was constant in his attendance on public worship, and gave good attention to what was preached. He felt himself to be a sinner, and the tear of sorrow for disobedience to the just commands of God, would often trickle down his cheek. Daily he read the Scriptures and daily offered his secret prayer, in thankfulness and praise, to his Father above.

Whenever a poor man came to his door, or an orphan solicited charity at his hand, his heart was ready to give relief. He would visit the sick and distressed, and do all in his power to alleviate their sorrows and their sufferings. The weary and the faint never went unblest from his presence.

Jones, on the contrary, was selfish and mean. He had driven so many poor and destitute from his door, that but few ventured to solicit charity of him. When a subscription paper was handed round to send missionaries to the heathen, or to support a school at Owyhee, he invariably put his name down for a few dollars. But he never visited the sick or the widow, excepting they were professors and members of his church, and then he would pray with them, and inquire if they were prepared to die — and comfort their poverty by informing them they should receive assistance from the parish — and perhaps go away and not mention their case. His family were dressed in the best the market could afford, and a spirit of pride was encouraged and fostered in his children. They were brought up to look rather with contempt than love on those who were beneath them. When of sufficient age, he sent his two sons to college. "It is my determination," he said, "that they

3*

shall be preachers of the gospel." With feeble talents, unbounded ambition, and unrestrained pride, they had but poor recommendations to the devoted life of a truly Christian minister. But it is a humiliating truth that we have more ministers of this description at the present day, than any other class. Rich professors deem no life so honorable as a preacher's, and being abundantly able, their children pass through college and come forth ministers, as destitute of the true requirements of a godly minister as it is possible for men to be. It is such who spend their lives in wrangling on doctrinal points — cause dissensions — and make the ministry a hissing and a reproach throughout the whole world.

During one year that business was dull, Mr. Watson had neglected to pay his pew tax, when it was due. Being called upon, he stated to the collector that he was unable to cancel the debt at present, but before many days he would pay it. A few weeks went by and on meeting the collector, Watson informed him that his tax money was now ready. To his utter astonishment, the gentleman replied, " Your pew was sold yesterday for the taxes."

" Indeed ! and who purchased it ? "

" Your neighbor, Mr. Jones."

" But has Mr. Jones paid his last year's taxes yet ? "

" Why — no — but he is good for them at any time."

Watson was grieved at this treatment, because he had never refused to pay his taxes, but merely put it off a few weeks, till it was more convenient. Instead of being angry and saying as perhaps Jones would, in such a case — " He may have my pew, he is welcome to it, I will hire a pew in some other church " — he went to Mr. Jones to purchase it again.

"You may have the pew," said the professor, "by paying me five dollars in advance of what I gave."

"But you are aware, Mr. Jones, I knew nothing of the matter. I would never have permitted it to be sold for that."

"I can't help that, Mr. Watson. The pew was sold and I bought it. If you will give me five dollars more than I paid for it, you may have it, if not I will rent it. There are three or four who have spoken to me about it already. You can do as you please."

"Well, rather than lose the pew, I will give you what you ask, although I do not think it right for you to take it."

"What! accuse me of doing wrong? I am astonished at you, Mr. Watson. I can get double for the pew at any time."

Without multiplying words, the poor man paid him what he asked and was once more the owner of a pew.

Time passed on, and the Christian and the sinner continued their business. The former adding wealth to wealth, while the latter continued poor. One was proud and overbearing — the other meek and condescending. One loved the praise of men — the other was ambitious for the praise of God. As usual, the church and society patronized the wealthy Jones, while they passed by the humble Watson.

One morning, quite early, the professor called at the store of his neighbor, informing him that he had purchased a lot of excellent land for two dollars an acre.

"As you find it rather difficult to get along," said Jones, "I will sell you half this land — about a thousand acres — on which you can double your money."

"But I am unable to buy land at present. I find it

exceedingly difficult to collect money enough to pay my just debts."

"No matter for that. I don't want the money at present. I will take your note on six and nine months, and, in the mean time, you can sell the land and double your money."

Here was strong temptation to Watson; but when he considered the dangers of speculation, and that the Bible said, that those who would suddenly become rich, should have many snares he replied, "I think, sir, I will have nothing to do with the land."

"You are unwise, very. Now here is a chance for you to make money — and make it, too, in an honorable way. If you neglect this opportunity, you may never have another."

"But suppose we should not sell the land, where could I raise the money?"

"Don't let that trouble you; I will see that all is right."

After a great deal of persuasion, Mr. Watson was induced to take the land and give his notes. He trusted altogether to his neighbor, who informed him that he knew the land to be worth more than double what he gave for it, and there was no doubt they would both realize a handsome profit.

A few days after this transaction, Mr. Watson was informed by a friend that the land he had bought of the professor was almost valueless, — that it was not actually worth one dollar an acre — and that was all that Mr. Jones had given for it. Watson could hardly believe that he had been so deceived, and on inquiring of his neighbor, he made it appear that all was right, and it would so prove in the end. But still Watson was fearful of the consequences, because he knew very well that he was unable to meet the notes when they became due, unless the land was sold.

Six months passed away, and the property was unsold; but Watson was told not to give himself any trouble, that perhaps they might dispose of it before long. He felt easy, thinking his neighbor would not present the notes unless the land was sold. But he was mistaken. At the end of the nine months, both notes were presented for payment.

"It is impossible for me to raise the money," said Watson.

"But you must dispose of some of your property," said Jones, "for I want my pay, and must have it."

He was reminded of the transaction, but Jones did not seem to recollect any thing further than this, that he was to pay the notes when they became due. His neighbor left him, and the next day he received notice of an attachment upon his house for two thousand dollars and costs of attachment. In vain did Watson see and converse with Jones. He could get no satisfaction. He owed him fairly, and he must have his pay.

"But you will have to sacrifice the house, for nobody will give what it is worth in these hard times."

"I can't help that. You must get some friend who has money to bid it in."

"I have no friend with that amount who can spare it at present. I know not what course to pursue, if I am turned out of the house."

"Oh, you will do well enough. You have money and friends, too — I will risk you anywhere."

When the church heard what Jones had done, they censured Watson for entering the land speculation. "It

is on account of his own folly that he is about to lose
his house.   If people will speculate with the expectation
of making money, they must suffer the consequences."

Nothing was said to the professor.   He was rich — in
regular standing with them — a brother in the church —
and could not do wrong.

The day of the sale had arrived, and the notes were
not taken care of.   Once more Watson called on his
neighbor to beg of him not to sacrifice the property, or
to turn him out of doors.   "For you know when I
bought the land, I was urged to take it against my will.
It was only the promise that I should not be troubled
that induced me to sign the notes."

"A likely story, Mr. Watson.   You know I want my
pay.   Whenever I sign notes, I expect to meet them,
and should do it, even though I had to sacrifice all my
property."

"But what can I do ?   I have a large family on my
hands ; and it is only by prudence that I am able to get
along without getting in debt.   The times, you know,
are exceedingly hard."

"The house must be sold, and there is an end of it.
'Tis no use to whine to death because necessity compels
us to give up our property.   'Tis better to meet it like
a Christian "— and so saying, he walked away.

The hour for the sale arrived, and the people had
gathered.   The first bid for the house was made by a
friend of Jones, whom he had probably employed to
buy it in.   One hundred dollars after another was bid,
until the sum reached to two thousand and twenty dollars.   And that was the bid of Jones' friend.   Just as
the auctioneer was striking his hammer for the last
time, a young man was seen coming up the street.

Just in time, he bid fifty dollars more, and now the contest was between him and Jones' friend; finally, the house was knocked off to the young man for three thousand dollars.

"Whose is it?" inquired the auctioneer.

"Charles Mason's," said the young man, and a frown was on the brow of Jones.

"What does this mean?" said he to the young man.

Without deigning to reply, "Mr. Watson!" said the purchaser—and the poor man stepped to him, weeping —"Mr. Watson, I have bought this house—it was taken from you by the spirit of avarice—I now make you a present of it—the house is yours."

The poor man fell on the neck of the young man, and embraced him, and wept like a child, while the spectators gathered round, unable to solve the mystery.

"Charles Mason," said Jones, as soon as Watson arose, "you are no longer worthy of my confidence, and from this time I forbid you an entrance to my house."

"Wretch! begone!" exclaimed the young man, "you will yet receive the just reward of your oppression."

Amid the hisses of a few, the professor hurried away, muttering something which could not be heard, but his anger was seen to be at its highest pitch.

"Come with me, my benefactor, my best friend," at last said Watson through his tears, and the young man followed him to the house.

The family were weeping. "Dry your tears and bless God," said the husband and father, as he closed the door, and bid the young man be seated.

"To this gentleman we owe every thing; he has bought the house—but, O sir, explain the mystery."

"You know, Mr. Watson," said Charles, "that I have been in the store of Mr. Jones for many years. I am knowing to much of his strange conduct, but I am well acquainted with the course he has pursued towards you — the manner in which he wronged you. I could not endure to see a poor man brought into difficulty, and then turned out of doors by the avarice of one who pretends to be a Christian. Sir, it is your self-denying, Christian conduct and his spirit of evil, that has moved me to thwart his designs, and make you still happy in your dwelling. It is yours. The deed I have done since I have entered this room, has made me the happiest of men."

There was not a dry eye present. The family gathered around their benefactor, and expressed their gratitude upon their knees, invoking the blessing of Heaven upon him — nor would they permit him to depart without his assurance that he would call and see them on the following day.

Charles Mason was the son of a rich man, who left him at his decease several thousand dollars, which was now at interest. He had spent several years in the store of Mr. Jones, to whom he had loaned part of his money. The next day, on calling upon him, he was coolly received.

"I have no further use for your services," said he. "Such conduct as yours merits my sovereign contempt."

"Your conduct, sir, and I do not hesitate to say it, is as far removed from that enjoined by Him you profess to serve, as heaven is from hell. It must be despised by all honorable men."

"Enough of your sauciness; let me have no more of it, or you shall leave the shop instantly."

"Mr. Jones, but give me a draft for what is due me, and I will trouble you no more."

As Jones handed it to him, he exclaimed, "Begone, you wretch!" and the noble youth walked away without deigning to notice his remark.

Charles immediately settled for the house he had purchased — took a deed of the land — and put the balance of his property into the stock of Mr. Watson, and entered into copartnership with him.

Day by day their business increased. Since Charles left Jones, many of the old customers had followed him to the new store, and now gave him their trade. They had as much as they could do. The conduct of Jones was spoken of and despised by all, while the noble course of the young man was commended as worthy of all praise.

A twelvemonth did not elapse after the young man went into business with Watson, before he led to the altar as gentle and lovely a creature as ever breathed. It was Eliza Watson, the daughter of the kind and benevolent man. She was every thing that heart could desire. Brought up by an estimable mother and a kind, benevolent, and Christian father, she inherited a sweet disposition, and a heart with no perceptible blemish. She was just such a being to make a good man happy. Two more contented, more affectionate beings never lived. For years they prospered; their course approved by man — and their walk and conduct consistent with the precepts of Christianity.

Mr. Jones' business gradually declined; but having amassed a large property, and being stern and unyielding in his disposition, and active in the church, he retained his standing until the close of his life. He died

4

suddenly, and was buried with great pomp. On his splendid tombstone was inscribed: "Blessed are the dead who die in the Lord."

Mr. Watson lived to threescore years and ten, and then died, trusting for salvation in his Redeemer. His last words were, "Into thy hands, O Lord, I commit my spirit," — and he breathed his last.

His remains were followed to the grave by the poor and the orphan whom he had blessed. An humble stone marks the place of his sepulture, on which is engraved — "For me to die is gain."

Charles Mason and his wife may be often seen on a summer day, bending over the grave of the good man. A little tree has been planted there, by their own hands, which grows and flourishes. They have cherished in their memory, the love and kindness of their father, which will never be erased till their bodies sleep beneath the sods of the valley, and their spirits are united to his in the paradise of God.

HONESTY AND DISHONESTY.

Oh, dark and fearful is the path
   That leadeth man astray ;
No blushing flowers to love it hath —
   No greenness spreads the way.

He is a brother and a friend
   Who, when our lot is low,
With pleasant words will aid extend,
   And wipe the tears that flow.

"Be a good boy, Henry. You are now fourteen years old, and I have made arrangements with Mr. Simonton to take you into his store. Be obedient to your master; in all things be just and reasonable. I have confidence in him, or I would not consent for you to go from home. He will be kind to you, and always treat you well if you do your duty. Be perfectly honest, Henry: never take the value of a copper from your master, even if you stand in great need of money. If you do your duty, and are faithful to Mr. Simonton, you will secure his confidence, and the respect of all who know you, and become a useful man. Mind what I tell you; be honest, be industrious, attend strictly to your business, and never associate with the vicious and unprincipled."

Thus spake Mr. Jones to his son, who was about

leaving the parental roof for a clerkship in a store. Henry was a dutiful child, and had received excellent precepts and good examples from his parents.

" I shall try, father," said the boy, " to please Mr. Simonton, and I think he will never have occasion to speak a cross word to me."

" You must do your best to give satisfaction to your master," said his mother. " Remember that you will have to put up with more inconveniences than you would at home, and that you cannot always do as you would desire. Endeavor to be obedient to Mr. Simonton, so that he will never have occasion to reprove you, and so conduct yourself that he will never hesitate to trust you."

With cheerful spirits and a happy heart, the youth left his parents and entered the store of the merchant. Mr. Simonton did an extensive business for the place, and employed another clerk, who was about two years the senior of Henry. His name was Charles Bedford. It was not long before Henry became the companion and friend of Charles ; the latter could not help loving the former, he was so gentle and amiable in his disposition. There was a difference in the feelings of the youths. Henry was strict in his adherence to what he considered correct principles. He abhorred deception and profanity, and strictly observed the sabbath by attending church, as he had been brought up by his parents. But Charles would often evade and equivocate, and sometimes utter falsehoods. When he was displeased, he did not hesitate to make use of profane words, and as for the sabbath, he did not believe in its observance, and would often pass the day in strolling about the streets.

The boys boarded together with their master. One night as they retired to rest, Charles remarked,—

"I don't see why you are so plaguy particular about what you do."

"In what respect, Charles?"

"In every thing. You wont stay at home on Sunday, you know, and seem to think it wrong to enjoy yourself on that day. I think, as we are confined to the store all the week, there's no harm in enjoying one's self on Sunday."

"But I take more pleasure in attending church than I should in loitering about. In a good sermon I feel considerable interest. I also like good singing. I would not stay away from church on any account."

"And then, Henry, you are so particular to speak just so. I don't know as I ever heard you swear. There is no harm in using a few trifling words."

"But what good do they do?"

"Oh! one appears better to use them—and then they come in so easy that I cannot help using them."

"If I cannot appear well without swearing, I shall be contented to appear badly. I know I shall never learn to use profane words."

"You will get over such feelings, by and by. You'll never be thought any thing of unless you do; and there's another thing, you will not smoke a cigar. What harm is there in smoking, I should like to know?"

"It does no good. I have heard it said that smoking leads to drinking, and that there are few if any drunkards who do not use tobacco in some shape or another. You wouldn't wish to be a drunkard, I hope?"

"No—and I never intend to. I don't exactly like
4*

your temperance societies; I wouldn't join one on any account. I like freedom from all restraint."

"I am sorry to hear you talk so. The temperance societies, I believe, are doing a great deal of good."

"You are foolish, Henry, to think so. But you will change your mind before long!"

Thus the two youths conversed till they dropped asleep. It was evident that Charles had had a different education from his companion. His parents were of that class who look upon mere morality as a virtue, even though the heart be depraved. If outwardly the man appeared well, it was sufficient — and thus they taught their children.

For a few months Charles and Henry moved on pleasantly together, but a keen observer could have noticed the bad influence that young Bedford exercised over his companion. Being with him constantly, and hearing his conversation and observing his conduct, Henry, by degrees, learned the disgusting habit of using profane words, and was less particular in his observance of the sabbath. He less frequently called upon his parents, and often spent his evenings walking in the streets, or in some improper shanty, where the rum glass was freely circulated. His mother saw the alteration in her son, but knew not to what cause to impute it. One evening, when he called upon her, she remarked, —

"Henry, where is it that you spend your evenings? You haven't been at home for more than a week."

"I generally go with Charles Bedford."

"Where do you go?"

"Sometimes to one place, and sometimes to another."

"I am afraid, my son, that Charles is not so good a boy as he ought to be, and that he will lead you astray."

"So you always say, mother, when I go with anybody I like."

"But, my child, I never speak unless it is for your good. It troubles me to have you away from home every evening."

"You no need to have any fears of me. I shall not go into bad company."

"I have known many a boy to be ruined by bad associates, and I fear that boy is not so upright as he ought to be."

Thus would Henry's mother talk with him. She was apprehensive that he would be led away by Charles and ruined. Her fears were not entirely groundless. Young Bedford was loose and irregular in his habits, and had so insinuated himself into the favor of Henry, that the latter did not hesitate to follow his advice and example. Charles was in the constant practice of using profane words, smoking cigars, and spending his evenings among those who did not hesitate occasionally to take a glass of cordial. Henry had learned to swear and smoke from his companion, and every night he accompanied him to his favorite resorts. Once Charles took a glass of wine, and invited his friend to partake with him.

"I should rather not," said he.

"Come — don't be afraid."

"No — I don't wish for any."

"It will not hurt you. Come — come, drink a glass with me."

Stopping a moment to think, he replied, "I will not drink any to-night."

"You are foolish, Henry."

"Yes, he's a devilish fool," remarked the retailer; "and I'll be bound he's been to the temperance meetings and heard that cursed Neal Dow, or that brawling John Walton, or that notorious Joe Lord speak. Drink away, Charles, and I'll drink with you."

"I am no fool, sir," said Henry to the barkeeper; "but what use is there for me to drink when I do not need it, and have not the least desire for it?"

"Then drink to please your friend, who has so kindly offered it to you."

"Suppose I drink one glass it may be the ruin of me."

"Who told you that story? John Crockett, I'll be bound to say. Let John look at home. He has enough to do to mind his own affairs."

"Who is John Crockett? I don't know him."

"You don't. He has been whispering in your ears more than once, that I can swear. Come, take hold and drink."

"Yes, don't be fearful, my little lad," said one who was lying upon a bench; "don't mind what the temperance folks tell ye. What do they care about you or anybody else? All they want is power to rule the state. Then they'll be satisfied. Come, my fine fellow," he continued, rising from his seat, and patting Henry on the shoulder; "take one glass, just to please us all."

"Do, Henry, do," said Charles, putting the glass to his lips; "there, drink. That's a fine fellow — I knew you were no fool;" he continued, as Henry took one or two swallows.

"I knew that youth was too intelligent," said the retailer, "to listen to the harangues of Dow and Walton.

Keep him from their influence, and he will grow up a fine fellow."

After conversing for about an hour in a like strain, cursing the temperance societies and all who addressed their meetings, — Henry remaining the most of the time silent, — he and his companions went to their lodgings and retired.

" What's the matter with you ? " said Charles, addressing his friend, as he jumped into bed.

" What would my mother say, if she knew how I have conducted ? I have tasted of ardent spirits tonight." And the poor boy could not help shedding tears.

" Your mother will never know it — and certainly, she would not object to your enjoying yourself, if she did."

" But what will it lead to ? Who knows but I may become intemperate ? "

" You'll be a fool if you do. Can't you now and then take a glass of wine or cordial, without being a drunkard ? I pity you, if you can't."

" The greatest drunkards commenced by one drop. If my mother knew what I have done to-night, she would not rest till I had left this place."

" Your mother is like the rest of the Orthodox, always borrowing trouble, and always afraid somebody's going to be ruined."

Without extending the conversation, Henry closed his eyes in sleep — not, however, without resolving in his mind never to go into a grog-shop again.

Early in the morning, as he was passing down the street to his shop, he met the retailer, who sold to his companion the spirit the night previous.

"Ah, my little fellow," said he, "I was much pleased with you last night, and should be happy to have you call on me again. That Charles Bedford is a capital fellow. Follow his advice, and you'll make something."

Henry made but a word in reply, and entered upon his duties at the shop. All that day he said but a few words, while Charles appeared to be as cheerful as a lark. He felt he had taken a wrong step, and disobeyed a kind mother, and he was unhappy.

But, by associating constantly with Charles, the idea that it was wrong to drink a little spirit occasionally gradually wore away, and he objected less to go into retailers' shops. With his companion, Henry denounced the temperance people as fanatical, and was as earnest in condemning their course as any of his associates. He now preferred the company of the profane and drinking to the steady and industrious, and often absented himself from church on the sabbath. So much for the influence and bad example of a companion. His parents noticed the change in their son; and entreated him to keep aloof from bad associates; but they knew not the extent of his departure from their precepts.

After they had got through with the business of the day, and supper was ended, Charles and Henry went into their chamber, when the former remarked, —

"I have an idea of taking a ride this evening — should you like to go?"

"I don't know but I should. But where can you obtain a horse?"

"Say nothing, and I will tell you. On the floor of the shop, under the money-drawer, I picked up a two-dollar bill."

"It probably belongs to Mr. Simonton."

"How do I know that? I found the money, and it is mine. If you will go with me, I will hire a horse and chaise."

After a moment's hesitation, Henry decided to go. That evening, they spent the two dollars. Henry, by the request of his companion, handed the bill to Mr. Plummer, the stable-keeper, to take out his pay for the horse.

Early the next morning, Mr. Simonton took Henry aside, and remarked —

"I have often missed money from my drawer. It is unpleasant for me to accuse you of dishonesty; more especially one as young as you are, whose integrity I never wish to doubt. But I must say, I have strong suspicions that you are not so honest as you ought to be."

"Sir, I have taken no money from you," said Henry, shedding tears.

"Look here," continued Mr. Simonton, taking a bill from his pocket-book, "did you ever see that before?"

Henry saw it was the very bill he had passed to Mr. Plummer the night before.

"Yes, sir," said he; "I think that is the bill I passed to the stable-keeper last evening."

"It is the very one, and it belonged to me, and you must have taken it from the money-drawer."

"It was handed to me by Charles, who said he found it on the floor."

"A likely story. But if it were true, you knew that it belonged to me. But the story I do not believe. Charles has been with me a number of years, and I have always found him trustworthy."

"It certainly is as I tell you," said the boy, sobbing aloud.

"You should have wept before. I cannot consent to have a dishonest boy in my employment. I shall directly send you to your father."

"I am not so guilty, sir, as you may suppose, and if you'll try me once more, I'll be more careful what I do. I am sorry I consented to go with Charles, and would not do it again for the world."

"I am aware, Henry, if I turn you away, and for dishonesty, too, it will nearly ruin you. Who will trust you again? Where can you get a place?"

"It is this thought that makes me feel so; and I know my mother would not sleep if she knew this. If you will try me again, I will study your interest, and never be guilty of a dishonest or improper thing."

"Henry, you know my feelings towards you. I have felt a deep interest in your welfare, and have always been kind to you."

"I know it, and for this reason, I feel so much the worse," said the boy, continuing to weep.

"If I should consent to have you remain in my store, you must turn over a new leaf to-day. I understand you have been in the habit of late of visiting the miserable grog-shops in —— Street, and spending your evenings among the people who meet there to drink and carouse—and also that you have sometimes partaken of the intoxicating cup. Is this true, Henry?"

"It is true, sir—I am sorry to say that I was led away, and over-persuaded to drink; but I will not do so again. I'm ashamed to think I have abused your kindness, and have come to this. If you'll forgive me this once, I will give you no future trouble."

"You know, Henry, I feel for your situation, and would not hesitate to retain you, if I were sure that you would be faithful to me and keep away from bad associates."

"Just try me, sir, this once."

"Well, Henry, as you are sorry for the course that you have pursued, and seem resolved to become a good boy, you may continue with me, and I shall say nothing about this affair. Henry, I wish you would listen to my advice, and never go near a grog-shop, or spend your evenings with a gang of unprincipled youth. Use no profane words yourself, and discountenance their use in others. When you came with me, you were free from this charge, and I feel sorry that you ever associated with other than upright and virtuous youth. Guard your heart and your lips — watch against temptation, and you will grow up an honest man, to be respected by all."

Henry thanked his master for his kindness, and resolved, as he attended to his duties, never to do any thing that would displease him.

When Charles had an opportunity of speaking to Henry, he remarked — "How did you like the old man's blowing up?"

"I don't blame him. We have both done wrong."

"He said but little to me, and he'll forget all about it in a few days. Don't be so chapfallen, Henry."

"Mr. Simonton has been kind to us, and it makes me feel unpleasant to know that he has had occasion to find fault. We must try to conduct better in future."

"Don't be frightened too soon. We've done nothing out of the way."

5

"We have not spent our evenings as we should, you know."

"What harm is there in enjoying ourselves? I sha'n't stay in the house for anybody, after my work is done."

"I shall visit the shops in —— Street no more."

"The bigger fool you are."

"There is one thing we should look at, Charles. While we disobey Mr. Simonton, and visit improper places, we are injuring ourselves. Suppose we continue in the course we have pursued the last two months — what will be the consequence? If we accustom ourselves to smoking, drinking, and swearing, the habits will grow upon us, and we may become unprincipled men and common drunkards. We should look a little ahead."

"Enjoy ourselves while we can, I say. This is what I intend to do; but you are at liberty to become a deacon if you please."

Henry did not feel like prolonging the conversation, but he was surprised and grieved at the language of his friend. He felt that he had erred, and was now resolved on a different course. In the evening, instead of going with Charles, he visited his parents; and when he retired to rest, he felt happier than if he had been with unprincipled associates. It was late before his friend came home. He remarked to Henry, —

"I have had a glorious time this evening. I never, in my life, enjoyed myself better."

"I am afraid you have not been in good company to-night?"

"If you were not a ninny, you might enjoy yourself too. Henry, why don't you join the church?"

"To tell you the truth, Charles, I wish I was good enough to."

"Ha! ha! ha! so I thought. Well, every one to his taste, I say."

Young Bedford continued to grow more unsteady, and stay out later at night. He was generally cross and disagreeable, and began to find fault with his companion. So different were the tastes and dispositions of the two boys, that they now associated together but very little, except in the way of business. Thus a few months passed away. The leisure time with Henry was passed in reading valuable books, and in various kinds of study, to improve his mind. Charles seldom took a book or a paper into his hands. Mr. Simonton was still kind to the boys, and seldom spoke a cross word to them. While in his shop, they attended to the business, and every thing seemed to go on prosperously. One day, as Henry was sitting at the dinner table alone — having been detained at the store later than usual — Sarah Simonton, his master's eldest daughter, a girl about eleven years of age, came running into the room, and spoke to Henry —

"Pa has lost some money, and you have taken it."

"What is it?" anxiously inquired the boy.

"You have been taking some money from his drawer at the shop."

That moment the girl's mother came into the room, and took her out, leaving Henry astonished beyond measure. He knew that he was innocent of the charge of theft, and without half eating his dinner he hastened to the shop. Mr. Simonton being alone, Henry stated to him what his daughter had said.

"It is true, Henry, that I have lost several dollars

of late, and it is unaccountable to me where it has gone. Last evening I called Charles to me, and made inquiries, but I could learn but very little from him. Have you seen Charles with money of late?"

" No, sir, I have not."

" Have you had any money?"

" The last I had was the three dollars you let me have a week ago last Saturday."

" Have you the bills now?"

" No, sir, I have but fifty cents in the world."

Upon his stating thus, Mr. Simonton took him into his counting-room, with Charles, who had just entered the store. Being seated, Mr. Simonton inquired of Charles, —

" Did you not tell me that Henry had some money?"

" Yes, sir — I thought I saw him put some bills in his trunk the other night."

" It is a mistake, Charles," said Henry ; " I have had no money since the three dollars Mr. Simonton gave me a little while ago, and my mother bought me some things with the money."

" What made you think you saw him have money, Charles?"

" I saw him put something into his trunk, and I had no doubt it was money, but I may have been mistaken."

" Now tell the truth," said Mr. Simonton, turning to Henry — " have you not money in your trunk?"

" Not but fifty cents, sir."

" Have you any objection to let me have your key and look into your trunk?"

" Do you not believe me? I tell you the truth."

" Just loan me the key of your trunk."

"I have nothing in my trunk but what is my own." The boy could not help from shedding tears.

By his reluctance to let him have the key, his master supposed he might be guilty, and insisted on having the key.

"Well, sir, you may take it; but you will find that I have not been dishonest or deceived you."

Mr. Simonton took the key, and went directly to the house. He opened Henry's trunk, and, after looking a moment or two, stowed away in one corner, he found a one-dollar bill. With more grief than anger, he locked the trunk, and took the bill with him to the shop.

Calling Henry into his room, he said —

"I am pained to the heart to find that you have deceived me."

"Deceived you I have not."

"Do not add lying to dishonesty, I beg of you. It will be worse for you in the end. It is better to acknowledge the whole."

"I have nothing to acknowledge," and the boy wept aloud.

"I found this bill in your trunk," holding it in his hand.

"Then it was put there without my knowledge."

"Henry, I am sorry to hear you talk so. For the last few months, I have put the utmost confidence in you. You remember your promise to me, when I concluded to keep you, and say nothing about the former affair? but I must dismiss you now."

"Say not so — it will ruin me."

"I have tried you, after I found you not to be trustworthy, and this is my reward. I regret you have done

5*

54 HONESTY AND DISHONESTY.

this, but I cannot keep you longer. You may take your trunk from the house, and go home to your father."

With his handkerchief to his eyes Henry left the store, and went directly to his mother. He told her the whole affair, amid sobs and tears.

"Never mind, my son," said she; "the really guilty person will be detected at last. It is hard to be accused of dishonesty, but it will be best not to say a word about it. Mr. Simonton is wealthy and we are poor, and, if he were disposed, he could injure us a great deal; but he is deceived. By and by, when he knows who is the really dishonest person, he will not hesitate to do justice by you. Dry your tears, and for the present you can assist me about the house. Perhaps you can find a good opening in the course of a few weeks."

Mr. Jones exceedingly regretted what had happened, when he came home to his dinner, but he whispered not a word of reproach against his son or his master. Like a Christian philosopher, he remarked, —

"Never mind, my boy, innocence will be vindicated in the end, while crime alone will be punished. Dwell not on the unhappy circumstance, but be happy at home, till you can obtain another place. It will turn out right in the end. Your motto always has been, 'Look on the bright side.'"

When Henry took his trunk away from Mr. Simonton's, he went into the parlor to bid Mrs. Simonton and her daughter good-by, but they took no notice of him. A tear in his eye told how keenly he felt the slight.

"But I'll not mind it," he said, as he brushed the tear from his cheek.

In a few days he met Charles.

"What a fool you was," said he, "to leave that money in your trunk. You might have known the old man would find you out."

"I didn't put the money there, and you know it."

"I know it? Tell me that again if you dare!"

Henry made no reply and passed on.

It was not long before young Jones obtained another situation. He went into the store of a gentleman, who, liking his appearance, asked him if he did not wish for a place in his establishment. Henry was pleasantly situated with Mr. Roberts, and gave perfect satisfaction to his employer. He was attentive to his business, and took care to improve the spare moments of his time.

Henry had been in his new situation about four months, when he received a request from Mr. Simonton for him to call and see him at his house, on the following evening. Without hesitation, Henry called on his old master. When he was seated, Mr. Simonton and he being alone in the room, the former remarked,—

"You may think it strange that I have sent for you, Henry, but I must tell you that I have done injustice to you. Until very recently, I believed that you were dishonest and lied to me. My opinion is now changed. Charles I believe to be the villain. I have missed money at various times, and a few days ago I accused him of being the thief; and I think I had sufficient proof of his guilt; but he used very insulting language to me, and during the day, took away his trunk, and went to the south, as I understand, in a steamboat that evening. Since then I have found that he was very dishonest. I have lost more than a little by him. Henry, I am sorry I treated you so unkindly. I think you told me the truth."

"Yes, sir; what I said at the time, was what I believed to be the truth. I never could tell how that money came into my trunk."

"From what I have learned of Charles, I have no doubt that he opened your trunk and put it in."

"I cannot believe that he would have done it."

"There is no doubt in my own mind. It has always been a rule with me, when I have wronged another, intentionally or otherwise, to ask his forgiveness; and it is my duty to ask yours, for I have seriously injured you."

"Say nothing about it, sir. With all my heart I forgave you a long time ago. I knew you had a wrong impression, and hoped the time would come when the real offender would be detected."

"Another thing I wish to say to you. I should be pleased to have you come and reside with me again. If you are not engaged for any length of time with Mr. Roberts, and will come with me, I will do well by you."

Henry thanked Mr. Simonton, and as he was always pleased with the general treatment he received while he remained with him, he concluded to go with him again. His present master regretted to have him leave, but finally gave his consent, and Henry was once more in the employ of his old master. ·

No man could be more kind to another than was Mr. Simonton to Henry. He treated him as a son, and favored him in a thousand ways.

Young Jones remained with his kind master till he became of age, and soon after, he was taken into equal copartnership with him. The firm of Simonton and Jones did as much business in their line as any two firms in the place. For moral worth and sterling integrity, no men in the community stood higher. They dealt fairly and honorably with all, and were perfectly free from those contracted views and mean contrivances that make so many detested and abhorred.

In a few years, Henry had acquired some little property, and in a pleasant part of the town, he built him a neat and commodious house. When his dwelling was completed, he married Sarah, the daughter of Mr. Simonton, than whom a kinder and more agreeable young woman could nowhere be found. She was well calculated to make him happy — and two more congenial hearts probably never came together.

Mr. Jones had been in business something like six years, when he took a journey to the south, partly for business and partly for pleasure. Among other states he visited, he went to Louisiana, and spent several weeks. One day, in New Orleans, he saw several persons gathering, and inquiring the cause, he was told that a thief had just been placed in the pillory. On his head was a paper cap on which was printed, in large letters, the word *voleuse*. Henry thought the countenance of the felon was familiar, and in a moment it struck him that it was his old companion, Charles Bedford. He could not be mistaken — it was he. But the marks of degradation were on his person. He had the appearance of a man of forty-five, when in fact he was not more than thirty. A tear or two struggled down the cheek of Henry as he gazed upon the miserable man. On the breast of the thief was a placard, upon which his crime and sentence were written. He had been stealing, and was to stand in the pillory one hour, and then receive twenty lashes. Henry waited and saw the punishment inflicted upon the person of the young man, nearly every blow of the whip drawing blood with it. Though a painful sight, he remained till he saw the poor fellow removed for the dressing of his wounds.

That day Henry called upon him, but he found him a miserably wicked and polluted being. Without at first making himself known, he remarked —

"My good friend, what has brought you to this condition? — if I may ask you the question."

"Intemperance and dishonesty. I have brought it all on myself."

"There is a chance for your reformation — why not forsake the bowl?"

"Sir, I am too far gone, now; I am houseless and friendless."

"None are beyond the reach of hope, while they can move and breathe. You may yet be a man again."

Seeing him in much pain from his chastisement, Henry left him, promising to call again in a day or two. But feeling a sympathy for the poor fallen wreck of humanity, the next day he was at his side, with some trifles he had bought for his nourishment. The unhappy man appeared exceedingly grateful, and thanked Henry with tears in his eyes.

"Who am I indebted to for this kindness?" inquired he.

"I am a stranger in this place."

"Sir, I can never forget you. No other person but yourself has shown me any pity. I have done wrong, I know. Once I might have been something. I commenced early a career of folly; but I knew not the bitter consequences till now."

"You are not now too old to reform. Give me your

word that you will from this time cease to drink ardent spirits, and become a reformed man, and I will see what I can do for you."

"Sir, your kindness astonishes me. Can I have one friend in the world? Is there yet hope for me? O sir" — and tears checked his utterance.

"You have a friend in me, if you will do your duty."

"I will try to with all my heart."

"There is one gentleman in New Orleans with whom I am acquainted. Upon my recommendation, he has agreed to take you as a porter in his store. If you are faithful, steady, and honest, he will do well by you. If otherwise, I am to sustain the loss."

"A thousand thanks, sir! I will become a man again. Such kindness I never expected to see. Sir, what may I call your name?"

"Jones — my name is Jones."

"Jones, did you say?" and the poor fellow looked up, astonished beyond measure. "I once knew a person by that name — a fine little fellow, too — would that I had been like him — but I wronged him" — and the tears continued to flow. "I will tell you what I did: I led him away from virtue. God forgive me! — I took money from our employer; for we lived with the same man — and to screen myself I placed a bill in his trunk — wretch that I was — and our master dismissed him as a thief. How can I be otherwise than miserable, when I treated a kind, honest, and virtuous youth in this manner? What has become of him, I do not know, but I trust he is yet virtuous and happy, while I am miserable and wretched. You are no relation to this Jones, who lived in a distant state?"

"I know him well."

"You astonish me."

"Charles, without longer deceiving you, I am the very person! Don't you know me?"

"True as I live, it is he"—and it was some time before he could speak—while the tears gushed in torrents from his eyes. "Henry, my benefactor and friend, forgive me! oh, forgive me!"

"My dear fellow, you have long been forgiven. I never harbor an unkind feeling in my heart, against a fellow-creature."

For an hour they conversed together, and each related the history of his past life. Charles had suffered every thing but death. He had been degraded and miserable in the extreme. Several times had he been imprisoned for his dishonesty. But now by the kindness of his friend he resolved to reform, and before Henry left the place, he saw him pleasantly situated in a store, where, if he should prove faithful, the prospect of a good living and something more was before him.

Henry returned to his native place after an absence of one or two months, and continued to prosper in his business. He occasionally received letters from Charles, who had faithfully kept his promise, and become an altered man. The last time he heard from him, he had been promoted to chief clerk in the establishment, and was about taking to himself a wife.

We have but little to add to our story. Though virtue for a time may be cast down, yet will she triumph at last. All should remember this fact, and let nothing keep them from the path of duty.

Kindness will work wonders in the human heart. When a man errs, reproach him, and you drive him further from virtue; but be kind; persuade and encourage him, and you change his heart and save a soul from ruin.

TEN THOUSAND DOLLARS.

However dark the cloud may be
That lingers o'er your head —
Bear up — beyond the cloud you'll see
Bright fields of sunshine spread.

DOROTHY HENDERSON was the daughter of a farmer who lived in Scarborough. Her parents owned the farm on which they lived; but as it was partly on a ledge and the land poor, it was only by the strictest economy that they made a comfortable living. In the fall of the year Mr. Henderson would carry produce to the Portland market, the proceeds of which enabled him to obtain the dry and West India goods that were used in the family. As Dorothy grew older, she was of much assistance to her mother in milking the cows, churning the butter, and the like. Although she was not handsome, the farmer's daughter was of an amiable disposition, industrious and attentive to the duties of the little farm. Not living in the neighborhood of fashion, Dorothy was not injured, either in body or mind, by its fascinating influence. She grew up, as nature designed her, and was therefore healthy and happy. When she was about nineteen years of age, her father took to board the schoolmaster of the district, a man prepossessing in his appearance and well calculated to win the

6

heart of a young woman. He was extremely partial to the daughter, and occasionally took her with him to Portland, where he had friends. The parents of Dorothy were delighted with the schoolmaster, and fondly cherished the hope that at some future day he would become their son-in-law. The daughter, however, was less pleased with him than her parents were, and treated him kindly, as a friend and nothing more. She did not wish to consider him in any other light than that of an acquaintance. There was a young man in the neighborhood, by the name of James Smith, with whom she had been intimate from childhood. He was quite poor but perfectly upright and honest. It was evident that James was attached to Dorothy, but his modesty and his poverty prevented his avowing his passion ; and it was only as a neighbor that he occasionally called at the house of Mr. Henderson. But when James saw the movements of Mr. Hobson the schoolmaster, his feelings were such that we cannot describe. He had cherished the hope for many years, that Dorothy, at some future period, might become his wife, although to no one had he made known the feelings of his bosom. Had he been made acquainted with the heart of the young woman, he would have had no trembling fears when he saw the attentions paid to her by Mr. Hobson.

One afternoon, as Dorothy and her mother were at work, one of the neighbors called in to spend a few hours. She brought her knitting-work with her, as is usual in the country, so as not to pass any idle moments. After conversing on various topics, the name of the schoolmaster was introduced.

"Mr. Hobson appears to be an excellent teacher," remarked the neighbor.

"He is, indeed," said the mother, "and a fine man in every respect."

"I see he is very partial to Dorothy," giving her a particular look.

"As to that I cannot say. She has been to Portland with him once or twice; but it may be on account of his boarding with us."

"There must be something else in the wind, I know; is there not, Dorothy?" addressing the young woman.

"What do you mean, Mrs. Stacy?"

"Why, don't you think highly of the schoolmaster?"

"As a friend I like him; I could not do otherwise, for he has always been kind to me."

"That's it, and you intend to marry him?"

"Why, Mrs. Stacy, you know better than to talk so. I wouldn't marry him, feeling as I now do, if he were worth as much as Captain Clapp or Matthew Cobb."

"Dorothy, mind what you say," said her mother. "Always speak the truth."

"That is the truth, mother. As true as I live, it is the truth."

"Nonsense, girl," said Mrs. Stacy, "you would have him in a moment. I have heard girls talk before."

"Mr. Hobson is a gentleman, every inch of him," said the mother, "and I should think myself lucky to have my daughter obtain so good a husband as he will make. But I don't expect any such thing."

"If that should happen, it would not be strange at all," remarked Mrs. Stacy. "Girls in love always talk like your daughter — that we all know."

"In love, Mrs. Stacy! — it is strange you talk so. You know better. I care no more about Mr. Hobson than I do for your husband; believe it or not."

"We'll see what a few months will bring forth. I know what young women are. You can't deceive me."

"Nor do I wish to. I have no secret to keep, and desire only to tell the plain truth."

At this moment the schoolmaster came in, and happened to take a seat next to Dorothy. Upon this, Mrs. Stacy gave a knowing look to Mrs. Henderson, and touched her with her elbow, as much as to say, " What I said was true — look for yourself."

" A fine day, Mr. Hobson," said Mrs. Stacy, as soon as he was fairly seated.

" Beautiful," the schoolmaster remarked, stretching his legs.

" What's the news to-day ? "

" I don't hear of any thing at all. I just saw Dick Parsons, who came from Portland, and he says hay brings a good price."

" I'm glad to hear that. When are you going to Portland again ? " and she touched Mrs. Henderson with her elbow.

" In a few days, ma'am."

" I suppose you will take Dorothy with you ? "

" Why, y-e-s — I suppose so."

" She'll be pleased to go, no doubt."

" You had better take Mrs. Stacy next time," Dorothy remarked ; " I think it would be highly gratifying to her."

" Well, she may go if she pleases."

" Dorothy would cry her eyes out, if I should."

" Perhaps I should ; try it, ma'am. You go, and we'll see what effect it has upon me."

" I'll see about it."

The conversation was interrupted by the appearance

of Mr. Henderson, who had come home to tea, after his
day's labor. It was not long before they all partook of
the supper prepared by Dorothy — soon after which Mrs.
Stacy took her departure. Mrs. Stacy was a distant relative of James Smith, whom we have mentioned before.

James was a constant visitor at the house of Dorothy;
but — poor fellow! — he noticed that since the schoolmaster had boarded at the house, the parents of the
young woman were not as social and as agreeable as
formerly. The reason he suspected, but he hinted not
a word. Hobson himself seemed to take particular
pains to treat him with contempt, and often in the presence of Dorothy and her parents, took occasion to speak
disrespectfully of the young man. He would ridicule
his dress, his manners, and his awkward appearance;
but Dorothy usually resented it and would speak in the
highest terms of her friend.

"There is not a better-hearted young man in town
than he," she remarked to the schoolmaster one day.

"Perhaps he is a fine fellow, but what does he
know?" inquired Mr. Hobson.

"More than he appears to know, that I can tell you.
He has read a great deal, and is very intelligent.
There is not a sum in Pike's Arithmetic that he cannot
do, and he is familiar with grammar."

"That may be, and yet he knows but little. He acts
like a simpleton."

"He has never been in much company, I know, and
is very diffident. But I should rather see a modest
man than an impudent fellow any time."

"Look at his appearance. His coat sets like a shirt
on a handspike."

"He is not able to dress well, I know; but the coat
6*

he wears, was made by a fashionable Portland tailor, Mr. Charles Rogers, I believe, and if it does not suit him, the tailor is in fault."

"Well, there is nothing prepossessing about the fellow —I know that."

"So I think," said the mother.

"Why, mother, how can you talk so? A few months since, you told me he was one of the best young men in the whole town of Scarborough."

"But I have changed my mind since."

"James has not changed. He is as industrious as ever, and I'm sure he's as kind hearted."

Her mother made no reply, and Dorothy was glad to drop the conversation. She now had a less favorable opinion than ever of the schoolmaster. A day or two after, he invited her to go to Portland, but Dorothy declined. Her mother, learning this fact, said, —

"What has got into you, child, that you act so strange? Why don't you go with Mr. Hobson, and thank him for his kind invitation?"

"For this simple reason, mother, I do not like him."

"Don't like him! what do you like, hey?—why, there is not a girl in all Scarborough, from Prout's Neck to Libby's Corner, who would refuse him; nay, more, there's not one, I'll be bound to say, who wouldn't esteem it a great favor to be waited upon by the schoolmaster."

"I can't help that, mother; I cannot go with him."

"What in the world have you against him?"

"Why, what he said about James, and the manner in which he has treated him has made me dislike him, and I was never very partial to him, as you know."

"I think you are unwise, and by and by you will

regret your conduct. Mr. Hobson is the son of a wealthy man and at some future day will have property left him."

"That may not be correct; but if it is true, I should not like him any better."

"All you care about, then, is that fellow, Jim, with not a cent in the world, and, who, from present appearances, will never be worth a second shirt to his back.

"That James is a fine young man, I cannot doubt. With all his poverty, I would give more for him than for a dozen schoolmasters like Mr. Hobson."

"You are a foolish girl; you talk more like Coot Moody than ever I heard a female before."

"I speak as I think, and I cannot help it. As for going with Mr. Hobson to Portland, I shall not do it."

"If you will be so foolish, you must take the consequences."

"In the end, mother, I believe you will acknowledge I am right."

Finding that he could make no impression on the heart of Dorothy, the schoolmaster treated her with indifference and affected contempt. At the same time, a keen observer could have noticed that he respected her in his heart. After the three months had expired, for which Mr. Hobson was engaged, he left the house of Mr. Henderson and returned to Portland.

On account of Dorothy's treatment to the schoolmaster, her parents had fallen out with young Smith, and gave him to understand that his company was not agreeable at the house. But lovers will meet, and many a happy interview did they have. At the house of a distant relative of James, Capt. Moses Libby, they often resorted to pass a pleasant evening. They had now made known their love for each other, and resolved, if their lives were spared, at no very distant day, to become man and wife.

Although the parents of Dorothy were in humble circumstances, the parents of James were still poorer. Having a large family of children, Mr. Smith found it exceedingly difficult to obtain the necessaries of life. But since his children had grown up, and could work for themselves and earn something, he succeeded better.

It was nearly six months after the schoolmaster had left Scarborough, that James ventured to call on Mr. Henderson. Dorothy had assured him of a welcome reception. She supposed that the old affair had been forgotten by her parents, and that now they would treat James with kindness and attention. But she was disappointed. No sooner was James comfortably seated by the fire, than Mrs. Henderson remarked — addressing her daughter, —

"There are some men who never seem to take a hint when they are not wanted."

"And you might have added, mother, some females too."

"I never wish to make any uneasiness, but I have often said, I did not wish you to invite persons to the house, that were not agreeable to your parents."

"You may as well say what you mean as hint it. James and I can understand you."

"I will be plain with you. Since you and James treated Mr. Hobson with so much indifference, I have not felt like seeing him, and have never wished to have him enter the house."

" I'm sure James had nothing to do with it. I don't think he ever spoke a dozen words to him. I thought by this time you had forgotten the schoolmaster."

" I can never forget what a fool you have been."

Dorothy said no more, and in a few moments left the room with James. The tears filled her eyes as she said,

" You mustn't mind what mother says; you know my feelings; we shall yet be happy."

" No," said James; " I am sorry she feels so, but it would be of no use for me to say a word. It would only make the matter worse. If I were you, I would not mention the subject to her after I am gone."

" I shall not. I am glad you take it so philosophically."

In a few moments, James started for his home, and Dorothy went back to her mother.

" I'm astonished that you should think of asking that fellow here," said Mrs. Henderson, " when you know how your father and I look upon him. I can't bear the sight of him."

" Mother, tell me what he has done that you feel so. Is he a rogue and a villain? Has he been guilty of theft, or of any impropriety? If you will point me to a single act of his, that would be condemned by people in general, I will have nothing to say to him."

" What and who is James Smith? He is thought nothing of by anybody. There is not a female who would keep company with him, if I may except Em Moody."

" You mistake there, mother. A dozen girls would be pleased to have him, he is so amiable, kind, and industrious. Why, he has fifty dollars laid by, which he has earned with his own hands."

"Compare him with Mr. Hobson — a gentleman you might have had for your husband — yes, you might have had him — and his father is wealthy. But no, you treated him with contempt, while you received the visits of that good-for-nothing Jim. I feel vexed when I think of it, and have no patience with you."

"I believe Mr. Hobson was not a good man. I did not like him, and I should never have been happy in his company. Would you have me sacrifice my happiness for money?"

"You didn't know what you liked. If you had kept company with Mr. Hobson, you could not help liking him, he was so amiable."

"I was with him more or less every day for three months, but disliked him more and more. So what you say could never have taken place. I never could like him."

"What I want you to do now is, to have little to say to James."

"I may as well tell you, mother, that I intend to marry him before many months."

"What is that you say?"

"I am engaged to James."

"If you talk so, remember you can have no home with your parents."

"If I were in the wrong I would not blame you; but I think I am in the right."

"I don't want to hear any thing more on this subject. Never mention the name of Smith to me again."

So saying, Mrs. Henderson left the room while her daughter remained indulging in no pleasing reflections. She was attached to James; he was upright and generous, industrious and prudent. What more did she want? He was poor, but that was a trifle in her estimation. They both were young, healthy, and strong; and if they ever should be united, she doubted not that they could make a comfortable living.

A week or two after James had received the hints from Mrs. Henderson, that he was not wanted in the house, as Dorothy and her parents were sitting by the fire, a neighbor dropped in, and inquired if they had heard the news respecting a recent bank robbery.

"We have not," said Mr. Henderson.

"I understand," said the neighbor, "that, on Saturday evening last, the Portland bank was broken open, and bills and specie to the amount of more than a hundred thousand dollars were taken from the vault."

"Is that correct?"

"I believe it is; for I heard it from a gentleman just from Portland. He states the bank was entered by means of false keys. The directors of the bank have offered a reward of ten thousand dollars for the recovery of the money."

"Have they any suspicion who the thieves were?"

"Not that I know of. I heard it hinted that possibly some of the money might have been brought to this town and secreted in the woods, and several people, in hope of rewards, will start to-morrow in search of the money."

While Mr. Henderson and his neighbor were talking, Dorothy slipped out and ran down to Mr. Smith's to tell James what she had heard. She met him in the road near the house, and related the story of the great robbery.

"To-morrow James," said she, "I would get up early

and hunt the woods, and if the money has been secreted here, you may possibly find it."

"I will, Dorothy; although there is no hope of such good luck. For your sake I wish I might be so fortunate as to find the money and get the reward."

In a few minutes Dorothy was with her parents.

Young Smith, thinking so much of the money that was stolen, could hardly sleep that night. He arose very early and went into the woods, without making known his object to any one. Hour after hour he searched where he thought it at all probable the money might have been secreted, but in vain. Being familiar with the woods, he knew almost every thicket, and every tree. After a search of many hours, he was about giving up and returning home, when the thought struck him that there was yet one place, where possibly the money might be concealed. He hastened to the place, lifted up the shrubbery, when to his amazement and joy, he beheld the bags that contained upwards of a hundred thousand dollars. What to do, James hardly knew. If he left the place, others might come, and he lose his reward. He waited a short time, when he heard voices at a distance. He looked ; they were strangers. When they came up, they stated that they were from Portland, (one of their number being one of the robbers), and had come for the money. But luckily, James had first discovered it, and was entitled to the reward. Dozens gathered about the spot, and the gentlemen removed the money, and carried it to Portland. Just as young Smith was going home filled with joy at his good luck, he met Dorothy and told her of his success. Nothing could exceed her joy as she bounded to her father's house. She resolved, however, not to mention the circumstance to her parents, knowing they would very soon hear of the good fortune of James.

A few moments after she had been in the house, her father entered and exclaimed, " James Smith has found that money, and will be entitled to ten thousand dollars ! "

" What ! James found it ?" said the mother, " you astonish me ! Dorothy, what do you think of that ? "

"I 'll tell you what I think ; he will be a fool, if he ever darkens our doors again."

" Why, we have always treated him well, you know."

" No, mother, no. It was only about three weeks ago that you did the same as turn him from the house, and you forbade me having any thing to do with him."

" You are wrong, Dorothy ; I didn't mean any thing. James and I have always had a pretty good understanding."

" O mother ! how differently you talk now. Ten thousand dollars in a young man's pocket makes him a gentleman. If it had not been for you, James would have shared the money with me."

" For me, child ; what do you mean ? "

" Why, you turned him away, and forbade my going with him when he was poor ; now he is rich, do you suppose he has forgotten your treatment ? I guess I must try to hunt up the schoolmaster."

" Don't be so foolish, Dorothy. I don't care any thing about Mr. Hobson."

" He's a fine man, and his father is rich, you know."

During the conversation between the mother and daughter, Mr. Henderson scarcely spoke a word : he knew that both he and his wife had not treated James

7

as he deserved, and now they felt condemned. After a moment's pause, he remarked, —

"There is no mistake about it, wife, we have not treated James as he deserved. We knew he was very poor, and, without looking at his virtues, or dreaming that he might become rich, have shunned and despised him, and fairly driven him from our doors."

"That is a fact, father; and not all my entreaties would induce you to do differently. Now, what have we lost? Think of it. A better, kinder, and a more good-hearted young man than James, cannot be found. I do not think I am the least to blame."

"I don't know but we have done wrong," remarked the mother; "and it is strange we should have treated James so, when we had nothing against his character. I wish we could see him, and acknowledge our fault."

"That would not answer, now," said the father, "it would look as if the change in his condition had changed our minds, as, indeed, it has."

"As you both regret the course you have taken with James," said Dorothy, "perhaps it would be better for me to see him, and explain all. If money has not changed his affections, I shall yet be his; and money has not, I know. Had James a million of dollars, and I were penniless, I know that he would stick by me to the last."

The parents appeared to be satisfied with this, and hoped the time might come when they could look upon young Smith as their son-in-law.

The next day Dorothy had an interview with James, when she related the conversation that had taken place between herself and parents. "Now," said he, "there will be no objection to our union."

"None in the least, I trust."

"I have learned from the directors of the bank, that I shall have my money in a few days. The whole reward they are unwilling to pay, because one of the robbers had confessed that he had taken the money, and was on his way to its place of concealment; but I shall receive more than enough to purchase a fine situation with all my farming utensils."

In the evening James called upon Dorothy at the house. As soon as he entered, he was met by Mrs. Henderson, who extended her hand, appearing very glad to see him.

"I am rejoiced at your good luck," said she; "but I feel ashamed of the treatment you have heretofore received at our house. You must forgive us."

"Say nothing about the past; I never treasured an unkind thought in my heart against you, and am as ready to forget any slight I have received, as you are to ask forgiveness. I always had the kindest feelings toward you."

The husband, coming in, was as free to confess his fault, and ask the pardon of James, who, with the family, was melted to tears.

"James," at last said the father, "we have been unkind to you heretofore, but as you have shown a kind and a Christian spirit, we cannot but admire your character. Any thing we can do in future to promote your happiness, we shall not fail of performing."

"Sir, there is one request I wish to make; if you grant it, I shall be happy; it is your consent to my union with Dorothy."

"Nothing could give us more pleasure. We shall

be proud of calling you our son.   Dorothy, what say you to this?"

"I'll give my hearty consent."

"And I'll agree to it, also," said the mother.

Never was there a pleasanter evening passed, and when James returned to his home, the thoughts of his future happy prospects so engrossed his mind that he found but little sleep.

In a few days young Smith received his money from the directors of the Portland bank.   The first thing he did was to purchase him a farm in the neighborhood on which stood a beautiful little house.

Not many weeks passed before he was united to Dorothy.   Old Parson Bradley was called upon to perform the marriage ceremony, and the evening passed off pleasantly and happily.   The couple were accompanied to their own house by several of the guests, where, after giving them three hearty cheers, they left them, and retired to their homes. ·

Some twenty years after James had met with his good luck, he was in Portland on some business, and was called to the poorhouse.   While there, he saw a miserable looking being, who appeared to be fast wasting away.   Struck with his singular looks, James approached him and entered into conversation with the poor creature.

"You appear to be very unwell," James remarked.

"I am feeble, and suffer a great deal."

"How long have you been in this house?"

"Several years.   I have seen better days, but intemperance has brought me here, and here I shall probably remain till I am carried out."

"Can the physicians do nothing for you?"

"No, nothing at all. A few months since as I was employed in the yard, throwing bricks into the cart that belongs to the house, our overseer spoke to me to do something else; but not understanding him, I continued my work. He ran up to me, and with all his strength kicked me so severely that I fell, in great agony. I never suffered in all my life so much as I did from that kick. Now I cannot work and the physician tells me it will be the death of me. I cannot inform you in what way I suffer from the wound; but no one can tell how painful it is. If I were prepared to die, death would be quite a welcome visitor."

"What may I call your name, sir? it seems to me that I have seen you before."

"My name is Hobson."

"Didn't you teach school some years ago?"

"Yes, sir; I taught in Gorham once, and in North Yarmouth, and also in Scarborough. Afterwards I followed the seas."

Mr. Smith at once recognized the sick man as Mr. Hobson, but not thinking it worth while to let himself be known, after making him a trifling present, he bid him good-by.

To his wife and her aged parents, that evening, he related this circumstance, when the old lady exclaimed, "I thought Hobson would come to some miserable end, for he had an evil eye! It was lucky for Dorothy that she had nothing to say to him."

A few months after, James learned that poor Hobson was dead and buried.

For many years, Mr. Smith and his wife lived on their farm, enjoying the blessings of an industrious and

7*

virtuous life ; and for aught we know, they are living to this day. The next time we take a ride to Scarborough we shall certainly inquire for them, and have the place pointed out to us where the hundred thousand dollars were deposited.

RELIC OF A BELOVED PASTOR.

'Tis every day the heart is pained
By word, or look, or deed ;
The real bliss that we have gained
Proves but a broken reed.

FOR many years the Rev. Mr. Johnson had been settled over the church and society in R——. Being a
man of talents, and devoted to his people, he was respected and beloved by his hearers. Around the sick-
bed, in the social company, at the place of business
— wherever Mr. Johnson was found — he had a peculiar
talent for making himself agreeable. His conversation was animated, and his heart warm. Everybody
spoke in the highest terms of praise of the excellent
pastor, generous citizen, and Christian teacher.

Among the warmest friends of Mr. Johnson, were
Deacon Peabody and his wife. Too much praise they
could not bestow upon his discourses. In their estimation, they were exactly suited to the wants of his large
congregation. Although the deacon and his family
were strongly prejudiced in favor of their minister,
this partiality was not a criterion of their piety. A
pastor, of a different persuasion, who resided in R——,
they looked upon as any thing but religious. In their
view, the Rev. Mr. Emerson was a blind leader of the

blind, and more fit for a money-broker than a preacher. In the presence of one of his friends, the good wife remarked, —

"I do not see how you can sit under such a man as that Emerson is."

"Why not? We all like him."

"He preaches abominable errors."

"How do you know?"

"So I have understood."

"But did you ever hear him preach?"

"No, and I never want to. I should feel guilty if I were seen going to his church."

"Then I must say, ma'am, you are not a proper person to judge."

"I believe Mr. Emerson is a wicked man, and I should feel dreadfully to have him a near neighbor of ours."

"I am sorry to say it, Mrs. Peabody, you lack that most essential trait of Christian character — charity."

Upon this the good lady manifested her displeasure by leaving the room. But Mr. Simons, who was well acquainted with the deacon's wife, thought but little of the circumstance, as he had often offended her before, by similar plain language.

Mr. Johnson continued to preach to the satisfaction and perhaps edification of his people, when, to their grief, he received a call from a church in a distant place to become their pastor.

"What will be the minister's reply? What will he do? Will he consent to leave us?" were prevalent inquiries.

"Nothing will induce him to leave R——," some

said. " We don't know about it," said others. " We are so united in him that it would be wrong for him to leave us," said one and all.

In a few days, however, the conjectures of the good people were silenced, by the pastor stating to his friends that he believed it to be his imperative duty to leave, as it was a call of divine Providence. He regretted it much ; but the peculiar circumstances of the case, and his duty to his family, led him to the conclusion.

Deacon Peabody and his wife could not be reconciled to the decision of their pastor. He had been their friend and counsellor in prosperity and adversity, in sickness and health, and never failed to make himself agreeable. Mrs. Peabody, with tears in her eyes, called upon Mr. Johnson, remarking, —

" I'm dreadful sorry you are going to leave us. Is your mind fully made up ? "

" Yes, ma'am ; I think it is my duty to leave R—— ; but I regret it exceedingly. I have found many fast friends among my people, and they have been very kind to me ; but I think my health would be improved if I should accept the call and settle in S——."

" Why don't you leave for two or three months, and then return to us again, and not take your final leave ? "

" I think it would be better for the church to release me and obtain another pastor."

" But it is so hard to part, we are so attached to you, and you have been with us so long. I can't help crying, when I think of your leaving ! " And the tears began to flow afresh.

" I regret exceedingly that necessity compels me to leave a people to whom I am so strongly attached ; but

when duty appears plain to me, it would not be right
for me to disobey."

" We must submit to God's will, although it is hard ; "
and, continuing in the like strain for a few moments,
Mrs. Peabody left the parsonage, and returned to her
house.

The thought of losing her beloved pastor preyed
deeply on the mind of the old lady, and it was many
weeks before she could feel at all reconciled to it.
Every time she thought of losing the " blessed good
man," as she called him, the warm tears would fall
from her cheeks ; but when the last sabbath came, and
he was preaching his farewell sermon, you might have
heard the old lady sob half across the meeting-house.

In a day or two after, the minister and his family
took their departure for the town of R——.   Hundreds of his parishioners called to bid the family good-
by — and many a heart was sad.

The Wednesday following, Deacon Peabody took up
his daily paper, and read, among the advertisements,
that all the furniture of the Rev. Mr. Johnson would
be disposed of at auction on the following Saturday.
Mr. Simons was to be the auctioneer.

As soon as the advertisement was read, " I declare, I
will go," said Mrs. Peabody, " and buy some article to
remember Mr. Johnson by — some little relic of his."

" So I would, wife," said the deacon.   " Buy a tea-set
or something else."

" I will, husband."

Till Saturday came, the deacon's wife was continually
talking of the auction, and occasionally remarking,—

" The best articles to remember a faithful pastor by,

will be something he used in his family. As we use it, it will remind us of the good old man and his faithful instructions."

Early on the morning of the auction, Mrs. Peabody was at the house so recently occupied by her beloved pastor. She passed from one room to another, examining the articles, till at last her eyes fell upon a tea-set.

" This I will purchase," she said to herself, " and use it only when I have company, so as to keep it whole for many years."

The bell rang, and Mr. Simons, the auctioneer, and near neighbor of the deacon, commenced operations. The articles in the kitchen were first sold, every thing bringing a good price, for nearly all the church and congregation were present, each determined upon purchasing something by which to remember Mr. Johnson.

Finally, the auctioneer came to the tea-set — a common affair,—

" Ah! " said he, " this is a beautiful set, what you all want, and yet it will go for nothing. Examine it for yourselves, ladies, and bid something generous for it. Mrs. Peabody, this is just what you want," seeing her pass through the crowd to get another peep at the set —" what will you give for it? Don't be afraid to bid, give us something."

" Three dollars."

" Thank you for a bid, Mrs. Peabody, although it is not half what the articles are worth. Three dollars — three dollars — three dollars — who will give four? "

" Four dollars."

" Four dollars, did I hear? — Yes, four dollars."

" Five dollars," said Mrs, Peabody.

" Five dollars! " repeated the auctioneer,— " not near

its value! Six dollars — six and a half — going —
who will bid again? Seven dollars — seven and a half
— eight dollars — nine dollars — nine, and it is a shame
to sacrifice this beautiful set! Ten dollars — ten and a
half — eleven — eleven and a half. Only eleven and a
half — going — going — it is your last chance."

"Twelve dollars," said Mrs. Peabody.

"Twelve dollars — going — going — gone! Mrs. Peabody, the set is yours — cheap enough."

Without stopping to purchase more, the good wife,
pleased with her bargain, went home to tell her husband, requesting a little boy to bring the set immediately to the house.

"Well, what did you buy?" inquired her husband,
as she entered the house.

"A splendid article — a beautiful tea-set, for only
twelve dollars! Ah, here it is," she exclaimed, as the
boy handed it in at the door, — "here it is, husband,
this is what I bought."

"Did you give twelve dollars for this tea-set?"

"Yes, and the auctioneer said it was cheap enough."

"Confound it, wife — 'tisn't worth three dollars!
Why, I can go down town and purchase a better article
than this for three dollars."

"But, husband, it belonged to our minister — and I
would give more than that for it on his account."

"Curse our minister, I had almost said."

"Mr. Peabody, don't get angry; I thought you would
be pleased with the purchase, I'm sure."

"Well, 'tis bought; I'll say no more about it, and
pay the bill when it is presented — although it is so provoking. It is not more than a year since I sold just such
a set as this to Parson Emerson for less than three dollars,

I'm positive. But there, we must make the best of a bad bargain, and keep it as a relic of our excellent pastor."

"I'm sure it is an excellent set; and Mr. Simons, the auctioneer, and our near neighbor, would not have deceived me so much as you think for."

"I have heard auctioneers talk before to-day, I assure you."

As the deacon's wife put up the articles, she found that several of them were cracked, which she had not before observed; but she said nothing about it to her husband.

A few weeks after the purchase, Mrs. Peabody had a few select friends at her house, and at supper time she placed before them her new tea-set, remarking, "This once belonged to our pastor, and on that account I value it highly. I use it only on particular occasions."

All the ladies admired it, because they loved and respected their pastor.

A month after, the deacon and his wife were invited to sup at her neighbor's, Mr. Simons. In the evening, as luck would have it, Rev. Mr. Emerson and his wife came in. Had Mrs. Peabody known that Mr. Emerson was to be present, she probably would have kept at home, for of all ministers, she abominated him. Several stories had been reported, prejudicial to his Christian character, and she believed them, and pretended to despise him. However, the company conversed on several subjects, when the purchasing of articles at auction, and the deception sometimes practised, was mentioned. This was a subject in which the deacon's wife felt no particular interest, but she listened to hear the others converse.

8

"Do you remember my purchasing a tea-set of you a year or two ago?" inquired Parson Emerson of Mr. Peabody.

"Yes, sir, I do."

"I gave you three dollars for it, I believe. Well, being tired of it, and, as part of it was cracked, I handed it to Mr. Simons to sell for me. What do you suppose it brought?"

"How can I tell?" answered the deacon, looking as though he was thinking of something not very agreeable.

"It brought the astonishing sum of twelve dollars!" Oh, what a moment for the deacon's wife!

"Mr. Simons took it into the room where Rev. Mr. Johnson's articles were sold at auction, and it actually brought twelve dollars — was it not so, Mr. Simons?" appealing to the auctioneer.

"Yes, sir."

"It must have been a fool who bought it," one remarked.

"I think so, too," said Mr. Emerson. "It was not worth over two dollars."

"Who bought it?" inquired one.

"A lady bought it," said Mr. Simons, a little embarrassed, and he tried to turn the current of the conversation.

In a few moments the deacon and his wife were on their way home.

"Did not I tell you, wife, that the plaguy tea-set you bought was not worth two dollars? And it turns out to be the very set I sold for three dollars so long ago to Mr. Emerson."

When they reached the house, Mrs. Peabody hastened to the closet to look once more at her tea-set.

" Yes," said the husband, " it is the very set I sold so long ago ; our pastor never owned it — it was merely put into the room by the plaguy auctioneer to deceive people and bring a high price."

" That's a fact," said the good wife, as she threw a saucer upon the floor, smashing it into a dozen pieces.

" I'll follow suit," said the deacon, and smash went the whole set upon the floor, making a tremendous noise.

Mrs. Peabody never attended an auction again — and whenever articles that were bought as a bargain at ven- due, were shown to her, she thought of her tea-set, and looked upon them with a feeling of contempt. Nothing will sooner vex the old lady, than to ask her if she has any relic of Mr. Johnson, her beloved pastor.

NOT ASHAMED TO WORK.

They wrong, who shrink from looks alone,
Or from appearance judge :
Virtue may have the brightest throne
In her we make our drudge.

" Now, mother, I am eighteen years old, and as you promised me, I should like to go to town and see if I cannot earn enough to support me."

" I know, Hannah, I made you such a promise; but I was in hopes you would give up the idea of going to P—— before this time."

" I am more anxious to go now than ever. I think I may do well."

"And you may be glad to come back again. You have no acquaintances in town, and I know you will be homesick. Besides, there are a great many temptations there of which you have no knowledge. I think you had better conclude to remain at home, for the winter, at least."

" No, mother, I insist upon you fulfilling your promise. Ask father to be in readiness on Monday to carry me to P——, and if I cannot get a situation I will return."

" Well, Hannah, if you are set upon it, I suppose you must go."

Mr. Warner lived in a country town, and being the owner of a small farm, barely made a living. Having a large family, it was impossible for him to do more than clothe them decently and comfortably. His oldest daughter had heard that females from the country could obtain employment as domestics, and realize for their services from fifty cents to a dollar a week. This appeared like a large sum to Hannah, who had seldom seen more than a few small pieces of silver together. As she had received the consent of her mother to go to town, she felt happy at the thought.

It was soon spread about the neighborhood that Hannah was going to P—— to live: all her acquaintances called upon her to bid her good-by, and among the rest, Jonathan Johnson, the son of a farmer in the vicinity, who had always chosen Hannah to escort to husking parties and Christmas dinners, and for whom he had not a little partiality. It was on the Sunday evening previous to her starting for town on the following morning that Jonathan called to see her for the last time. As they sat together before the fire, talking about the intended journey, Hannah's success, and like topics, the lover remarked, " Now, don't forget Jonathan when you are away, but let me have a letter as soon as you get a place. Now you will, wont you, Hannah, let me hear from you right away? but I hate most awfully to have you go — you don't know how I feel about it " — and then he took from his pocket a large cotton handkerchief, which had not been opened before since it was ironed by his mother. After unfolding it and shaking it before the fire, he put it to his eyes, and wiped away the big tears that were gathering — " you see, how I feel, Hannah, I do so masterly hate to have you go " — and then he took hold of her hand and squeezed it.

8*

"Don't cry, Jonathan," said the girl, "for I shall write you just as soon as I get a good situation."

"You may think so now, but among so many fellows down there, you may forget me, and how should I feel ; " and Jonathan found use for his handkerchief again.

"Now don't feel so bad about it ; I wont forget you."

"Wont you, certain true ?   Now, Hannah, jest tell me, do you love me ? "

The poor girl blushed — but it was an innocent one — and looking up, said, " You know, Jonathan, without asking the question."

"But I kinder felt you wouldn't go way off if you cared any thing about me."

"You must not think so.   In P—— I can get from fifty cents to a dollar a week, and can be able to lay by a good part of it ; it is for this that I am anxious to go."

"I am proper sorry you are going to go so soon as to-morrow, but I shall expect a letter right off, and don't forget it."

As it was getting late, the lovers thought it best to retire.   Jonathan took his hat — looked grieved to death, and turned it over and over while he held down his head ; " Oh, how I hate for to go and leave you, but I s'pose I must ; don't forget me," and he made use of his handkerchief again, and bidding Hannah a good-night, and a pleasant day's ride on the morrow, he was on his way to his father's house.

Early on Monday morning, Hannah arose, got break-fast, and was ready to start for P——.   Her mother, after putting her bundle in the wagon, and seeing that she had left nothing behind, said to her — " Be a good girl, go into no bad society, and obey your master and mistress, wherever you may be. If you are homesick you can come back immediately — if not, write home and let us know how you get along."

Hannah could not help weeping as she bade her mother "good-by," and she and her father started on the journey.

Arriving in town about the middle of the afternoon, Mr. Warner put up his horse at the "Farmer's Tavern," and left his daughter in the house, while he went in search of a situation. About dark, he returned, and informed Hannah that he had secured her a place for the present at fifty cents a week, and that she might go with him and commence her duties.

It was in the family of Mr. Nelson that Hannah went to work. She felt very unpleasant when her father left her alone, and she almost wished she had never left home. Every thing was new and strange to her; but after learning her duty, she labored to perform it to the satisfaction of Mrs. Nelson and the family. At first what she did was awkwardly performed, but in a short time she learned to do her work as others did, and she became excellent help. For a week or two, Hannah thought a great deal of her home, her friends, and particularly of Jonathan Johnson, but gradually becoming acquainted with the family, and going out occasionally, she was more reconciled to her situation.

She addressed a line to her parents and also to Jonathan, expressing herself as being contented and happy, to both of which letters she received an answer. They were all well at home; one of her neighbors was about being married, another had a new gown, while her father's hogs grew finely. Jonathan wrote, that he was anxious to see her — he had thought of her day

and night, and dreamt of her besides. He concluded
by expressing his love for her, and hoped that she would
prove faithful to the last.

Mr. Nelson's family, beside himself and wife, consisted of two children, James and Olive — who were
about the age of Hannah. The daughter had been
brought up in a round of folly, and looked upon those
who worked for a living — more especially upon domestics — as beings far inferior to herself.

It was not often that she spoke to Hannah, except
when she informed her what to do, or scolded at her
for something that was not done exactly to her liking.
Olive had a great deal of company. Her father was
wealthy, and he indulged her in all her foolish caprices
and desires. He spared no expense to please her.
Books of all kinds she had in the house, but she seldom
perused them. An occasional tune on the piano, a call
or two, or the reception of company, served to pass
away the day. As for labor, she seldom performed any
excepting to work lace, or do some fine sewing.

Her brother was of a different disposition. He was
not proud, and thought it no disparagement to converse
occasionally with Hannah. As she was a modest girl
and behaved herself, he occasionally sat down in the
kitchen to have a chat with her. He inquired about
her parents, her friends at home, the size of the town,
or any thing to make conversation, and he seemed
pleased with the disposition and the spirit of the girl.
Olive would reprove him for his familiarity with the
kitchen girl, and tell him she wished he had more respect for himself— more honorable pride ; but James
would reply that so long as a girl was industrious, and
behaved herself, whether he found her in the parlor or

kitchen, in the palace or the hovel, he would treat her with respect.

To speak the truth, Hannah was a pretty girl — was kind in her disposition, and given to no foolish airs. She strove to please, and in this way she could not but win the esteem of the kind-hearted. Olive was plain in her person, and had not only a violent temper, but a thousand disagreeable airs. Her brother, when he had been censured for his kindness to Hannah, often told her, he wished her disposition was as good, her temper as even, and her heart as humble.

After residing in the family of Mr. Nelson for about a year, Hannah concluded to learn a trade, and at the same time to work for her board. She had no difficulty in obtaining a place, although the family were sorry to lose her — if we may except Olive, who, on account of her good behavior, and the attentions she received from her brother, was in no degree partial to her. For some time before she left, Olive had not spoken a pleasant word to her, and expressed her joy when she left the house.

After completing her trade, Hannah concluded to pay a visit to her parents. She had seen her father occasionally, since she had resided in P——, and as often as once a month received a line from him. But now, as two years had expired, she came to the conclusion once more to see her native place, and converse with those kind friends with whom, so long ago, she parted.

Starting early in the morning, she arrived at her father's towards sundown. The family were rejoiced to see her — the poor mother wept tears of joy when she embraced her child once more and saw by her looks that she was happy, and heard from her lips that she

had been well, and enjoyed herself. She had brought
her mother calico for a new gown, and several articles
for her younger sisters, with which they were much
pleased. All the neighbors began to crowd into the
house when they heard of Hannah's arrival, and asked
her a thousand questions, all of which she answered as
well as she was able. Among all the neighbors who
had come to welcome her home, she found that Jonathan Johnson was absent. Hannah was astonished
that he who professed so much regard for her two
years ago had not yet called, but it was too delicate a
question for her to inquire respecting him.

The day after her arrival, Hannah concluded to call
on Mrs. Johnson, and on inquiring for Jonathan, she
was informed that he was at work in the field. "But,"
said the mother, "you have heard, I suppose, that he is
to be married next Sunday to Abigail May?"

"No," said Hannah, greatly surprised, "is it indeed
so?"

"Yes, and they are to board with us."

"This," thought Hannah, "accounts for his not calling upon me."

She did not express any regret, or censure him to his
parents, although she felt that he was unworthy of her
love.

Jonathan saw Hannah enter his mother's house, and
ran to the window to look in, so as not to be observed.
The injured girl saw him, and without manifesting any
anger or displeasure, went to the window and called him
in. When he saw he was discovered, Jonathan turned
all manner of colors, and could hardly speak.

"Come in, Jonathan," said the mother, "come in and
see Miss Warner, your old friend."

He came, and when he saw her pleasant countenance, her neat dress, and heard her animated conversation, he would have given the world, had he been its possessor, to recall the step he had taken.

"What a fool I am! — what a beautiful girl! — how handsome she has grown! — how tidy she looks!" said Jonathan to himself.

"Why didn't you call to see me?" said Hannah, addressing Jonathan. "Didn't you hear of my arrival?"

"I was going to call, but I thought I wouldn't," said he, and he appeared very uneasy.

"Call and see me to-night, Jonathan, I should be happy to have you."

"Well — may be I will."

As he did not seem inclined to talk, Hannah resumed her conversation with his mother. As she left, she overheard Mrs. Johnson say to her son, "What a fine girl Hannah is! How far superior to Abigail May! If she had been your choice, I should not have a word to say."

She saw Jonathan peeping from the window as she passed by. The moment she looked up, he turned his head away.

Jonathan did not call on Hannah, but she was invited to the wedding on the following Sunday. She went, and the look of Jonathan told plainer than words could speak, that he was unhappy. Abigail May was half a head taller than himself, stooped over, and looked any thing but neat in her apparel. But they were married, and the evening passed off very well. Hannah was not sorry that she had got rid of her lover for since her return, he seemed to have grown stupid, and had lost his former ambiton. Everybody spoke

well of Hannah, and there was not a young man in the
village who would not have been glad to take her as
his companion.

Hannah had been at home but two or three weeks,
when one day a chaise stopped at her door. She looked
and there stood before her no less a personage than
James Nelson, the son of the merchant, and the brother
of the proud Olive. After the usual ceremonies of the
meeting of two friends, James was invited in, and introduced to the parents of Hannah. By his pleasant
manners, his freeness of conversation, and his manly
looks, he won the respect and the love of the family.
For a few days, he stopped at the farmhouse, and during that time, had made arrangements for the wedding.
All the neighbors were surprised at the good fortune of
Hannah; but they said she was worthy of as fine a
man as ever lived. In three weeks after, at her father's cot, Hannah Warner was united to James Nelson.
It was a happy season to them both. Although when
they became acquainted, one was comparatively poor,
and in an humble but honorable situation, the other
was the son of a rich man, with bright prospects before him. But he was won by the virtues of the heart,
and two happier souls never came together. Their dispositions and tempers were alike.

When Nelson took his wife to his father's house, she
was received with great kindness. Olive at first was a
little offish, but she soon lost these feelings, and loved
Hannah as an only sister. She regretted her past conduct, and by her acts of kindness, her endeavors to
please, made up for all her past folly and unkindness.

Mr. Nelson had realized a handsome fortune by industry and success in his business, and now gave his

store and its contents to his son, and retired from active life. Prosperity attended his steps — as it always does the virtuous and the diligent, and James appeared to be perfectly happy. Once or twice a year, Nelson and his wife visit her parents, and spend a few weeks in their society. He usually carries with him presents to the old folks and younger children, and is so cheerful, pleasant, and sociable, that his visits are always looked forward to with a great deal of pleasure.

A few years passed away, and Jonathan Johnson parted from his wife. He had become intemperate, and his wife was little better, and the last heard from them was, that they were supported by the overseers of the poor.

Mrs. Nelson belongs to one of the first families in town. She is industrious and benevolent. She never feels ashamed of having worked in the kitchen, or of having learned a trade, and whenever she sees the pert miss or the haughty girl, she does not hesitate to check her pride, and recommend her to work. "Be industrious," she says, "and you will succeed; but nurture pride, and despise those who work for a support and you will come to naught." She inculcates these virtues in her own family, and you can always tell her children by their neat and simple attire, their modest behavior, their industrious habits, and their respect for all classes, whether rich or poor, high or low, black or white. They have a smile for everybody, and everybody loves them.

9

THE TAILORESS.

Cold as the grave must be the heart
That pity never moves,
Which in distresses bears no part,
But self, self only, loves.

"MOTHER, I think I will go to the shop to-day; I am much better than I was yesterday; and you know what Mr. Emerson will say if I am absent two days in succession."

"I don't know what to think about it, Mary. I am afraid you are not well enough to work, and, besides, it is rather an unpleasant day to go out. You may do as you think best, however."

"On the whole, mother, I think I will go. By wearing my thick shawl, I shall be warm, and if it should storm a little to-night, there will be no danger of my taking cold."

"Be sure and tell Mr. Emerson the reason of your absence yesterday, and I don't think he will be offended. If it had been possible for you to go out, you might have taken cold and been laid up for a week. Don't work too hard, and remember that you have a slender constitution."

Mary Jones was the only daughter of a poor widow. Her mother had seen prosperous days, but losing her husband when her child was but two years old, she gradually became reduced in her circumstances. Mary was a dutiful and affectionate girl, ever attentive to the wants of her mother. She possessed a feeble frame, and it was only by taking particular care of herself that she was enabled to enjoy a comfortable degree of health. At the age of seventeen, she obtained her mother's consent to work in a shop, and learn the trade of a tailor. She was induced to take this step on account of the extreme poverty of her parent. "You know, mother," said she, "that you are not able to support me without working very hard yourself, and as you are often unwell, after a day's labor, I am afraid that you will not long be able to do any work. If I could learn a good trade, and have constant employment, I might be able to earn enough to support us both, without your being obliged to go out to wash, or take in work. Then we could enjoy ourselves and have all the necessaries and comforts of life."

Mary did not think of her own feeble constitution, when the idea of learning a trade first presented itself to her mind; and when she obtained her mother's consent, it was a happy day to her. She looked forward to the time when she should be able to earn her own living and support her aged mother, while neither should suffer for the necessaries of life. Full of spirits she visited the various tailor shops in town, and at last engaged a situation at Mr. Emerson's on these conditions: to work twelve months in acquiring the trade, in the mean time finding her own support; at the expiration of which period she was to be employed on wages. The appearance of the mechanic was not altogether prepossessing, in Mary's estimation. He was particular to tell her what he should expect, and among

other requirements, she must be at the shop precisely
at seven o'clock in the summer and precisely at eight
o'clock in the winter. If she lost a single day, it was
to be made up at the expiration of her apprenticeship.
On inquiring how long she must work each day, Mr. Emerson remarked, " Our girls work till sundown in the
summer season, and in winter till seven or eight o'clock,
except occasionally when we are in the drag, and then
they work a little longer."

The following Monday found Mary Jones in the tailor shop of Mr. Emerson, with some twenty or thirty
females, all of whom were strangers to her. As she
was put on plain sewing, she did not find the task difficult, and by degrees, with the assistance of more experienced shop girls, was enabled, in a short time, to do
her work to the satisfaction of her employer. Mary
heard a great deal of complaint made by the apprentices and those who were hired, against Mr. Emerson,
which but confirmed her in the opinion she had entertained of him. They accused him of meanness, of
want of principle, of avarice, of caring for nothing but
making money. He would hurry his girls to throw off
as much work as possible, and when called upon for
their hard-earned money, it was said he would oblige
them to wait, or put them off with miserable orders.
But as Mary had seen none of this herself she never
repeated a word of what was intimated in the shop.
She continued to work constantly and closely for a
month or two, when she found her health began to
fail. Going out in all weathers, sunshine and storm,
cold and heat, was what she had not been accustomed
to do. Besides, she lived a long distance from the
shop. Her mother was obliged to engage a cheap rent,

and this she could not find except on the outskirts of
the town.   Walking so far in the rain, and then attending closely to her business, without scarcely mov-
ing from her seat during the day, it is but natural to
presume, had a deleterious effect upon Mary's health.
She was obliged by sheer necessity to keep her house,
and her bed occasionally ; but feeling better the following morning, she would renew her task.

One day, after being absent, her employer said to her,
as she entered the shop, " How is it, miss, that you absent yourself so often from the shop ?   It appears to me,
whenever you know we are more hurried than usual,
you take that opportunity to stay away — a little fearful, perhaps, that you may have to work a few moments
longer at night, and stir your lazy bones."

With tears in her eyes, Mary replied, " I was extremely unwell, so that it was not possible for me to
come.   I do not intend to leave my work for any reason except utter inability to perform my duty."

" A likely story for a stout, hearty girl ; but you
must mind your p's and q's in future, or I shall be under the necessity of getting another hand to supply your
place."

Mary said nothing more, but resumed her work.
She saw there was sympathy in the countenances of
her fellow-apprentices, and when Mr. Emerson left the
room, they with one voice condemned him, and begged
her to think nothing about what he said.

" We have all been treated as unkindly as you,"
they remarked, " and there is scarcely a day passes,
that we are not scolded, or harshly reproved, for being a minute or two late, or for not doing the work bet-

9*

ter than it is possible to be done, or for some other trifling cause, when he is in an unpleasant mood."

Mary continued to go to the shop, although on some
days she was hardly able to sit up.

She was determined to learn her trade, and earn a
support for herself and poor mother, and, without
dreaming of the injury she was doing to herself, she persevered like a martyr. One day it was exceedingly unpleasant. In the night a severe storm from the north-
east had commenced, and when Mary awoke, the snow
was nearly two feet deep, and so drifted that it was
with difficulty that one could pass along the streets.
But Mary, knowing the disposition of Mr. Emerson, resolved that she would go to the shop. Her mother endeavored to persuade her not to think of such a thing.

"If I don't go, mother, I shall certainly lose my
place ; and the hope of earning something for our support will assuredly be cut off. You are aware of the
temper and disposition of Mr. Emerson, and if he as-
certains that I was able to sit up, and did not go to the
shop, he will discharge me at once. I must go, mother."

She went. Toiling on through the snow, the poor girl
reached the shop, more dead than alive. No inquiry was
made how she got along or whether she had not better
rest a few moments, and warm herself. No ; but she was
immediately put to her task, and as some of the girls
were kept at home that day, Mary was obliged to stay
much longer at night, and go home alone through
deeper snow and heavier drifts. When she arrived at
her mother's she was nearly exhausted and by her appearance one would have supposed her to be in a rapid
decline. Her mother had prepared for her supper the best

her little means could afford, of which she partook and retired. The next day Mary was too sick and feeble to leave her bed. She attempted to rise two or three times, and as often sank on her pillow exhausted.

" O mother ! " said she, " I am afraid I shall lose my place now, I cannot go to the shop to-day."

" Never mind, Mary, don't worry yourself about it. If you should be turned away, Providence will never let us suffer."

" It is not so much for myself that I feel, mother. It pains me to see you work so hard ; you will wear your-self out in a short time."

" Perhaps, after an hour's rest, you may feel better. Try to obtain a little more sleep."

But through the day Mary was sick and feeble and scarcely left her chamber. The following day, however, she was a great deal better, and thought she was able to work. It was at this time that the conversation took place at the commencement of our story. She started for the shop, but all the way she dreaded to meet Mr. Emerson. " What shall I do," she thought to herself, " if he turns me away ? What will become of my poor, feeble mother ? She cannot now perform the work she could in years past, for sickness and age have worn upon her constitution, and almost broken her down. But I will trust to Him, who knoweth my situation, and who never will forsake me in trouble." And then she breathed a silent prayer to Heaven as she passed along.

As she opened the shop door, the first person she saw was Mr. Emerson. An angry frown was on his coun-tenance. " Mary," said he, " I came to the conclusion yesterday to discharge you. You are more plague than profit to me. While the other girls work, you are away, idling your time, probably, with some half-crazy lover. I can stand it no longer."

Mary, half sobbing, replied, " Sir, I was not able to work yesterday. My mother will tell you my anxiety to come ; but I sat up very little all day. That is the truth."

" A likely story. You are the picture of health, a stout, hearty girl ; able to perform the work of a man, and yet complain ! O God ! what a world this is ! No, no ; some country lover was in to see you, and yet you try to palm off this story upon me. I can't stand every thing."

" But, sir, try me once more. I am poor, or I would not ask for work. I am willing to labor to the utmost of my ability, in hope at some future period to do something for the assistance of my mother. But try me once more, and if I am absent, I will not solicit work again."

" Well, I'll try you ; but remember the first day you are absent, let me never see you darken that door again. Go to your work ; " and as the poor girl hurried along, he muttered something to himself, which she could not understand.

Mary had now more than half completed her trade, and as warm weather was approaching, she felt encouraged that she should soon accomplish her object, without any further sickness to put her back and displease her master. On and on she toiled at her task, early and late, until the twelve months were completed, and all the time she had lost had been made up. Mrs. Jones was obliged to live sparingly, and deny herself many comforts to enable her daughter to appear decently through the past year, while learning her trade, and now it was accomplished, a smile of joy — of triumph

—lighted up their hearts and made the little room they occupied, a paradise to them.

"Mother, now we shall be happy," said Mary; "I shall have wages, and the last quarter's rent, which I have promised in six or eight weeks, I shall be able to pay."

"Or it may be that I shall yet earn it."

"No, mother, you must not labor now, as you used to do. I will work, and can earn sufficient, if God gives me my health, to supply us abundantly with all the necessaries of life."

Full of hope, Mary entered the shop, and informed Mr. Emerson that her time was out, and, according to his agreement, requested employment.

"But have you made up all your lost time?" inquired he.

"Yes, sir," said Mary, "every hour that I was absent I have fully made up."

"Well, I must look into it. As I am busy now, call some other time."

"Can I not go to work to-day?"

"I can't attend to it now. Don't bother me — I'm busy."

The poor girl left the shop in tears. Her hopes were almost blasted. She had not doubted but she should find employment, since she had given a whole year's work, and received not a farthing; she did not expect to be treated in this unkind manner. Her mother endeavored to console her by saying that perhaps in a day or two Mr. Emerson would have something for her to do, and that he was doubtless exceedingly perplexed when she called upon him.

Mary saw Mr. Emerson in a few days, and all the re-

ply he made to her urgent request was — "I have not
yet attended to it; call next week and I'll let you know."

It was three or four weeks after Mary left the shop
before she entered it again to work. She had thus
been put off from time to time. She was to receive for
her labors but twenty-five cents a day. But then she
thought that that amount, well spent, would make herself and mother comfortable. She had pledged herself
to pay five dollars which was the last quarter's rent, and
this she could obtain in three or four weeks. Punctual
and constant to her task, the four weeks soon passed,
and the landlord called for his pay.

On asking Mr. Emerson for the amount, he answered
her, shortly, "I have no money now!" and left the
shop. What to do the poor girl did not know; the
money was promised, and she could not obtain it. Her
landlord was a rich and oppressive man; he had threatened to turn them from the house a month before,
and it was only the solemn promise of Mary that he
should be paid in six or eight weeks, that induced him
to be lenient, and permit them to occupy the house.
Now, he was expecting the money; it had been promised that very morning; for Mary had no doubt, as her
employer was wealthy, that he would pay her at any moment. What could she do? She waited a whole hour
for another interview with Mr. Emerson, and then made
known to him her case. But he was perfectly indifferent, said he did not wish to be eternally dunned, and
never intended to pay her wages in money. Perhaps in the course of a few days he would give her an
order. Such treatment was more than a sensitive girl
could bear. She went home, bathed in tears. Her
mother could not pacify her, although she endeavored

to do so. "But I have promised to pay our landlord. He expected it to-day; and he will certainly turn us out of the house."

"I will see him again, Mary."

"It will be of no use. You know his disposition — that what he says, he will do at all hazards."

While they were conversing, and Mary was in tears, Mr. Power, the landlord entered, and asked for his rent.

"Be seated a moment, sir," said Mrs. Jones, "and I —

"I can't stop," interrupted Mr. Power; "hand me the money and I'll go."

"Mary could not obtain it to-day."

"What! not ready yet! Leave the house instantly! Start! bag, baggage, and all! You've imposed on kindness too long! Away with you! Don't shed those crocodile tears, but pack up your duds and start! I'll not be treated in this manner any longer."

"O sir!" cried Mary, "do have pity — do pity my poor, aged mother. I pray you, don't send her into the street this bitter cold night. Wait but one day longer, and we will pay you, or go."

"I wont wait, and there is an end on't. I have been wronged and cheated, times without number, by just such spongers as you are, and when it comes to this, your pretended tears you think will save you. Away! out of the house!"

"I beg you, dear sir, to hear me. I have the amount due me, and expected to receive the money this day from Mr. Emerson; but he declined to pay me and says he will give me an order. If you would only accept that, sir, I think I could satisfy you to-morrow."

"Pretty well, too, to tuck off an order upon one who has worn out all his patience in waiting upon you.

But if you will certainly hand me in a good order to-morrow, I will let you remain; but remember, I will never take an order again; and the moment you refuse to pay your rent punctually, that moment you shall leave the house. This is the last time I will be fooled with by you." So saying, he left the house.

But little rest did Mary and her mother obtain that night. Perhaps Mr. Emerson would refuse to give the order the next day; and if so, what would become of them? With broken slumbers, the morning dawned. After partaking of her scanty meal, Mary went to the shop. She commenced her weary task with feeble spirits. Her peculiar look was noticed by her shop-mates, but not knowing the weight that preyed like an incubus upon her mind, they failed to administer proper consolation. As soon as Mr. Emerson came in, Mary left her work, and trembling with fear, she made known her object.

" When I get leisure, I'll attend to it," he replied. " Have I not told you repeatedly not to dun me to death? You are more trouble to me than a little. I tell you once for all that I will not be so tormented by you; when it is convenient, I will give you the order, and not before."

" Sir," said Mary, " I am peculiarly situated; if it were not so I would not ask you for the order."

" That's your eternal plea. There is always something urgent about your business. You want to buy some dainties, maybe, to entertain a country lover. If you were half as interested in your work, and consulted your employer's interest, you would be a great deal better off. When I am at leisure I'll attend to you, and I hope in mercy this will satisfy you."

The tears came in Mary's eyes as she stood before the unfeeling man.

"I could tell you, sir, my object in requesting the order to-day, if it were necessary; and then you would not censure me. A great deal hangs upon this decision."

Calling his clerk, he said — "Give this girl an order on Mr. Gooch, the grocer, for five dollars. I shall never have any peace until she is paid. To be so tormented with the plaguy girls is enough to make one tired of life; but, thank Heaven, she is the only pest I have in the shop."

Mary took the order, but she could not restrain her tears as she renewed her task. The girls pitied her, sympathized with her, but yet knew not her sorrow. When night came, she carried the order to Mr. Power, who, as he took it from her hands, remarked, " This is the only thing of the kind I shall ever take. If the next quarter's rent is not paid on the day it is due, I want you to understand distinctly, that you must shift your quarters forthwith. There will be no mistake about it."

Mary flew to her mother to tell her the glad news of her success — that she had received the order, and paid the landlord. Happiness was in that cot that night, as with gratitude they raised their thoughts to God.

Early the next morning, Mary and her mother were greatly surprised on seeing Mr. Power enter their door. By his looks they were prepared for something unusual, when he exclaimed, "Am I thus insulted! — Is my kindness and lenity to you thus repaid? Wretches you are, to give such an order as this to me! — Why, Mr. Gooch charges me ten per cent higher than I am charged at any other store in town. He says it is an

10

express understanding between himself and Mr. Emerson, as he makes the deduction in his favor on settlement. This you must have known when you palmed the order off on me! Out of the house instantly, and take your miserable order. I'll never let my house again unless I know who's going into it, and I can secure the rent. Out of the house instantly, or an officer shall be called immediately."

In vain did Mary and her mother plead; the hardhearted wretch was invulnerable to the calls of pity. He even seized their only bed, and threw it on the floor, declaring that unless they exerted themselves, every article should be thrown into the street.

"I shall retain enough of your furniture," said he, "to cover my debt, and when you settle you may have it, and not before."

A neighbor kindly consented to take Mary and her mother into her house, and permit them to occupy a little bedroom. Thankful for such a favor, they expressed their gratitude in a flood of tears, and soon removed what little they possessed. But her hard work and confinement, her exposure to all weathers, and the sufferings of her mind, soon brought the dutiful and affectionate Mary to a sick-bed. That very day she was taken with a slow fever, and was obliged to absent herself from the shop, though with great reluctance, as the little she could earn would so materially assist them, and of which they now were in peculiar need. Her mother was obliged to take the order returned by Mr. Power, and purchase those articles necessary to the sustenance of life, and she found that the grocer did, indeed, charge her a great price for her goods. Once she remonstrated a little, but received only an insulting reply. It was a bargain between Mr. Gooch and the tailor, that the latter should have a certain per cent deduction by ordering goods at his store, and there was no remedy for the poor woman.

For three or four weeks, Mary lingered on her bed, when her disease took an unfavorable turn, and her situation was pronounced dangerous by her physician.

"It is no unwelcome news to me," said the noble girl; "but on your account, dear mother, do I wish to live. It pains me to think of dying and leaving you to the charities of a cold world."

"Fear not for me, my dear child," said her mother, who was almost inconsolable by the thought of losing her affectionate child, "God will take care of me — and if we part, it cannot be for a long season. I feel my days are nearly numbered."

"If I die, I know our Father above will provide for you. He never forsakes those who put their trust in him."

Many a time did the poor mother take herself from the bedside of her child, that Mary might not see the grief of her heart. It was like death — yea, harder than death, to part with one so kind, so dutiful, so affectionate; an only prop, an only counsellor in her declining years.

As the days passed away, Mary grew weaker and weaker; a few only called to see her, and among these the females who worked in the shop, who by their little presents and kindnesses manifested how much they loved her. They seldom left her couch with dry eyes. Her resignation, her trust in God; her patience; her Christian character throughout, so wrought upon them that they almost envied her situation. Mr. Emerson never visited her, never inquired for her health, and

was as indifferent to her circumstances, as if she were
a brute. Mary censured him not; nor manifested any
other disposition than that of kindness towards him.

Mary Jones died — she died in faith and in triumph.
Her last words were, " Lord Jesus, receive my spirit,"
and the struggle was over.

A few followed her to the grave; for she was known
by a few only. But their sorrow was sincere. Even
now when her name is mentioned, it brings a tear to the
eye, and a sorrow to the heart.

The mother survived her daughter but a few months,
most of which time, she kept her bed. She now re-
poses by the side of Mary, in the house appointed for
all the living.

The case of Mary Jones is not a solitary one. Hundreds of feeble and tender girls are induced to go out
to work, in all weather, by the hope of a future support. They are poor, but they are industrious and virtuous. There are many who take advantage of their
circumstances, and give them but trifling pay for their
services. When money is justly due them, and they
are in pressing need of the necessaries of life, justice
is denied them day after day and week after week.
They turn them off with miserable orders, or pursue
any other course whereby they can make money, without any regard to the oppression which they exercise.
We verily believe that, like the subject of the above
tale, scores of poor females thus suffer and thus die.
But few know them, and their wrongs are suffered to
die with them. If we can awaken an emotion of pity
in a single breast, or induce one heart of avarice to
melt in love and tenderness, or to sympathize with the
suffering poor, we shall not have written this story in
vain, and our reward will be incomparably great.

BEAUTY AND DEFORMITY.

Trust not to beauty ; it will fade
Like rainbow tints away ;
While virtue, in perennial bloom
Lives through an endless day.

" WILL nobody love me, mother ? " said Ellen to her
only parent, as she came running into the house —
" will nobody love me ? " and she hid her face in her
mother's lap and wept.

" Yes, my child, your mother loves you ; but why these
tears ? "

" As I was at play on the bank, a lady passed by, who,
as I looked up, exclaimed ! ' What a horrible creature ! '
O mother ! nobody will love me but you."

Mrs. Mansion had but one daughter, and that was
Ellen. She was extremely plain. Her hair was coarse
and of a flaxen color, and always looked in a snarl. Her
eyes were very large, and of a homely gray, her mouth
wide, and her nose flat. Besides, her face was completely covered with freckles, which altogether made her
one of the plainest children ever created. To a stranger,
she had a very unprepossessing appearance, which often led people to make remarks similar to the above,
and which gave the sensitive girl a great deal of pain.
But Ellen Mansion possessed a sweet and amiable disposition ; she was kind, benevolent, and generally cheer-

10*

ful, so that she won the affections of her neighbors and companions. It was only when an unkind remark was made in her presence, that sorrow seemed to enter her heart, and then she would give full vent to her feelings in tears.

Within a short distance from the cottage of Mrs. Mansion, lived a wealthy farmer by the name of Johnson, whose only children, Edward and Jane, were brought up in the indulgence of all their hearts could desire. The daughter was pretty,— some called her beautiful,— and she was the idol of her parents. But she was a proud and envious child. As she grew older she was fully sensible of her beautiful face, and was aware that she attracted a great deal of attention and many admirers. Once she was the playmate of the widow's daughter, and together they would cull flowers, attend school, and make themselves happy in various ways. But as years flew by, and she could distinguish between riches and poverty, beauty and deformity and saw that caresses were bestowed upon her, and denied to her friend, she began to treat Ellen with coldness, to call upon her less often, and finally, in her social parties, to refuse to give her an invitation. The poor girl felt it all, and said but little. Instead of engrossing her mind with the fashions ·and the follies of the day, she spent her leisure hours in reading and study — in improving her mind. As she grew older, she became more intelligent, but her homely features remained. When Ellen and Jane were about eighteen years of age, there seemed to be a perfect coldness existing between them — they would speak when they met, and that was all. Occasionally, Ellen would endeavor to throw out some pleasant topic of conversation, but Jane appeared so indifferent to the poor girl, that she, without appearing to notice it, would part with her as pleasantly as if she had always been kindly treated. It was her disposition to return kindness for ill-nature, while she endeavored always to speak well of her neighbors. She was well aware, if she had possessed beauty and wealth, she would have been treated differently; but she remembered that she was created as God saw best, and a murmur never escaped her lips.

The village church had recently been deprived of their pastor by death. The venerable rector was a good old man, and Ellen appeared to be his especial favorite. By his request, she attended upon him during his sickness, administered to his comforts; and did all in her power to alleviate his sufferings. As he was a single man, his little property, by his will, was given to Mrs. Mansion and her daughter.

The good pastor had been dead some months, when a call was given to a young man, who had supplied the pulpit for a few sabbaths, to settle over the church and society. Mr. Clark accepted the invitation, and became more and more attached to the people the longer he continued among them. Mr. Johnson was the principal supporter of the ministry, and Mr. Clark boarded at his house. The young pastor was a well-educated man, and possessed fine talents. He was what might be termed handsome. It was the village talk, that Mr. Clark would take Jane to be his future companion, and as her father was wealthy and a man of influence in the town, all the neighbors thought it would be a wise choice. Jane had received a number of offers, none of which she would accept, as they were mostly from farmers and mechanics, who did not possess much of this

world's goods. What was whispered by her neighbors,
Jane partially construed into a reality, and really supposed Mr. Clark was in love with her. Of course, as
he boarded in her father's house, it could not be otherwise than he should treat her with politeness and occasionally accompany her on a visit to her friends. These
common attentions led Jane and her parents and her
neighbors to presume that their pastor intended to make
the beautiful girl his companion. A few of the judicious thought otherwise, and even expressed it among
themselves. "Jane is not suitable for a pastor's wife.
She cannot work — she is too proud and too self-willed,"
would be their remarks. In his pastoral visits, Mr.
Clark made no distinction between the wealthy and the
poor, and would as often be found in the humble cot as
in the painted dwelling. Mrs. Mansion seemed to be a
particular favorite of his, and it was noticed that the
parson never appeared to be more happy than when
conversing with her and with Ellen. The latter was
remarkably intelligent, and appeared more like his equal
in conversation, than any other member of his parish.
Then, too, Mr. Clark seemed to sympathize with the unfortunate girl and her poor mother.

One day after Mr. Clark had been settled nearly
a year, in conversaing with Mr. Johnson, he asked
him what he thought of his entering the matrimonial
state. Supposing the good pastor had his daughter in
view, he replied very favorably to his query, recom-
mending him to enter that state without delay.

"Before many months I think I shall take me a wife,"
said the pastor.

Mr. Johnson mentioned the conversation to his wife,
and both concluded that Mr. Clark had their daughter in

his mind. Nothing was too much for them to do to please their minister, and make their house agreeable; but he, good man, had not the least suspicion of their conjectures, but pursued the same course as he had heretofore. Jane was too vain and too proud for him, and, besides, she did not possess sufficient intelligence to make her company agreeable. In fact, she had nothing but beauty and wealthy parents to recommend her, and these were nothing in comparison to a well-informed mind, a gentle disposition, and a humble heart. One evening Mr. Clark remarked, "I think I shall call on Mrs. Mansion; should you like to accompany me?" addressing Jane.

She hesitated a moment, and then said, "I should be pleased to go," but her look and manner gave her words the lie.

When they arrived at Mrs. Mansion's, Ellen and her mother received them with smiles, although many a day had passed since Jane had had an opportunity of conversing with her friend. The evening passed pleasantly away to all but the haughty girl. As they returned to their homes, the pastor inquired of Jane, "How are you pleased with Ellen Mansion?"

"I like her very well, but you know her situation has been such that she has never seen much company. She is so distressingly homely, few care about visiting her."

"Don't you think she has a fine mind?"

"Why — as to that, I don't think she is any thing remarkable. To be sure, she has studied a great deal, and ought to know something."

From Jane's conversation, Mr. Clark saw that her own condition in life and her personal beauty had so

carried her away, that she could not look on poverty
and deformity with any degree of complacency. But
as for himself he looked to the mind, and not to its
rough shell, and although Ellen was plain, he had resolved long before to make her his wife.

The next sabbath, when it was announced that Mr.
Clark was about taking to himself a wife, and the lady
of his choice was Ellen Mansion, nearly the whole
parish was struck with astonishment. When Mr. Johnson announced it to his family, the proud Jane was
completely overcome, and if it had been fashionable in
those days, she would have fainted and fallen, and not
have recovered so as to see company for a whole week.
"Can it be possible?" exclaimed her mother, "only
think how much we are doing for Mr. Clark — and now
he has gone to that old lady and taken her daughter.
Why, Ellen is nothing but a heap of deformity."

"'Tis laughable, truly," said the father; "where can
be his discernment? He must be ashamed to walk with
her in the street. But every one to his taste."

"I don't care," at last said Jane, "let him have the
creature, if he likes her, and good luck to them. Mr.
Clark is no great things after all."

Mr. Clark found he was treated rather coldly by the
family, but could not divine the reason. Certainly,
thought he, Mr. Johnson can have no objection to
my marrying, since he expressed himself favorably
of it.

A day or two after, when the subject was introduced,
Mr. Johnson ventured to express his surprise at the
choice he had made, and stated that many of his parish
were of the same opinion.

"I tell you, Mr. Johnson," said the pastor, "there is

not that young woman's equal in town. She is plain
to look at, I know, but she possesses a superior mind,
and a most excellent disposition. She is perfectly humble ; she is kind and obliging, and is more anxious to do
a favor than to benefit herself. It is her delight to visit
the sick and the distressed and use all the means in her
power to benefit them. Your former pastor loved her ;
there was not a member of his church he esteemed more
highly than he did Ellen. I believe she possesses every
requisite for a minister's wife, and I know she will
make me happy. If there is a person in our society
who can say aught of her I should like to see that individual, for I am certain he cannot know her."

Mr. Johnson made no reply ; he was a little vexed,
because, in his own mind, he had selected his only
daughter for the pastor's wife, who possessed both
wealth and beauty. To have a very plain and humble
girl take a place he had expected Jane to fill, was hum-
bling indeed. If Mr. Johnson thus felt, the haughty
girl felt it so much the more keenly, and no language
was too harsh for them to use in reference to Mr. Clark.

Without much ceremony or parade, Mr. Clark and
Ellen were married. The neighbors remarked that she
never looked better, and that as she grew older, she was
less plain. Certain it was that the virtues of her heart
made up for the deficiencies of her person. Ellen made
a most excellent wife, and by her counsels and advice
contributed greatly to the happiness of her husband.
The church and society now approved of his choice, and
seemed to be as devotedly attached to the wife as they
were to the pastor. In her benevolent acts her kindnesses and her charities, her looks were forgotten, and
her plainness was never mentioned or thought of by the

people. In a few months, Mr. Johnson and his family
buried all their hard feelings towards the pastor, and
Jane herself became a constant visitor at Mr. Clark's.
She had altered materially within a few months, and instead of that haughty look, and that unbecoming behavior which formerly characterized her, she manifested a
humble temper, and lived a consistent life. She united
herself to the church of Mr. Clark, and with his wife
went about doing good.

Jane has often acknowledged her errors to Mrs. Clark,
and confessed her sin in slighting her on account of her
poverty and deformity. " But," she has often repeated,
" you have been the making of me. When I treated
you with contempt, the forgiving disposition which you
always manifested, made me ashamed of myself; and
although I knew your mental superiority, I would not
acknowledge it, and so I shunned and endeavored to
despise you."

A few years passed away, while peace and prosperity
attended the good pastor and his people. They loved
him and his wife, and used their endeavors to sustain
and encourage them. To be sure, his salary was small
and his pay was mostly received from the farms of his
parishioners, yet he had plenty to sustain himself and
asked for no more. But in the midst of their happiness,
the good and devoted wife of the pastor sickened and died.
It was a severe stroke to Mr. Clark, for he was devotedly attached to his wife, and the society mourned her
loss as if a parent or a child had been taken from
their own families. Hundreds followed her to the
grave, and never before was there such a sad day to the
poor villagers. It could be read in every countenance;
it could be noticed in every word. Mr. Johnson, at

his own expense, erected a monument to her memory, on which her name and her age were inscribed with the following simple line : —

"BLESSED ARE THE DEAD WHO DIE IN THE LORD."

A year had elapsed since the death of the beloved Ellen, when Mr. Clark led to the altar another bride. The reader will not be greatly surprised when he is informed that her name was Jane Johnson — the once proud and unsanctified girl; the now humble and Christian woman. She had been so long intimate with the pastor's first wife, that she caught her very spirit, and became so much like her that the good man has often said, "It seems as if the soul of Ellen had passed into another body." Every one approved the pastor's choice; for Jane was as much respected and beloved now, as she was condemned before. For many years they lived happily together, and spent their days in following the example of their Master in going about and doing good. Their influence is felt to this day among the people of that devoted parish.

Let young women learn, that though beauty may entice the eye, it cannot win the heart; but real goodness, though clothed in a plain exterior, commands the love and respect of all.

11

A TALE OF MOOSE ALLEY.

CHAPTER I.

A little word in kindness spoken,
  A motion or a tear,
Has often healed the heart that's broken,
  And made a friend sincere.
A word, a look, has crushed to earth
  Full many a budding flower,
Which, had a smile but owned its birth,
  Would bless life's darkest hour.
Then deem it not an idle thing
  A pleasant word to speak;
The face you wear, the thoughts you bring,
  A heart may heal or break.

"THERE is some one knocking at our back door, Sarah; go and see who it is."

The little girl ran to see what was wanted, and in a few minutes, returned to her mother, saying, "It was only a dirty beggar boy, who asked for cold victuals."

"What did you tell him?"

"I told him we hadn't any, and that he must come again."

"But perhaps his parents are very poor, and he may not have had any thing to eat to-day. You should have given him something."

"He looked so ragged and so dirty, that I was almost afraid of him."

"If he ever calls again, ask him to come in, and if he is really deserving of charity, we will pick up something for him."

The parents of Sarah Griffin were not wealthy; they made a comfortable living and yearly added a little to their property. The father was a mechanic, and by his industrious habits and correct moral principles, had gained the respect and confidence of all who knew him. Whenever he undertook a piece of work he was particular to have it faithfully done, so as to give entire satisfaction to his employers. By this means, he was never out of work, and was gradually becoming independent. His wife was prudent and industrious. She did not follow the foolish fashions of the day, but was neat in her dress, having every thing that was comfortable and necessary. Whatever was brought into the house was taken care of; nothing being wasted or destroyed, that would prove beneficial either to her family or her neighbors. Mrs. Griffin never had a desire to make a show in the world, and to pass for more than she actually deserved; but her ambition was to please her husband, to bring up her family to industrious and virtuous habits, and to exert a good influence about her. She lived on the best of terms with her neighbors, and never had the least unpleasant feeling towards them, while they esteemed her a pattern of gentleness and kindness.

One day as Sarah was looking from the window, she exclaimed, "O mother! here comes that ragged beggar boy again; do go to the door and see what he wants."

Mrs. Griffin went to the door, and presently the little fellow made his appearance in the kitchen, where he had been invited by the mother. Sarah stared him in the face, and with reluctance handed him a chair, where he seated himself, holding his torn hat in his hands. The poor boy hardly ventured to look up, when he replied, " Joseph Lanford," to the question, " What is your name ? "

" Where do your parents live ? " inquired Mrs. Griffin.

" In Moose Alley."

" What does your father do ? "

" He don't do any thing, he can't get any thing to do. He used to work on the wharves loading vessels and piling boards, but now he can't get any thing to do."

" How long is it since you have been obliged to beg your bread ? "

" All winter ; but I don't get much."

" Do you attend school ? "

" No, ma'am ; my clothes are not suitable. I did go once to Master Winslow, but he was so cross and whipped me so hard, that mother kept me at home. But I think if I had good clothes, I would go again — and perhaps I might learn."

After giving the poor boy a supply of food, and advising him to learn no bad habits, Mrs. Griffin told him that she should call on his mother in the course of the week.

" I'm much obliged to you," said the poor boy with a bow, appearing exceedingly grateful for the lady's kindness.

" I do pity that boy," said Sarah, " for he looks kind and pleasant. I wish he had better clothes."

" There is a great deal of poverty about, and multitudes of children who suffer for the necessaries of life. I have no doubt the parents of this boy are extremely poor, and I shall call upon them."

"Mother, may I go with you, when you call on them?"

"Yes, my child, if you wish to go."

"And perhaps I can do something for them. I can sew and knit, and assist them, I know."

A few evenings after, Mrs. Griffin, accompanied with her daughter, went to the house of Mr. Lanford.

Moose Alley was a narrow lane, especially at the head, but it was found without much difficulty.

"But how do you know which house to call at?" inquired Sarah.

"I don't know, but we will inquire."

At that moment a gentleman passed by, of whom Mrs. Griffin inquired — "Can you tell me where a family by the name of Lanford lives?"

"No, ma'am, I cannot."

"Who lives in this small black house?"

"Mr. Leach, the sexton," and the man passed on.

"Inquire of Mr. Leach, mother, perhaps he can tell you."

She knocked at the door, and a tall, dark-eyed man came, of whom she made her inquiry, but she could not get the information she desired. "There are several families who live at the bottom of the alley," said the tall man, "but I am not acquainted with their names."

Mrs. Griffin passed down the alley, and meeting a little black fellow, who told her his name was George Gardner, she inquired for Mr. Lanford, and was directed to the house.

When she knocked at the door, the little boy, Joseph, came and invited her and Sarah to walk in.

"Here, mother, is the lady I told you about," said the boy; "she has now called to see us."

11*

Mrs. Lanford expressed her gratitude for the visit, and requested them to be seated. The house was very old, and the room but poorly furnished, and every thing betokened extreme poverty.

" For the last six or eight months," said the woman, " my health has been feeble, and my husband finding but little employment, I have been obliged to depend upon others for assistance. Our neighbors are very good, but most of them are poor, and my little boy has been obliged to beg sometimes. We feel grateful for what you have done for us, but cannot repay your kindness."

" I liked the appearance of your boy," said Mrs. Griffin, " and promised him I would call and see you. I shall be pleased at any time to render you what assistance I am able."

" I thank you kindly; I am in hopes my husband will obtain work. Being a laborer, he has scarcely done a day's work the last two months, but we live in hopes that times will be better."

Mrs. Griffin had brought a few little things which she gave to the poor woman, who expressed her gratitude in tears; and little Sarah opened her bag and drew forth a few dainties for Joseph, who thanked her for her kindness. Mrs. Griffin after spending an agreeable hour with the poor woman, went home; not, however, until she was strongly invited to call and see them again.

" What a pleasant woman Mrs. Lanford is, " I should like to call at her house very often."

" If we could do her any good," said the mother, " it would be worth while to call upon her."

" But you gave her something."

" Yes — that was but a trifle, however. But we will

see if we have not some old clothes of your father's, that will answer for her son."

" And let me carry them down ? "

" You may if I can find any thing suitable."

Mrs. Griffin mentioned the visit to her husband, who united with her in endeavoring to assist them, for she believed them to be not only poor and needy, but honest and industrious. In a few days a suit of clothes was made for the boy, and Sarah was happy with the thought of carrying them down. She tripped through the alley and the first person she saw was the black boy, George, who smiled at her as she passed along. Mrs. Lanford was overjoyed with the present, and thanked the little girl a dozen times for the kindness.

" Come, Joseph," said the mother, " and see what the little girl has brought you — a pair of trousers."

The little fellow looked at them with astonishment. " Are they mine, mother? did the good lady send them to me ? Now I shall be able to go to school," and he thanked Sarah for bringing them down. " Tell your good mother," continued the boy, " that I hope to be of some use to her. If she wants anybody to go of errands, or split her wood, or bring her shavings, tell her I shall always be happy to do it." And pleased with her visit, and the gratitude manifested by the family, the little girl ran home.

" I do love to visit Mrs. Lanford, she is so pleasant," said Sarah to her mother ; " and little Joseph says he will do any thing for you."

A number of months passed away, and Mrs. Griffin continued to send food, or clothing, to the poor family in Moose Alley, when one day, she was informed by Mrs. Lanford that her husband had made up his mind to re- .

move to Boston, where he thought he should find employment the year round, and be able to support his
little family. She expressed a great deal of regret to
leave one who had been so kind to her as Mrs. Griffin,
and said she never should forget her kindness.   Sarah
and her mother were sorry to lose the poor family, for
they had become attached to them, and felt a pleasure in
visiting and assisting them.   The first packet that sailed
for Boston took the poor family, together with the little
furniture they possessed.

CHAPTER II.

What beauty and what heavenly grace
Beam in a virtuous woman's face !
True index of a heart devout ;
As pure within as fair without.
Methinks the holy angels vie,
As on a mission from the sky,
To lift above her humble prayer,
And gain for it admission there.

A FEW years passed, and Sarah left her school to commence doing something for herself.   Although her
father was in good circumstances, it was her choice to
learn a trade ; "I may see the necessity of it, by and
by," said she.   She chose to be a mantuamaker, and by
diligence and industry, soon acquired it.   Sarah was an
excellent girl; she was kind and accommodating, possessed a sweet temper, and was calculated to win the
respect and love of all who became acquainted with her.
She was not beautiful; her beauty was centred in the
mind — the true seat of worth and excellence.   But,

notwithstanding, there were several who thought they should obtain a prize, if they could but win the affections of Miss Griffin. In some things she was peculiar. She said but little to those young men who have no steady employment and strive to live by their wits, or sponge their bread from the hands of honest industry. She labored herself, and she was determined, if she was ever married, to be united to an industrious and useful man —one who was not ashamed to work, providing the employment was honorable. While two or three young gentlemen, whose parents were wealthy, were constant visitors at her house, there was one whom they occasionally ridiculed on account of his peculiar notions. He had been brought up with them, but chose to keep aloof from their company, when he had a leisure hour, and spend it in some useful employment. He was a young mechanic, and not unfrequently visited the house of Mr. Griffin. Of all her male acquaintances, Sarah was more partial to the mechanic, Edson by name. This was noticed by those who thought themselves superior to him, and they put forth their strongest efforts to bring him into contempt. He never heeded their remarks, but pursued his business, regardless alike of their smiles or their frowns. When it was a settled point, that Sarah was to become the happy wife of Edson, the envy of the foppish and idle young men was excited to its highest pitch.

"She has a singular taste," said one.

"She'll miss it," said another.

"And she is a fool," said a third.

But she knew her own business best; she had consulted her own happiness; and the young mechanic became the husband of Sarah Griffin. It is needless to

say they prospered — for as certain as the day succeeds
the night, so sure will prosperity follow in the train of
virtue and industry.   They commenced life in a humble
way, purchased but little furniture, and hired a small
house — the very house, which had been thoroughly re-
paired, once occupied by the Lanford family.   Here
they lived pleasantly and happily.   Edson, being a good
mechanic, had as much work as he could attend to.   In
a few years after his marriage, he had saved enough
from his earnings to purchase the house in which he resided.   Although it was not so pleasantly situated, still
it was convenient for him, and with peace of mind, true
contentment, and an affectionate wife, it was his paradise.   But this happiness was not long to last.   That
insidious disease, consumption, which yearly sweeps off
so many of our citizens, seized the frame of Edson, and
his constitution bowed to its mandate.   He was sensible that he could not live — that his present sickness
would be his last; but he was resigned.   He had placed
his hopes in a better world.   It was hard to leave his
wife and only child, but he knew that He who taketh
care of the sparrows would not suffer them to come to
want — His care would be over them still.   And the
good man died — died in faith and triumph.   But

"When such friends part, 'tis the survivor dies."

It was so in this case.   Sarah suffered in mind, but
she looked above the earth for comfort and consolation.
The thought that at some future time she should be re-
united to her husband gave her peace, and in some measure abated the waters of affliction that rolled over her.

Mrs. Edson continued to reside in the house bought
by her husband, and by taking care of the little property

left at his decease, and working more or less at her trade she was enabled to live comfortably and pleasantly.

Sarah had been a widow something like three years, when on one summer day, as she was sitting by the open window, she observed a stranger pass, looking rather thoughtfully at her house. He went by, and seeing her, turned and inquired, "Can you tell me what became of the family that lived in yonder black house some twenty odd years ago?"

"No, sir, I cannot," said Sarah, "for I have lived here but six or eight years. What was the name of the family?"

"Gardner; there was one member, a boy then, who appeared to be a fine fellow. His name was George."

"Oh, I do remember him. He died a great many years ago, when quite a youth. I have heard him spoken of by many of his old playmates as a very exemplary boy."

"Is he dead? I have played with him for many an hour, and though he possessed a dark skin, a kinder and better boy never lived."

"Did you formerly reside in this place?"

"I did, but it is many years since."

As the stranger seemed anxious to make inquiries, he was invited to step in, and gladly accepted the invitation.

"I perceive many changes," he continued, "since I was here before. What has become of the old sexton who lived in the black house at the head of the alley?"

"He is also dead."

"And his sons?"

"They dropped off one after another, and not one of them, I believe, is left."

" And where's the merry shoemaker who kept below ? "

" He is gone also."

" There was the S—— family, the H——'s, the M——'s, and I forget how many more who formerly lived in this neighborhood. Are any of them living ? "

" Yes ; some of them are alive, but where they reside, I cannot tell."

" But there is one family I feel particularly interested in, of whom I have thought many and many a time since I left Portland ; but you probably don't know them. The name was Griffin."

Sarah was struck with astonishment. " You cannot mean the Griffin who formerly resided on —— Street ? "

" The same ; where are they ? and what has become of their daughter, Sarah ? Do you know her ? "

" I am their daughter."

" Gracious heavens ! can it be possible ? " and he extended his hand, saying, " My name is Lanford ; I am the poor beggar boy that you felt so much interest in years ago," and tears of joy checked his utterance.

After a few moments of silence, the young man related to Sarah the principal incidents in his life. When his parents removed to Boston, they were as poor as they could be, but his father got work and prospered. When Joseph was old enough, he went to a trade, completed his apprenticeship, and commenced trading for himself. He was now doing a good business, and felt anxious once more to see his native place, and converse with those friends with whom, years before, he associated. For two or three hours did Sarah and her friend converse upon the past, and when he left, he promised faithfully to call and see her again.

Lanford remained but a few weeks in the city, and

when he left for Boston, Sarah had become his wife. They now live happily together.

Lanford is doing an excellent business, and has prospered beyond his most sanguine expectations. Once a year they visit their friends in Portland, and we often hear the remark, when referring to old times, and bringing to mind the playmates of our youth — " Lanford has turned out well. From a poor, destitute boy, by industry and integrity, he has amassed a large property, and is respected and beloved by all who know him."

12

WIDOW AND SON.

CHAPTER I.

Oh, let me die the death of those
    Who calmly sink to rest,
Like placid summer evening's close,
    That fades so gently in the west.
With not a pain, with not a care,
    To ruffle life's decline,
But soft as dews of heaven are,
    Oh, be the last repose of mine.
As gently as the voices fall,
    Of seraphs on the ear,
Be the commissioned angel's call —
    As soft, as melting, and as clear.

"Listen to me, Henry, and do not indulge the thought of leaving your place. True, you may do better, but there are ten chances to one that you will not succeed as well — that you will bitterly regret it in the end."

"I am so confined, mother, that I don't like to stay with Mr. Walker. I should rather go to sea. You know I always had a desire to see the world; and I told you I did not think I should stay, when you put me to a trade."

"You have been there some time, are acquainted with the family, and your master is a good man and appears to be attached to you."

"But I cannot stay. I am determined to go to sea, and you may as well give me your consent."

"That I can never do, Henry. You are my only child, and to have you follow the sea would be as severe an affliction as could happen to me."

Henry Norton lost his father at an early age; and the care of an only son fell upon one of the best of women. His mother was kind and benevolent, and a pattern of industry. Having been left with but little property on the death of her husband, by taking in work, she was enabled to live comfortably, enjoying all the necessaries of life. Henry was a good boy, but rather too headstrong, and when bent upon pursuing any course, it was a difficult matter to turn his mind. At an early age, Mrs. Norton placed her son, as an apprentice, to a worthy mechanic, and for the first year or two Henry was contented and happy. But an associate of his had obtained the consent of his parents to follow the sea, which at once unsettled the mind of the apprentice and made him discontented with his place. He had often endeavored to get his mother's consent to leave Mr. Walker and go with his companion, but the good woman would not hear a word about it. Finally, seeing the determination of her son, she made known to him her feelings. But Henry was resolute.

"If you do not give your consent," said he, "I will run away."

"Remember," said his mother, "the consequences of disobedience to parents. If you should so far forget me and disregard my feelings, perhaps it may be a thorn in your flesh the rest of your days. I have told you repeatedly that I can never give my consent for you to follow the sea. If you ever go, it will be contrary to the express wish of your mother, and God will never bless you."

"Well, I don't care, I will go to sea, if I can get away, whether you give your consent or not," said the stubborn boy, leaving the house.

A day or two after, Mrs. Norton heard from Mr. Walker that her son had run away from his place, and shipped on board a vessel and before he was apprised of it, had sailed. The poor woman burst into tears, and wrung her hands, exclaiming, "What shall I do? Oh! how can I bear this affliction?" And it was a long time before she could be comforted. She thought how poorly her son was clad — of the privations and dangers of the sea — of the company of profane men on board the ship, with none to counsel or advise him — and she was sad indeed for many a day. She had no heart to work, lost her usual vivacity, and her neighbors pronounced her in a decline. However, the poignancy of her grief wore away, although she never ceased to think of her erring boy.

After a twelvemonth had passed, the vessel returned; but to open afresh her lacerated heart, Mrs. Norton was informed that her son had left the brig in a foreign port, and it was uncertain what vessel he had shipped on board. Those who have a mother's feelings, and those alone, can realize the sorrows of her heart. Perhaps her son was dead, or, if alive, in the company of the vile and unprincipled, or it may be that he was suffering from disease, with no kind hand to administer to his wants. Such feelings burdened her soul, and gave her anguish inexpressible.

Another year passed and not a word had been heard respecting Henry. Mrs. Norton, true to a mother's love, had made up various things for him, should he ever return, and what little she earned, beside what was sufficient for her own support, was treasured for his benefit. But her son came not. Year after year passed by, and no tidings of her boy came to her ears. She finally gave up all hope of seeing him, presuming he had come to his end in a foreign port, among strangers. But Mrs. Norton continued to work for a support, till she was induced by a friend to give up housekeeping, and reside with her, where she should do but little, and enjoy herself in her declining days.

It was upwards of twenty years since Henry left his mother, and no one supposed that he would ever be heard from again. In fact, but few remembered the boy; and the circumstance of his leaving was treasured only in the breast of the mother, and the few friends with whom she was intimate. Mrs. Norton had grown old. The afflictions of her early years — the loss of the best of husbands and an only son, the idol of her heart, had so worn upon her spirits, that she seemed but a wreck of humanity. Still she looked up to God in thankfulness for the blessings she enjoyed, and was ever striving against sin, and endeavoring to live the life of a Christian. Threescore years had passed away, and the good woman was taken sick. It was evident to her physician, and to all who saw her, that her sands had nearly run out, that death was fast approaching. She was told that she would probably never recover. But death had no terrors for her. She had always lived a consistent, Christian life, and now said — "I am going to my Father and my God."

"Have you no desire to live?" inquired her friend.

"Not the least. My Saviour is waiting to receive

12*

me. The thought that I shall see my Maker and enjoy his presence forever, gives me joy that I find it utterly impossible for me to express."

Seeing her friend weeping by her side, the dying woman said, " Do not weep because I go; it will not be long before you will meet me in heaven.   Oh, how blessed it is to die ! "

Full of praise, and without a seeming doubt of a happy state beyond the grave, Mrs. Norton, after lingering a few weeks, fell asleep in Jesus.   Her last words were — " Come, Lord Jesus, come quickly."

Everybody who knew this good lady loved her.   The old and the young surrounded her bed while she lingered, catching the heavenly strains that fell from her lips.   Her little property was left to the marine society for the benefit of the poor sailors.

CHAPTER II.

What is your life ?   A vapor's breath —
The passing of a cloud at morn ;
You smile, you weep, lie down with death :
The traveller of a night is gone.

WHEN Henry Norton parted from his mother, he came to the determination to leave Mr. Walker and follow the sea.   The first opportunity that presented, he shipped on board a vessel, and, without informing his master, sailed for a foreign port.   Every thing was new to him on board the vessel, and it was some time before he was able to take hold and work like the rest of the crew.   He experienced that unpleasant sickness so common to fresh hands; but when fully recovered, he was as hearty and active as any of the crew. Before he had reached his destined port, however, he found that sea-faring life was not what he had anticipated on shore. Watching by night, in the storm and cold, and continually exposed to the weather in all seasons, made him regret more than once that he had left a pleasant trade and a kind master. Above all, he regretted most bitterly that he had disobeyed his kind parent, and pursued a course which he knew must fill her soul with sorrow.

When the vessel reached her destined port, the young sailor went ashore with the crew, and in a round of pleasure forgot his serious emotions. He had learned the follies and the vices of the sailors, and would drink and swear as heedlessly as the most abandoned. The vessel being bound home, Henry abandoned her, and shipped on board another. He felt ashamed of his course and conduct, and was determined not to return at present. Henry was soon upon the ocean again, but had not been out many days before the vessel experienced a severe gale. The captain thought it was not possible for the ship to live, the wind was so tremendous, and the waves beat over them with so much fury. One poor fellow was washed from the deck into the sea, and was never seen again. However, the storm abated, and the craft survived, with the exception of the loss of one or two of her sails. Our young seaman had never before seen a storm at sea, and he was terribly frightened. He wished a thousand times that he had obeyed his parent and continued his trade. When a fellow-sailor — one with whom Henry had been intimate — was swept instantly away, and launched into eternity, it affected him to tears.   But when the storm ceased, and the vessel moved on smoothly as before, he forgot his danger, and was as lively and as careless as ever.

For ten years Henry was a rover upon the seas, seldom remaining on land but a few days at a time, and contriving in that short space to spend his hard-earned money.   During all this period he barely clothed himself, without laying by a single copper for his own use or to assist his poor mother.   Having arrived in a vessel within a hundred miles of his native place, he resolved to take the stage and see his mother.   It was the first time, since he left home, that he had come to this conclusion.   Arriving in town at the close of day, he bent his steps towards the cot his mother occupied ten years before.   As he approached the house, he saw a glimmering light from the window, and curiosity prompted him to look in.   There sat his poor mother, intent upon her work; he knew her as soon as he cast his eye towards her, but his heart misgave him.   His error rose up before him, and the thought of his vicious life, and the manner in which he squandered all his money, not possessing a single dollar to bestow upon his kind mother, made him resolve to go no further.   The calm, sweet look of his parent, as she bent over her work, would not suffer him to intrude.   With no money, with no character, to come before her was more than he could bear.   Perhaps she would sink under the thought, and it would destroy the little happiness she seemed now to partake.   The sailor wept and turned away.   Again he returned, and looked once more upon his dear mother, and sank down in grief.   In a moment, he was gone, and the next day he was on his journey to the vessel he had left.   From that hour, Henry was an altered man.

He had seen his mother, and while looking upon her pleasant countenance, he resolved to be a better man —never to swear again, but to go away and take care of his money, and return, a son worthy of such a woman. He determined to save all his earnings, that the latter days of his parent might be cheered by his smiles, his virtuous conduct, and his prosperity. It was exceedingly difficult for Henry to overcome his bad habits, but hard as it was, he conquered them. He never drank again, and an oath was never heard to pollute his lips. He was frugal and industrious, and strove to do his duty. From a common sailor he rose by degrees, till he commanded as fine a vessel as ever whitened the seas. Yet he toiled on, accumulating money, till in the course of eight or ten years from the time he saw his mother, he was the owner of a beautiful vessel. We will not follow Captain Norton through his voyages, nor recount the many dangers he escaped, nor the shipwrecks and trials he encountered. He was a superior officer and a real gentleman.

Once more, with a light heart, he was bending his course towards his native place, which, ten years before, he had left under peculiarly distressing circumstances. He arrived there in the morning, and putting on his best clothes, started for the dwelling of his mother. He was on the point of lifting the latch and walking in, when the thought struck him that perhaps his mother might have removed. He rapped at the door, and a stranger came. On inquiry for Mrs. Norton, Henry was told they knew of no such woman; they having resided there for about three months only. The thought struck him that he had better call at the house of his old master; and on going round he passed the graveyard. Curiosity prompted him to enter. On many a stone he read a familiar name; many had been sleepers there for years, whom he supposed were living, active beings. After wandering about the tombs for upwards of an hour, he saw a funeral procession enter. He walked to the new-made grave, waiting pensively for the approach of the dead. But a few followed. The coffin was laid beside the grave, and Henry stepped forward to read the inscription. It was — "Mary Norton, died May 4, 1840, aged 60 years."

"Oh! my mother! my mother!" — the captain exclaimed, falling prostrate on the coffin.

The little group, being astonished beyond measure, instantly raised him from the abode of the dead, and discovered that life was extinct. The poor man had died of a broken heart.

From the papers found in his pocket, and from his general features, it was ascertained that he was the long-lost son of the widow. In a few days his body was placed beside the grave of his mother. But few dry eyes were present.

THE OLD KEY.

Thy modest virtue and thy grace
How dearly do I prize!
The very soul of loveliness
Beams in thy sparkling eyes.

MARY JOHNSON was a plain, modest, unassuming girl of fifteen years; and poor, of course, as all modest females are. Her parents lived in a small house, and by industry and economy made a comfortable living. In the neighborhood were many wealthy females, who were proud and fashionable, and therefore took but little notice of the Johnsons. Occasionally, Mary would associate with the children of her neighbors, but seldom received an invitation to visit them at their houses. There was one young lady, however, who seemed extremely fond of Mary, and although her parents moved in a higher circle, and never visited the Johnsons, yet she was often found in the humble tenement with her companion. Mary was often invited to her house, and was kindly treated. Ellen Jameson loved her on account of the good qualities of her heart. Mary was kind, sweet-tempered, and perfectly amiable. But among her neighbors there were those who treated her with much indifference, if not contempt, and they would take pains to let her see the bad feeling of their hearts. Mary paid but little attention to what they

said or did; minded her own business, worked for her
mother, and improved her leisure hours, not in writing
silly letters to the beaux, and reading the trashy novels
of the day, but in perusing valuable works, or attending to some useful branch of study.

When Mary was about sixteen years of age, a gentleman by the name of Aubert, reputed to be wealthy,
paid a visit to his relations in the neighborhood. During his visit, the young ladies of fashion had several parties, to each of which the stranger was invited. Aubert was about thirty-five years of age, and
possessed the elements of a real gentleman. He was
not haughty, and knew well what belonged to good
manners. A short time before he left the village, it
was Ellen Jameson's turn to invite company, and, of
course, she had her modest friend, Mary Johnson,
among the number. The poor girl had never before
been introduced to the stranger — she being the only
female in the place, who had not found an opportunity
of conversing with the accomplished Aubert. During
the evening, but few noticed the humble Mary, who enjoyed herself as well as she could. Occasionally, she
would notice the haughty look and contemptuous smile
of some of her neighbors, who had elegant and fashionable dresses, and sometimes a remark not very pleasant
would reach her ear.

"I should not have come here," said one, "if I had
known one of the Johnsons was invited."

"I like to keep better company," said another.

"It is provoking," said a third, in which remark all
appeared to concur, excepting Ellen, who did not happen
to hear the conversation.

Before the company broke up that evening, Aubert

stated that on the morrow he should depart from the village, and perhaps should never see any of them again. "I have passed a pleasant season among you," said he, "and I shall always look back with pleasure to the time I have spent here. Before I go, I wish to leave you all something as a token of my regard.— a trifling present. But in the first place, young ladies, I wish to ask you all a simple question which I trust you will gratify me in answering."

All the girls at once consented.

"The question I wish you to answer is — What do you most desire in life? That which you think will afford you the most happiness? Now," he continued, "I wish you each would answer this question on a slip of paper, and leave it with our friends here to-morrow, and before I depart, you will each receive in return, a trifling present."

The girls were pleased with the idea, for they all respected the gentleman, and on the morrow each one left her answer to the question. One wrote "Riches," another "Beauty," another "Accomplishments," and so on. But Mary Johnson being singular in her choice, wrote, "Modesty and Virtue."

Aubert departed that day, and left presents for all the females who wrote answers to his question. To one he gave a watch, to another a chain, to a third a ring, etc., but to the modest Mary he left nothing but a common key.

When it was whispered about the neighborhood that each one had received a present, the fashionable girls had a hearty laugh over poor Mary's. "Yes," said they, "she thought by her silly answer that she should receive the handsomest present, but she got nothing but an old rusty key. It was all she deserved."

But Ellen Jameson told her friend that she was welcome to her own present; for she felt grieved that she should be slighted more than the rest.

"I am perfectly satisfied," said Mary; "I did not expect much, and I assure you, the key is as good a token of remembrance as I could have. I shall never be tempted to part with this; 'tis of so little worth that no one will desire it."

"But you know how our neighbors feel about it. It pleases them much."

"You also know, Ellen, that if I had been presented with a gold watch, it would have excited their envy, and they would have made more unpleasant remarks than they possibly can do about the key."

"True, and I am glad you feel so pleasant about it; but I confess I was disappointed and sorry when I heard what had been left for you."

Mary continued to pursue her course in an humble way, and although her neighbors laughed a great deal about her present being an old rusty key, she heeded them not, but minded her own business. It was Mary's ambition to earn her own living, to do all the good she could, and exert a happy influence around her. She was devotedly attached to her parents, and when they were ill, all her endeavors were put forth to alleviate their sufferings.

Year after year passed on, bringing various changes in the neighborhood. A few of Mary's companions were married, while the remainder were still living in hope, but as yet no one had offered his hand to the humble girl. Had wealth been showered upon her, had her parents moved in the fashionable circles, she would have found a dozen suitors. But no; she was a hard-working, poor, and industrious girl, whose highest ambition was to do good and promote the welfare of her parents, and make those around her happy.

It was now a dozen years since the visit of Aubert to the village. A great many had forgotten the circumstance of the question and the presents. But occasionally the fact that Mary Johnson was presented with a rusty key, was kept alive by those who styled themselves the "first classes," in the neighborhood.

A young man by the name of Derby had but recently removed into the village, and commenced trading. He was poor, and while so was modest and humble. He was thought but little of by the wealthy, from the fact that he had no property, and was intimate at the house of Mr. Johnson. It was said that he had engaged himself to Mary, and there was good foundation for the report. While matters were in this train, his business began to increase and Derby was very successful in many of his trades. In two or three years, he had collected quite a handsome property. When it was circulated in the village that Derby was "well to do in the world," the rich girls courted his society, and by degrees, so turned his affections from poor Mary, that he finally left her for the company of her wealthy neighbors. Mary was grieved to the heart at the conduct of one in whom she had placed implicit confidence, and to whom she had always been kind and agreeable. But the poor girl did not reproach him, or threaten to revenge him, or her neighbors, but bore her affliction with a true womanly spirit. If this is his disposition, she thought, it is lucky he has left me. If he does not love me, why should I wish longer to cultivate his acquaintance? It is better for me to suffer a little now than to endure a lifetime of sorrow. Glorious girl! we wish there were ten thousand like her in the world.

Within a year after Derby's cruel treatment to Mary, he was married to the daughter of one of the most wealthy men in the place — to the very girl who, so many years before, had said the most she desired in life was riches. We need not say there was little real affection existing between the newly married couple; that the reader will surmise. With them the greatest enjoyment of life consisted in the accumulation of dollars and cents, and the carrying out of the fashions of the day. It was said by those who knew the parties best, that their house presented any thing but scenes of love and kindness. Happiness was a word neither of them could comprehend.

About this time, the death of Aubert, the gentleman of reputed wealth, was announced in the neighborhood. He had made his will, one clause of which ran something like the following: "The large iron trunk which has remained for years in my private room, I desire to be forwarded to the village of ——, and to be presented to the lady, if living, who has a key that will unlock it." The trunk, with a copy of the will, had been forwarded to a gentleman in the neighborhood, with the necessary instructions. After a few inquiries, he learned that Mary Johnson had, years before, been presented with an old rusty key. He hastened to her, and made known the death of Aubert, and the clause in his will respecting the key. Full of surprise, she ran to her drawer and produced the key. The gentleman immediately employed a carter to bring the trunk. The key fitted it exactly.

"Miss Johnson," said the gentleman, "I know not the contents of the trunk. It is yours. For your sake and your parents', I trust it contains something of value." So saying, he left the house.

As soon as her father came home, Mary related what had transpired, showing him the present, and desiring him to look into it.

The old gentleman unlocked the trunk, when lo! gold coins and rare jewels presented themselves to the astonished gaze of the family. Suffice it to say, that after a thorough examination, the contents of the trunk were valued at no less sum than ten thousand dollars — no small amount for a poor girl. There was a little note at the bottom which read as follows : —

"This is the reward of modesty and virtue."

If we had the power, we would portray the feelings of young Derby and his wife on hearing of this good luck. But we cannot. The girls who once turned from Mary Johnson with contempt, desired to court her society; but she treated them kindly, without referring to the past, or desiring such acquaintances.

Mary is as modest and unassuming as ever, and uses her wealth to promote the happiness of others. There is not a family on earth where more real comfort is enjoyed than in the newly shingled and white-painted cottage of the Johnsons.

We shouldn't wonder if the next mails bring us the news of the marriage of Mary Johnson to a worthy and industrious mechanic, who, but a short time previous to her good fortune, had secured her affections by his rare virtues and accomplishments.

Modesty and virtue — what females will not prefer them to riches, fashion, and impudence ?

13*

THE REFORMATION.

In kindness breathe a word; it may
   Sink deeply in the breast
Of one who long has been astray
   In paths of vice unblest.
Drop but a tear, and it may fall
   Upon a stony heart,
That long resisted wisdom's call,
   And life and joy impart.

MARY JOHNSON was the pride of the village. Gay and cheerful, she had culled the flowers of eighteen summers, without scarcely realizing the flight of time, or the reality of existence. Surrounded by kind friends, and blest with wealthy parents, she was contented and happy. Possessing a mild disposition, and being courteous in her deportment, Mary received the praise, and won the affection of all who knew her. Being an only child she was the idol of her parents, who spared no pains in her education.

From early childhood, Mary had been intimate in the family of a neighbor by the name of Elson. The oldest son, Henry, had been her companion in early youth, and they had grown up together, with scarcely a day passing when they were not in each other's company. They had now pledged their love, and the day was appointed when they should become man and wife. The parents of each were well pleased with the union, and had used their influence to bring it about. The marriage-day was one of interest to the whole village. Everybody loved and respected the happy couple. They had grown up in their midst, and not a word had ever been lisped to their discredit. They were kind and obliging, sociable and pleasant, and possessed that disposition which always secures the esteem of others. When the ceremony was over, all the invited guests formed a procession and escorted the young husband and his wife to their future abode. Their parents had erected a neat and commodious dwelling, which they presented to the happy couple. It was neatly furnished, pleasantly situated, and surrounded by beautiful trees. And here Elson and his wife were happy. They had every thing to make them so. In the morning, Henry would go to his business, while Mary found pleasure in attending to her household duties, or taking care of the various plants, which adorned their gardens.

Thus month after month passed away, while prosperity attended their steps and happiness brightened their glorious sky. Every day their kind neighbors would call to see them, while they in turn visited their friends. From so auspicious a beginning, one would predict the lives of such would be no other than happy — that peace and contentment would continue to linger around their door. It was thus for two or three years. As long as Henry continued in humble life, felicity dawned upon them, and each day brought new pleasures to their delighted dwelling. But Elson had become popular with the villagers; they all loved him, and as a mark of their respect, he was nominated as a candidate to fill the highest office in town. Without the least opposition he was elected. This was a mark of honor

wholly unlooked for, and it elated Henry not a little.
He had never moved in any other but the humble walks
of life ; and to be so distinguished — to be looked up to
by the whole village, made him feel the importance of
his office, as it naturally would one who had been un-
accustomed to receive such a distinction, and more especially as it was never expected and had never been
sought.

At this period it was customary whenever an individual had received a mark of honor from his fellow-
citizens, to manifest it, by occasionally inviting those in
high standing, such as the selectmen of the town, to
his house, and giving them a treat. Elson commenced
this practice, and for the first time in his life partook
of the social glass. As his associates increased, his
taste for spirits began to strengthen, till a little every
day seemed to him indispensable. Mary thought her
husband was less attached to his home than formerly,
and that his love for her was gradually diminishing.
The reason why she could not conjecture. She labored
to please him, and did all in her power, to make home
happy and her company attractive. One night she was
astonished and grieved beyond measure to discover that
her husband was a little intoxicated, and on asking him
a question, she received an angry reply. It was the
first time that a cross word had escaped his lips. Mary
burst into tears. She remembered the past ; the happy
hours and pleasant days they had enjoyed. Henry, instead of feeling regret for the misery he had brought
upon his wife, spoke unkindly to her, which only increased her sorrow, and brought the tears to her eyes.

"O Henry, how can you talk so?" said she ; "what
have I done to merit such treatment? You know my

attachment to you, and yet you reproach me. I try to do only that which will please you."

Her husband made no reply; and on the next day he was more pleasant, acknowledged his fault, and promised to drink no more. But he had now acquired a habit which it was no easy matter to conquer. Henry determined in his own mind, come what would, to resist the temptation; but it was too powerful. He yielded, and continued to use a little every day. It could not but be noticed by his devoted wife, who entreated and begged of him to resist the tempter, and forsake the practice which was growing upon him, blasting his prospects, and bringing her to the grave; but she pleaded in vain. The people lost their confidence in Elson, and his office was given to another. He now neglected his business, associated with the low and spent much of his time at the tavern. As is the case with those who give themselves up to strong drink, Elson became unkind and abusive to his family. He found fault with every thing done for his comfort by his devoted wife, reproached her wrongfully, and from the best of husbands, became one of the most abusive and tyrannical of men, especially when under the influence of spirit. To see the lovely wife was enough to make the heart ache. From the cheerful, contented, and perfectly happy woman, she was almost the victim of despair. The conduct of Elson so preyed upon her spirits, that the flush of health had forsaken her cheek, she grew thin and cadaverous, and seemed to be fast wasting for the tomb. Her parents endeavored to persuade her to come to their house, and leave a man who conducted so basely. But to them she would not hearken. She loved him yet; she clung to him in his degradation, and strove with all her strength to please him and make him happy.

One day Mary called upon the keeper of the tavern, where Elson spent his money and watsed his time, and requested him not to furnish the means of intoxication to her husband.

"You know," said she to the keeper, "that it is injuring his health and destroying my happiness; as a great favor, then, I will beg of you not furnish him with the means of intoxication."

"It wont do for me, situated as I am, to refuse liquor to any gentleman who may call. I don't calculate to sell to those who have enough already — but I can't refuse gentlemen, ma'am, any way."

"But couldn't you persuade my husband not to drink? Can't you tell him the consequences?"

"Oh, he knows the consequences better than I can tell him; it's no use to try to compel men not to drink when they will have spirit. Why, if I should refuse to sell him, he would go somewhere else, you may depend upon it. He may as well obtain it here as in any other place."

"But you know there are very few places where it could be obtained, and I am confident if you refused it to him, he would not drink one-half as much as he does now. O sir, if you knew my sufferings, I am confident you would oblige me in this thing, and not sell any more spirit to him."

"It is my business to sell, and I cannot refuse when a gentleman calls for a glass of liquor. You had better go home, and not try to prevent what you cannot help."

"Sir, if you will but refuse to furnish him with the means of intoxication, I will assure you that you will not be the loser by it. I, myself, will agree to pay you double what you would make by selling spirit to him."

"'Tis no use talking, I shall sell it when purchasers are gentlemen." So saying he left the room, while the good woman turned her steps homeward. Sorrow pressed hard upon her, and the tears would steal down her cheeks. "Oh, what shall I do to reclaim him?" was her constant mental inquiry.

That night Elson came home more intoxicated, and, consequently, more abusive than ever. His language was coarse and profane in the extreme. He even threatened to strike the wife of his bosom.

"I understand," said he, "that you have had the impudence to call at Mason's tavern, and try to persuade him not to trade with me. A pretty trick, indeed, for a woman. What do you mean by such conduct, I should like to know?"

"You are aware, Henry, that of late I have led a miserable life, produced by the course you have pursued, in partaking too freely of the intoxicating cup. Once I never dreamed of such a thing."

"It is all a lie, and you know it," said he, in a passion. But Mary said no more, merely asking him to retire.

It is useless to converse with a drunken man. He has no reason; and so she perceived, and concluded to postpone conversing with him. Perhaps on the morrow she would have an opportunity. That night was a sad one to Mrs. Elson. Sleep refused to come to her swollen eyelids, and tears were her repast.

The mother of Mary had died about a year previous to this period, and her father was so much displeased with his daughter for living with Elson, while he continued to abuse her, that he declared he would do nothing

towards her support, even if she should come to want.
The parents of her husband had become reduced, so
that they by prudence only were enabled to live from
day to day. It was the love that Mary bore to Henry,
and the dark prospect that was before them, which
pressed so heavily upon her spirits — that refused to
give rest to her limbs or slumber to her eyes. As Elson had been a long time out of business and his funds
were exhausted, she knew not what would be the result
of his course. The thought, however, that they owned
a house, from which none could expel her, was some
source of consolation, and she resolved never to forsake
her husband as long as she lived, and she could obtain
her daily bread. Mary had moved in the first circles of
the village; had always been invited to the parties of
her friends, and was received with pleasure. Everybody
loved her then for her circumstances were good, and her
husband steady. But now her friends seemed to forsake
her; partly because she would not listen to their advice
and have Elson put in the workhouse, but mostly because
she was the wife of a drunkard, and, consequently, reduced in her circumstances.

  The next day Henry came home as much intoxicated
as ever. His wife, as usual, endeavored to persuade him
to live a new life, and give up his present evil habits.

"I will do every thing to make you happy, if you
will," said she. "I can take in work, if it be necessary;
I can do any thing to support us. I don't care how
hard I work, if you will be as kind, as affectionate, and
as cheerful as formerly. I am certain, if you continue
to drink, we both shall be utterly ruined. Now, my
father will not assist us; our friends are forsaking us;
our health is declining, and our prospects are dark and
discouraging."

" 'Tis no use to talk, Mary. What did you do yesterday, but call on Squire Mason? that was a kind act; wasn't it? What do you suppose he thinks of me? No, never will I reform, so long as you act so much like a plaguy fool. What if I do drink a little, there is no harm in it; we're none the worse off."

"Oh, yes, we are. We are very poor now, when we might have been rich. Look at my dress and your clothes! Do they not bespeak poverty? Once we were as decently clad as any of our neighbors; we had all we could desire, and prospered abundantly. But since you have given up business, and taken to drink, we are miserably poor."

"I would work if I could get any thing to do, and you know it. 'Tisn't my fault because we are poor."

"But none will employ an intemperate man. If you will leave off drinking, I will insure you work, and a good support. Above all, we shall be happy. We shall enjoy ourselves as in days that are past."

"Well, I will leave off drinking."

"But you have said the same a great many times; and when you have gone into bad company, and visited Mason's tavern, you have broken your good resolution and drank as much as ever. If you are determined not to drink, and will not visit such places, there is hope. Why wont you keep away from Mason's? You can get all we want elsewhere, without calling upon him."

"I will drink no more, you may depend upon it."

"Then we shall be happy, supremely so; the past will only be remembered with joy to think you have broken away from that curse which has well nigh ruined us."

"I will keep the house to-day, and shall be sure not to drink."

"Now," thought Mary, "there is some hope. If he remains in the house, it will speak well for his resolution."

And so she endeavored to interest him through the day, and they both appeared happier than they had for months before.

In the evening Elson remarked, "I believe I shall take a little walk. I know you think I shall drink — but I will not — I am determined to leave off."

"You better not go, I think."

"I shall go but a little way and then return."

Mary said no more; but the moment he left the house, she hurried on her cloak and bonnet with the intention of following him unobserved. She hoped he would not drink, but she was fearful of him. She thought if she could prevent it now, there would be some hope. As she followed just so far behind her husband as not to be observed in the dusk of the evening, she saw him pass the tavern of Mason. He had hardly got by, before he was hailed. Elson stopped and conversed for some time, and at last she saw him go in. The poor woman hurried to the door, and on looking in, beheld a group of inebriates, who had probably come to spend their hard-earned money for that which would prove their greatest curse. She observed Mason by the side of her husband, patting him on the shoulder, saying, "Don't mind the old woman — don't give up your liberty — come take a glass to cheer you," — and he pulled him along towards the bar. "Here, take this, 'twill warm you and do you good," handing him a glass of spirit he had just drawn.

Elson took it in his hand, and was about raising it to his lips, when his wife sprang in, and with a single blow, dashed it to the floor. It was breathless silence for a few moments, when Mary, giving Mason a piercing look, exclaimed — "Wretch that you are, thus to destroy my peace, and ruin my husband! If the curse of Heaven falls upon guilty man, surely, such a wretch as you cannot escape."

Soon as she thus spoke, Mrs. Elson and her husband departed, leaving the rumseller and his company, who stood like so many marble statues, to their own sober reflections.

Neither Elson nor his wife spoke a word that night. They retired early. In the morning, Elson thus addressed his wife — "You have saved me, Mary. The temptation last night was too strong for me to resist. I shall never touch the glass again. And never will I pass the threshold of Mason's door, till he relinquishes the sale of spirit. He has almost proved my ruin," and the tears were in his eyes as he spoke.

The intemperate made good his resolution. From that day, he became a sober man and was one of the most active agents in the temperance cause. His former kindness to his wife returned, and nothing did he leave undone that could in any possible way contribute to her welfare or happiness. Mary has often said that she was more than repaid by his kindness for all she had endured during the years in which her husband partook of the intoxicating cup.

Mr. Johnson was so well pleased with the reformation of his son-in-law, that he exerted himself in his behalf, and obtained for him a situation where he made a comfortable living. From the day that Mary dashed the fatal glass, a reformation commenced in the village which did not cease until nearly every man who had been intemperate, signed the pledge and became sober and industrious. Even old Mason himself pulled down his bar, declaring that he would no longer stand out against duty and reason, and was as zealous in promoting peace and happiness, as he had been for years active in destroying the health and reputation of the village.

THE PROMISE FULFILLED.

How sweet and tender are the words
   Which flow from hearts that feel!
They vibrate on the tenderest chords,
   And only bruise to heal.
Bring these, and like rich music's swell
   Upon a placid lake,
They'll sink within the heart and dwell,
   And grateful thoughts awake.

CHARLES EMERSON was the son of a mechanic. When he left school, he entered the store of a merchant in Fore Street, as his clerk. Bright, active, and intelligent, he secured the favor of his master, and the good-will of those who traded at the store. For six or seven years, Charles was attentive to his business, and exerted . himself for his employer. When he arrived at one-and-twenty years of age, he came under an obligation to remain with his employer another twelvemonth for a specified sum. The year passed, and young Emerson concluded to commence business in his own name. The merchant did not wish to part with one who had been so faithful to him for a series of years, but as he thought it might be advantageous to the young man, he encouraged him to go into business for himself.

In a few weeks, Charles was in his own store. His goods had been well selected, and purchased low. By the assistance of a few friends, he commenced business with a good capital, and the prospect for him appeared to be excellent. His acquaintances were numerous, both in the city and country. His noble character was appreciated by all with whom he had dealings.

A few years passed away, during which time the young merchant prospered beyond his most sanguine expectations. His business had increased year by year, and his stock was as large as any merchant's in the city. No man's credit was better than his. Amid his prosperity, however, Charles was not unmindful of others. He was always ready to assist honest young men who were striving for a livelihood. And he had facilities for being useful to others. Being chosen a director in one of our banks, he was extremely careful how he refused small notes from young men. These he preferred to discounting paper for a large amount from wealthy capitalists. One day something like half a dozen notes were presented at his bank for discount. The largest note was for four or five thousand dollars, drawn by a very wealthy man, and the remainder were for small sums, ranging from fifty to a hundred and fifty dollars each. The directors, with the exception of Emerson, were in favor of taking the large notes and refusing the small ones.

"My friends," said he, "the gentleman who wants the large amount can obtain it elsewhere, if we do not discount his note, and, of course, it will be but little disappointment to him — whereas these young men, all of whom I know personally or by reputation, are in need of this money to carry on their business. They have no friends to call upon for money, and if we refuse it to them, it may be of serious inconvenience. I am in favor of refusing the former, and discounting the latter notes."

"You know, Mr. Emerson," said one of the board, and we should like to give his name, but it will not be prudent, "that Mr. —— is a wealthy man, and it will be perfectly safe to trust him. These small fry are not worth looking after. It is just as much trouble to look after fifty dollars as five thousand."

"I grant, sir, that it will be more for our interest to refuse to accommodate poor young men, and loan all our capital to a few rich men; but I am in favor of accommodating those who are in need of money, and in a small degree help them to acquire property."

The directors coincided in favor of Skinflint, telling the cashier to give as a reason why the small notes were not discounted, the lack of money, or that they discounted but little on that day.

Mr. Emerson made no further remark, but in a short time, whispered in the ear of the cashier — "You may draw from my private account money sufficient to accommodate all these young men. I have been in a situation, when fifty or a hundred dollars were of incalculable service to me."

The cashier did as he was directed by the merchant, and every note was promptly paid when due.

It was in this way that Mr. Emerson did a large amount of good without having it known, and set a most admirable example to others.

The merchant had been in business something like a dozen years, and was supposed to be worth from forty to fifty thousand dollars. He gave employment to a number of hands, not one of whom who did not speak of him in the best of terms. But in the midst of his prosperity, the land fever began to rage in Maine. Everybody was buying land, and making thousands of dollars a day. Mr. Emerson stood aloof from the speculating mania for a long time, although frequently solicited to make a purchase. But at last he yielded, and bought largely. It was too late. The fever began to subside, and he was left with large tracts of land on hand. He had paid out many thousand dollars, and given his notes for as many more. The money he depended upon to meet his demands, could not be collected. Others had suffered and were not able to pay their just debts. What could be done? Must the merchant fail? There was no help for it; he made known his situation to those he owed; made a plain statement of his affairs, said he was willing to give up all his property, and commence business again. Would they accept his proposal? He wrote them that any thing in his possession would be theirs, if they would relieve him from his liabilities, and give him a chance to continue his business, assuring them that, as soon as he should be able, he would fully make up the loss with interest. Those who had long traded with the merchant knew him too well to think he wished to deprive them of their just dues. They felt for his peculiar situation, and came forward manfully, with but a single exception, and released him.

But *one* exception, we said, and who was he? The very same director in the bank, who refused to loan money in small amounts to young men. He went to Emerson after he heard of his misfortunes, and requested an immediate payment of what was due him.

"I cannot pay you now, Mr. —— " said Charles,

" but as soon as I can get through my affairs, and see a possible way to move, you shall be paid in full — this you may rely upon."

" But you can pay me now."

" I cannot, sir. It would afford me a great deal of pleasure to do it, but it is utterly out of my power, without making a great sacrifice of my property."

" What did you give your note for, if you did not expect to pay it? I always pay *my* notes."

" But perhaps you never met with any losses. Had my note been presented six months ago, it would have been paid in an hour."

" I shall not be put off. If you do not settle that note by to-morrow night, you will be put to trouble. I shall not be treated in this way."

" Sir, I cannot pay you by that time, whatever course you may think proper to take."

" The world is full of scoundrels," said the fellow, as he went from the shop, " but I will see what effect a writ will have upon him."

Skinflint — there is no more appropriate name for flesh and bones made up of such materials — Skinflint revolved in his own mind who would be the best lawyer to undertake his business. He finally hit upon a being, who had no more mercy or kindness than himself — a man destitute alike of principle and feeling — a hard-hearted, mean, blustering wretch, who had gained admission to the bar by his brass, impudence, and interested friends. Such was the being who had been selected to torment one of the best and most honest men that ever lived.

In a short time, Mr. Emerson was waited upon by the sheriff, who informed him that his instructions were

to attach whatever property he could find in his possession.   As the merchant had concealed nothing, but was
on the point of compromising with his creditors, the result was that the property of Mr. Emerson was sacrificed, and Mr. Skinflint, the laweyr, and the sheriff, received their pay in full, while the honorable creditors
received but a very small part of theirs.   It was exceedingly trying to the merchant to submit to the proceedings, but he bore it calmly, looking forward to the
day when he expected to regain his property, pay his
debts, and be in comfortable circumstances.   Mr. Emerson did not lack courage and perseverance.   These traits
were admirably developed in his character.   When he
was apparently on his back, and all was dark above
him, he did not despair.   He looked ahead, and put
forth exertions, and was determined, if his health
should be continued, to rise above every adverse circumstance.

We should have mentioned before, that although the
young merchant was a single man, he had contemplated
entering the married state the very year his business affairs assumed their dubious character.   He was engaged to Miss Mary, daughter of the very man who had
instituted legal proceedings against him.   The day that
Skinflint heard of the failure of Charles, he took his
daughter into the parlor, and there made her promise
to discard him.   Mary was unwilling to listen to her
father's proposal, but finally gave him to understand
that he should be obeyed.   What arguments he used
to his daughter, we never knew.   Though his loss
pained him sorely, yet it was nothing to Charles in comparison with the coldness of one he had tenderly loved
— one who seemed to be perfectly amiable, and as much

unlike her father as it was possible for one to be. Mary was an only child; her mother had been dead several years, and on the death of her father, a very large property would fall into her hands.

When Charles found that both Mary and her father preferred that his visits should be discontinued, he was philosopher enough to act accordingly, and make the best of it. Attention to business gradually wore away the unpleasant feelings produced by the treatment of one to whom he had been ardently attached, and Emerson was the same high-minded and respected citizen. All felt for his circumstances, and not a few exerted themselves in his behalf. His old master did much for him by loans and purchases, and his credit was soon established. He was prudent, and very attentive to his business, and began gradually to acquire property. In a few years he had settled off with his old creditors by paying them the full amount of their dues. He was enabled to do this sooner than he anticipated, from the fact that many against whom he held demands proved to be honest men, and were able to pay him. Now Emerson seemed to prosper more than ever — his business greatly increased, and the amount of his trade brought in large profits.

Mr. Skinflint — would that we dared to give his real name! — still made gold his god and continued to acquire property. Oh, the mean man! He is before us in our mind. Day by day he might be seen in Fore, Exchange and Middle Streets; and his very looks would betray his grovelling mind. His daughter was married to a man of great wealth, so it was said. Mr. Cooper had in some way or another wound himself round the affections of the old gentleman, who looked upon his future son-in-law as the paragon of perfection. Yes, Mary was married to Mr. Cooper, and the wedding was as splendid a one as the city had witnessed for many a year.

Bad and unfeeling men are sometimes punished in this life. We are sure Skinflint was. His precious son-in-law proved to be a notorious villain. He worked his card so successfully, that the old gentleman's property was entirely gone before he had any idea of it, and he holden for some thousands that he could not pay.

What became of the accomplished Cooper, no one could tell. He had money, and a heart black enough to know how to use it without the assistance of any-body. The old man was nearly distracted when he was made acquainted with the course and conduct of Cooper. But what could he do? He trusted him, and had no one to blame but himself. Now his money was gone — his all — and his pleasant and beautiful house must be sold to pay his just debts. How did Skinflint feel now? Did he not remember his treatment to the young merchant, who failed a few years before, and a thousand other hard-hearted acts? We know he did ; and he would gladly have repented, could tears and regrets restore to him his lost wealth.

It was not more than a year after Skinflint had lost his property that his house and furniture were advertised for sale. His situation was a beautiful one, and on that account, many rich men were anxious to pur-chase it.

The auctioneer commenced with the furniture which took the whole of one day to sell ; after which he gave notice that on the morrow at ten o'clock, the house would be offered for sale.

The next day arrived — a crowd was assembled, and the house was put up. Three thousand dollars — four thousand — and finally five thousand three hundred and fifty dollars were offered, and the house knocked off.

"Who is the bidder?" inquired the auctioneer.

"Emerson."

"Mr. Charles Emerson," said three or four voices, to the astonishment of not a few.

When the house was sold, to the first man who entered the room where Skinflint and his daughter were sitting, the old gentleman inquired who had bought the house, and when told, he turned quite pale, but uttered not a word.

His past conduct undoubtedly rushed to his mind, and his sensations at that moment, who for the world would have felt?

Mr. Emerson in a few days paid for the house, and took the deed in his own name. Five or six weeks elapsed, when one day as he was passing the street, whom should he meet but Mr. Skinflint. The old man stopped and said, apparently with much agitation, —

"You have purchased the house I formerly owned?"

"Yes, sir, I have."

"When shall you want to take it?"

"I am not particular about it. If you are so disposed, you can remain there for the present."

"I thank you, sir," said the old man, and it was evident that he felt the kindness he received.

In a day or two, Charles called to look at the house. As he entered the door, he remembered the happy seasons he had passed there, and a tear came to his eye. He had sat with the old gentleman but a few moments

15

when Mary came into the room. She was so overcome she could hardly speak. They had not met before for several years. The bloom was still on the cheek of Mary, but the impress of grief was on her brow.

Charles addressed her kindly, and she instantly burst into tears, and the old man mingled his tears with hers.

"Mr. Emerson," said he, "I never thought I should come to this."

"Never mind, sir; misfortune is the lot of man. Sir, I have been unfortunate."

"It grieves me when I reflect on my treatment to you when you were in affliction — it was — O God! forgive me — God forgive me" — and the tears fell fast from the eyes of the old man — "will you forgive my unkindness — will you forgive me?"

"O sir, trouble not yourself. I never had other than feelings of forgiveness towards you."

"And me, too," said Mary, "Charles, will you forgive my unkindness?"

"With all my heart."

"Ah, Emerson, the girl is not to blame for the course she pursued. I alone am guilty — on my wretched head is all the blame. I have been a wretch indeed, and now I am punished — punished as I deserve — oh, that I had never lived to see this day!"

"Sir, do be calm; you are not so wretched as you might have been. This house I have bought, and you and your daughter are welcome to it while you live; and most of the furniture I also bought, and it shall not be removed."

"You astonish me beyond measure. What means this kindness to one so undeserving, and by one whom

I have wronged — shamefully wronged?" and the old man wept like a child.

"Mr. Emerson, how can you be so kind," at last said Mary, through her tears, "when we have treated you so shamefully?"

"Say not a word. You are not to blame; you shall never suffer while I live."

"I cannot speak. I feel —"

"Enough has been said. Be calm and collected. Forget the past, and Heaven grant that the future may be bright before us."

Charles left the house, assuring Mary and her father that he would call again in a few days. As he passed to his store, his former feelings began to revive. Mary appeared the lovely and affectionate being she once was, and doubly dear since he heard of her sufferings. Her husband had deserted her, and was probably dead, as a man answering his description had been killed in a street fight at the south — and should he offer to marry her now? Did she love him? Could he doubt it? Thus reflecting day by day, he made up his mind what to do. It was not long before he was sitting with Mary in the house.

"I have come, Mary, to ask if you will fulfil your promise?"

"And what, pray?"

"That you would be my wife."

"You astonish me."

"Will you make good your promise?"

"O Charles, would you now accept me — as ungrateful as I have proved? If you were serious, my happiness would be complete."

"I mean what I say; Mary, will you fulfil your promise?"

"Dear Charles, Heaven knows I will, most sincerely," and she fell in his arms, while the old gentleman exclaimed, —

"God be praised — it is the happiest moment I ever knew."

A few months passed away, and Charles was united to Mary. They live in the old house, and two more congenial souls it would be difficult to find.

Mr. Emerson is now one of our rich merchants, and one of the best-hearted men in the city. To young men of enterprise and correct habits, he is extremely partial. He often assists them in their business, and encourages them to persevere and surmount the obstacles that occasionally rise in their path. Everybody respects and loves him. You never hear his name mentioned except in connection with a good deed, or to lavish praise upon his benevolent heart. Would that our city possessed more characters like this. Then prosperity would be seen in our streets — pleasure and sunshine mantle the brow — and hundreds would be in the path to competence, who now labor under a load which it is next to impossible to remove.

THE GOLD RING.

CHAPTER I.

How greatly wise, who never move
When stern misfortune lowers;
Who see the same kind hand of love
In sunshine and in showers.
When shadows veil the burning sky,
Behind the clouds they know
Bright fields of golden grandeur lie,
And seas of splendor flow.
They only bend, but never break,
When angry storms arise —
Prepared the hand of grief to take,
And wait for brighter skies.

EMILY ACTON was an excellent young lady of some eighteen years of age. Her parents, though in humble circumstances, were industrious, and the daughter was early taught to employ herself about that which was useful. She took pride in rising early, and getting breakfast ready by the time her mother arose; after which she would employ herself in the kitchen, or sew, or knit. Unlike a great many of her sex, she was seldom seen at the window, to watch the young men who passed, dressed in the height of fashion. It was not because Emily was poor, but she had a different taste, and thought more of her character and the assistance she might render to her mother. Her dress was always neat, but never gaudy; and it did not trouble her if she could

15*

not follow the foolish fashions of the day. Emily was also interesting in her conversation. You would not hear her talk about the fashions and the beaux from one month to another; nor remark what this person and that wore at church. She attended meeting to hear, and not to see and be seen; and what she heard was treasured in her mind. Miss Acton was called a little odd by some of her flirty young friends, who were all for fashion and show; but they loved her, nevertheless. Emily had an excellent disposition; she was kind and accommodating, and never indulged in angry words or manifested unpleasant feelings.

Mr. Acton was a worthy shoemaker, but as his business was not very good, and he not an expert workman, it was with difficulty that he paid his debts and lived comfortably. To purchase the necessaries of life requires no little sum, especially when rents are high and wood and flour are dear. To help him in the family, Emily was in the habit of taking in work, and often earned from twelve to fifteen shillings a week. This she gave to her mother to spend in any way she might think proper.

One morning as Emily was returning some work that she had done, she picked up a small gold ring. On examining it, as she returned home, she discovered the initials "J. S." engraved on the inside. "Mother," said she, "this may belong to some one who prizes it highly; otherwise, I think, the owner would not have had his initials engraved upon it."

"If so you may find the owner, for it will certainly be advertised."

"Do you think one would go to that expense for so trifling a thing?"

"Not unless it is valued more as a gift than for the gold it contains."

Emily carefully put away the ring in her box and thought but little of it for a few days. On Tuesday morning when the *Gazette* came, — for Mr. Acton was a subscriber to this paper, — on looking in the advertising columns, Emily exclaimed —

"Why, mother, the ring I found last week is really advertised."

"Are you sure of it?"

"Yes; it describes the ring perfectly."

"Run and get it, and then read me the advertisement."

Emily brought the ring and handed it to her mother, and read as follows : —

"Lost. — A small gold ring with the initials 'J. S.' upon it. The ring is prized as the gift of a friend, and whoever has found the same shall be liberally rewarded by leaving it at the store of Mr. ——, in Middle Street."

"It must be the same, Emily, and you had better carry the ring to the store this morning."

"I will, mother; but I shall charge nothing for finding it."

Putting on her things, Emily started for the shop in Middle Street. On entering, she made known her errand, and the storekeeper remarked that the gentleman who lost the ring had left two dollars for him to pay, should any one present it. But Emily refused to take the money, and left the ring. The shopkeeper insisted on her taking the two dollars. "The gentleman is rich and able to pay it," he said.

Finding that she refused and was leaving the shop, he called her back and requested her name and residence, which she did not hesitate to give, and then left the shop and returned to her home.

The following Monday, when Emily and her mother were at their washtubs, some one knocked at the door. The old lady went to see who was there and presently returned, telling her daughter a young gentleman was in the front room, who wished to see her. Wiping her face and hands on her apron, she hastened into the room, without unrolling her sleeves or unpinning her gown. Yet she did not apologize for her appearance, taking it for granted, that if a real gentleman wished to see her, he would know that to work was no disgrace and that on Monday morning she must of course be found at the washtub.

As she entered the room the gentleman remarked — "If I mistake not, you are the young lady who recently found a gold ring and left it at the store of Mr. ———."

" Yes, sir."

" But as you refused to take the two dollars I left, I didn't know but you might think it too small a sum, and I have called to present you with five dollars."

" O sir, I did not think I ought to be paid for doing my duty, and therefore I refused to take it; and I shall now certainly refuse your liberal offer."

" But I insist upon you taking it. Here, accept this bill."

" I cannot consent to take it. It wouldn't be right for me to be paid for discharging my duty; do you think it would, sir?"

" The ring I value at ten times that sum. It is a ring worn by a very dear friend who died about two years since, and on that account I prize it. But I

merely ask you to take this bill as a present, not as pay
received for a very honest act — and take it you must."

" Do not urge me to take it, sir."

" Take it — take it — and say not another word."

Reluctantly Emily held out her hand and took the
five dollars, remarking that she would endeavor to
make good use of it.

" I have no doubt of that," said the stranger, seeming but little inclined to leave ; " you have probably
learned how to make good use of money."

" Yes, sir, as my parents are poor, I am obliged to
earn my own living by sewing and knitting, and I expend but very little for what I think is not really useful."

" You take in work, then."

" Yes, sir, all I can get to do."

" I have some shirting I should like to have made up.
Can I get you to do it ? "

" I should be happy to do it for you."

Bidding Emily good-morning, the stranger left, and
the industrious girl returned to her washtub.

" Mother," said she, " who do you suppose this
stranger is ? He appears to be an excellent man, and
insisted upon my taking five dollars for finding the
ring."

" I cannot tell ; he must be some rich man's son, or
he could not afford to give you so much."

" Besides, mother, he says he will give me some
work."

" If he should, and you do it well, it may open the
way for more employment. I should as lief you would
work for gentlemen as take it from slop shops."

Cheerful and happy, Emily continued at her work

day by day.   She never had a moment to spend to walk
the streets or gossip from house to house.   Her thoughts
were how she could make herself more useful, and
better promote the welfare and happiness of her worthy
parents.

CHAPTER II.

I seek a female in whose heart
Domestic virtues share a part ;
Not fond of gaudy dress or show,
To please some foppish, senseless beau ;
Who rather at her work be seen,
Than pace the town with haughty mien,
Addressing every male she meets,
In bustling mart, or crowded streets.

CHARLES SIMONTON was the son of a rich man ; but
unlike the children of many wealthy parents, from his
earliest years, he was obliged to work.   His judicious
father had been brought up at a mechanical trade, and
had made his fortune by diligence and industry, and he
was determined his son should not be ruined by idleness and improper associates.   When he was old enough
to learn a trade, he put Charles to Messrs. Gould & Web-
ster to learn the mysteries of making hats.   With these
gentlemen he worked hard, but at this he did not murmur.   Sometimes his fellow-associates would joke him
on account of his steady habits, and even laugh at him
for not touching the ardent spirits which they daily
used.   But he had seen the evil of intemperance, and
warned them to beware.   They heeded him not.

One day two of the apprentices, young Woodman and Hanes, determined they would make Charles take a glass of bitters with them, but he stoutly refused. They held him and endeavored to pour the poison down his throat, but could not succeed.

"You will be sorry for this," said Charles, "for I am certain unless you forsake your practice, you will become intemperate and die drunkards."

"We'll risk that, young Morality," they replied. "Who wont enjoy themselves when they can, must be fools."

Charles made the best of the treatment he received, and was so kind-hearted, it was seldom that he was treated roughly. His most excellent mother had taught him lessons of wisdom which he could not forget. When tempted to stray from duty, her image and her counsels were before him, and he turned from the wrong path and pursued a virtuous course.

When Charles had finished his trade, his masters offered to give him employment, but his father had business for him, which he thought would be more congenial to his feelings; he took him into partnership with himself. Their business was good, and prosperity crowned their efforts. About this time, Charles met with a severe loss in the death of his mother. She had been sick for some months, and her death had been daily expected. She gave her son some excellent advice, and begged him never to deviate from a virtuous course.

"My son, I am dying," said she, "and when I am gone, remember my words to you, and always practise according to the dictates of wisdom. Follow the Bible and treasure in your heart its holy truths, which if obeyed will make you happy in life, cheerful in death, and blessed forever. Here, Charles I give you a ring I have worn; keep it to remember my precepts."

Charles loved his mother affectionately. She had been a devoted parent to him, and when she was dead, his grief was poignant. He placed her gift upon his finger, resolving to part with it only in death.

Mrs. Simonton had slept beneath the clods of the valley for nearly two years, and Charles had safely kept this relic of his mother; but one day on going to his supper, he discovered that he had lost his ring. He looked for it in vain. Charles went directly to Isaac Adams, proprietor of the *Portland Gazette*, and paid him for an advertisement stating his loss, requesting the finder to leave it at a shop in Middle Street.

In a few days, Charles called at the store, and ascertained that his ring had been found. "But," said the shopkeeper, "the young woman who found it would not take the two dollars reward you ordered me to pay her."

"Wouldn't take it? — and why not?"

"It is more than I can tell. She seemed to think it was not one's duty to receive pay for what was found. And, faith, Charles, she was a very pretty girl."

"But she shall be paid. Just inform me where she lives, and I will see she is rewarded for her honesty."

The shopkeeper informed Charles of her residence, and on Monday he called at her house. The result of that visit the reader learned in our first chapter.

When young Simonton left the house of Mr. Acton, he resolved on one thing — to marry the interesting and domestic daughter, as he found her to be, providing he could obtain her consent. Her beauty and her modesty, her industry and her humility, struck him at once, and he could not forget her. At night he thought of the beautiful girl, and in the daytime she was before him. "She is just such a woman as I need," said he to himself, "and she suits me better than any of the dozens I am acquainted with, who fill the circle of pride and fashion."

In a short time Charles called at Mr. Acton's with the shirting he wished to have made up. It was in the evening. He was politely invited in, and gladly embraced the opportunity. While sitting with the good lady, Emily busied herself with ironing the clothes, now and then stopping to converse with Charles. Every thing was neat about the house, and spoke of industry and not of poverty. In taking leave he was invited to call again by Emily and her mother, the former stating that his work would be finished in the course of a week.

"What a fine young gentleman Mr. Simonton is," said Mr. Acton, after Charles had gone; for on that evening for the first time, they had learned his name.

"He is very pleasant and very kind," remarked Emily. "How different he is from many of our rich men. I really begin to like that young man."

"I certainly do," said the mother. "You seldom see a man of his wealth so pleasant and agreeable to poor folks."

"If ever I should be so lucky as to get a husband, mother, I know of no one who comes up to my ideas of what a husband ought to be as this Mr. Simonton."

"I fear, my child, you will not get such a gentleman as he."

16

"I do not expect it. I never dreamed of such a thing. It was only some of my foolish talk."

One week passed away, and Mr. Simonton called for his work. It was done and well done; for which he paid Emily liberally — she, however, refusing to take more than it was worth, until being over persuaded.

When Charles took his leave that night, he remarked to Emily, "On Sunday evening next, Dr. Deane delivers a lecture before the Benevolent Society. I should be happy to have your company there."

"I should be pleased to go," said Emily, and they bade each other good-night.

Charles and Emily went to the lecture. A door was now opened for his frequent visits at Mr. Acton's, and every week he spent two or three evenings there.

A year passed away — just one year from the day that Emily picked up the gold ring in the street. There was a wedding at the house of Mr. Acton, and Emily was the happy bride. She never looked handsomer and Simonton's joy was complete. Mr. Kellogg united the happy pair, and then invoked the blessing of the Almighty upon them.

As Mr. Simonton was a wealthy man, he purchased a fine house in Back Street; thither he took his excellent companion, where they lived in peace, prosperity, and happiness for more than half a century. It was but a few years since that they were deposited in the narrow tomb, followed by numerous friends and relations. They died in Christian faith, the precepts of the Bible cheering them in their sickness, and giving them an antepast of those joys which are in reservation for the righteous.

THE HUMPBACK.

What are another's faults to me?
  I've not a vulture's bill,
To pick at every flaw I see,
  And make it wider still:
It is enough for me to know,
  I've follies of my own —
And on my heart the care bestow,
  And let my friends alone.

SARAH EDGAR was a young girl very much deformed in her person. When quite a child, she had a fall which nearly cost her her life, and from that time she became humpbacked, and grew but very little in height. Sarah possessed a kind disposition, and was so much beloved by her young associates that they never thought of the defect in her body. She was active and cheerful, and appeared as happy as if she were as perfect in her form as her companions. But as Sarah grew older, she felt her situation more sensibly, as many of her early friends who seemed to be the most partial to her, gradually forsook her society. There was one girl whose name was Jane Coburn, with whom Sarah had been intimate from early childhood, who, since she had grown up, seemed more than all her other acquaintances to avoid her company. The poor girl was at a loss to conjecture the reason; for she was sure she had neither said nor done any thing to make her act so

strangely.   When they met, a few words would pass between them, but Jane never seemed disposed to prolong the conversation.   To be sure, Sarah was deformed
and poor, and lived in a small house, while Jane's parents were reputed to be wealthy, and owned the large
dwelling they occupied ; but this should have been no
reason why Sarah was treated so coldly.

The mother of Jane was very partial to the humpbacked girl ; she could appreciate her virtues, and pity
her misfortunes.   Many a time did she present her
with a new gown or a new bonnet, and no person was
ever more grateful for a present.   One afternoon, Sarah
called on Mrs. Coburn ; but she had hardly seated herself before Jane remarked in the presence of her
mother, —

" I wish folks knew when they were wanted, and
would stay until they are sent for."

" Why, Jane, what do you mean ? " inquired her
mother.

" Nothing particular ; but I hate intruders."

Mrs. Coburn immediately remarked — " Jane ex-
pects some company to-day, and every thing has gone
wrong with her, and she hardly knows what she says.
I am determined that this shall be the last time I consent to have her receive her friends unless she can show
a better feeling."

" If I do expect company, I don't want any to come
but those I invite.   Who wants everybody and every
thing ?   I don't, I'm sure."

Jane's mother thought it was not necessary to reply
to her daughter, and continued to converse with Sarah
who, although she understood Jane's remark, was as sociable and as pleasant as ever.

Although Sarah was urged to remain with her during the afternoon by Mrs. Coburn, she would not consent, knowing that it would be disagreeable to her daughter.

As Sarah's constitution was feeble, she was over persuaded by her friends not to learn a trade, as she contemplated, but to do something else to support herself; but what business to engage in she did not know. Plain sewing she could do, but while so many were depending upon their needles, it was but poor encouragement to her. But a trifle only did she earn in this way.

One day a thought struck her as she was passing one of the principal streets in her town; it was this: perhaps she could make a living by keeping a small fruit and candy store, at the corner of some street. The more she thought of the subject, the more favorable it appeared to her. Her mother thought it was a good idea, and encouraged her to undertake it. Sarah was not long in finding a suitable place; but all the money she could raise to commence business with was seventy-five cents. With this sum, she purchased a few apples, and some other fruit, and also some candies, and commenced trading. The first day she sold nearly all her articles, and made twenty-five cents. Day after day her business increased, so that she was enabled to keep on hand a larger assortment and a greater quantity. Every summer day, Sarah Edgar might be seen trudging to her little stand, where she would remain all day, selling to the passers-by. In winter she was permitted to occupy a corner of a gentleman's shop, who, out of kindness, charged her no rent. Now Sarah had but little time to see her friends, excepting in the evening;

16*

and when she called upon Mrs. Coburn, she was pleasantly received by the good lady, who still felt a deep interest in the unfortunate girl.

But Jane had grown more and more haughty. One
evening she asked her in the way of ridicule —

"How many sugar-plums have you sold during the
day?"

"About a dozen cents' worth," said Sarah.

"It must be pleasant business for a lady to follow."

"It is not so disagreeable as to be idle; but while I
make my own living, and assist my mother, I feel quite
happy."

"You will make your fortune, yet, by retailing peppermints and candy, no doubt."

"Perhaps I shall."

"If I were you, Sarah, I would be looking out a
house to buy, you are making money so fast. Perhaps
father would sell you this," and then a scornful smile
played upon her face.

"I do not wish for a house at present, and you know,
Jane, I may never earn a hundred dollars in my life."

"Great profit is made on sugar-plums, you know. It
is a very fine business."

"If I were not deformed, I assure you, I should do
something else for a living. I could learn a trade, or
work in a factory."

"You wouldn't stand half the chance to pick up a
beau."

"I never thought of one."

"Don't tell me. When the sailors pass, you look up
smiling enough, I know."

"Jane, you are too bad."

"Not when I am talking with a merchant."

Sarah did not care to prolong the conversation, and so she was rejoiced when Mrs. Coburn came into the room. The good woman made her usual inquiries respecting business, and she was glad to learn that it had been very much increased.

Occasionally, Jane would pass the stand of Sarah, with a few of her companions, and cast a sneering look at the humpbacked girl, and sometimes make a remark which was not pleasant for Sarah to hear. One day she came up to the stand, throwing down a silver dollar, saying —

"Give me a pound of peppermints."

"I haven't a pound."

"Give me half a pound, then."

"I haven't that quantity even; it is seldom that I have a call for more than two or three cents' worth at a time."

"Oh! you don't keep but a few cents' worth, then," said Jane, winking at one of her companions. "Well, give us a pound of almonds."

"I haven't a pound of any thing."

And off the girls went, laughing loud enough to be heard across the street. Sarah was a little mortified, but yet she pitied the folly of the proud and haughty Jane and her companions.

A few years passed, and Sarah continued her business, and with great success. She was so kind and pleasant, that all the children loved to trade with her. When they had a penny to spend, they would run down to Miss Edgar's stall, and were always satisfied with their bargains.

About this time, the good mother of Jane was called from her family by death. She was an excellent woman, and all the neighbors mourned their loss; none felt her loss more severely than Sarah. Next to her mother she loved Mrs. Coburn; in all her trials she had been her friend and counsellor. It was to be regretted that her daughter possessed none of the excellent qualities of her mother. Not long after her decease, Jane mingled in the gay circles, and did not appear to be half so deeply afflicted as the poor humpbacked girl.

Charles Somers, the son of a merchant, had for some time been partial to Jane. She was a pretty girl, as far as outward beauty was concerned, and this attraction affected young Somers. Occasionally, as he passed by the stall of Sarah, he would stop and purchase a few articles — such as peaches, apples, and pears. He seemed to pity the unfortunate girl, and sometimes stopped a few moments to converse with her. At one time he passed with Jane, and stopped to buy something, when Jane made some unkind remark. Charles checked her by saying, "That unfortunate young woman deserves a great deal of credit. She not only supports herself and mother, but actually gives something to those poorer than she is. Besides this, she has a well-cultivated mind, and were it not for her humpback, there is many a man who would rejoice to make her his wife."

"I don't think much of her myself," remarked Jane; "I never saw any thing so attractive about her. She always obtruded herself into our house when mother was living, although we hinted to her repeatedly that she was not wanted. We haven't seen her much of late."

"I never heard her spoken slightly of before."

"The reason is people don't know her. She always

looks so modest and saintlike that I have no patience
with her. To hear her talk, you wouldn't think butter
could melt in her mouth. You may depend upon it,
she is a self-conceited, deceitful creature — that I
know."

Being but little acquainted with Sarah, Charles took
to be correct what Jane had told him, and after that was
cautious how he spoke to her, and never again purchased
an article at her stand. Sarah noticed the appearance
of the young man, and supposed he had been influenced
by Jane; but not hearing what had been said, she had
no opportunity to defend herself. She continued to
sell and to buy, while her business rapidly increased
year by year. Every Saturday night, she would place
in her mother's care, what she had made during the
week, which was carefully put aside in silver money.

For ten years, had Sarah been attentive to her little
business, and no one but herself and mother knew how
well she had succeeded, and how much money she had
in her mother's chest. During this period, Mr. Coburn had married a second wife, who was called an extravagant woman, and it was thought he had not prospered of late as in former years. Jane was still waited
upon by Mr. Somers, who, it was said, was worth property and intended to be married in a short time. Jane
and Sarah seldom met; they had scarcely exchanged
words for two years. But Jane, according to all appearances, had not changed for the better. She was
still proud and haughty, and looked with contempt
upon Sarah, and all those she considered beneath her.

In the course of time, Mr. Coburn failed in business, his creditors having attached his stock and house.
This put a damper upon the haughty spirit of Jane,

who had never dreamed of such a thing. She thought her father's affairs were on a perfectly safe footing. And now she even flattered herself that his failure would not be a bad one, and that in the end he would make money out of it, as some others had done before him. But when her father told her that his house must be sold to pay his debts, she began in some measure to realize her situation.

The beautiful house of Mr. Coburn was advertised for sale "at a bargain," and those who wished to purchase were invited on the premises to see the house. Among others who called was Sarah Edgar. As soon as Jane saw her, with a curl of scorn upon her lip, she said —

"Well, I suppose you intend to buy our house; you have made enough selling candy."

"Well, Jane, that is not an impossible thing."

"*Per-haps* you may, miss; it would be a fine place for an apple-woman."

"I think so too. I should like to be the owner of as fine a house."

"Oh, lordy, and *you* should. I guess it would take all the candy-women in town to buy it, even if part of them were sold for what they think they are worth."

"Perhaps it would, Miss Coburn; but we shall see."

"Impudence! — I detest those low-bred people," muttered Jane, as she closed the door in the face of Sarah.

As Mr. Coburn and his family were sitting in the room a day or two after this conversation, the gentleman who had been appointed to sell the house was introduced.

"Mr. Coburn, I come to inform you that I have effected a sale of the house," said he.

"Ah!—and how did you sell it;—for cash or credit?"

"For cash, as soon as the deed is made out. It was sold for forty-five hundred dollars."

"Who was the purchaser?"

"Miss Edgar."

"Who?" said the astonished man.

"Miss Sarah Edgar, the young woman who keeps a little stall in —— Street."

"Is it possible? Where in the world did she raise that amount?"

"I cannot say; but she has bought it, and tells me that the money is ready as soon as she can have a deed."

Who can describe the feelings of Jane when this fact was announced? We shall not attempt it. It will be sufficient to say that she was fully repaid for all her unkindness to the once poor and unfortunate girl.

The next day Sarah took possession of the house, but told Mr. Coburn that he need not be in a hurry to remove. "On account of your wife's kindness to me in years past, you may remain in the house at present, and nothing shall be charged you for the rent."

Mr. Coburn thanked her with tears.

After the failure of the merchant, Charles Somers was less attentive to Jane, and finally forsook her; he could not feel any confidence in a woman who had deceived him, as Jane had done repeatedly, more especially in what she said respecting Sarah Edgar.

In a year after Sarah purchased the house, Mr. Coburn removed into a smaller dwelling, while Sarah and her mother took the house. Not many months passed before the humpbacked girl was married; yes, Sarah became a happy bride, the wife of one of the best and most influential men in town.   Charles Somers was her husband.

Females should learn a lesson from this story. Never look upon the deformed and the poor as beneath you ; especially if your parents are wealthy.   The time may come when you will be reduced while they are exalted.   Never ridicule poverty or deformity.   It was this disposition that ruined — utterly ruined Jane Coburn.   She is now a woman of some fifty years of age, and is so poor that she is obliged to take in shirts to make, at twelve cents apiece, or she would suffer for the necessaries of life.   There are scores just like her, proud, superficial, and overbearing.   Unless they reform, and begin to live as they ought, and that speedily, we can safely predict for them a life of poverty and wretchedness.

POPULAR AND UNPOPULAR.

CHAPTER I.

How beautiful, when life and mind
  Conspire to make the wretched blest !
With acts of mercy, unconfined,
  Reaching to every sorrowing breast !
The heart thus nurtured in the school,
  By wisdom and by mercy taught,
Obeys the Saviour's golden rule,
  In life and act — in word and thought.
This lesson be it mine to learn,
  With love to God and faith sincere ;
In every form, a friend discern,
  That pines in want or sheds a tear.

"To tell you the truth, Somers, I am not partial to this dull sort of life. Law is a dry study, more especially to a person of an active temperament."

"Law is just the thing for me, Mason. I like it. There is no labor, comparatively, — no hurry about it ; you can take your own time to study."

"It is exceedingly difficult for a young lawyer to get ahead. If he have talents and ambition, they are crushed before the learning and experience of the older members of the bar. It is one of the poorest professions in the world in which to succeed, or to make money."

"You mistake altogether. I shall go ahead in a few

17

years and become wealthy. What do you prefer to the study of law?"

"A mechanical trade, Somers; give me the mechanic to the lawyer. His business is much more pleasant, his time better employed, and he is not perplexed and harassed almost to death to make a living."

"A foolish idea, Mason. Who would be a mechanic? They have to dig and dig, from one week to another — year in and out — and then they make but a poor living. Besides, they are not half so much respected as lawyers are. Who are the candidates for most of the important offices? Lawyers. Who receive the largest salaries for public services? Lawyers. Wherever you hear of good speeches or able arguments, you will find they are by members of this profession."

"I might inquire, Somers, who have been the most beneficial to society, mechanics or lawyers? And you cannot deny that the former have been of the greatest service to our country. Franklin and Sherman, you know, were mechanics, and although they did not make speeches, what they said was to the purpose; and because they were short and comprehensive, everybody listened to them. Give me a trade to the law."

"And give me a profession to a trade. I like the law and there's no mistake."

"As soon as I can get father's consent, and a good opportunity presents, I will throw aside Coke and Blackstone, for something more congenial to my taste."

James Somers was the son of a merchant. His father had given him a college education, after which he put him into an office to study the profession of the law. Here he became acquainted with Henry Mason, a young man of his own age, who had a good education, and had been over persuaded by his father, who possessed a handsome property, to study the profession of the law. Henry despised the business, and had often told his parent that a trade would be more congenial to his feelings, and more profitable and useful in the end. But his father would not listen to him. Being a proud-spirited man, the idea of his son's working at a trade was something he could not endure. It was not respectable enough. All the arguments Henry could produce had not the least effect upon his father; so he continued at his studies.

At the expiration of two or three years, Somers was admitted to practise at the bar, and removed to a country town and commenced business. In the mean time, Mason, who had never relinquished his determination to learn a trade, received permission of a friend, a printer, to enter his office and work. Having naturally a quick turn of mind, it was not many months before he became an expert workman. With not much effort he could pick up a thousand types in an hour, and work off a token at the press in about the same time. When Henry thought he had become master of his trade, he removed to a large town and established a paper. Possessing a strong mind, and having the advantage of a good education, he made an interesting and popular sheet. By his industrious habits, he secured a great deal of work, and being a man that everybody respected, he commanded as much influence as any person in town, and in a few years was put up as a candidate to the State legislature. He protested against it; said he could not leave his business and questioned his ability to discharge his duty as he ought. But the people would not excuse him, and

Henry was elected. He did not seek the office; he was no politician, but as he was chosen by the vote of the inhabitants, he went to his task. It was said that Mason was one of the ablest men who represented the state. Calm and dispassionate, he never let an act pass—he never made or seconded a motion even—without forethought and deliberation. He consulted no individual interest, he approved of no mere party measure, and so he gained the respect of all. When he spoke, it was to the purpose; he never descended to scurility or low slang; but was perfectly honorable in all his acts. Seldom did one of his speeches last over ten or fifteen minutes. He was short, comprehensive, and to the point, and was a mortal enemy to inflated words, long arguments, and extended debates. No persuasion would induce Mason to be run as a candidate for office again. He was offered many high and important situations, but he turned a deaf ear to them all. He could do more good in an humble sphere, exert a better influence, and enjoy more of life. He might have been a senator in Congress, but he rejected the offer at once; but such an office as a school committee or an overseer of the poor, he willingly accepted. Here was where he could be useful, and see the happy effects of his labors. In his paper he strove to awaken the sympathy of the public in behalf of the suffering and needy, and through his efforts, many a widow's heart was made to sing for joy, and many an orphan child was housed, clothed, and instructed.

Mason chose for his bosom companion, a lady who had been brought up by sensible and judicious parents —a woman who had been taught to work from her earliest years. Sarah Averd had learned a trade, and by her habits acquired the name of a worthy and capable woman. Her time had not been spent in idle visits or senseless gossiping; she did not consult her glass oftener than her heart. It was not Sarah's ambition to shine in the ballroom, or at the public assembly; but it was her pride, to earn her own living, assist her parents, and live a useful and virtuous life. For many months had Mason watched the conduct and studied the character of Sarah; but no one knew it but himself. Many a proud and fashionable lady, dressed most expensively, and putting on a thousand airs, crossed his track, in hopes of winning the talented and popular man; while the neighbors wondered which of the wealthy girls would be so lucky as to win him. No one had the most distant idea of his choosing the poor, retired, and modest Sarah Averd, who had learned a trade, and now supported herself by her needle. And she as little thought of what was about to take place, as any of her neighbors. When Mason sent some poor child to her to be clothed at his expense, she never once dreamed that he was penetrating her character and studying her habits, as it proved to be in the sequel. Sarah loved Henry, but she never dared to hope that he would prove more than an acquaintance. But to the utter astonishment of the rich and fashionable, and proud and self-sufficient young ladies of the town, Mason became the husband of the poor tailoress, Sarah Averd. Henry was an excellent husband, and Sarah made him one of the best of wives.

CHAPTER II.

Oh, let me know there is but one,
　One friendly heart to sympathize,
And make my daily cares its own,
　And bid my drooping spirits rise —
To speak when others are unkind,
　In melting tones of tenderness,
And round the stricken soul to bind
　The cords of love, to heal and bless :
Oh, let me know but this, and I
　Shall joyful pass the vale of tears,
See light beyond each frowning sky,
　Dispelling doubts and gloomy fears.

JAMES SOMERS, after he had opened an office in the village that he had chosen for his future residence, used the most strenuous efforts to make himself popular. He exerted himself to become acquainted with the prominent men of both political parties, and generally coincided with their views. He pretended not to be a strong advocate on either side ; waiting, before he took a stand, to ascertain which was the stronger party, and which the most likely to put him into office, for to be elected to some lucrative office was the height of his ambition. He attended meeting one sabbath with one denomination, and the next with another. He had no preference. This was his policy — if he should become a candidate for office, his religious views should be no objection to his receiving the votes of the people. By pursuing this course, Somers gained the respect of but few, excepting those, who, like himself, were ambitious and selfish, and who hoped, by favoring him, in turn to receive a like reward.

The time approached when it was necessary to determine upon a candidate for the legislature. But among three or four prominent men, it was difficult to make a selection. Each had his friends, and it was the object with the people — at least with many of them — to put up the individual who would run the best, and not the best man. Finally, they pitched upon Somers, but others taking offence, voted for another candidate, and the poor fellow was defeated. Contrary to the expectations of many, the opposing gentleman received a majority of the votes, which showed the unpopularity of the young lawyer. Somers was extremely mortified; his ambition received a check, and he raved for many a month against a few individuals, whom he supposed were chiefly instrumental of his defeat.

For sometime Somers labored to get into office, but the more he labored, the less popular he became. If the people disliked him as a man, they detested him as a lawyer. He would frequently sue and serve a writ, when, by a milder course, he would have better succeeded and made fewer enemies. He was poor, but he should have studied his interest. Sometimes he would go to the clerk of a militia company and request a job to sue those who did not appear in the ranks on review or muster-days, pledging himself not to charge for services unless he succeeded in getting the case. Such proceedings, together with his generally niggardly conduct, secured him the title of the "mean pettifogger." At a town-meeting, the citizens, who had noticed his treatment to others as well as themselves, and knew his ambitious turn of mind, nominated him for the of-

fice of hogreeve, and he was chosen almost unani-
mously. When the vote was announced the house rung
again with the shouts of the people.

When Somers was informed of his promotion to the
important office, he was so full of wrath that he actually struck the informer a severe blow, which was instantly returned, and a regular fight ensued. The
lawyer was fairly beaten, and bawled lustily for quarters, which brought out the neighbors, and further
blows were prevented. Somers was prosecuted and
paid his fine for the attack.

Among the few friends of Somers in the town, was a
Mr. Blake, one of the richest men in the place. He
had a daughter, for whom the lawyer had manifested
some partiality. Jane was the very counterpart of her
lover. She had a violent temper, was vindictive and
resolute, and as proud as Lucifer. Jane had nothing
to recommend her but her father's property, he being very rich, and she the sole heiress. As there was
nothing prepossessing about her, it was evident to all
but herself and her parents, that wealth was the magnet
that drew the lawyer to the house of Mr. Blake.
Jane had been indulged in all she desired, scarcely
was a wish ungratified. To balls, to parties of pleasure — anywhere and everywhere, unmindful of expense — would the daughter be gallanted. She seldom did any work. It was not necessary, she thought,
as she would have no occasion to labor. Her father's
property was sufficient to make her comfortable, without her putting forth the least exertion to keep herself
from rusting out, and promoting her health.

Somers was married to Jane. We need not say the
wedding was a splendid affair ; we wish we could say as

much of the sequel; but the truth will not permit us. They began housekeeping on an extensive scale; hired a large dwelling, furnished it throughout, and employed one or two domestics. If there were no counter currents in life, they might have gone on smoothly, but not pleasantly, for their dispositions forbade their being happy.

The father of Jane met with two or three reverses the same year of his daughter's marriage, which sunk the larger portion of his property. About the same time he was involved in a lawsuit, and losing his case, it cost him a large amount, so that he had barely enough left to make himself comfortable. Somers, who had depended mostly on Mr. Blake to support him in his extravagances, now found it impossible to pay his debts. Being dunned every day, with no means of paying, and having an expensive wife, he was obliged to give up housekeeping and go to her father's. They lived upon the old gentleman about a year, when one day, being a little piqued, he told Somers he could not support them much longer. "I am willing to let Jane stay here," said he, "but as for keeping you both, I cannot do it; I am not able."

Exceedingly unpopular as the lawyer was, and having no business to speak of, and about being turned out of doors, he hardly knew what course to take, especially as he had no money. Jane appeared perfectly indifferent to him; for of late he had taken to drink, and it had been said that he went home occasionally a little intoxicated. Somers still continued to live with the old gentleman, till a quarrel ensued, and then he forbade his entering the house.

The lawyer left the house in a rage one morning. and

no one knew whither he went, and but few felt interested enough in him to inquire. It was his determination
to go to some small village, and if he could find an opening, establish himself in business. He travelled from
one town to another, without determining where to
stop, till at last his small amount of funds was entirely
exhausted. In despair he resorted to the intoxicating
bowl, and was beastly drunk about the streets for a few
days, till at last he was taken up by the overseers of the
poor, and sent to the almshouse. He was ragged and
dirty; an entire stranger to the people. When he became sober, he refused to give his name or his business. One of the overseers approached him, spoke
kindly to him, and seemed to feel for his peculiar situation. He thought he could discern in the face of the
poor man something that indicated intelligence, and
he did not doubt that he had seen better days.

"Friend," said the gentleman after he had conversed
with him kindly for half an hour, "tell me where you
came from and who you are, and if I can render you
any assistance, it shall be done."

"I cannot tell you; I am ashamed to tell," said the
man, weeping.

"Perhaps I can be the means of benefiting you; certainly it will not be for your disadvantage to inform me
of your true situation."

"Sir, I have seen better days. I have been prosperous; but my ambition, my love of gain and pleasure,
have ruined me."

"I thought as much. Your language, your whole
appearance indicated that you were once happy and
prosperous. But pray tell me your name!"

"You shall hear it, sir, for you appear to feel for

the unfortunate, the poor, and the destitute. My name is Somers."

"What! James Somers?" and the truth flashed at once upon the gentleman that an old friend was before him.

"That is my name, sir," said the poor man, somewhat agitated.

"Can this be my early friend, Somers?" and he fell upon his neck and embraced him, though the poor fellow was covered with nothing but rags.

At such strange conduct, Somers wept aloud. "Pray, sir, what can this mean?" he asked in astonishment.

"I am your old friend, Henry Mason."

"Good Heaven! can it be? God be praised that I have fallen into such hands! My kind friend — but I cannot express the feelings of my heart."

"O James, I never thought to see you in such a condition; but come with me, you shall have a home in my own house. Come with me."

"I dare not go. Look at my condition," and he wept like a child.

"Come with me — you shall come," and Mason led him from the house, helped him into his chaise at the door, and drove to his dwelling, where he was treated with the greatest kindness and attention.

Mrs. Mason interested herself in his behalf, and in a few days the poor outcast became an altered being. He was furnished with suitable clothing, encouraged to hope for the best, while Mason exerted himself to the utmost to get his friend into business.

The lawyer had learned an important lesson during his past career and now resolved to pursue a different course. Through the instrumentality of Mason, who furnished him an office, he commenced the practice of law, and his business gradually increased. Somers being perfectly attentive to his affairs, he prospered beyond his most sanguine expectations. After a year had gone by, he sent for his wife, who had materially changed for the better since he parted from her. She had seen the effects of her folly, by her parents being reduced in their circumstances, and she resolved to work and support herself by her own hands. But it came hard upon her at first.

The lawyer and his wife removed to a small tenement, were prudent and frugal, and succeeded better than they had anticipated. In the course of a few years Somers was able to purchase a dwelling, and for a long period was considered one of the ablest lawyers in the county. He never forgot his old friend; but years after his kindness to him, expressed his heartfelt gratitude in tears.

Mason became one of the wealthiest, as certainly he was the most influential man in the place. Everybody loved him. Wherever there was sickness, or distress, or sorrow, he was ready to render assistance and do good. His whole life was spent in acts of benevolence, and thousands were made better and happier through his instrumentality.

THE IMPRUDENT STEP.

The flower when crushed will send perfume,
  The riven tree may sprout again,
And spring will raise to life and bloom
  Bleak autumn's melancholy train ;
But human hearts whene'er they feel
  The frosts of unrequited love,
No earthly power the wound can heal,
  Till death the malady remove.

Harry Heywood! how I loved him when we were
boys together, sporting over the fields and hills, chasing
the bee and butterfly, or culling the new-blown flowers!
Then he was happy. The future was pictured bright
before his young imagination. He saw no cloudy sky
—no chilling storm—no winter of gloom; but a
bright sun and a pure heaven were ever above him.
The green earth, sprinkled with ten thousand flowers,
smiled before him. A kind father and an indulgent
mother doated upon an only son. Nothing was denied
to him that would gratify his desires. In a round of
pleasure, the years flew by, and Henry was on the verge
of manhood. Genteel and accomplished, possessing a
good disposition and a fine mind, he won the respect
and love of all who knew him, particularly the affection of the kind and gentle Louisa. Miss Mentor was
the daughter of a neighbor in comfortable circumstances, where Henry had been a constant visitor from

18

his childhood. Now that he had grown to manhood, his feelings had changed somewhat in regard to Louisa. His regard to her had ripened into an attachment; and throughout the village it was understood that young Heywood and Louisa were destined for each other. "It will be a fine match," was the common remark; "their dispositions are so nearly alike, they cannot fail of being happy." The young lady was not handsome, but she was good. Possessing a generous heart and an agreeable disposition, she was calculated to make any one happy who should cultivate her acquaintance.

About this time the father of Louisa sickened and died. The faithful daughter watched beside the bed of her parent day and night, administering to his wants and smoothing his dying pillow. A short time before the fatal termination of Mr. Mentor's illness, a day had been appointed by Henry for an excursion of pleasure. Presuming that her father would be better in a few days, Louisa gave her consent to accompany her friend; but when the time arrived, she told Heywood that she must be excused on account of the illness of her father. "When I made the promise," said she, "I thought he would be better by to-day, but he has been growing worse, and now it would not be prudent for me to leave him in his present critical situation."

The color rushed to Henry's cheeks, as he said, "I have made all the arrangements and you must go; you will not be missed one day, and certainly your father will be no worse."

" I cannot leave him. I could not enjoy myself when father is so feeble, and then if he should be worse, I should have it to reflect upon through life. Can't you put off going till some future day?"

"No, I cannot put it off. Come, get ready and go; it is getting late."

"I must decline, unwilling as I am to do so; for I cannot leave my father."

"Then you will not go, I am to understand?" said Henry, manifesting a little displeasure.

"With all my heart I would go, if it were not my duty to take care of my father. It will not do to leave him, and sorry as I am to do it, I must decline;" and a tear was in her eye as she spoke.

"Very well, you will be sorry for it."

"Now don't censure me, Henry, because I do what I believe to be my bounden duty."

"You could go as well as not if you were so disposed, but I sha'n't ask you again," and so saying, the young man left the house, leaving the dutiful girl in tears.

Henry went directly to Mr. Howell's and invited his daughter Jane to accompany him, who readily accepted.

The Howells were noted for their pride and poverty, and Jane was disliked among her acquaintances on account of the foolish airs she was accustomed to put on, and for her envious disposition. She had more than once circulated a story, which, among those who were not acquainted with both parties, would reflect upon the character of Louisa Mentor. These two young ladies spoke when they met, but were not on the best of terms. Louisa had often condemned Jane's deceitful, tattling disposition, and Henry had always coincided with her. Perhaps it was for this reason that he now had invited her to accompany him. He knew the feeling it would produce in the breast of the sensitive girl, and he thus cruelly revenged her. When it was known throughout the village that Heywood had gone in company with Miss Howell, it opened the door for a great deal of gossip. A few who were envious of those whose characters stood higher than their own, were much delighted and hoped it would tend to break up the match between the young man and Louisa, and these encouraged Henry. " I approve of your choice," said one. " She is much more accomplished than Miss Mentor," said another. " It is the best step you have taken for many a day," continued a third. These individuals were all of a meddlesome disposition, and the more unhappiness and misery they could produce, the better they enjoyed it. Henry was unwise enough to consider them his friends and listen to what they said. He ceased to call on Louisa, and was a constant visitor at Miss Howell's. When he heard of the death of Mr. Mentor, he was on the point of calling at the house, — for he really loved the dutiful girl, and felt sensibly her situation, being deprived of a kind parent, — but self-will predominated over his better nature and he yielded to his bad disposition.

The parents of Miss Howell did their utmost to please Henry so that he might be induced to continue his visits and finally take their daughter for his companion. When he was present, all was love; there was no unpleasant look or word; every wish of his was gratified.

In the mean time, Louisa looked on calmly and lisped not a word against the man she loved. The loss of a tender parent had filled her heart with grief, and the thought that her attention to his sick chamber had driven her friend away, gave her pain and sorrow indescribable. But she could not see that she had erred.

She had but done her duty, and so every one thought who knew the circumstances of the case.

A month or two passed by, and Henry was as attentive as ever to Jane, and it was settled in the minds of the neighbors that he was engaged to the haughty girl. The thought preyed deeply in the breast of the dutiful Louisa, but she suffered it not to interfere with her duty. She bore it like a philosopher, and was determined, whatever the result should be, to submit without a murmuring word. There were peace and happiness in her cot. The thought that a devoted father and excellent husband had been removed by death, would sometimes cause a feeling of sadness, but the mother and daughter looked to Him who gave and took away, and felt it was for the best. But when Louisa thought of the past — when she was happy in the society of Henry, and of his present alienated feelings, it made her sorrowful indeed. Save these hours of sadness, none were happier than they — none had a better circle of friends — none lived more peaceably with their neighbors. There were two or three young men in the village who would have esteemed it an honor to win the love and approbation of Miss Mentor, but she would encourage the visits of none, save those who called upon her as neighbors and friends.

Henry would often pass the home of Louisa, with the vain Miss Howell hanging on his arm, while their conversation appeared to be deep and earnest. It was evident that Henry wished to be seen by Louisa, and make her feel regret for once refusing to accompany him on an excursion of pleasure. But she witnessed the young man's conduct without manifesting the least displeasure. She never moved aside to be unnoticed or to make him

18*

feel that she was angry, or regretted the step he had taken. She thought such a course would be for the best in the end, whatever might be the consequences. Miss Mentor continued her duties, slept as soundly as ever, and gave no one occasion to say that the conduct of Henry had worn upon her spirits or broken her heart.

One evening Louisa attended a social party where Henry and Jane were present. They both took particular care to let her see their affection for each other; just as the reader has often seen two simpletons conduct when they thought they were made for each other. When the party broke up, in going home Louisa happened to be but a short distance behind the lovers. They were talking very earnestly, and did not seem to care if they were overheard.

"I wonder how Miss Louisa enjoyed herself to-night?" inquired Jane.

"I don't know, I'm sure," said Henry; "she tried to appear cheerful, but I saw that she was not very pleasant."

"Perhaps she regrets her past course."

"I have no doubt she does."

"She is a foolish girl, and I always knew it."

"It is certain she doesn't study her interest. She will never get a husband; she was cut out for an old maid. No young man who thinks any thing of himself, ever goes with her. She has been trying a long while to get one of the Goodings or Charles Hamilton to gallant her, but they know better."

This was all of the conversation Louisa heard; it was enough to convince her that she had lost nothing when Heywood left her society for the society of another. It was so untrue that it pained her to the heart. But it did not trouble her long. She did not look alone to earth for perfect happiness.

The day was appointed for the union of Henry and Jane, and it was understood to be their intention to have a splendid wedding. A week previous to the celebration of the nuptials, a young man made his appearance in the neighborhood. He was dressed in the extreme of fashion, and appeared to be in independent circumstances by the manner he expended his money. He had lately graduated from a lawyer's office, and had come to the village to commence practice. He hired a room, and put up his sign, which was very neatly printed in gold letters. In looking round for a boarding-house, he was introduced to Mr. Howell, who took him into his family. It was said that the landlord's head was more erect than ever; he was honored by having a lawyer board at his house, and he mentioned the circumstance so often, that the whole village was made acquainted with the fact in less than a week.

Mr. Edwards, the lawyer, had not been in Mr. Howell's house more than two days, before he was quite intimate with Jane, and when Henry called he was treated with not a little coolness.

"Father," said Jane one day in private, "what must I do? I am engaged to Heywood, and have no affection for him, and Mr. Edwards, whom no one could help loving, has offered me his hand. What shall I do?"

"By all means, tell Henry your feelings towards him, and as he is a reasonable fellow, he will not censure you. Of course, you need not mention the honor you have received from our distinguished boarder, the lawyer."

After thinking over the matter, and conversing with Edwards, they concluded to drop a line to Henry. It was written by the lawyer and copied by Jane, and sent forthwith.

Poor Heywood was thunderstruck. Though not accustomed to use harsh words, he could not refrain, declaring first that he would sue the girl for a breach of promise. But when cooled down a little, he declared she was not worthy of his attention, that he did not care a fig for her, and would return to his old friend, Louisa, not doubting that she would gladly accept of him; for notwithstanding his strange conduct he had really loved her.

The young men of the neighborhood laughed heartily at the affair, and said it was just right, as he had long before been so unkind to Miss Mentor, one of the best girls that lived in the village. No one sympathized with him, except his own relations, and even they declared it was a just punishment.

Few thought much of the lawyer. He was genteel, dressed well, talked loud, and knew a little more than every thing. He was married to Jane in the course of a few months after his arrival in the village. Having no property, and business being dull, he was obliged to sponge his living out of the old gentleman. Howell was tired to death with supporting him, and he finally removed to another place with his wife. They did not live very happily together, as the dispositions of each were any thing but agreeable. The last heard from him was that he just made enough by his profession to keep his family from starving, and was disliked by everybody on account of his niggardly behavior.

Full of hope, Heywood went to the house of Mrs.

Mentor, and was cordially received by Louisa. She was a young woman who never retaliated, and you could not tell by her conduct that she had ever been wronged by another. After conversing on various topics for nearly an hour, Henry introduced the one that lay near his heart.

"I have thought a great deal of late," said he, " of the course I pursued towards you last summer. That I did wrong, — was altogether too hasty, — I am free to confess."

"I always thought you were too hasty in the step you took, for my poor father was so unwell that I could not have a heart to leave him."

" Although we have hardly seen each other for many months past, for one I should be pleased to have that friendship renewed."

"I have never been otherwise than friendly to you ; if you thought otherwise you have been mistaken."

" But I should be pleased to be on the same terms of intimacy."

" Henry, there is a serious objection to that ; I am now engaged to another."

" Is it possible ? "

" It is so, and I expect shortly to be married to one who I have reason to believe loves me — who will never forsake me ; who will never prove treacherous."

Henry's heart was too full for utterance. He left the house after being kindly invited to call again by Louisa and her mother, who, if they remembered the past, did not have any feelings of unkindness towards Heywood, nor did they wish to reproach him.

During the year there was a wedding at Mrs. Mentor's. Louisa, the sweet-tempered, the amiable and lovely girl, was united to James Eldwell, the village pastor, a young man of fine talents and consistent piety. A better match was seldom formed. Poor Heywood was invited to the wedding, but he could not go. His imprudent step had sealed his fate and made him miserable.

From the day that Louisa was married, Henry was an altered man. He was seldom seen in company, and always preferred to be alone. It was his practice to walk in retired places, where the voices and the footsteps of men were seldom heard. He had few associates, and said but little. Apparently worn down by sorrow, he lived but a few years, and found that repose in the grave, which had been denied him on earth.

A MAN AGAIN.

No more will sorrow dim thine eye,
   Or grief thy heart oppress,
And bright as once shall be our sky,
   And every thing shall bless.
Forget the past — thy tears refrain —
   Come to this sheltering breast ;
For know, I am a man again,
   And still shall make thee blest.

It was a beautiful evening in May.   Couple after couple were seen wending their way to the mansion of Capt. Mould.   His daughter Ellen was to be united to the accomplished Edward Simonton.   Miss Mould was young, pretty, and prepossessing in her manners.   She had been blest with parents who had taken particular pains with her education.   Though not wealthy, Capt. Mould was in good circumstances, and had ever been indulgent to his daughter.   Young Simonton was the son of a merchant, who had amassed considerable property by strict attention to his business and frugality in his habits.   He brought up his son in his own counting-room, where he did pretty much as he had an inclination ; his father not often checking him in any irregular course.   Edward possessed a good disposition, but would doubtless be easily led away by a companion, although he was never known to be guilty of any particular vice.   His father was exceedingly liberal to his son ; permitting

him to take money whenever he was disposed, presuming that he was careful to expend nothing for useless
or vicious purposes. A short time previous to his marriage, the merchant took his son into partnership, to
share with him equally the profits of the business.

With bright prospects before the young couple, it
seemed impossible for them to be otherwise than happy
—that a single cloud should linger in their bright sky,
or that a single thorn should spring up in their pleasant
pathway. But there are many reverses in life. The
poor and forsaken to-day, may be the rich and happy
to-morrow. Those who can nowhere find a friend to
whom they can unbosom their sorrows, may in a few
days be surrounded by sympathizers and friends. We
cannot tell what the future may unfold. They only
who are prepared for joy or grief, for poverty or riches,
really know how to live and enjoy the blessings of life.
A few years passed by, and Edward prospered in business with his father. They not only made an excellent
living, but they were daily adding to their property.
In the midst of their prosperity, Mr. Simonton thought
he noticed a careless, indifferent spirit in his son; he was
absent frequently from the shop, and appeared to neglect his business. One day, when they were alone in
the shop, Mr. Simonton spoke to his son respecting his
seeming indifference to the concerns in the store, and
made the inquiry of him, why it was so.

"I was not aware," said Edward, "that I had been
careless or neglectful."

"You may depend upon it, it is so; and others have
noticed it beside myself. Where are you generally
when absent from the store?"

"I often associate with a few friends, and go to the

island on a sailing excursion, or take a chaise and ride."

"I am afraid that some of those young men do not sustain the characters they should. Are they not wild and headstrong and bent upon vicious pursuits?"

"Oh, no, father; they are as respectable and as virtuous young men as can be found in the city. Do you think I would associate with any but such?"

"No, I am sure I should not; but when young men are wild and careless and pursue courses without looking to the consequences, they are very apt to form bad habits, and if not utterly ruined, become unfitted for their business. And yet they do not perceive the stain which is gradually imprinted upon their characters. How true, Edward, is that familiar passage: —

> "'Vice is a monster of so frightful mien,
> As to be hated, needs but to be seen;
> Yet seen too oft, familiar with her face,
> We first endure, then pity, then embrace.'

It is only for your good that I speak thus plainly to you."

"As I said before, father, I am not aware that I have done wrong, that I have neglected my business; but if you think so, I will endeavor in future to conduct differently."

For a few months after this conversation, Edward was very attentive to his business, but he began gradually to slacken away, until his father found it necessary to check him again; but it had not the desired effect. His wife, too, had noticed the difference in her husband. He was less attentive to her, and appeared to take less interest in his domestic affairs. He would of-

19

ten keep late hours, not returning to his wife until near midnight. She, with a woman's love and solicitude, often inquired where he had been, but he merely replied, "In the company of a few friends." But not feeling satisfied with his answer, she was still unhappy and expressed the wish that he would return home in better season.

Thus young Simonton continued for nearly a year, when his father learned that he was in the constant practice of visiting the gaming-room, where he had met with frequent and heavy losses, and that he still continued the practice. Finding that what he now said to his son was of no avail, and that he persisted in the sin, he told him frankly that their copartnership must be dissolved for the present. But Edward appeared perfectly indifferent; he had been so long accustomed to the vice of gambling, that he preferred to be thrown out of business rather than relinquish his growing passion.

In settling up the accounts of the firm, Mr. Simonton found that by his son's irregularities and the debts he had contracted, they had met with a loss of several thousand dollars. When his father related the circumstance, Edward said not a word. He knew that he had wronged his parent and himself, that he had neglected his family, and brought disgrace upon his friends. As a natural consequence of the course he had taken, he resorted to the fatal bowl to drown his feelings, and it was not unfrequently that he was seen intoxicated. To save him from ruin, his father made him excellent offers. If he would forsake the gaming-table and touch no spirit, the past should be forgotten with all his losses, and he should still share one-half the profits of the concern. His wife also pleaded eloquently with her husband, and with tears entreated him to forsake his injurious habits, that he might be again respected and happy.

"Just think how much we once enjoyed," said she. "We had every thing the heart could desire. Every day's sun renewed our joys. Oh, how happy we were! Now, Edward, we can again enjoy life; pleasant will be our path, and bright and cheering our prospects, if you will only refuse to associate with those wretches — I can call them by no milder name — who have plotted your ruin, taken your property, and brought sorrow into our family. You cannot realize your altered appearance, since you have become addicted to the vile habits of drinking and gambling. How often have I of late thought of those lines of the poet: —

> "'A night of fretful passion may consume
> All that thou hast of beauty's gentle bloom,
> And one distempered hour of sordid fear
> Print on thy brow the wrinkles of a year.'

Every time I reflect upon your appearance, and know what you once was, I feel more than I can express. Now do, Edward, hearken to me, and not associate with the gambler. Depend upon it, we shall be happy if you only pursue a right course."

"I know, Ellen, that I have done wrong, I am fully sensible of it, and will try to keep away from those fellows who have professed to be my friends."

But habit is strong. When once accustomed to walk in the downward path, it requires great effort to retrace the steps and return to the true path. Habit —

" Does often reason overrule,
And only serves for reason to the fool."

If Edward did try to forsake his pernicious practices, his efforts were of no avail; he continued to associate with the unprincipled and became quite intemperate in his habits. His poor wife suffered in her feelings more than can be described; for she really loved her husband and did all in her power to promote his happiness. The father of Ellen endeavored to persuade her to leave one who had become so lost to shame and self-respect and so abusive to her; but she would not hear to them. "Perhaps he will do better," would be the reply to her parent.

Having pursued so degraded a course for so long, and having received a large amount of money from his father, at different periods, which he had wasted, Edward had become entirely penniless. His father would allow him no more.

"What I give in future shall be to your wife," said he. "Not another cent of my property shall you receive until you have altered your course."

This had no better effect upon Edward. Among those who had used their influence to lead him astray, he found some who would not hesitate to treat him to spirit, and he might be seen daily going home in a state of intoxication.

As the best course to be pursued, his father had him placed in the house of correction, he being complained of as a common drunkard. After remaining in this place for a few days, the young man began to realize his situation. He had lost his character, injured his father and almost broken the heart of his wife. No one respected him now; he was degraded. Those who in years passed had professed so strong a friendship for him, forsook him when his money was gone. Not one of his associates had called to see him. But his wife, she who had suffered and borne with him, was the only friend he found in his loneliness. Not a day passed that she did not call upon him, and bring some dainty which she had made especially for him. While in the house of correction, Edward promised his wife faithfully that he would pursue a different course as soon as he was permitted to have his liberty.

"If I will exert myself," said she, "to have you liberated will you promise to associate no more with gamblers?"

"I am determined to forsake them altogether. I will have nothing more to say to them."

"Will you drink any more?"

"No, never will I touch a single drop if I can possibly avoid it."

"There is one safe course and only one, to sign the pledge, and be firm in your resolution. Will you do this?"

"You know, Ellen, I have always said I would not sign the pledge. You would not have me tell a lie?"

"No, Edward, I would not have you tell an untruth; but if you have said you would not do a right act, there is more sin in keeping the resolution than in breaking it at once."

"But I cannot sign the pledge."

"Then I certainly cannot exert myself to have you released. It is only on condition that you will sign the pledge, that I will do any thing towards your liberation. This is my only hope."

"Well, I don't care then. I wont sign the pledge,"

19*

he said, with a little anger, and turned away from his wife.

Ellen left her husband, exceedingly sorry that he would not come to the good resolution. She knew that unless he signed the pledge, he would not resist the temptation, and it would be better for him and for her that he should remain in his present situation. She was determined to do nothing towards having him released from the house of correction unless she had real evidence of his reformation. It was out of pure love to him that she pursued this course.

For two or three days Ellen did not see her husband, when one morning the keeper of the house called upon her and told her that her husband was quite anxious for her to come and see him.

"Tell him I will come to-morrow," said she.

The next day she procured a Washingtonian pledge, and called upon her husband. He appeared glad to see her again.

"I have concluded to sign the pledge," said he, "and not only to sign it but to keep it."

"It is the only safe course, Edward."

"So I now believe."

"I have brought the pledge with me, and will read what you are to subscribe to, that you may not put your name to that which you do not perfectly understand."

After reading the pledge, Edward took the pen and signed it.

"There!" he exclaimed, throwing down the pen, "I am a man again! I feel new life in all my limbs. I bless God for what he has given me a disposition to do," and the poor fellow wept like a child. "O Ellen, forgive me, for all the injury I have done you — for all the suffering and sorrow I have brought upon you. Never, never again will you have occasion to grieve over my departure from the path of virtue. Never will I refuse to listen to your counsels, and to take heed to your advice."

"With all my heart I forgive you. This hour of joy more than repays me for all my sufferings."

Together they left the house and returned to their home, which had been so long the habitation of sorrow.

Edward went immediately to his father, told him what had taken place, and begged forgiveness for his undutiful course.

His father fell upon his neck and embraced him. Tears came freely to his eyes, as he said, "My son that was lost is found again."

His mother, poor woman, was so overcome that she could not for a long time give utterance to her joy.

If happiness was ever felt on earth, it was in the dwelling of Mr. Simonton, on this occasion of the reformation of his erring son.

A few months elapsed and Edward continued firm in his resolution, and became one of the most active members of the temperance society. In relating his experience, he has often brought tears to the eyes of many. "I would advise all to sign the pledge," he recently said in a public assembly; "it was the means of my reformation. Had I adhered to the resolution formed while associating with the intemperate, never to put my name to the pledge, I had still been an irreclaimable drunkard. The pledge alone has saved me. I can never be too thankful to Heaven that I was blest with those friends, who never forsook me in my lost condition, but labored with me till I was induced to become a man again. For I *am* a man now, who but recently was a brute — a brute in actions, pursuing a brutish course, and being brutal to all my real friends."

Edward and his father are now in business together, and by appearances are doing exceedingly well. The former course of young Simonton will be but an incentive to his usefulness. With the industrious habits, benevolent feeling and desire to do good and be useful to others, that now characterize him, the prospect is that he will be eminently useful in the world, and exert a wide influence in behalf of temperance and virtue.

THE ORPHAN.

There's not a heart, however drear,
 The hand of friendship may not bless;
No breast, if touched by Mercy's tear,
 That will not move in thankfulness.

JAMES STANFORD was an orphan. His first recollection was when running about in the almshouse at the age of three or four years. He had been told his parents died when he was an infant, and that he was placed in the hands of the overseers of the poor. James received but few tokens of kindness; most of the inmates being cross and snappish to him. If any thing went wrong with the miserable inmates, and he was near, he was always sure to receive a kick or a cuff. As he grew older, he was obliged to work about the establishment, under the direction of the overseer, Mr. Langdon, a complete tyrant. When the child was too weak to lift, or too unwell to work, this man would growl at him, and call him a lazy wretch, "a young viper," a " good-for-nothing puppy," and the like, and not unfrequently box his ears, or throw a cowhide about his legs. The child feared this wretch as he would an unchained tiger, and trembled like a leaf when he saw him approach. One time the little fellow accidentally broke a bowl, in which he was eating his supper, which circumstance soon came to the ears of the overseer.

James was ordered into his presence. He came pale as death and weeping most bitterly. "You little good-for-nothing wretch you, what did you break that bowl for?" said Langdon; "it had better been your neck."

"I didn't go to, and I will never do so again. I never will, sir."

"Not a word, you dog you. I'll teach you better than to break up all the crockery in the house. Off with your jacket instantly, or I'll skin you alive. Be quick."

The poor child more dead than alive with fear, attempted to pull off his torn and dirty jacket, when the overseer grasped his arm and tore it off.

"I'll never do so again."

"Hold your tongue; I'll teach you to break another bowl, that I will."

With these words, he laid the cowhide over the child's back, while the little fellow begged earnestly and affectingly for mercy. "You'll kill me — I shall die — Oh, do have mercy." But the wretch continued, till there was scarcely a place on his back that had not been lacerated, while the blood ran down to his feet. When Langdon had ceased whipping, the child was senseless. He knew nothing until the next morning when he awoke in intense pain and so stiff that he could hardly crawl out of the bed when he was called.

When Langdon saw him, he exclaimed, "I have a good mind to whip you again, you dog, this morning! I'm altogether too easy with you young scamps. But I'll try you again."

About once a week the overseers of the poor visited the workhouse to see if every thing went on regularly, and to supply the food and clothing that were needed.

Before these men, Mr. Langdon was as mild and ami-able as a saint. He would show them about the differ-ent apartments, that they might see the regularity and order of the house. As one of these gentlemen noticed the deathlike appearance of James, soon after he had been unmercifully flogged, he remarked — "You ap-pear to be sick, my little fellow."

"Sick!" said Langdon, "I guess you wouldn't think so, if you knew how much he eats. Jim is a roguish boy, too, and very saucy sometimes."

"You feel happy, do you not, my lad?" said the gentleman.

"Why don't you speak up and say Yes, sir, to the gentleman and not be sulky? Tell him you are per-fectly happy," and then turning to the man, he said, "That boy appears really to enjoy himself among us. We have to humor him a good deal, and you know it is best to do so with small children. Poor child! he has no father or mother to look after him, and I pity the boy," and the tears ran down the cheeks of Langdon.

"That is right, my friend. While you thus feel and act towards those whom heaven has afflicted, you will not lose your reward." And then placing his hand on the head of the lad, he said — "Always be obedient to your kind and indulgent master, and he will treat you the same in future."

James trembled when he thought that he should re-ceive the same treatment, and could hardly stand, which the gentleman observed, when Langdon re-marked —

"The poor child is unwell; he has been ill for two or three days past. I shall give him some castor oil to-night."

After the overseers had left, Langdon had James brought to him.

"Why didn't you speak up, and tell the gentleman, when he asked you if you was contented and happy? I'll teach you better manners," grasping him by the arm and severely shaking him — "a little more, and you would have got me into difficulty, you dog you. What did you mean by not talking up, hey?" shaking the trembling child again — "Why don't you tell me? I'll shake you to pieces, if I am to have this trouble with you."

Giving him one or two cuffs, he sent James to bring in some wood, telling him to be careful and not pretend to be sick, or he would be under the necessity of using the cowhide again.

It was some weeks before James recovered from the effects of the whipping given him for the crime of accidentally breaking the bowl. In the mean time, he had received several kicks and thumps from his master, and also from some of the inmates of the house, who, from their bad characters, had won the good-will of the tyrant. It was not half the time that the boy had enough to eat, yet he dared not complain. One day he requested a little milk in his molasses and water, which coming to the ears of Langdon, he declared that, for his impudence, the boy should go without sweetening for two months to come, and so the child drank nothing but water. But just so much bread and gruel was allowed him daily. If he asked for another mouthful, his next meal would invariably be taken from him. James was not the only child treated in this way. There were several, besides the aged and infirm, who suffered for the necessaries of life, and yet they dare not complain, lest they should be more unkindly treated. There was one poor afflicted man who was deficient in sound common sense, and the treatment he received was barbarous. He was ordered out in the cold and wet, and compelled to labor when he should have been on his bed. One time as he was stooping down, throwing some bricks into a cart, he was spoken to by Langdon, but being a little hard of hearing, did not notice it; whereupon the wretch ran up behind him and gave him a severe kick in the groin. The poor man fell to the earth in extreme agony, and was obliged to be carried to the house and placed on a bed. From this kick .he never recovered, but languished, at times, in excruciating pains, for a year or two, and finally died of his wound.

Time passed on, but it brought no blessings to the orphan boy. His life had been the scene of pain and sorrow from the dawn of existence. As he grew older he saw the injustice of his master more and more, but he could not speak out his mind. He was tempted time and again to mention his case to the overseers, on the day of their weekly visit, but he could find no opportunity; Langdon being always present and compeling him to lie to their faces.

James was now twelve or thirteen years of age, and while at work chopping wood one morning, a chip flew up and broke a pane of glass. What to do, the frightened lad could not tell. He knew he should be severely punished for the accident; but he had hardly begun to reflect on his situation before he was called before Langdon. "You're a pretty boy, aint you?" said the stern old reprobate; "you've broken a window, you dog you?"

20

" Sir, it was accidental."

" Hold your villanous, lying tongue; you know you
lie.   Do you think I'm fool enough to believe you ?   It
is pretty well too, to imagine that a lie will screen you
from a just punishment.   Off with your jacket — off
with it, or I'll tear you limb from limb."

" O sir, I — "

" Hold your tongue.   Open your mouth again, and
I'll tie you up naked by your thumbs, and whip you
till you have learnt better manners.   Come, off with
your jacket.   I sha'n't wait many moments for your mo-
tions, that I'll have you know."

" Sir, I — "

" Dare you speak again ?   I'll learn you who is your
master," and with these words, he flew at the boy,
tore off his jacket, and stripped him completely, continually muttering, " You villain, you dog, you rogue, I'll
learn you something."   He then tied his hands, and
drew them up to a spike in the wall, and made the rope
fast, while his toes just touched the floor, the poor boy
begging for mercy all the time.   He now took his cowhide, and commenced whipping.   Nearly every blow
brought blood from his back.   The child cried and
plead, till nature was nearly exhausted but he plead in
vain.   It was more than an hour after that reason returned to him, and then he was lying upon some straw.
But he could scarcely move a limb.   It was several days
before he could walk, and for weeks he was unable to
work.

When the overseers of the poor should call at the
workhouse again, James determined to show them his
back and tell them of the treatment he had received;
for he could not believe, if they knew his sufferings,

they would justify the tyrannical man. It was not long before Langdon and one of the overseers were standing before him.

"James, my lad, how do you feel to-day?" said Langdon, pretending to feel compassionate towards him.

"*Feel*, sir, how should I *feel* after being beaten almost to death?"

The wretch was thunderstruck. He turned all manner of colors — hemmed and stammered — "How — what do you mean to say?"

"Mean to say? That you have almost killed me. It is true, God knows."

"What does this mean, Mr. Langdon?" inquired the gentleman.

"It is one of his villanous lies. Miss G——," said he, calling one of his favorites to him, but who was as vile a woman as could be found, — "Miss G——, that boy accuses me of beating him. Have I done any thing more than correct him mildly for his faults?"

"Oh, no, Mr. Langdon, you never have; and I can tell this gentleman how kind you have always been to him — watched over him as a father, and done more, too."

"So you see, sir," said Langdon, "that this is a trick of the boy to injure me in the estimation of the overseers."

"But I can show my b—"

"Hold your lying tongue!" exclaimed the wretch, "this gentleman shall not hear you lie any more. You may go now and pick the rest of that oakum."

Young Stanford went with a heavy heart; he dared not do otherwise; but how bitterly did he regret what

he had said.   He thought of the punishment he should
receive that night, — his body being already lacerated
from his recent flogging, — and he thought of an escape from the house.   He had nothing but an old cap,
besides the clothes that were on him.   But while thinking of escaping, word was sent him to go to his master,
and be punished for his impudence.   Immediately, James
started for the door and the gate.   He ran as fast as
his sore back would permit him ; but he had not ran far
in the wood, when looking back, he saw three or four
men after him at full speed, and among the rest old
Langdon himself.   They gained rapidly upon him.   At
this moment, a wagon with a gentleman in it came up.

"O sir, take me in — take me in, I pray you," said
James.

"Why, what is the matter?"

"Take me in and I will tell you all."

"But who are those men behind?"

"For God's sake, save me — take me in — do, sir,
do!"

"Jump in, then."

And in he jumped, and off they rode when Langdon
was not two rods from the wagon.   James related his
sorrows to the gentleman who took him in, whose name
he ascertained to be Ingman.   He appeared to feel a
deep interest in the lad, ragged and dirty and miserable as he was.

"I live about seventy miles from here on a farm,"
said the gentleman, "and if you will go with me and be
contented to work with me, you shall be welcome."

James thanked him with tears in his eyes, for such
kindness he did not expect, having through life experienced nothing but savage looks, hard words, and severe beatings.

Late in the evening Mr. Ingman put up at a private house, and the next morning started on his journey, taking James with him, whom he found to possess a good mind, but without culture. They conversed freely, and their journey soon terminated; for about sunset, Mr. Ingman arrived at his home. When he informed his family what he knew of James, they appeared to feel a deep interest in him, more especially when they saw the wounds on his back. Mrs. Ingman dressed them as well as she could, gave him clean and tidy clothes, which she had in the house, while the tears of gratitude ran down the cheeks of the poor boy.

"I cannot tell you how grateful I am for what you have done for me," said he, "and I will try to repay you as soon as I am able to work."

With a good suit of clothes and a clean face, and receiving kind treatment, James improved in every respect. Mr. Ingman sent him to the district school, where his daughter, Sarah, attended, and purchased him books to study. Young Stanford did all in his power to please the good people who had been so kind to him, and each felt strongly attached to the other. James was industrious and labored diligently on the farm, and also improved what leisure time he had in reading and study.

A few years flew rapidly by, and James had grown up to manhood. He had passed very happily the last years of his life; but he could never look back upon his childhood without feelings of horror at what he had passed through, nor upon old Langdon, but with deep indignation, and he often thought he should like to see that man punished as he deserved. Since he had been with Mr. Ingman, he had not heard from him.

20*

Mr. Ingman and his wife were so well pleased with Stanford, that they readily consented to the request of their daughter, that he should become their son-in-law. When Sarah's father had completed a small house which he was building about a mile above his dwelling, he said to his daughter and James, "I make you a present of this house and a hundred acres of land. Be prudent and industrious and you will prosper." The young couple thanked him sincerely for his liberality and kindness and said they would endeavor to profit by his advice and the example he had always set before them.

That night Sarah Ingman was married to James Stanford, and removed to their new house, as happy as fond hearts and virtuous characters could make them.

Young Stanford went diligently to work on his farm, dressing and improving his land, so that it yielded abundantly. The produce he raised, he was obliged to carry fifty or sixty miles to find a good market.

One evening, as he was returning to his village, at a late hour, he was overtaken by a man on horseback who appeared very sociable. James thought he knew the voice, but it being dark, could not recognize the person. For several miles they conversed on various topics, till they approached a piece of thick woods.

"Young man," said the stranger, "I'm a robber, and I would thank you for the money you received to-day," at the same time drawing a large horse pistol from his saddle and cocking it.

Stanford was a man of some nerve and not easily frightened.

"Sir," said he, "I have but little money about me, and it is hardly worth taking."

"Out with what you have instantly," said the robber, pointing the pistol towards Stanford, " or your life is not worth a fig."

James immediately took out his purse and handed it to the robber, who was about putting it in his pocket, when Stanford grasped his pistol. In attempting to wrest it from the hands of the stranger it was discharged, the ball just grazing his cheek. In an instant the robber jumped from his horse, followed by Stanford. The former attempted to draw a knife from his pocket, and the latter clinched him. There was a severe struggle. At one moment the robber had the advantage, but it was now recovered by James, who threw him down and held him firmly.

"Villain," said the farmer, "it is in my power to take your life."

" Sir, spare me and let me go and I will reward you. Five hundred dollars that are in my saddle-bags shall be yours."

"Do you think I am a knave like yourself? Not ten thousand dollars would be a temptation for me. Vile wretch to make such an offer, when in an instant you would sacrifice my life. No, I shall hold you here until some one passes, if it be till to-morrow noon."

"I will reform, and pay you well for letting me go. I will give up my pistol, my knife and every weapon I have about me, so you need not fear."

"I have no fear, this is not your first attempt to rob, and the law shall take its course with you."

For an hour or more did the robber beg for liberty, but in vain, when a gentleman with a wagon came up, which proved to belong to Mr. Strong, a distant neighbor of Stanford. The farmer related his adventure, and asked for assistance. Mr. Strong readily granted it. They tied the robber's feet and hands, he making but little resistance, put him into the wagon and carried him to Stanford's house — his own wagon and the robber's horse had arrived there an hour before, having started the moment the men had sprung at each other.

In carrying the robber to the house where there was a lamp, and he could be seen distinctly, James recognized the villain at once. It was the wretch, Langdon, who treated him so unkindly, and beat him so unmercifully years before, when he was an inmate of the almshouse.

Langdon pretended to feel penitent, and even wept, supposing he was not known.

"It was my first offence," said he, "and I was driven to commit the act by sheer necessity."

"We know more about your past life than you are aware of," remarked Stanford. "Were you not the keeper of the almshouse in ——, a dozen or fifteen years ago?"

This question made the villain uneasy. He hesitated to answer, but finally said, "I was."

"Do you remember a little boy by the name of Stanford that was an inmate of the house about that time?"

This was an uncomfortable question, but the robber replied: "There were so many there that I cannot recollect them all."

"But don't you distinctly remember James Stanford, the orphan boy?"

"Yes, I think I do."

"Do you remember the unmerciful beatings you gave him?"

Langdon made no reply.

"If you have forgotten them, I have not. I am that orphan boy, and shall never forget your cruelty. But justice has overtaken you at last."

This announcement had an astonishing effect upon the robber. He knew that he was discovered—that his true character was known, and that strict justice would be done to him.

Two or three of the neighbors set up with Langdon that night, and in the morning an officer was found to carry him to the county jail. He was tied hands and feet, and put into a wagon with the officer; but as they were passing over a bridge, Langdon gave a sudden spring from the wagon, and before he could be secured, plunged into the water and immediately sunk. His body was recovered a few days after and interred on the bank of the river.

Thus closed the days of a wretched being, who passed from one degree of crime to another until he perished by his own hands.

The horse of the robber was a fine one, but his saddle-bags contained but very little money. Stanford heard that for the last five years, Langdon had been an outcast and a robber, but had thus far escaped the vigilance of his pursuers.

Many years have passed away since the events we have recorded, but James Stanford and his wife still live in happiness and prosperity. He is esteemed as a valuable citizen and an excellent neighbor. In any important transactions, he is consulted by the villagers, and his opinions are given with caution and forethought and carry with them great weight. We trust that he

will live to a good old age, and that his life will continue to be useful and happy. When he is removed by
death, we know many a heart will be sad, and many a
tear will moisten his grave.

WHICH SHALL I MARRY?

CHAPTER I.

I seek a female in whose heart
Domestic virtues share a part;
Who loves her home, and there will shine,
A devotee to Wisdom's shrine.

"I CONFESS I am at a stand, Henry," remarked William Emerson to his intimate friend; "for the life of me, I do not know which I like best of those two girls — Sarah Talbot or Jane Emery. They are both capital girls in their way, and would both make excellent wives — so I think. All the fault I can find with Sarah is, that she is rather too fashionable, and not quite so domestic as I should like to see her."

"That I consider a serious objection to a female, and to be frank, I must tell you so," remarked Henry Willard. "What does a man in your circumstances want of a girl who cannot work? If you marry, you should have a wife that can bake and wash and iron, and do a thousand little things that a fashionable lady will not put her hands to without fainting. What kind of a girl is Jane?"

"As fine a young lady as you will find in the city. She is not so handsome as Sarah, I confess; but then she is not carried away by the fashions of the day.

Visit her when you please, and you will find her busy about something."

"I know whom I should choose," remarked Henry; "and it would take me but a few moments to decide, if I were you. Does Sarah ever do any thing?"

"To tell you the truth, I have visited her house more or less for two or three years, and never have I seen a thimble on her finger or a needle in her hand. She is either braiding her hair or adjusting her dress before the glass, or poring over some silly novel. Sometimes she will sing and dance, but never have I seen her at work. Yet Sarah is a beautiful girl; I am strongly attached to her, and I think she will make me a good wife."

"We are apt to be carried away by a pretty face and a fine form and a sweet voice, I know; but what are these, William, in comparison with some other qualities? You have told me that Jane is an industrious girl?"

"She certainly is, Henry. I think I never went into her house when she was not busy about something. She always has work in her hands. Her mother, with Jane's assistance, does all the work in the family, and that is not a little, as you must know."

"With the description that you have given me of the two girls, I think you cannot do better than select the one who will be of the most advantage to a person in your circumstances. You are not able at present, if you should get married, to support a fashionable wife in all her whims and follies. If she must follow the fashions of the day, it will take more than you can possibly earn to support her. What a person of your circumstances needs, is a helpmeet and not a doll, a willing worker, and not a fine singer; one who can make bread, and not a dancer. If I were better acquainted with the young ladies, however, I should be better able to judge which of the two would make the better wife for me."

"Go with me to the Cape some evening, and I will introduce you to them."

"Agreed. When will you go?"

"To-morrow evening I will call on Sarah, if you are not engaged."

"I shall not be engaged, and will accompany you."

The next evening found the two friends at the house of Mr. Talbot. Sarah was a fascinating girl; she was pretty and had a sweet voice, of which she seemed to be particularly proud. She sang about a dozen different songs during the evening, and displayed herself to no little advantage Her hair showed the work of hours, and her fingers were adorned with costly rings. In short, Sarah was such a girl as was well calculated to captivate the heart of a young man who looked merely to the outward appearance.

"Well, Henry, how are you pleased with Sarah?" inquired William of his friend, as they left the house.

"To tell you the truth, I was not remarkably well pleased with her. I must acknowledge that she is pretty to look at, has a sweet voice, and is well calculated to please a young man who looks only to appearances. She must have spent hours in adjusting her hair and her dress. Her hands looked as if they had never known work. And then her conversation was any thing but agreeable to me. What do I care about the latest fashions, and the appearance of this young woman or the other — the characters in this novel and in that, and the like? It would cost more to support

21

a woman like her, William, than you will be likely to earn for many years to come."

"I don't know but you are correct in your opinion, but, notwithstanding, I am attached to her. But I wish you to-morrow evening to go with me to Miss Emery's. Will you go?"

"Yes. I think I have nothing particular to do to-morrow evening."

The friends parted. On the following evening, they visited the house of Jane. The young lady, when they entered, was seated by the table with her mother, diligently at work. Occasionally she would stop a few moments, while they were conversing, but again ply her needle.

The hours passed pleasantly away, and William and his companion took their departure.

"Well, Henry, how did you like the appearance of Jane?" inquired his friend.

"Very much indeed. To be sure she is not what people would call handsome, but she appears so agreeable and pleasant, that no one could help loving her. She converses intelligently, and during the whole evening she never spoke of balls or novels, or said aught of any one. She was neat in her dress but not gaudy. Her hair was done up with taste, and had not the appearance of two or three hours' labor in fixing it for the occasion; and her fingers betrayed but a solitary plain ring. More than all, she is an industrious girl. She continued with her mother to work, which plainly shows her industrious habits. From what little I have seen of the two girls, I should by all means choose Jane, if I wished for a companion and a wife."

"Do you really think she would make the better wife of the two?"

" Most certainly I do."

" Well, I shall see before long. Should I prosper in my business, I think I shall take me a wife before many months."

" Be careful how you choose. Remember your future happiness depends mainly on this important step."

CHAPTER II.

Bow not to Fashion; they who feel
The influence of her ban,
Are in a thraldom more debased
Than the chained African.

CAPE ELIZABETH is a beautiful place. It is a long neck of land about a mile from Portland, Maine, and is so situated that it breaks up the sea that would otherwise make Portland harbor unsafe for vessels, instead of being one of the best harbors in the world. In Cape Elizabeth and round about it, are many delightful spots which never weary the heart or tire the eye, when gazing upon them. You have a view of the ocean and the islands, and vessels are continually passing, so that a ride over to this place is one of the most delicious that can be enjoyed. Thousands resort thither in the warm days of summer, and are refreshed by the cooling breezes and the delightful scenery.

There are many excellent farms and noble-hearted farmers in this place. Several years ago, we became acquainted with some of the people, and now often pass a happy day in their society.

In the town of Cape Elizabeth, lived a Mr. Talbot, a
farmer, who had become independent. He had several
sons and but one daughter. Unlike many of her companions, from her childhood Sarah was proud and indolent. She would sit and read from morning till night,
while her mother was obliged to wait upon her. When
she arrived at the age of fourteen or fifteen, she was
sent to the city to board, that she might learn to play
on the piano and to dance. These amusements highly
delighted her, and she became what is so common now-
a-days — a fashionable lady. Sarah had a near neighbor, Jane Emery, who was as much unlike her as possible. She was always at work. Her parents were in
humble circumstances, and she had always been taught
by an excellent mother to be industrious. The girls
were about the same age, and for a season attended the
same school. At one time they both boarded in Portland, and received instruction from a high school for females taught by the Rev. Mr. Adams.

"Jane, you will never be any thing but an old maid,"
remarked Sarah to her one day, "unless you spruce up
a little. Who will ever think of having you for a companion, looking as you do? who, except that great calf
of a fellow, with owl's eyes and a mouth like a hinge,
who called to see you the other day? You should fix
up your hair, and sit upright, and not be everlastingly
at work."

"Let me be an old maid, then, Sarah. I am sure I
can never consent to look as you do. Why, you are
now so small round the waist that your system must
suffer, I know. And then, look behind you — when I
saw you pass the house to-day, I could not but laugh
outright at your ridiculous appearance."

" Why, Jane, it is all the fashion, now ; you are behind the age. Stooping over the washtub, has made you
almost as round as a hoop."

" You mistake ; I do not stoop, although I do a large
part of our washing. I should be ashamed to let
mother do it all."

" But she might employ some poor woman to do it,
or part of it, at least."

" So she could, if she were able. But you know it
is as much as we can do to get along and pay our expenses ; and I would rather work than not. I take a
great deal of pleasure in assisting about the house."

" Your taste is different from mine — that's all I have
to say."

" I am sorry that we think differently, for all physicians tell us that a little labor is conducive to health,
and I know I feel much happier when I am about
something."

" Jane, I wish to ask you a question ; how are you
pleased with young Emerson ? "

" Why, I don't know much about him. He appears
to be a likely man."

" Ay, that he is — and between you and I — but
don't mention it, for the world — I intend to have him
as my beau."

" To do that, Sarah, you must be a different girl, in
my way of thinking. He is an industrious, prudent
young man, I judge, and when he takes a wife, he will
select one who is not ashamed to work."

" You know nothing about him. He has money
enough, and will not want his wife to work herself to
death."

" True, but he will want his wife to know *how* to
21*

work and oversee the domestic concerns. With your present tastes and feelings, you cannot do either."

"I'll risk myself, Jane. If I were obliged to be a slave, if I became a wife, I should rather be an old maid all my days."

"But, Sarah, why don't you learn to work in the kitchen ? Perhaps you may never be obliged to do this kind of work ; but it is necessary for you to know how to do it."

"If you begin to work in the kitchen, you are not thought any thing of, but few call to see you, and no respectable young man thinks of waiting upon you."

"You have mistaken notions entirely. I don't like to offend you, but I know your mother is a very domestic woman. I venture to say when she was young, she knew all about culinary employments."

"Times have altered since then."

"Times may have altered, but I know that a woman who is not too indolent to work, and who spends a portion of her time usefully, feels happier than the fashionable lady, and finds more true friends. An industrious young man is generally more partial to her. If Mr. Emerson is such a man as I think him to be, he would much prefer to know you spent the larger portion of your time at home, assisting your mother."

"Poh, I know better."

"We shall see."

By the above conversation the reader will learn the characters of Sarah and Jane. One had been brought up in fashionable indulgence, without scarcely lifting her finger to help herself. Dress she considered the criterion of character. The other had been taught by a judicious mother to improve her mind — to work in the kitchen, and employ herself about something that was useful during her evenings. To dress decently and modestly was all she desired. No new fashion turned her head; no fop captivated her heart!

CHAPTER III.

Let others sing of lips and eyes,
As more than half divine;
The virtues of the heart I prize,
And these, I know, are thine.

ONE evening, a few months after the conversation related in the last chapter took place, young Emerson called upon his friend, William. "I am decided, Henry," said he; "my mind is now made up."

"What do you mean, William?" inquired Henry.

"Why, don't you recollect the conversation we had several months since respecting Miss Talbot and Miss Emery?"

"Oh, yes, I remember."

"Well, I have decided in favor of Jane, the industrious and domestic girl. I have watched the movements of both for a long time, and Jane, I am confident, is the girl for me. She will be a companion and a friend, if I am so lucky as to obtain her."

"I cannot but commend you for your choice, William. What little I saw of Miss Talbot, convinced she was not the girl for you. But pray tell me what induced you to decide in favor of Miss Emery?"

"To tell you the truth, I saw nothing in Sarah, if I

may except her pretty looks, her singing and her dancing, that I cared a fig for. As many times as I visited
her house, I never saw a needle in her hand. I verily
believe she cannot darn a stocking or make a batch of
bread. For me to have selected such a girl for a wife
would have been the height of folly. Besides, Sarah
has had several suitors, but they were either disgusted
with her manners, or she turned them off for new faces.
Our neighbor, Edward Simons, told me that he was
once favorably struck with Sarah's appearance, and for
several months visited her house, but when he learned
her disposition and character, he immediately forsook
her company. There is nothing pleases her so much as
balls and cotillons, where she can go and display herself in dancing. I have known her to spend half a day
in preparing for one of these exhibitions. Her hair,
of which she is exceedingly proud, employs many hours
of her time. Every braid must look just so. Nothing
short of two hours before the glass, will satisfy her in
adjusting her braids and her curls. And then, too, she
has a pleasant voice, of which she is very particular to
give a stranger notice, especially when she has an opportunity of thumping on the piano."

"I recollect, William, her displaying herself when I
called on her with you. If she had not exerted herself
for effect, I should have been pleased with her voice;
but as it was, I was rather disgusted."

"And then, too, Sarah wants everybody to wait
upon her. She tells her mother to do this thing and
the other, as if she were sole mistress of the house.
If her brothers do not run at her call, or obtain what
she requests, she is very angry, and makes use of
words that would shame another girl. I feel thankful

that I found her out, and I believe it was by your sug-
gestion that I was more particular."

"How is it, William, with Jane? Are you well
pleased with her?"

"I never saw a girl I liked so well. She is always
busy and always pleasant. Visit the house when she
is about her work, and she never colors and never
makes apologies. Instead of conversing on frivolous
subjects, she always has something interesting to communicate. She has read a great deal and of the right sort.
She knows nothing about Ingraham's or Bradbury's
last work; but she will converse on any department of
science or history. Instead of devoting her time to
dress and the various follies of the times, she improves
her leisure hours in study, or in perusing valuable
works. And then she is always agreeable. You never
find her in the sulks — never. She is cheerful and
happy, and instead of calling upon her mother to bring
her this article and the other, she goes after it herself
and assists her parent all in her power. I never heard
her speak an unkind or an unpleasant word to any
member of the family. She is the girl for me."

"As I said before, I highly approve of your choice.
If you get that girl, you will have a prize indeed.
Does she seem to favor your suit?"

"Certainly she does, and there is a right understanding between us. Since Sarah has noticed my partiality to Jane, she takes every opportunity to treat us
both with contempt. Poor girl, she is her own worst
enemy, and is not worth minding."

CHAPTER IV.

One error, when persisted in,
Though trifling it may be,
Will lead to dangerous paths of sin,
At last to ruin thee.

In the fall of 183–, there was a marriage in Cape Elizabeth — William Emerson was united to Jane Emery. There being no minister in the place, Rev. Mr. Adams, of Portland, was sent for, who solemnly united the happy couple. A number of friends were present, and among the rest was Henry Willard. Every thing went off well, and all the guests appeared to be happy. The parents of Jane were humble people, but they assisted her all in their power, and she had almost every thing that was necessary for her to commence housekeeping with. William had been doing business for himself for some time, and had prospered. As soon as the company broke up, Emerson and his wife rode to Portland, and commenced housekeeping in the dwelling that they occupy at the present time. It is said that he has made money, and is in a fair way to become one of our richest merchants. We hope it is correct, for a better-hearted man we know not where to find.

Last summer, as my friend Becket and myself were riding leisurely along, enjoying the beautiful scenery on the Cape, we met Mr. Talbot in the road, and being acquainted with him, had quite a chat. He finally insisted on our taking tea at his house. The pressing invitation we could not resist, and we therefore hitched our horses and went in. And there were Sarah and her mother, whom we had not seen before for many a day. The old lady was sociable and agreeable, but her daughter seemed averse to talking. The rose had faded from her cheek, and her hair, which was once so beautiful, was sprinkled, we noticed, with gray. Two or three wrinkles had been added to her forehead, and she seemed the completest specimen of an old maid we had ever seen. With every thing to make her happy, she seemed determined to be miserable, at least so we thought.

After spending an agreeable hour with the old folks, we arose to leave. At that moment Sarah left the room.

"Don't you think Sarah has altered a great deal in her looks?" said the old gentleman, addressing me.

"Very much," I replied.

"Poor girl! she has endured every thing with that rascally husband of hers."

"Indeed! Is she married?"

"Why, she was married three years ago to one of your Portland men whom we all considered an excellent character; but he turned out a villain. John Alson is a drunkard, and abuses his wife; so much so, that we have now taken her home."

We expressed our surprise and regret, when the old gentleman continued, —

"I fear it will be the death of the girl."

We knew Alson, but for the first time we learned that he was the husband of Sarah. He was indeed a villain; no one could depend upon him; and how in the world Miss Talbot could ever have fancied him was a mystery to us.

We drove into Portland, conversing all the while upon the ill-luck of Sarah and her rascally husband.

She had false notions. She did not begin life aright, and this was her ruin. Had she been industrious and prudent, like her young companion, Jane Emery, it is more than probable she would have succeeded as well and been as happy.

There are many girls who are now as frivolous and as idle as Sarah was. Let them take warning. Few industrious and worthy young men can approve of your conduct. If you wish to secure good husbands and happy homes, be industrious, and discard the foolish fashions of the day. Live not to please the eye alone, but to improve and elevate the heart.

STORY OF ELLEN.

If but a single thought I drop
    Into a drowsy ear,
It may revive the spark of hope,
    And the desponding cheer.
A word may save where volumes fail,
    If spoken from the heart,
And with the dying soul prevail,
    And life and joy impart.
Ye all can speak a gentle word,
    To bless the weak and low,
And o'er life's dark and thorny road
    Sweet flowers and sunshine threw.

It was the custom in my early days for children of both sexes to attend the same district school. And I remember distinctly the happy faces that congregated every day to gather instruction from our worthy master. Among the females there was one, who, for her beauty and modest deportment, had secured the love and respect of the whole school. She had a dark, brilliant eye, a beautiful forehead, and a pleasant countenance. Rich auburn hair fell in graceful curls about her neck. It was not often that Ellen received a reprimand from her teacher, whose partiality was evident, from the frequent smiles he bestowed upon her. While her companions were at their plays, or were carelessly wasting their time in frivolous amusements, Ellen was attentive to her studies, and treasuring up

22

useful information. As her parents were in rather indi-
gent circumstances, she was sometimes slighted by her
more wealthy schoolmates, but, notwithstanding, she was
cheerful and pleasant, and even grateful for the smile
of love or approbation. For years I attended this
school with Ellen, and during all the time, I do not recollect of any impropriety in her conduct, but on the
contrary, she was a. pattern which would have done
honor to any female to follow. Amiable, kind, and affectionate, she secured the friendship of many, so that
when she finally left the school, she had not an enemy
behind. About the same time I went to learn the mysteries of a mechanical trade. Not hearing the name of
Ellen, I seldom thought of her excepting when, meeting with an old schoolfellow, we would name over the
companions of our early days. I finished my trade, —
having spent seven of my best years in its acquisition, —
and "set up" for myself, but never saw or heard of
Ellen. I made frequent inquiries of my friends, but
no one had heard from her since she was a playful girl.
It might be that she had died early, or that she had removed to a distant town, or that she had become the
amiable and accomplished wife of some devoted husband. At times, I would feel anxious to know what
had become of the beautiful being, whose opening
youth seemed to be the precursor of a glorious sequel.

Years passed away, and I was fast verging to the meridian of life, when one day an opportunity presented
itself to visit the poorhouse, belonging to my native
town. It contained a number of sick, aged, and
wretched beings, who had been placed there on account
of their friendlessness and poverty. Others had become
victims of intemperance, and were thus shut out from

temptation to prevent the further inroads of disease, and to stay the steps which were fast tending to shame and infamy. In visiting the several departments, I was struck with the misery that seemed depicted on many a countenance, which once doubtless was the index of a happy heart. In an upper room, which I came near passing without entering, on a low pallet, I observed the wasted form of a female, who appeared to be in the last stages of consumption. As I approached her, she cast her hollow, glassy eyes upon me, and in a moment I discovered the countenance of my early schoolmate, the once happy and beautiful Ellen. Her former beauty had not forsaken her, but disease, or sorrow, or infamy, had traced, in lines too legible to be misunderstood, its desolating imprint upon her hectic brow. As I approached her, she recognized me instantly, and a tear came in her eye.

"Ellen," said I, "can it be possible? my early schoolmate and friend in so wretched a condition? am I not deceived?"

"Ah no — no," said she, "you are not deceived — it is indeed Ellen, or the shadow of what she once was, — but I'll tell you all," and a flow of tears checked her utterance. I was fearful lest the excitement of the occasion should have a deleterious influence upon her feeble mind. Indeed, her exhaustion was so great that it was impossible for her to proceed, and I left, after faithfully promising that I would soon call and see her again. As I left, painful thoughts entered my bosom; to think of the end to which this once beautiful being was approaching — in the poorhouse — away from her friends — with no kind hands to minister to her wants, and with no hearts to truly sympathize in her condition.

The keeper of the house informed me that this young woman had been an inmate of the establishment but a few weeks, — that she was brought there in a state of beastly intoxication, and that the language which came from her lips was the most profane and impure that he had ever heard, — that she soon after took to her bed, and would probably never be removed from it, till carried out to the grave.

In a few days, as I had promised, I called again to see Ellen. She had grown weaker in the interim, and was rapidly wasting for the tomb. When I approached her bedside, 1 saw a smile of gratitude play upon her countenance, as she expressed her joy in seeing me again.

"I cannot live long," said she, "but once I little thought of this!" and she sobbed aloud; but my anxiety to know what brought her to her present miserable condition, induced her to relate what follows: —

"I was poor, but I was happy; indulgent parents caressed me. Had they lived, my course would have been virtuous, my end glorious. But at an early age I was doomed to be an orphan. Within a few months of each other, both my parents died, and left me with none to guide or counsel me, but a distant relative, who treated me more like a slave than a friend. I had no protector, and was obliged to remain in this situation, and bear as well as I was able, the unpleasant dispositions of the family. This relative had a daughter a few months older than myself, who was full of pride and vanity, and seemed to think herself far superior to the rest of her sex. Her father was rich, and bestowed upon her all her heart could desire. 1 was constantly employed in some menial service, and it was exceed-

ingly difficult for me always to obtain clothing necessary
for my comfort. When I was about eighteen years of
age, a young man of gentlemanly appearance came often to the house to see my relation's daughter. They
were very intimate, but I never had spoken to him.
One evening, I happened to meet him at the door; he
spoke kindly to me, and inquired for Jane, who immediately came, and they entered the parlor together.
I indistinctly heard him inquire respecting me, when
Jane remarked, 'She is our servant girl only,' and immediately turned the conversation to another subject.
Occasionally, I saw this young man, whose name was
L——. He was attentive and polite, which was very
gratifying to one who seldom received any thing from
human beings, but an unkind look or an angry word.
From the time that L—— first spoke to me, I noticed a
change in Jane's conduct. No pleasant word escaped
her lips when I was in her presence. I bore it all
without complaint, although at times a tear would fall,
when reflecting on my lonely lot. Thus time passed
on, and L—— was as constant as ever in his attention
to Jane, who, day by day, grew more irascible in the
house, and treated me with more contempt than ever.
Pride lived and reigned in her heart. But I noticed
that L——, now seldom spoke to me, and was inclined
to pass me by without uttering a word. This I could
not understand, especially as I had given him no occasion to slight me, and I conjectured it was on account
of what Jane might have said of me. I was determined
to know the truth. Accordingly, I sought every opportunity to hear the conversation that passed between
them, to know the cause of L——'s indifference. But
I could ascertain nothing definitely. One day when
22*

Jane had gone out, L—— unexpectedly came in. He
seated himself and began to converse freely with me.
It was not long before Jane returned and found us together. I saw the fire in her countenance, while she
affected perfect good feeling, and as I left the room, I
heard her harshly rebuke L—— for his familiarity with
the kitchen girl. I was grieved to the soul. I knew that
my character was as irreproachable as hers, and that
the only difference between us was, she had wealthy
parents and I was poor. The first opportunity I had
of obtaining a place, I was determined to improve. It
was not long before I succeeded. Not many days after
I had been pleasantly situated in a fine family, I was
one evening surprised at the appearance of L——, who
seemed pleased at the happy change I had made. He
was free and sociable, and when he departed, remarked
that he would call upon me again. He did call, and I
encouraged his visits, when one evening he informed
me that he had become disgusted with the society of
Jane, and had entirely broken off his visits to her. He
made a certain proposal to me, to which I acceded, little thinking what would be the result. I became
strongly attached to L——, and had no doubt but at
some future time I should become his wife. But after
his purposes were accomplished, he cruelly deserted me.
I was stung with remorse, and grief preyed deeply
upon my spirits. I had but few friends, and they
looked upon me with suspicion, and finally forsook me.
I left my place, not knowing where to direct my steps,
and finally took up my abode with those who live on
the profits of crime. I now gave myself up to every
evil propensity — would drink and swear with my miserable associates, until I became as great a proficient

in vice as the most abandoned. But I was far from being happy. Misery was my constant companion, and I would often resort to intoxicating drinks to drown my sorrow. For a number of years I continued to live in this miserable condition, an enemy to God and man, till in one of my drunken revels I was brought, unconscious, to this house. Soon after, I was taken sick, and I have been growing weaker and weaker ever since. My sins rose in terror before me, and when I thought of death, an awful feeling came over me. What could I do? I looked to God — that God I had cursed and despised, and I prayed for forgiveness. Oh, the rich mercy of Christ! I am now, as I humbly trust, a redeemed sinner. I cannot express the gratitude I feel to him for his great mercy to me, an unworthy worm of the dust. It is marvellous to me that Heaven should spare me through all my vileness, and then show unto me his great, inexpressible mercies."

Thus did this poor, forsaken girl speak of her deliverance from the thraldom of sin, till weak nature was nearly exhausted. And often during her sickness, did I visit her bed, and find the same strong faith and hope in her Redeemer. As she grew nearer to her end, she was much engaged in prayer, never expressing a desire to recover, excepting that she might prove useful to those deluded creatures, in whose society she had spent many of her precious days. The last time I saw her, she could scarcely speak, and I conversed but little with her, but she seemed already ripe for the kingdom of God.

She died without a struggle, and was interred in the cemetery connected with the poorhouse.

GOOD FOR EVIL.

Envy, a cursed plant at best,
Is never favored friendship's guest ;
It lives and flourishes alone
Where virtuous love is never known.

" WELL, Harry, I have seen Mr. Favor, and he agrees
to take you on trial. He is a very strict man, and will
keep no boy who is not perfectly willing to obey him,
and is honest and trustworthy."

" 'Tis just such a place as I want, father. I know I
shall like to retail goods."

" You must always remember that Mr. Favor is your
master, and whatever he tells you to do, you must not
hesitate to perform. A stranger will not overlook a
great deal that your parents would. If you should be
neglectful, or contrary, or disobedient, he will not keep
you, and it will be far more difficult to obtain another
situation. Few persons will have confidence in a boy
that often changes his place. They come to the conclusion at once that he is either shiftless, or dishonest,
and think it unsafe to employ him."

" But I shall be careful to do what Mr. Favor requests me, and will never disobey him."

" I trust you will obey him," said his mother, " for it
would nearly kill me to have it said that my son was a
bad boy, and was turned away from his place. If you

are obedient, attend well to your business, and feel interested in your master's welfare, it will be for your happiness and interest. If you live, it will be a pleasant thought to reflect upon, besides gaining for you many friends. I have heard it said that men take more notice of clerks and apprentices, than they are aware of. If they are steady, and attend punctually to their duties, they observe it; and so, too, if they are lazy, shiftless, and idle. I do hope and pray, Harry, that you will be a good boy. Be sure and not stay out during your leisure evenings, but read useful books, and endeavor to improve your mind."

"You need have no fears about me, mother; I shall try to do my best."

Henry Safford was fourteen years of age. His father, an humble mechanic, had obtained for him a place at the store of Mr. Favor, an English goods merchant, where he was to commence his duties on the following Monday. Harry had been taught most excellent precepts from his parents, who ever set before him a good example. He was not given to any bad habits, and the prospect was that he would grow up a good and useful man.

On the following week, Henry left the roof of his parents, and entered the store of his master. He found there another boy, about two years his senior, by the name of Francis Bradley. This youth took particular pains to initiate Henry into the business. He told him the prices of the goods, and taught him how to measure them off.

"The old man is an odd crony," said Francis, "and to get along with him, you must keep a sharp lookout. Whenever he is in the store, always be busy putting up goods or cleaning up the shop, and be as spry as possible when you wait upon customers. If they don't want one thing, show them another, and be sure and tell them we sell cheaper than at any other store. This will please the old man, and he will like you."

"But mustn't I do the same when Mr. Favor is absent from the shop?" inquired Henry.

"Why, as to that, you needn't be so particular about it. If we can make him think we do the best we can, it will answer as well."

"That doesn't seem to be hardly right."

"You're green yet, Harry. By and by, you will understand matters, and find that my advice is good. Now, mark my word."

"Perhaps I may. But I shall always try to do my best for Mr. Favor, and then he will not censure me."

"This selling dry goods is curious business, Harry; one must understand it pretty well or he cannot make a living. You will understand it all in time."

Henry busied himself through the day in his new employment, and being quick to learn, and feeling an interest in his business, he succeeded admirably. At night, when he and Francis retired, he felt a little unhappy. It was the first time that he had ever slept from beneath his father's roof, and no kind mother came into his chamber to see if he were warm, and lay comfortably. But he soon lost himself in sleep. In the morning he rose early to open the shop, and attend to his business. After a few weeks had passed away, Henry was quite contented and seemed to enjoy himself. He liked his master, who seemed to be always agreeable. Francis and he lived very pleasantly together, although he noticed that his companion was not particular always to

speak the truth, and accustomed himself to use profane language, and sometimes associated with young
persons who did not sustain good characters. One day
he said to him — "Francis, I don't see how you can enjoy the society I saw you in last evening, as I was passing Mr. ——'s confectionery."

"O Harry! they are clever fellows. Sometimes they
treat me to a pie, or to cake, and we pass our time
in real enjoyment."

"Do they usually spend much money there?"

"Not a great deal. But they always seem to have
money enough. Their parents are rich."

"Do you ever treat them, Frank?"

"Yes, occasionally. It would be mean and niggardly if I did not. I should like to have you go with
me some night. I am sure you would enjoy it. Mr.
——, who keeps the shop, is as fine a fellow as ever
lived. Will you go?"

"I should rather not."

"Why, what makes you hesitate?"

"One reason is, I have no money to spend, and besides, I don't think my father would like to have me go
there."

"What, Henry, do you care for your father when you
want to enjoy yourself a little? Everybody will laugh
at you. Come, go with me to-night."

"No, I cannot."

"You're a fool, and will never be any thing; that I
can assure you."

Henry knew the wages of his companion were small
and that his parents were poor, and he wondered where
he could obtain his money to spend at the confection-
er's. He dare not question his honesty, and yet he

could not account for his having money to spend so freely. After his meals, he would often bring candy and cakes into the shop, and give part of them to Henry. One day he asked Francis where he could get the money to purchase so much.

"Oh, I pick it up in various ways," said he, "I sometimes make little trades with companions, and my father gives me part of what he receives from the old man."

"But I think I would not spend it so foolishly, if I were you."

"Money is good for nothing but to spend. I may as well enjoy it as others."

"You will need it perhaps at some future time."

"Oh, no; I can always get a good living."

Henry mistrusted that Francis came by his money dishonestly, and to ascertain, he frequently counted the money in the drawer when he went out and often found from ten to fifty cents gone. Sometimes he came to the conclusion to mention it to his master, but was afraid he might incur the displeasure of his companion, and so kept it to himself.

Months passed on, and Francis continued to visit the confectionery shop with those young men who had but little to do, and there spent the larger portion of his evenings. Coming home one night, Henry found a twenty-five cent piece on the floor of his chamber, and taking it up he discovered it was the very one he had taken that day of a customer. He knew it by the letters R. S. which some one had stamped upon it. Now he was certain in his own mind, that his companion was dishonest, and he resolved to charge him with it as soon as he returned.

"I've had a fine time to-night," said Francis as he entered the chamber. "If you had been with us, Harry, you would have enjoyed yourself, I know."

"What have you been doing?"

"We've been down to ——, where we had as fine an oyster soup as ever I tasted. We had every thing else to correspond. It was glorious, I tell you."

"But who paid for it all?"

"Oh, we each put in so much."

"I tell you what, Frank, I don't believe you all came by your money honestly."

"What is that you say, Harry? Do you accuse me of stealing, I should like to know?"

"I do not actually accuse you of stealing, but I do seriously question your coming honestly by all the money you spend."

"That is the same as accusing me of stealing — and I will make you prove it. 'Tis the first time I have ever been charged with dishonesty."

"Perhaps it would be an easy matter for me to prove it, should it be necessary."

"What do you mean, hey?"

"To be plain with you, Frank, I am knowing to the fact that you take money from the drawer."

"You're a liar," and the language he used was profane in the extreme.

"I will convince you in the morning that what I say is the truth, but not to-night."

"And I should really like to have you."

Nothing more was said until morning, when on rising, Francis said — "Now I should like to know what you meant last night, when you accused me of stealing?"

23

Henry took the piece of money he had found on the floor, and showing it to his companion, said — "This is what I took of a woman yesterday, for some calico — I know it by the letters R. S. which you see are stamped upon it, and when I came home last night, I found it on the floor. No one had been in the chamber but yourself."

Francis colored a great deal when this evidence was produced against him, but said, in a subdued tone — "I know nothing about it ; the probability is that you stole it from the drawer yourself, and now, for fear of being detected, wish to accuse me."

"You know better, Frank. I never took a copper from Mr. Favor in my life. But I have often missed change from the drawer."

Without saying more Francis hurried down. As Henry reflected on what had been said, he felt grieved, but hoped this detection would effectually check his friend in his career. As soon as Mr. Favor came to the store that morning, he said to Henry, "I wish you would go with me." He followed him to his father's house. Such proceedings were unaccountable to the honest boy ; he could not conceive the intention of his master.

When they were seated, — his father and mother being present, — Mr. Favor said, "I have come to discharge your boy. I am sorry to inform you that I have detected him in theft, which I never suspected till this morning."

The poor boy burst into tears, exclaiming, " It is not so! It is not so ! "

" O my son, my son ! " said his mother, " how could

you do so? I never thought it would come to this; it will be the ruin of us all."

"Mother, I am not guilty," said the boy, weeping still more, — "I am not guilty."

"He must be hardened, indeed," said his master, "to lie so deliberately about it. There is no manner of doubt of his guilt, and that, from time to time, he has taken money from my drawer."

"Sir, I never took a cent from the drawer in my life; you are deceived."

"Hush, boy! don't add sin to sin."

"What I say is true," he added, while the tears were flowing fast.

His parents were somewhat encouraged to believe that Mr. Favor was mistaken, for they never knew their son to be guilty of uttering a falsehood, but the gentleman immediately said, "Yesterday I had a quarter of a dollar in my drawer, on which the letters R. S. were imprinted, which has been seen in the possession of your son."

"That money I found — "

"Hold, hold," said Mr. Favor, "don't add falsehood to falsehood. Now I propose to have the boy searched; if the money is found on his person, can there be any doubt of his guilt?"

"Let me tell — "

"Not a word," said Mr. Favor, "till we get through."

"This will be the death of me," said his mother, as Henry emptied his pockets.

"Here is the money," exclaimed his master, as he held up the twenty-five cent piece, "and here are the very letters, R. S. I never expected to find so much deception and wickedness in that boy. But there is no

doubt of his guilt.   I thought he would make a smart,
active man, and felt interested in him ; but now I cannot longer keep him.   I will not have a thief in my
store."

"My son, oh, how could you do so?" inquired his
mother.   "There is no affliction so great as to have a
dishonest son in the family."

"If you will hear a word, mother, I will explain it.
I have not stolen a cent from Mr. Favor.   It was Francis who took that money."

"Oh, the depravity of his heart!" exclaimed his
master.   "He now is endeavoring to accuse another
boy, who has been in my employ some two or three
years, and against whose character I never heard a lisp.
I am indebted to him for the information which led to
the detection of your son.   Had he been given to dishonesty, I might have been ruined.   I never wish to
see the face of that rogue again," pointing to Henry.
"I know he will come to a bad end," and bidding the
family "good-morning," he left the house.

"What shall we do?" said his father.   "It will be
whispered all over town that Henry is a thief; that his
employer has turned him away, and it will be impossible to obtain for him another place."

"It will worry me to death," said his mother.   "How
could you do so, Henry, when we have cautioned you
so much, and ever implanted in your mind virtuous
principles?   How could you be guilty of stealing?"

Henry told his parents the whole truth respecting the
affair; what he had seen in Francis, the conversations he had had with him, and finally, how he became
the possessor of the piece of money.   They believed
him, and pressed him to their bosoms.   How could

they do otherwise ? They knew him to be an injured boy, and they embraced him as a wronged but virtuous and honest child. Mr. Safford went directly to Mr. Favor, and explained the whole matter, but not a word of it would he believe.

"Your son is a deceptive, artful boy, that you may rely upon," said he; "I am perfectly satisfied of his guilt, and that he is endeavoring to screen himself by attempting to injure the character of Francis."

"But time will determine who is innocent and who is guilty," said the father.

"Certainly; if we live a few years, I should not be surprised to learn that your son had found his way to the State Prison."

It was rumored about the town that Henry had been turned away from his place for stealing; and while the few believed his story, the many thought him guilty. Of course, it injured him exceedingly, and was a source of much pain and sorrow to the honest and virtuous lad. He consoled himself with the reflection that he was innocent, and at some future day his innocence would be established.

Among those who believed that Henry had been injured, was a Mr. Jones, who frequently observed his attention to business while with Mr. Favor. He also kept an English goods store. Meeting Harry one day —

"My good fellow," said he, "how would you like to enter my store?"

"Very much indeed, if you dare to take me, considering what has been said."

"If you please, you may come to-morrow morning."

23*

"Thank you, sir," said the lad, running home to communicate the pleasing intelligence.

The next day found Harry in the store of Mr. Jones. His new master being a pleasant man, and feeling interested in the boy, endeavored to make his situation agreeable. Henry did his best to give satisfaction, and labored not in vain. Occasionally, Mr. Favor would come into the store, and, without speaking, would give him a suspicious look. It was evident that he believed him guilty of the charge he laid to him. And Francis passed him by without speaking a word. But he knew the innocence of Henry.

A few years passed by, and Mr. Jones still retained the young man in his employ, and for no consideration would he part with him. Pleasant in his disposition, industrious in his habits, and capable in his business, his employer loved him as a son. One evening, he was invited to a social party, where he found among the guests Ellen Favor, the daughter of his former master, who went in company with Francis Bradley. Henry was not only genteel in his appearance, but was really handsome, while his former friend was directly the reverse. Ellen noticed that the ladies were partial to Henry, and her envious disposition was aroused. The young man happened to be near her person, while she was conversing in a rather loud tone with one of her female acquaintances. "Only think," Henry heard her say, "why, only think, it is the very individual who stole from my father a few years ago. If his character was known, I guess but very few would wish to associate with him; for my part, I wont speak to him, or even notice the fellow."

It is true Henry's feelings were injured, but he said

nothing, and endeavored to pass the evening as pleasantly as possible. He noticed that he was slighted
by one or two, while others appeared not to mind what
was said about him. He felt innocent of the charge
laid to him, and knew there was one present who, if
he had his just deserts, would be detected as the thief.

Francis continued to be flush with money. His companions were of that class who think nothing of spending, providing they partake of a momentary enjoyment.
He would often ride out for pleasure, without reflecting
on the expense incurred, and purchase whatever he had
an inclination to buy. Such a course cannot last for a
great length of time; the older a person grows, his acquaintances and his expenses naturally increase. It
was so with Francis. Still his employer placed implicit
confidence in him; it could not well be otherwise, for
he expected at some future day to claim him as a son-
in-law.

Henry became of age, and the story of his supposed
dishonesty had nearly died away excepting with a few
who were envious of his success, his personal appearance, or his irreproachable character. They kept it
alive, and always exerted an influence prejudicial to
him. None were more active in their slanders than
the children of Mr. Favor, who had looked up to Francis as a pattern of honor and integrity. But Henry
had given them no occasion to censure him; he had always treated them with respect. It was his disposition
never to speak against another, or he might have ruined young Bradley. Though the falsehood spread rapidly, he thought the truth would finally come out and
triumph over every thing false. He did not mistake.

He became an active partner with Mr. Jones, and prospered abundantly, as virtue and integrity always will.

One day, a little boy came into his shop and left word that Mr. Bradley wished to see Mr. Safford immediately, and requested that he might call at the house of Mr. Favor, where he was boarding. It was a singular request, but Henry resolved to go.

As he entered the house, he understood by the young woman who came to the door, that Francis was very sick — that it was apprehended he would not recover — that something seemed to trouble him exceedingly — and that he said he could find no peace until he had seen Henry. As he entered the sick-chamber, he observed Mr. Favor and his wife and their daughter Ellen in the room. They received him more cordially than he anticipated.

"Henry," said the sick man, stretching out his hand to Safford, "Henry, I have wronged you" — and he wept. "In the presence of these witnesses I acknowledge my sin. I cannot die without it. Mr. Favor, I have wrongfully accused this young man. It was not he who took that money from you seven years ago, but it was myself. I am the guilty person. He was always honest — I was the thief," and he sank down, exhausted.

The family were thunderstruck. They had always looked upon young Safford as a thief and a villain, and had circulated the story of his dishonesty far and wide. Now to have it contradicted — and the guilty individual to be the person they had cherished and nursed — on whom not the slightest suspicion of evil rested — was what they could hardly comprehend. They were dumb with confusion. They saw before them an example of suffering virtue — a meek and kind heart, which they had contributed to lacerate and goad even to bleeding — and the author of the crime on his death-bed.

Francis raised himself again, and weeping, asked, "Will you forgive me, Henry? Oh, will you forgive me, that I may die in peace?"

"With all my heart do I forgive you," and the tears filled the eyes of the noble-hearted young man.

"And will you forgive me the injury I have done you?" spoke Mr. Favor.

"Most assuredly."

"And me, too?" said his wife.

"Certainly."

"And me, also?" said Ellen. "For oh, how basely have I acted! Will you forgive me?" and she extended her hand.

Henry grasped it, and melted to tears as he said, "Most heartily do I forgive you, Ellen. From my soul I forgive you all." And the family stood around him weeping like children.

When Henry left they followed him to the door, entreating him to call the next day without fail, which he assured them he should be happy to do.

It was soon noised about the town that the sin that was laid to the charge of young Safford years before, was committed by another. Those who had circulated the report to his injury, and shunned his society, now came forward and acknowledged their sin. None stood higher in the estimation of the people than Henry. His virtues were everywhere spoken of.

When he called to see Bradley the next day, he found him very feeble. He extended his hand to Henry, ex-

pressed his regret for the course he had pursued, but
was too feeble to say much. The family were all kindness to Safford, and expressed their gratitude to him
again and again.

Every day he called to see Francis, and once or
twice watched by him during the night. The poor fellow died. His excesses brought him to an early
grave. But he regretted his past course, and if a
death-bed repentance can atone for a life of sin and
folly, his Creator forgave him. He died at peace with
the world, though none cherish his memory. For they
cannot look back upon his life with pleasure or profit,
and the stain he inflicted on the character of his early
associate will never be forgotten.

Henry followed his friend to the narrow house, and
manifested, by his attention to him in his sickness, and
in the last sad services paid to mortality, a disposition
which accords strictly with the gospel of peace; but
which is altogether too rare in this selfish, unforgiving
world.

Not a day passed that Mr. Favor did not call upon
Henry. He told him repeatedly if there was any
thing he could do for his interest or happiness, it
should be done with pleasure. "I should be happy,"
said he, "to have you connected with me in business;"
but Henry could only thank him for his kindness.

Safford became a constant visitor at the house of his
friends, who seemed never to be tired of his company.
Ellen was particularly attentive, and always strove to
please him. None enjoyed his society better than she;
but her parents dared not flatter themselves that he
would deign to connect himself with the family, yet
nothing would have been more congenial to their feel-

ings. But Henry was really attached to Ellen. She had materially altered for the better since the death of Bradley. She had thrown aside her foolish airs; was pleasant and cheerful in her conversation, and bid fair to make a useful woman.

Ellen did not forget the manner in which she had treated Henry in years past, and the influence she had exerted against him. She felt ashamed and grieved at her conduct, and times without number expressed her regret in tears. Now she labored as hard to counteract her past influence, and thought no praise too extravagant to bestow upon him.

Many months did not elapse before Safford was married, and Ellen Favor was his happy bride. Truer and fonder hearts were never united. The past served as a magnet to draw them closer together. The father and mother of Ellen were never happier than on the day of the wedding — for they both loved Henry as they would an only son.

Safford continued to prosper in his business; but unlike many, he did good as opportunities presented. The poor and distressed were relieved by him. He was devoted to the cause of benevolence, and lived not so much to accumulate property and enjoy the blessings of life himself, as to add to the sum of human happiness. He was an example of kindness, benevolence, and virtue, and no one was ever heard to lisp a word to his injury. The praise of men and the blessing of Heaven continued to rest upon him, and his example will never cease to exert a benign influence, till time shall be no more.

THE OLD BOOKS.

To know we've dried a single tear,
  And made one moment bright,
Or struck a feeble spark to cheer
  The darkest hour of night
Will give to us more joy at last
  Than Cæsar's triumphs gave;
The memory of such deeds will live
  In worlds beyond the grave.

"Do you buy old, second-hand books?" inquired a
boy of Mr. Letford, the bookseller.

"Not very often," was the reply. "Sometimes we
take schoolbooks that have been used a little in part
pay for others."

"Can't you buy these books of me?" said the boy,
placing six or eight volumes on the counter.

Mr. Letford took one up to examine, saying—
"These are very old books, and I could never sell
them. They are not worth two cents apiece to me."

"They are good books. Some of them are old sermons. Perhaps you could sell them. What will you
give me for them?"

"I don't want them."

"I must have a little money, will you give me sixpence apiece for them?"

"No; I will not give you but three cents apiece. At
that price you may leave them, or take them somewhere
else."

"Where would I be likely to sell them?" anxiously inquired the boy.

"The best place would be to put them in the auction-room. Carry them down to Mr. Bailey, the auctioneer, and ask him to sell them. You can get more than I would allow you."

"I will see Mr. Bailey, then," said the boy, tying up his books and putting them under his arm, "for I feel unwilling to sell them for what you offer me, although I want the money."

Mr. Letford attended to his business and thought no more of the lad, till about two or three weeks after, when the same boy came into his store with the very books he carried away.

"Sir, I have not yet sold my books," said the boy. "I carried them down to Mr. Bailey, and requested him to sell them at auction; but he said they would bring little or nothing. I left them, telling him I would call again in a short time and get my pay, if he could dispose of them. To-day I called and was handed my books. Mr. Bailey said he offered them for sale, but no one would bid over two cents apiece, and he couldn't let them go. Now I've come to sell them to you. Can't you give me over three cents apiece?"

"No; they are not worth more than that to me."

"Well, take them, then."

The bookseller counted out twenty-four cents, and handed them to the boy, while he placed the old volumes under the counter.

The boy appeared pleased with his money, thanked the gentleman and was leaving the store when Mr. Letford asked him, "My lad, what is your name?"

"Charles Merrill."

24

" Where do you belong ? "

" In North Yarmouth."

The boy immediately left the shop, while Mr. Letford
waited upon his customers.

Six months and more had expired, since the bookseller had purchased the books of the boy, when one
day, as he was cleaning up his shop, his eye chanced
to meet the old volumes.   Taking one up, he found it
to contain sermons printed about a century before.
As he was looking over the pages carelessly, he found
concealed between two of the leaves a ten dollar bill.
On examining it, he discovered that it was a genuine
bill, although about twenty-five years old.   Curiosity
led him to examine the book more closely, when to his
astonishment, he found in all fifty ten dollar bills of
the same bank, making in all five hundred dollars.
The other volumes were searched as carefully, but
they contained nothing.

" Where can I find the boy of whom I purchased
these books ? " was the first question Mr. Letford put to
himself, after his surprise was over.   He recollected the
boy's name was Merrill, and that he informed him he
resided in North Yarmouth.   That very day, he addressed a line to the boy, stating he had something of
importance to communicate to him, and requesting him
to come immediately to Portland.   He waited a week
or two, but received no answer.   The first opportunity
he took a chaise and rode out to make inquiries respecting the youth.   After spending several hours, he
learned that a boy by that name lived with a Mr.
Mitchell about six or eight months before.   On Mr.
Mitchell the bookseller immediately called.   From him
he learned that a poor boy by that name came to

him one day and solicited employment, stating that he was poor and destitute. Out of pity, Mr. Mitchell employed him several months, when the boy left, stating that he intended to go to Readfield, or Bangor, and study. Mr. Mitchell spoke well of the boy, said that he was industrious and pleasant, and spent much of his leisure time in reading. He could not remember where he was born, but believed that Charles was an orphan.

Without ascertaining any thing more particular as to the whereabouts of the boy, Mr. Letford returned to the city. The next day he addressed a couple of letters to him; one was sent to Readfield, the other to Bangor. To these letters he never received any answers. The bookseller deposited the money in the bank, and made use of it, as occasion required, determining, if possible, to find out where the boy resided, and always to have · at his command the amount he had found. If Charles were an orphan, perhaps that money had been left him by his parents, but he being young when they died, knew not that they possessed this amount; or it might be that he had purchased the books of another, or that they had been given to him. At any rate, Mr. Letford hoped the time would come when the mystery would be solved and the money be given to its rightful owner.

Year after year passed away; and although Mr. Letford had made numberless inquiries, he could not ascertain any thing definite respecting the youth of whom he purchased the old books. About ten or a dozen years had gone by, and the bookseller had almost given up the idea of ever seeing the individual, when one summer he visited Boston, for the purpose of purchasing a stock of books. As he was conversing with a wholesale dealer one morning, a gentleman came into the store, with whom the dealer appeared to be intimately acquainted. He introduced him to Mr. Letford as the Rev. Mr. Merrill, of A——. After a short conversation, the minister inquired if he were not the Mr. Letford who formerly traded in Portland.

"Yes, sir; I still trade there."

"Do you remember a little boy selling you some old books about a dozen years ago?"

"Perfectly well."

"I am that boy."

"Indeed! you astonish me. I have made more inquiries than a few, and have never been able to learn what became of him."

"Soon after I sold you the books, I went to the eastward, with the intention, if possible, to attend school. The money that I obtained for those books was all I had to defray my expenses. Taking my bundle in my hand, I started. In a few days Providence provided me a friend, who took me to his house, gave me schooling, and prepared me for college. I graduated at Dartmouth, and for the last year I have been pastor of a church in this state."

"I am really glad, sir, I have met you at last! Do you remember what books you sold me so long since?"

"I do not—only that some of them were volumes of sermons. They were books that belonged to my father. When he died, they came into my possession. Was there any thing remarkable about the works?"

"About six months after I purchased them, I took one volume up to examine, and folded between the leaves, I found fifty ten dollar bills."

"You astonish me."

"These bills must have been placed there by your father."

"It was said that he had money by him when he died, but we never could find any."

"That money, Mr. Merrill, has been kept at interest most of the time since I found it, and now I am indebted to you to the amount of something like eight hundred dollars, which I will forward to you as soon as I go to Portland."

"Sir, I cannot consent to take that amount. That the money rightfully belonged to me, I have no question, but I shall insist on your keeping at least one-half the amount."

"On no consideration will I take it. I presume you are in debt for your education."

"Yes, sir; I owe several hundred dollars."

"You will now be able to square up, and have something left."

Mr. Merrill thanked his friend in tears, and pressed him, but in vain, to keep a portion of the money for his own use.

In a few days Mr. Letford returned to Portland, and the first thing he did was to return to Mr. Merrill the money which he had kept so long in his possession. The amount exceeded eight hundred dollars, every cent of which he gave to the rightful owner — feeling a satisfaction and pleasure in so doing, which a mean, dishonest man could never appreciate.

In a few months after, the pastor left his congregation for a few weeks to visit some of his eastern friends, and for several days, he stopped at the house of Mr. Letford; an acquaintance had been formed which could not be easily broken.

24*

Had we not read the following in the newspapers some years since, perhaps this story would never have been given to the world : —

"Married, in Portland, by Rev. Mr. Dwight, Rev. Charles Merrill of A——, Mass., to Miss Eliza, daughter of Mr. James Letford."

THE WOOD-SAWER.

Oh, harbor not a base-born thought —
 Win grace to make you strong,
That every virtuous act performed
 Bring holy fruit along.

"I KNOW my business is not looked upon by the majority as so respectable as a trade, a clerkship, or a profession; but you know I was not put to a trade, and have always been obliged to work at any thing I could find to do, to help support my mother."

"But you might find something else to do besides sawing wood."

"What can I do at present that would be as profitable? I have always told you that I did not intend to follow this business through life. Just as soon as I earn money sufficient, I shall engage in something else. Once you didn't feel and talk as you do now."

"As I grow older, and associate more with young women, I perceive, by their actions and language, that they do not respect young men who dress meanly, and are engaged in low employments."

"Why should you mind what they do or say? My business, if it is low, is an honorable one, and I earn every dollar I receive. I owe nothing. But the same cannot be said of many of those young men who dress extravagantly, display gold rings and chains, and spend

so much time and money in riding and other amusements."

"I don't know how that is, but they appear to get
along well, and always have money to spend."

"Appearances are very deceitful. You cannot tell
how much grief it has caused me to see the change that
has been wrought in you the last few months. You do
not meet me with your accustomed smiles, and often
seem indifferent when I call upon you. Is it solely on
account of what other girls — and very foolish girls, too
— say, that you thus appear?"

"I confess I do not like your business, and since I
have grown older and heard so much said, my mind has
changed materially."

William Nelson was the son of a poor woman. From
early life he was accustomed to work and earn whatever
he could to support his parent. He would run of errands for the neighbors, bring water, wheel stones, or
do any thing that would bring him a penny. Every
Wednesday and Saturday afternoon, before he went to
play, he would take his basket and run down on Long
Wharf, or Portland Pier, where men were stubbing
boards, and load it with chips for his mother. William
was always industrious, both at home and at school.
Master Patten often said he was one of his best scholars.

When young Nelson was fourteen years old, he left
his school and exerted himself to get employment, so as
to be of some assistance to his widowed parent, and often
found employment by the day, working hard for fifty
cents. When he became a little older and a little stouter,
he bought him a horse and saw, and undertook the business of sawing wood. He went round among his neighbors and solicited their work, most of whom employed

him. There were two or three, however, who depended upon Sam Freeman, a singular character, who made it his business to saw wood about town, never receiving any pay for his services.

The next-door neighbor of Mrs. Nelson was a Mr. Richards, by whom William had been often employed. He not only sawed his wood, but brought home his flour, provisions, etc., and the whole family appeared to be attached to the widow's son, none more so than his young daughter, Sarah. For years she had been accustomed to give him a slice of pie, a bit of cake, or an apple, whenever he went into the house, and she really appeared to be attached to the poor boy. It was certain William loved her, for many an evening has he employed himself in painting pictures or making boxes for little Sarah.

As William and Sarah grew older, their attachment for each other increased; he not thinking of his poverty, his patched jacket, or his low employment, and she not dreaming that show and parade make the man, that dress and fashion influence the heart, or that honest industry and poverty are a disgrace. But as Sarah mingled more in society, and understood the manners and customs of the fashionable world, she began to look with more indifference upon the wood-sawer; but still she treated him kindly, and really seemed to be strongly attached to him. William was a likely boy, and given to no bad habits, he had treasured in his mind a fund of knowledge, gleaned from useful works which he had perused during his leisure time.

Nelson had become of age and was still attached to his early friend, but any one could observe that although Sarah loved him, she wished to give out the impression

that such was not the case. Many of her female companions would sneer at her, throwing out some unpleasant remark about the wood-sawer, while they
were gallanted about by the gay and the fashionable.
Whatever was said, Sarah never lisped a word against
her humble friend.   She knew that he was good, and
she often contrasted the language that fell from his lips
with the conversation of other young men of her acquaintance, and she was struck with the difference.
He was sensible, and his language good and solid.
They spoke the common topics of the day, and criticised
the dress and manners of others.   On one occasion,
when Sarah was in conversation with a neighbor of his,
Jane Waters, the latter remarked, —

"I do not conceive how you can speak to that wood-
sawer.   He appears to be a low-bred fellow."

"What do you mean, Jane?"

"Mean?   Why, Nelson associates with the low and
vulgar.   His business, you know, brings him in contact
with a certain class that are not thought much of by
people in general.   I am surprised that a girl of your
taste should have any thing to say to him."

"Jane, you surprise me.   I know of no better-
hearted young man of my acquaintance than William.
I have known him, as you are aware, from childhood,
and I never saw a mean action in him, or heard him
utter an angry word.   I know he is not as fashionable
as many other young men, but his business will not
permit him to be."

"Would you marry a wood-sawer?" said Jane, laughing heartily — "now tell me, Sarah, would you marry
a wood-sawer?   I know you would have too much

sense, and more respect for your friends than to think
of it."

"I don't know what I should be tempted to do, if I
had the offer."

"You know you would not disgrace your family and
friends so much."

"There is no disgrace in marrying an honest man, in
my way of thinking. Let me ask you a question: would
you marry a simple-headed fop?"

"Do you mean that as an insult to me, Sarah?"

"Not at all."

"I would marry a gentleman — one who had sense
enough to keep himself decent, and pride enough to
keep himself clean and tidy."

"Well, if you ever marry, it is my wish that you may
get a good husband; but from what I know of you, I
fear you will be terribly deceived. I would rather
have a man with a good mind and correct habits, with
but one shirt to his back, than a person with fine exterior and plenty of money, possessing a base heart."

"You talk like a simpleton, I'm sorry to say, and
we'll drop the subject now," said Jane coloring, as if in
passion.

"I wish to say to you, Jane, that I did not introduce
the subject, and shall not get angry, whatever you
may say against William. Although you have been
waited upon by one whose conduct and manners I am
displeased with, you cannot accuse me of treating him
but with the utmost kindness. You have not thus been
kind to young Nelson; he has seen it, and so have I;
but neither of us has complained."

"Well, I cannot treat him with respect. He is altogether too low for me to associate with."

"You may feel so, but I do not. Time, perhaps, may yet teach us some severe lessons. As I have often said to you, I prefer a kind and good heart, that I have known and tried, though dressed in rags, to a fashionable and foppish person I know but little about."

"Every one to her liking," said the scornful Miss Waters, tossing her proud head, and turning up her nose.

A day or two elapsed after this conversation, when another female friend called upon Sarah, and spoke in like terms of William. The same day, meeting one or two others, they expressed themselves in a similar manner. Who could wonder, then, that Miss Richards was depressed in spirits, and that she used the language at the commencement of our story, the next time she saw William? Poor fellow, he was sad indeed, and hardly knew what course to pursue. For a long time he had received ill-treatment from the friends of Sarah, and unpleasant epithets had been heaped upon him, as he passed along; but he murmured not, still pursuing the even tenor of his ways.

The next time Nelson called upon Sarah, she appeared more depressed than he had ever seen her. On inquiry why she was thus cast down, she replied, "Ever since you were last here, I have been thinking of what I said to you, and have condemned myself times without number. I had been spoken to by a number of my young companions, and what they said induced me to talk in the manner I did. I shall not heed them again, whatever they may say."

"I have been no less grieved than yourself. I knew something had been said, but by whom, I know not."

"Be assured, William, that I will not again wound

your feelings. We have been intimate from childhood, and never before, I believe, has a word passed between us that caused the least painful emotion, and this shall be the last."

Jane Waters and her lover were invited to a social party at the house of Sarah. John Elkins scarcely noticed William, and took occasion to show off his wit at the expense of Nelson, and the merriment of Jane, and one or two kindred spirits. Occasionally, you would hear "wood-sawer" spoken loud enough for the company to hear; but William had good sense enough to heed it not. He treated them all with that respect which is due from one person to another. Just before the company dispersed, Elkins, Jane's beau, remarked to Nelson, loud enough to be heard by all, —

"We have a load of wood at our store to saw, and we should like to have you come up to-morrow and saw it."

"Very well, sir, I will come with pleasure," remarked William; "I am always glad of a job."

"I suppose you wont charge more than old Jameson, or Boze, the negro?"

"Oh, no, sir; I always charge moderate. I find it is more advantageous. I'm much obliged to you for the job."

In a few minutes the company had retired, when Sarah remarked to William, "I was astonished at the impudence of Elkins, but more so to see how calmly you bore it."

"Never mind; John has a lesson yet to learn in life, and the day may come when he will bitterly regret his course. He is not worth minding."

On the morning of the next day, William went early
25

to the store of Mr. Fosdic, the gentleman with whom Elkins was clerk, sawed the wood, and received his pay. He observed, however, as he occasionally saw John and the other clerk, that no little sport was made of him, all of which he bore with a magnanimous spirit.

In process of time, Sarah Richards became the wife of William Nelson, and Jane Waters the wife of John Elkins. Sarah's was a simple wedding, with a few friends to witness the ceremony; and she commenced housekeeping in a small dwelling with but little furniture, which her husband had bought, having laid by enough in a few years from his laborious business. But Jane made a great display on her wedding-day, and hired a large tenement, and had it filled with the best of furniture.

What changes a few years produce! As the wheels of time roll on, the poor of to-day become the rich of to-morrow, and the most wealthy end their days in poverty and rags. None can fathom the future; none can lift the veil and penetrate the secret recesses. Elkins, the husband of Jane, was set up in business by his father. He occupied one of the best dry-goods stands in Middle Street, and for a while had a large run of business. But he became inattentive to his affairs, and spent a large portion of his time away from his store. It was said he gambled, and one or two of his friends had seen him disguised by liquor. Pursuing such a course, he could not long sustain himself, and was obliged to fail. In settling his affairs, it was found that he did not possess half enough to cancel his debts. Out of employment for several months, he might be seen hanging round the groceries, till at last he removed into the country, his father purchasing for him a small farm.

Nelson prospered. By diligence and prudence, after a few years, he gave up sawing wood and entered into business more congenial to his taste. By strict attention to his concerns, he gradually accumulated property, and was considered one of the first merchants in Portland. In his prosperity he did not forget that he was once poor. The saw and horse that he used so many years, were placed in a chamber of his house, that if ever he should grow proud and treat others with unkindness, he might take a look at them and remember what he once was. No money would have tempted him to part with them.

Mr. Nelson had been in mercantile business for more than a dozen years, and during that time had not heard a word respecting Elkins. One morning, on taking up the *Advertiser* he read a paragraph, stating that one John Elkins had committed some crime in North Yarmouth, and was brought to the city, and committed to jail to await his trial. "That must be my old acquaintance," said Nelson; "I will call to see him."

In a few days, Mr. Nelson went up to the jail, and entered the cell of Elkins. But he was so altered that he hardly knew him. The marks of intemperance were prominent on his face and in his tattered dress. Without making himself known, Nelson said, —

"Sir, I have called to see some of the prisoners, and I have brought you a few things which, perhaps, may be acceptable."

"I thank you for your kindness," said the prisoner. Nelson made but little conversation, and was about to leave, when the prisoner remarked, —

"Do not leave yet, sir. I have been here several

days, and you are the first person I have seen, excepting the jailor and one or two prisoners."

"You appear to have suffered a great deal in your lifetime, if I may judge from your appearance."

"Ah, sir, I have, I have! and a great deal of it is owing to intemperance and gambling. In early life my prospects were bright, but I ruined myself by bad associates."

"Have you no friends living?"

"Very few, sir; my parents have been dead several years."

"You have a family, I presume."

"I had once, but where they now are I cannot tell. My wife left me on account of my habits, and it is more than two years since I have seen her. I understood that she was living with a friend of hers in Biddeford. O sir! I never thought I should come to this;" and the poor man put his hands to his face and wept. After a moment he continued, "If there was any hope for me, I know I should be a different man; but no, I am too old in sin — too degraded. I have no friends."

"It is never too late, my friend, to reform," said Nelson. "When you again have your liberty, if you are really determined to be a different man, you can yet be happy."

"Sir, who would employ a person of such habits as mine have been?"

"I would employ you if I were convinced of your reformation."

"Are you in earnest, sir?"

"Most assuredly."

"I thank you with all my heart;" and a beam of hope lit up the countenance of the man, as if he had never before heard the words of kindness. "This seems like a dream. Degraded, ragged, friendless as I be, you have promised me employment, should I live to enjoy my liberty again."

"Upon this condition, you know, that you will be steady, and do your best to respect yourself."

"I will with all my soul; and I feel more than I can express the kindness you have shown me."

"Have you any acquaintances in the city?" inquired Mr. Nelson.

"Not any now. I used to be acquainted with a great many, but what has become of them I do not know. It is more than fifteen years since I was in the city. There is one man — I always thought I should like to know what became of him."

"And who was he?"

"His name was William Nelson, and he used to saw wood some twenty years ago."

"Why do you feel a more particular interest in him?"

"I'll tell you why, although I feel ashamed of myself, and have repented of what I did times without number. He was a fine young man, of an excellent disposition, but poor, and was obliged to saw wood. I ridiculed him in company and before others. He bore it all without a harsh word or a single retort. Would to Heaven I had possessed a spark of his excellent disposition. I'd give worlds to see him, and ask his forgiveness on my knees. Had I treated him well I should not have suffered half what I have gone through. It has always troubled me."

"I know that man."

25*

"You do? Pray, tell me something about him. Has he prospered?"

"Oh, yes. He gave up sawing wood some years ago, and is now engaged in mercantile business."

"If I thought he would speak to me, and think it no disgrace to him, I would send him word to come and see me. Nothing would give me so much pleasure as to ask his forgiveness."

"He would grant it, I know."

"Do you think so, sir?"

"I know so. And if he knew you had reformed, you would nowhere find so true a friend." ·

"I am more and more anxious to see him. Shall I trouble you to ask him to call and see a degraded being?"

"Mr. Elkins, you shall see your old friend, Mr. Nelson. He is here now; it is he who has been conversing with you. I am the wood-sawer!"

"Good heavens!" and the degraded being fell upon his knees and wept aloud.

In a few moments he recovered himself, and in broken words, and with streaming tears asked forgiveness of Nelson, which was readily granted.

After remaining with Elkins two or three hours, Mr. Nelson left the cell, rejoicing that his friend had come to his senses at last, and devising a plan for his release and future welfare.

The crime that Elkins had committed was a trifling theft, while under the influence of ardent spirits. On the day of his trial no one appeared against him, and he was discharged. Nelson immediately took him to his house, gave him a new suit of clothes, and employed him in his store. Poor Elkins' heart was filled with gratitude to his benefactor, and he exerted himself to the utmost to please him.

Elkins had been in the store of Mr. Nelson some twelve or fourteen months, and conducted himself with the utmost propriety, when, by the arrangement of his friend, his wife was reconciled to him, and came to the city to reside with her husband.

Now they are happy. The past is forgotten, or remembered only to bless Heaven for the great change that has been wrought. Few that see Elkins day by day know the sorrow that he endured, or feel the joy that continually thrills his happy bosom.

THE CLAY COVE MECHANIC.

The sunshine of kindness,
More precious than gold,
Has thousands directed
To virtue's sweet fold.

" Do you think I would have any thing to say to young Clinton ? He must know I do not wish to see him, and yet he persists in calling at the house."

" But Charles is a fine young man. He has an excellent disposition. You have noticed his kind feelings and generous character. And there are no bad traits about him. Why, I am surprised to hear you talk so."

" Charles is well enough in his way ; but you know his father and mother ; they still live in that wretched old shell in Clay Cove, and haven't decent furniture. I should be ashamed to call there."

" I know his parents are very poor, and that his father has been a drinking man. But he has joined the temperance society, and I understand he provides better for his family, and is striving to obtain a good living."

" That may be true, but I can never forget old Clinton, even though he has reformed. He has always belonged to the lower classes."

" But I'm sure Charles behaves like a gentleman. If his parents are poor and wretched, he should not be treated unkindly, provided he behaves well and sustains a good character."

"True; but he has got nothing, is only a mechanic, and will always have to work for a living."

"Only a mechanic, you say. But what was your father and my father?"

"But they worked only a little themselves, and employed others. Now they are independent. No matter what our fathers were. Time has changed. I shall have nothing further to say to Clinton. If he calls at the house, I shall contrive to be busy up-stairs. You may see him and talk with him as much as you like, but I wont."

"You talk foolishly, especially as Charles is as likely a young man as we have in our neighborhood."

"Every one to her liking," said the girl, as she left the room.

Clara and Mary Edwards were cousins, and about the same age. The former had been brought up with false notions. Her standard of respectability was a fine exterior, graceful manners, and a heavy purse. She had often declared in the presence of her cousin, that she would never associate with a mechanic, more especially if he sprang from a poor family. But Mary had different views. She respected all men, whether dressed in broadcloth or homespun, and was as particular in her attentions to the day laborer of good character as to the individual who prided himself on his birth, wealth, and education.

Charles Clinton was the son of a poor sailmaker. His father had been in low circumstances for many years, brought on by his intemperate habits, and he could barely earn sufficient to keep his family together. His mother was a prudent and industrious woman, and it was mainly owing to her exertions that they had kept together for so long a time. At an early age Charles left school, and went to learn the trade of a printer. He was industrious and obliging, and gained the respect not only of his master but his fellow-apprentices. Instead of spending his evenings or his few leisure hours in the day among the vicious and profane or in walking the streets in idleness, he would obtain some useful work and peruse it. He would frequently carry home the newspapers of the day, when he had nothing else to read, and thus endeavor to improve his mind. In this way he became intelligent, — how could it be otherwise? — and won the good-will of all who knew him. At times he would take a sheet of paper, and sit in the little room of his mother, endeavoring to place his thoughts upon paper. Charles was never idle; he was either at work with his hands or with his mind.

When Clinton became of age, he was employed by his master and received good wages for his services. At this time Charles was acquainted with but few females; among these, however, was Clara Edwards, at whose house he occasionally visited, he being more particularly acquainted with the father. He was cordially received by the family, but Clara endeavored to manifest her dislike to him in various ways. He held to no views which she did not oppose, and was not inclined to converse with him on any subject. Once he invited her to accompany him to a pleasant place of retreat, but she refused, by saying she was engaged; but remained at home all day.

One evening he found most of the family had gone out, and she was alone. He endeavored to interest her by introducing various topics of conversation, but she manifested no interest in his remarks, and he remained but a short time. This was before her cousin had arrived from the country. When she came, he found one who was willing to converse, who behaved like a lady to all who visited the house.

Mary Edwards had been at her cousin's about a week when the conversation at the commencement of our story took place. A day or two after, Charles called at the house, but the moment Clara saw him enter the door she left the room. Mary accepted a polite invitation to accompany him to a concert, and in a few moments she was ready. They passed an agreeable evening. She had no sooner returned to the house than her cousin exclaimed, —

"What a fool to be seen with Charles Clinton! I should be ashamed of myself. No one who thinks any thing of herself will go with him. I don't believe our kitchen girl would have gone with him."

"To speak as I think, Clara, Charles is a gentleman, and I esteem it an honor that he should invite me."

"Oh, luddy, I shall faint!" exclaimed Clara.

"You are a strange girl. Since I have been in Portland this last time, I have seen no young man with whose appearance I am so favorably impressed as with Clinton's."

"Then, really, you are in love with the mechanic — the son of a Clay Cove sailmaker."

"In love with his appearance, I am."

"And you may marry him in welcome. Oh, dear, what strange things will take place!" said Clara, with a contemptuous smile.

"Marry him! I am not worthy of so fine a gentleman. He is my superior in every respect. If I should be so fortunate as to obtain such a man for a husband, I should esteem myself the most fortunate of girls."

"Distressing! No decent girl would have the fellow. You would marry him, hey?"

"Perhaps I would, if I could get him."

"Well, really, I can't help laughing. A genuine love-scrape. I shall give up. It will be a beautiful place, I must confess, to live in — that hovel, setting in the mud; and to have so beautiful a father-in-law! Well, I declare, it will be fine."

"You anticipate too much for me, cousin. I do not expect to have Charles. He looks higher than a country girl. But if he *should* marry, he will not probably take his wife to live at such a place as you describe; although I don't know where Clay Cove is."

At this moment Clara's parents entered the room.

"Have you heard the news, father?" inquired the proud girl.

"No, child, I have heard nothing. What interests you so much?"

"You'll laugh well when I tell you. It is no less than this: Mary has got a beau."

"Indeed! and who may he be?"

"Who should you guess?"

"I'm sure I cannot tell," said the father.

"It is not so," replied Mary. "I have been to the concert to-night with young Clinton, and Clara is making all manner of sport about it."

"Well, Clinton is a fine fellow, and you could not get a better sweetheart."

"What! Charles Clinton?" inquired the mother.

"Yes."

"Why, he is only a mechanic. We have known his father for years, and he is a miserable shoat. They live very meanly. No respectable people ever call upon them."

"You know, wife, a great change has been wrought in the character of the old gentleman, since he joined the temperance society. Now he is industrious, and does the best he can to obtain a living. His wife, I have always heard, is a prudent, active, and industrious woman and keeps her house as tidy as she possibly can."

"But they are not genteel, and never will be."

"That should be no disparagement to the son. Charles has ever behaved like a gentleman, and there is no young man of my acquaintance that I would sooner Clara would marry."

"Father, you are joking," said the daughter. "It is the most absurd idea I ever heard you advance."

"My child, there is *worth* in that young man. He has talents that will yet shine in the world. Mark what I tell you, for I know him well."

"I would rather be an old maid all my days," said Clara, "than have such a fellow — the son of a miserable drunkard."

"Clara, you must not talk so. Mr. Clinton has reformed, and I understand is doing well."

"But no one will forget what he once was," said the mother; "and for my part I think Clara is right in her views. I should feel dreadfully to know she was waited upon by such a young man as Charles. And I know Mary's father would feel highly indignant if he knew who his daughter had been with this evening."

"No, no, aunt," said Mary; "my father has always taught me to respect and love all who are kind and vir-

26

tuous, without regard to their situation in life. But he has always cautioned me to beware of those who show a fair exterior, but are corrupt within."

"Mary is determined to have her way," said Clara, "and she will probably dream of Charles to-night."

But little more was said, and the family retired.

The next day Clara would often inquire about "the Clay Cove mechanic,"and throw out insinuations upon her cousin for consenting to go with him; but Mary heeded her not, simply remarking, "The sequel will tell who is right and who is wrong in her views."

Mary Edwards continued her visit several weeks with her cousin, and during that time Charles called often to see her, but as usual was treated with neglect and contempt by Clara. He pretended not to notice her coolness and indifference, and never lisped a word to her discredit to her cousin. Before Mary left, it was well understood between her and Charles that she was to be his future wife. The day for her departure arrived, and bidding her friend good-by, she took the stage, and was on her way home to Lewiston.

Her cousin had not been gone many weeks before a young man by the name of Henry Watson commenced his visits to the house of Clara. He had made her acquaintance in a ballroom, and was just such a character as suited the foolish girl. His father was a man of wealth, who resided in a large house, and who had brought his son up to live a life of idleness. Instead of putting him in a counting-room or a mechanic's shop, he suffered him to walk about, doing little, until he was eighteen or twenty years of age; and then he was too old to learn a trade. He was furnished with pocket-money, and dressed extravagantly, associating mostly with those who had no regular business.

In the course of a few years, both Clara and Mary were married, one to the industrious mechanic, the other to the fashionable fop. As the tastes of the two girls were so different, they seldom saw each other. Clinton took a small house, and commenced life as he thought he was able to go through. But Watson hired a large house, and had it elegantly furnished.

Ten or fifteen years have passed away since the cousins were married. As you pass up one of our most pleasant streets, you will notice a beautiful white house, with healthy trees before it. Every thing is neat and commodious about the dwelling. It is the residence of Charles Cinton. He owes not a dollar for it. Besides his independent circumstances, he is honored and respected by all who know him, and has frequently been promoted to offices of trust. By his industry and energy, the mechanic has risen to his present respectable standing in society.

Pass down to Clay Cove. Do you see the small black house, once the residence of Charles Clinton, when his father was nothing but a sailmaker and an inebriate? That now is the residence of Henry Watson and his wife. They are poor and destitute, and live mostly upon charity. It was not long after he was married, that his father failed in business and lost his property, and Henry; being brought up to no particular business, took hold of what first presented, but did not succeed, and was obliged to remove from one house to another, not being able to pay his rent, until he accepted the little house in Clay Cove, rent free, from his friend, Charles Clinton.

Poor Clara has been doubly paid for her folly, and repented in dust and ashes the stand she took against the poor mechanic.   Her husband has but little education and no energy, and is, in every sense, a poor tool.   Mary Clinton has too good a heart to reproach her cousin, and has been uncommonly kind and generous to her.

All is not gold that glitters.   Let the reader learn this lesson from the above story.   Judge not a man by his business or profession, but look to his heart and disposition.   Reproach no man on account of the sins and poverty of his parents.   The rarest gems are often found on a dunghill.   Let this be the lesson you learn, and our story will not have been written in vain.

THE LAWYER.

CHAPTER I.

His aim is high ; no low desire
  Prompts him to choose the right;
His acts pass through detraction's fire
  Unscathed — without a blight.
He cannot suffer, for within
There is no curse from practised sin.

"Hurrah! there's old Johnny Avery singing one of his songs!" exclaimed John Edson to his companion, one Fourth of July ; "let's go and hear him."

"Agreed," said William Stacy, and they both ran up the hill, where, beside old Ma'am Shepherd's tent, the old man was singing one of his favorite songs.

When Avery had finished, he handed round his hat for the change which he usually received for a song, and one and another dropped in a copper or two for the old fellow ; when unobserved, John Edson hit the hat a knock, and sent it to the ground. While Avery was picking up the change, the little boy contrived to get two or three coppers, which he put into his pocket and ran off.

When he saw his companion, he told him what he had done, laughing heartily at the joke, as he called it.

"You did wrong," said William Stacy, "to take the

26*

poor man's money; and if I were you I would go directly back and give it to him."

"That I will not do," said John; "and I wish I had got more of it. I also contrived to take two or three of Ma'am Shepherd's eggs, when she was looking another way."

"You do wrong, John, to steal and you will be sorry for it."

"No, I sha'n't. There is no harm in taking two or three cents from anybody."

"It is as much stealing, as if you took two or three dollars."

"But I don't consider it so; and when I can get something so easy, I always intend to," and so saying, he ran off before his companion could reply.

John Edson and William Stacy were neighbors and playmates. The former was the son of a merchant; the mother of the latter was a widow. The father of John expended a great deal of money on his boy, determining to give him a good education. He fitted him for college, and in his seventeenth year he entered. He barely passed an examination, for John was a dull scholar, and hated his books. On leaving home, his father gave him money to spend, telling him, if that was not sufficient, to write him, and he would furnish him with more.

About the same time, William Stacy was placed with a mechanic to learn the mysteries of a trade. His poor mother was obliged to labor with her hands to support her little family; but she felt encouraged that her son would do well, and in the course of time, if she lived, be able to render her some assistance. William was always good to his mother, and, when he earned a few coppers, invariably gave them to her to purchase something for the family. He regretted leaving his parent when he went to his trade, but he felt that he should have the privilege of seeing her often, and in the end of being able to assist her, and so he kept up good spirits. His master was a kind man, and finding his apprentice honest and faithful, did much to encourage him. The boy was fond of reading, and his master assisted him in obtaining those works which pleased him the most. He was delighted with Rollin's History, Plutarch's Lives, Josephus, and like works, from which he could gather information. Instead of spending his leisure time in idleness, or in vicious pursuits, he was storing his mind with knowledge, and preparing himself for a useful life.

At the expiration of each college term, young Edson would visit his parents, and spend a portion of his time with his old playmate, William. But as he grew older, he became less intimate with the apprentice, doubtless feeling that William was engaged in a less laudable pursuit, and withal he was not so particular as to his dress and the following out of the fashions. The young mechanic noticed the indifference of John, but always treated him with kindness and respect. He learned from various sources that the collegian did not stand high in his class. Instead of giving his attention to his studies, he looked more for his present gratification in pleasure and folly. He was not a very moral youth, and therefore gained the friendship of but few. When he graduated, he took no part in the exercises at commencement, but returned to his father what is called an educated man. It was some time before John concluded what profession to follow. He thought first of being a preacher, then a doctor, or teacher, but finally, decided upon the law. He had brass and impudence enough for any pursuit, and these are two essential qualifications to make one eminent at the bar; so John thought, and so thought his father. There was no difficulty in obtaining a place in an office; and the young man soon commenced the perusal of Coke and Blackstone. In the same office with John were several other students, who, observing the carelessness of their companion, endeavored to play tricks upon him, and were at times successful. He was so indifferent to what he read that, had he been questioned at night what subject he had perused, he would not have been able to say. John always kept a mark in his law book, for otherwise he could not tell how far he had progressed in the mysteries of the profession. Observing this, the other students often placed his mark some twenty or thirty pages back, so that Edson perused the same pages several times without being conscious of it. He would sometimes remark, "I think I have before read something similar to this," and proceed in his studies. John had good abilities, but he was lazy and heedless, and exerted himself but little to improve his mind. He better understood the fashions, and moved in what are termed the higher circles. After remaining in the office three years, — the time specified by our wise lawmakers, — young Edson was permitted to practise in his profession.

About this time John's father died, leaving him several thousand dollars as his portion of his estate. Upon the strength of five or six thousand dollars, Edson married a fashionable girl, and commenced living in an expensive style. At the same time, he hired a room, and placed over his door, in large letters, JOHN ED-

SON, *Counsellor at Law.* He also made known the fact
in all the newspapers published in the vicinity. The
young lawyer lived as if he thought his capital would
never be exhausted, and so he paid but little attention
to his business. He was occasionally consulted by some
straggling sailor, or forlorn negro, and he gave them
advice as readily as if he had been master of his profession; but no sooner had his clients departed, than Edson was seen whipping into the office of his next-door
neighbors in the profession, to inquire if he was right.
If so, it was well and good; if not, he would endeavor
to correct his mistake at the next interview.

By the course that Edson pursued, in a few years
his six thousand dollars were expended. When the
fact came home to him, he was much depressed in
spirits, but contented himself by saying, " Well, I've
done the best I could, and been as prudent as possible."
Now, from sheer necessity, he was obliged to live in a
small tenement, and to stick close to his profession, or
he could not get along. It was humiliating to both
himself and his wife, but it could not be avoided. To
increase his law business was a difficult matter; but
nevertheless, it must be done. He had thoughts of leaving the place, but was fearful it would not better his
prospects. Edson went round among his friends and
solicited their business. " I should like to do your collecting, or any business in my line that you can give
me. I will do my best for you, and be prompt in paying
over," he would remark, and sometimes he secured a
job.

Before military inspection and review days and general musters, he invariably called upon the clerks of the

several ward and independent companies, to solicit their business and collect the fines. "I will do my best," said he, "and if I do not succeed in collecting I will not charge you for my services."

Some took pity on him and threw their business into his hands; but he thereby made enemies. Men who were exempt by law from performing military duties, were alike sued with those who wished to evade the law, and although Edson could not get his cases, he put the gentlemen to no little trouble and expense to defend themselves.

There is no greater plague to the community than a miserable pettifogger, and such a character Edson proved himself to be. He had wasted a handsome property, and was now starving for business. So he eagerly grasped at low and miserable cases, and secured the name of a mean and low-lived attorney.

As long as his mother survived Edson had the means of a comfortable living, but at her death, when her little property was divided among a number of children, he was poor indeed. The vicious habits he had contracted in early life grew upon him, and he was occasionally seen overcome by ardent spirits. Thus, in the meridian of life, he had lost his best friends, and associated mostly with the low and abandoned. As his only hope of a livelihood, and to be saved from unpleasant associations, he concluded to remove to another place, and exert himself to get more practice. Accordingly, without making it known excepting to a very few, — for he was indebted to a large amount, — he left his native place for another town. Having arrived, as soon as possible he obtained a small tenement for his wife and children,

agreeing with his landlord to be punctual in the payment of his rent as soon as it became due.

Entirely unacquainted in the place, he sought business in his profession, but was unsuccessful. His family were destitute and suffering, and, as a last resort, he
came to the conclusion to act as porter in the store of a
merchant, for a small salary. As this was not sufficient
to support him and pay his rent, he knew not what step
to take, for he had resided in the place three months,
and daily expected a visit from his landlord.

Once evening he heard a light rap at the door. On
opening it, he discovered the gentleman of whom he
hired the house, who asked for his rent.

"I am sorry to disappoint you to-night," said Edson,
"but if you will call day after to-morrow, I will be ready.
I have been disappointed in my expectations, but then
you shall have it without fail."

The gentleman left, remarking simply that it would
be just as convenient for him to wait.

The poor man did not know where the money would
come from that he had promised so soon; but Edson
had no correct principles, and at once he came to the
conclusion to take the amount from the store of his employer, if he could possibly get an opportunity. Watching his chance, he slyly purloined the amount from the
merchant, and paid his landlord as he had promised.

On the following Saturday night the money was
missed, but how to account for it was a mystery to the
merchant and his clerks. The account of sales was examined again and again, and the money counted over
and over, still twenty dollars were gone. No one suspected the "honest porter," as he was called, and he
would probably have never been detected if he had

stopped here.   But when one wrong step is taken, it opens the way for another.   Edson not only took money from his employer, but articles from the store to a considerable amount at different times, till at last he was suspected and known to be the thief.   He was accused of it, and, although he denied the truth, was arrested by an officer and lodged in jail.

CHAPTER II.

We all can give — the poor, the weak,
    And be an angel guest;
How small a thing to smile, to speak,
    And make the wretched blest!
These favors let us all bestow,
    And scatter joys abroad,
And make the vales of sorrow glow
    With the sweet smiles of God.

WILLIAM STACY continued a faithful and industrious apprentice.   He gathered up knowledge year by year, devoting all his leisure time to the improvement of his mind. When he became of age I doubt whether a college-educated young man had a more thorough knowledge of the mathematics, of Greek and Latin than himself.   He pursued those studies which are usually taught in college, and by diligence and industry had become master of what he attempted.   Soon after his freedom he left his native town to reside in another city, thinking that better prospects would be held out to him at his trade. But in this respect he was disappointed.   He could get no work. A thought struck him. Perhaps I can study a profession; and, entering the first lawyer's office he came across, Stacy made known his intention. The gentleman was prepossessed in his favor, and agreed to take him, provided he would do his writing, collecting, etc. When he understood the young man's situation, he gave him permission to board at his house, if, at some future day, when he became able, he would cancel the debt. William expressed his gratitude, and immediately commenced his studies. A young man of so amiable a disposition, and possessing so many admirable qualities of mind, could not but secure the good-will of the lawyer. He became a favorite in the family of Mr. Lager, for that was the name of the attorney, a man who had an extensive practice, who was a perfect gentleman in all his dealings and behavior. Feeling an interest in the young student, he used his exertions to interest and inform him. He saw that his young friend was a man of no ordinary talents, and he treated him as a companion. When he had studied the usual time, he was admitted to the bar, soon after which Mr. Lager took him into full copartnership.

Perhaps I should have stated before that Mr. Lager had a daughter to whom Stacy was quite partial. He had been in business but a little more than a year when he was united in marriage to Elizabeth Lager. It will be enough to say that she was an excellent woman and made her husband one of the best of wives.

The business of Lager and Stacy was extensive; they had more practice than any three lawyers in the place. For years they prospered and accumulated money. Stacy had made enough by his profession to build him a handsome house, where he now resided. But amid

27

his prosperity he did not forget his mother. Every year she visited him, and received enough at the hands of her son to support her comfortably. No man stood higher at the bar than William Stacy. He had eloquence and power, and proved eminently successful in all his cases.

We have now come to that period in our story when poor John Edson was carried to prison for theft. In his gloomy cell he reflected on his past life, his vicious and profligate course, his once bright prospects, and his present blasted hopes, and there alone and in solitude he wept like a child. "Oh, that I had been wise, that I had been indutsrious, that I had been conscientious, that I had consulted duty and not pleasure; but there is now no help for me." Poor man! he now felt his case to be severe, and he knew not what to do. He had no friends who could assist him.

A few days before his trial came on, a young man who was clerk in the store where Edson was employed, called to see him. Although he knew that he must be guilty, he felt for Edson's condition, and when he saw his tears and his anguish, his heart was moved.

"Have you any counsel employed?" inquired the young man.

"No, I have none."

"But you had better employ one."

"I cannot pay him, and what man would exert himself in my behalf?"

"But you must have counsel. Suppose I call on Lager and Stacy, and tell them you wish to secure their services?"

"If you think it would be of any avail, and they would consent to defend me, if ever I am able, I will pay them."

"Then I will call upon them. They are the best lawyers in the city. If there is any hope for you, the junior partner can succeed."

Edson was a little encouraged. As the young man departed, he expressed his gratitude to him in tears. Since his confinement, this was the first time he felt that any one was interested in his welfare, aside from his wife and children.

The next morning the jailer announced to Edson that his counsel had arrived, who soon seated himself beside the miserable man.

"Sir," said he, "I am sorry to see you in this place, and if I can be of any service to you, I will use my exertions in your behalf."

"I thank you, sir," said Edson.

"But I wish to know if you are really guilty of what has been charged to you, and if so, whether you have ever made it known to another."

"I am guilty; but poverty alone prompted me to commit the deed. A wife and two children are dependent upon me, and I am poor indeed."

"Have you ever been guilty of like offences?"

"Never, since I was a child. Then upon several occasions I took what belonged to others; but it was from mere roguery or thoughtlessness, for my parents were wealthy."

"What is your name?"

"Edson."

"What! John Edson?"

"Yes, sir."

"Indeed! it is my old playmate, as true as I live."

Tears fell from the eyes of both as they at once recognized each other, and the mind flew back to other days when they were happy in their sports, when one

was the son of a rich merchant, the other the son of a
poor widow.   It was some time before they could speak,
but through his tears, Edson related all the circumstances of his checkered life, since he last saw his early
companion.   "Oh, that I had been wise," he continued,
"and pursued an upright course ; I should not now
have been in this wretched state."

His friend assured him that he would use his strongest exertions to clear him, provided in future he would
pursue a different course, and live an honest and upright life.

" With all my heart, I will.   Your example, if nothing
else, will induce me to do so."

After a long conversation, Stacy left his friend, and
bent his steps to the wife and children of the prisoner.
He found them poor and miserable indeed.   In years
past he had been acquainted with Mrs. Edson, and knew
her to be a proud and haughty girl, one who sneered at
him because he was a poor mechanic.   But he treasured no ill feeling in his heart, and when he visited
her, he found her almost the victim of despair.   Her
spirits had been broken and her health impaired, and
with brimful eyes she expressed her gratitude to Mr.
Stacy for his kindness, and begged him to do all in his
power to release her husband.

The kind lawyer sent her various things for her present necessities, and requested his wife to call upon her
and render what assistance she could.   Mrs. Stacy, ever
prompt to do a generous deed and alleviate suffering,
hastened to the poor woman, and, by her kindness, in
a great measure removed the burden from the heart of
the suffering wife.

Before Edson's case came on, his old friend called

often to see him. On the morning of his trial, Stacy was in the courthouse, prepared to do his best to liberate the criminal at the bar. The indictment was read by the clerk, and when the question was asked, " Guilty or not guilty," the prisoner, in a tremulous voice, replied " Not guilty." The evidence was brought forward, and the witnesses examined. It could be seen by the questions put to the witnesses by Stacy, and the manner in which he conducted his case, that he was deeply interested in his subject. When the examination of witnesses was closed, the lawyer commenced his argument. It was not long, but it was full of power and eloquence. He portrayed the situation of the prisoner, poor and friendless, in such vivid colors that tears were seen to trickle down the cheeks of the jury. After the argument from the opposing counsel, the jury retired, and in a few moments returned with the verdict in favor of the prisoner. There was not a man present who did not rejoice to hear it, not excepting those who had accused the prisoner of theft.

Stacy wept for joy, and hastened to carry the good news to his family. From this period commenced a new era in the life of Edson. By the advice of his friend, he was persuaded to renew his profession, which he did with zeal and energy. He now began to study in right earnest in the office of Stacy, and in a few months was able to practise. Although he never made an eminent lawyer, by his virtuous course and industrious habits, he was able to earn a comfortable support.

Now, the two early friends are on the strictest terms of intimacy. Notwithstanding Stacy is rich and independent, he remembers his poverty and is humble and generous. Edson looks back on his past life with regret

27*

and sorrow, but strives to make amends for a profligate course, and by his good habits and attention to business, has secured many kind and excellent friends. May they both live long, and exert an influence that will continue to be favorable to truth and virtue.

THE AGREEABLE DECEPTION.

Good thoughts and generous deeds alone
 Survive when we are dead;
These will around our memories
 A glorious halo shed.
If we have raised a sinking form,
 Removed a single tear,
A spot of sunshine long will rest
 On paths we wandered here.

" I FEEL no better, mother, since I took the last medicine."

" I cannot account for it, Sarah. The advertisement in the paper says the pills are a certain cure for diseases like yours, and that hundreds have been benefited by them."

" Since I took the pills, I don't think I am so well."

" Perhaps you did not take sufficient. I will send for another box."

Widow Mason lived in a small village. She had but one daughter, a young woman about twenty years of age. Mrs. Mason was very careful of the health of her child, and whenever she complained of the least illness she would run to the pill-box, this being in her view the sovereign remedy for all the ills of the flesh. The mother was altogether too credulous. What she read in the papers she believed. She never doubted the truth of the recommendations attached to the advertisements of medicines, and did not doubt that the makers and venders of the pills were actuated by the purest motives of benevolence — that they had the real good of suffering humanity at heart.

As Sarah had been complaining for a day or two, her mother had given her a dose of pills, and was surprised that she was no better. As she was about sending to town for another box, she took up a paper and saw a flaming notice of a new medicine, called the "Universal Vegetable Pill." "How fortunate, Sarah," said she, after she had perused the advertisement, "here's just what is wanted in your case. I must get Charles to go to-morrow and purchase some."

"So you must, mother," said the daughter, after she had cast her eye over the paper. "It is what I have needed for some time. Just see the recommendations; multitudes have been cured."

When Charles came in, and Mrs. Mason made known her wish, the young man replied, "I think you miss it to buy so much medicine. The pills that Sarah took yesterday were of no service to her, and she may continue to take them, and still be as feeble. I think it rather injurious to take so much stuff. I would not purchase more."

Charles Sumers was the son of a neighbor, a man of sterling integrity, who had seen something of the world and knew the deceptions and frauds which were too often practised on the credulous and unsuspicious. For some few years he had been a constant visitor at the house of the widow, and it was believed that he was engaged to Sarah. As he was aware of the amount of money the mother expended for medicine at various times, he often reminded her of the folly of thus throwing it away; telling her that those men she considered as philanthropists, were generally avaricious and unprincipled, and did not care how much misery and poverty they produced, providing it put money into their own pockets. But the widow could not believe it possible. Notwithstanding his aversion to pills, Charles consented the next day to purchase a box of the last advertised.

By her mother's request Sarah took a dose, and the next day she appeared better. "What did I tell you, Charles?" said the mother; "those pills have been of great service to Sarah. I shall never be without them."

For fear her daughter might yet grow worse, Mrs. Mason continued to dose her day by day, so as to purify her blood and strengthen her. But in a week or two Sarah was as feeble as ever, and a larger quantity of pills was given. Occasionally, the girl would appear much stronger and better; but her old complaint returned again. Charles insisted that she took too much medicine, and would never be well until she quit it. But her mother would not hear to him, and repeatedly said, her daughter would have been in her grave had it not been for the pills.

"Well, Charles, what do you think of Sarah this morning?" said the mother; "doesn't she look brighter and happier than she has done for some time past?"

"She appears pretty well, if it would only last. She will never be better, I am afraid, until you relinquish the use of those plaguy pills."

"These have kept her alive, I am certain. The reason why Sarah is so much better this morning is, she has been taking some new pills, the very best ever invented, the Indian Vegetable Pill. I saw them advertised last week, and sent and purchased a couple of boxes, and they have produced a wonderful effect."

" What! have you been trying more of those rascally pills? It is a wonder that Sarah is not in her grave. I verily believe if you do not stop dosing her you will kill her outright. For the last two years you have expended more than a hundred dollars for medicine, most of which has been taken by her. If that is not enough to destroy the constitution, I don't know what is."

" How singular you talk, Charles. It is for her good that I sacrifice this money."

" Yes, but you are mistaken. You have tried no less than a dozen kinds of pills, balsams, jellys, etc., and the last is always the best. So you may keep trying, and you will find that Sarah will never be any better. Of this I am certain."

His words were true. The daughter grew weaker and weaker day by day, and it was evident that the medicine given her by her mother had contributed to injure her health, but she could not believe it. Sumers felt that something must be done, or Sarah could not long survive. As for convincing her mother that she was wrong, it was an impossibility. He knew that the stuff given to the daughter had a deleterious effect, and utterly prevented her restoration to health. There was scarcely a day passed when, to please her mother, she did not swallow one pill or more, and she had thus practised for two or three years, so that now she was unfit for the duties of life. After reflecting what course to pursue, he hit upon a project.

One morning he called upon Mrs. Mason with a newspaper in his hand, and inquired of her if she had heard the news.

" I have heard nothing. What is it ? "

" Here is a paper which I have just received, which contains an important discovery — no less than a recipe, found after many years, for making what are called ' Life Pills,' left by a celebrated man, who died in 1535, at the advanced age of one hundred and fifty-two years."

" I want to know ! Are they to be sold in town ? I will certainly try them."

" They are advertised for sale by ——, and on the morrow, when I go to town, I will call, if you would like to have me."

" I should, by all means."

" Perhaps pills so celebrated may produce a better effect than such as you have purchased in months past, and Sarah may yet recover her health."

" True. I am really rejoiced that you called this morning to let me know of the discovery. I should like to have you leave the paper, that I may read the advertisement at my leisure."

The next day Sumers went to town, and called at the shop where the pills were kept for sale. The following morning he carried a box to the widow, who appeared exceedingly rejoiced. Sarah took a dose that day, and when Charles next called, her mother remarked, " I think these pills are admirable. See how much better Sarah looks, and she says she feels better too. I think she is smarter, and if she gets well, you will certainly put confidence in one kind of pills."

A month passed away, and the daughter rapidly recovered. Her buoyant spirits revived, the color came to her cheeks, and she was enabled to go out. No praise was too great for Mrs. Mason to bestow on the wonderful medicine. She told of it to her neighbors, and no one could dispute that they had a wonderful effect upon her child. After using about half a dozen boxes, in three or four months, the girl recovered, and it was thought unnecessary to take more.

It was whispered round the village that Sumers kept a quantity of the new pills at his store, and whenever there was sickness in the place, he was sure to sell a number of boxes. He kept an exact account of the boxes he sold, and to whom he sold them. The average amount of sales was a hundred dollars a year, which was no inconsiderable amount for a small town; but frequently individuals from neighboring villages would call upon him for the new article. And from many persons to whom he sold, he received testimonials of their value and efficacy. They had removed a hundred disorders, and were taken for all manner of diseases.

After a few years the sale of the pills was very meagre; scarcely an individual was sick in the village, and it was accounted for by the use of the efficacious medicine. About this time, Sumers, having amassed some property, came to the conclusion to be united in marriage to the beautiful and accomplished daughter of the widow, Sarah Mason. Arrangements were made for the wedding, and a large number of the villagers were invited as guests.

The evening came, and the happy hearts were united. After partaking of the festivities of the occasion, where every thing was joyous and pleasant, the company were invited into a chamber, where a large table in the centre was overspread with a white cloth. The people gathered in a circle around the room, wondering at the singular request, and anxious to know what was on the table. Charles stepped up and removed the cloth,

when lo! the table was loaded with silver money, separated into more than fifty piles, large and small. To
each lot was attached a piece of paper.

"Gentlemen and ladies," said Charles, "you may
wonder at this singular proceeding, and be astonished
at the quantity of change before you. But it is not
mine. Here are rising five hundred dollars, and it belongs to you. Some of you are the owners of a larger
portion than the others, but it shall be divided justly."

The company looked around and questioned among
themselves what this singular conduct could mean,
when Charles continued, —

"You are a little astonished at what I have said, but
I will explain it. You all know that for the last five
or six years I have kept for sale an article called the
Life Pill, which you considered an invaluable medicine.
Those pills were nothing but stained peas, which I put
in boxes myself. Having so long deceived you, I now
refund you each the money which has been paid me for
the worthless article."

He then commenced, and distributed to each individual his portion, which, like Franklin's whistle money, had
been parted with so foolishly.

"Some of you may censure me," continued Charles,
"for the deception I have practised, but it has been for
your good. The people in the village were never more
healthy than at the present time, which has convinced
me that the pills you have bought in years past contributed to disease. I have analyzed the various pills
which have been the most popular over the country, and
find their ingredients very similar, and all concocted and
vended for the sole purpose of making money. The
pills of each make are so nearly alike, that it is in the

28

name where all the difference lies; and neither of them
I am perfectly convinced, ever did or ever will do the
least particle of good. I have the testimony of you all
that the peas I have sold you for years past have been efficacious in removing countless diseases, and in restoring
your health; and I believe you were correct. Imagination did the work. Had I dealt out the pills with which
our community is flooded, I should have taken your
money and kept it, and, instead of promoting your health,
I should have increased your disorders and sent many
of you to premature graves."

As Sumers concluded, the whole company expressed
their admiration of his course, and thanked him a
hundred times. They saw how easy it was to be deceived, and resolved never again to touch a single article conspicuously advertised in the newspapers, but if
they were sick to employ a regular physician, and abide
the consequences.

When the company retired, Charles's wife and mother
laughed heartily over the circumstances, for they had
been deceived with the rest, and both declared they were
cured of pills and quack medicines forever.

Charles made an excellent husband, and Sarah was
one of the best of wives. Peace and prosperity attended
their steps and they were both respected and beloved by
the whole village. Nothing seemed too much for the
people to do for their welfare and happiness, and they
all acknowledged for years after, that Charles had been
a great benefactor to them. He had saved their money,
preserved their health, and made their path of life more
pleasant and happy.

Those who spend their money for the various pills
and nostrums of the day, will find in the end that they

not only lose their money but their health.   Let no one
be foolish enough to purchase those highly recommended
nostrums that are so conspicuously and prominently
placed before you in our newspapers.   They never did,
they never will, prove beneficial.   Their ingredients have
a deleterious tendency.   Better diet yourselves, if unwell, and exercise yourselves every day in the open air.
This will be better than all the quack medicine in the
world, and so you will confess after you have given them
both a fair trial.

JOB DOBSON.

Behold him with his treasure there,
IIis only comfort and his care ;
Daily he counts each portion o'er,
Though he but adds a sixpence more.
Poor man ! 'tis all his bliss below
To add, and watch his treasure grow.

WHEN Job Dobson was born, whence he came, or
who were his parents we never knew.   It is sufficient
for our purpose that such a being as Job existed, did
business in the town of B——, made money, and got
to himself an unenviable name.   The first we recollect
of him was many years since, when, passing old Horton,
the apple-man,— everybody knows Horton,— we heard
an individual vociferating loudly and vehemently against
the deaf old gentleman for not giving him his right
change ; he had wronged him, cheated him, and deserved a sound thrashing.   Stopping a moment to ascertain the occasion of such hard words, we learned that
the fellow had purchased a cent's worth of apples, gave
Horton fourpence halfpenny, and received five cents
as his change.   The man insisted on another apple for
the quarter of a cent, but, on being refused, he commenced the hue and cry.   When the trouble was made
known to the two or three spectators, the fellow sneaked
off like a whipped cur.   We then marked a man so

mean, and curiosity lead us to inquire his name. It was Job Dobson.

Occasionally, in our intercourse with the world, we have come in contact with Job, and wherever we found him, he was disputing bills, insisting on the half-cent, or quarreling about the price of an article; and he would invariably look with a peculiar countenance, as much as to say, "You see I am right." But we always avoided dealing with Job, for we well knew to have transactions with such a character was a certain loss.

Dobson made money; and who cannot, if he will stand for mills, dispute about fractions, and neglect the payment of debts until he is threatened to be sued? In a few years, Job had picked up change enough, in one way and another, to open a little shop, which he was careful to fill with those articles that would quickly turn his money, and yield a handsome profit. It was said that when he bought articles, he would insist upon good, heavy weight and overflowing measure; but when he sold, he was extremely careful that his customers should not accuse him of cheating himself. He had on hand two . sets of weights and measures — one for buying, the other for selling. One day he bought some coffee of a sailor, which had been smuggled ashore, agreeing to give him a specified price per pound. After the coffee had been carried to his shop and weighed, Dobson said to the sailor, "I can give you but so much for this coffee, now; that's all it's worth;" naming a less sum.

"But the agreement was that I should have four or five cents more on a pound," said the sailor.

"I can't help that," said Dobson. "You had no duties to pay, and you may take what I offer you, or I shall

28*

complain of you for smuggling, and you will lose the whole."

"Very well," said the tar; "give me what you say, and I'll be off."

Dobson was mightily pleased with his trade. He said to himself, as he examined the coffee, "I shall treble my money on this. 'Tisn't every one that knows how to work it. I'm the chap for trade."

Dobson might have spared himself those golden dreams in this instance; for as soon as the sailor had received his money he rendered a complaint against Job, for purchasing coffee which he knew to be smuggled; and for thus informing the proper authorities, he received a larger amount than if Dobson had paid him what he agreed. The poor cheat was thunderstruck when he learned what the sailor had done, and spit out his vengeance in a flood of profanity; but he was compelled to pay for his villany, which gave him no peace for many a summer day. A curse was on his tongue for every sailor he met for at least a twelvemonth afterwards; and when one entered his store he could hardly refrain from throwing out his spite.

This would have been a good lesson to Job, had he been at all disposed to improve upon it. But no, his love of gain, his parsimonious disposition, led him on to other deeds of folly and crime. On whatever Dobson purchased, he was pretty sure to make a large profit. A hundred-weight of tea, sugar, or coffee, would turn out at least a hundred and fifteen pounds. He was determined to make money; how, he did not care, so long as he was not detected. He would as soon take the bread from the widow's or the orphan's mouth as to accumulate property in any other way.

Job had now become quite independent by his course of cheating and lying, so that he was better able to carry on his knavery. In his shop he kept a little of every thing,— hats, clothing of all kinds, shoes, crockery, West India and English goods, etc., etc. He bought articles in every line, whenever he thought he could turn them to a profitable account. Old iron, copper, rags, and whatever the boys or older thieves could plunder, he would purchase at a reduced price, and keep them concealed until the inquiry for them was silenced, and then offer them for sale. In this way he encouraged youngsters to steal whatever they could lay their hands on, such as lead from the tops of houses, copper spouts, old sails, and in fine any thing and every thing that fell in their way. On such thing, she would more than treble his money.

One day, in the presence of another, he bought a piece of rope of a boy, telling him it weighed a dozen pounds, and giving him twelve cents for it. Just as the lad went out, a gentleman called on Dobson for just such a rope as he saw in his scales.

"What do you ask for it?" inquired the buyer.

"Three cents a pound."

"How much does it weigh?"

Dobson turned the scales, worked on them a second or two, and said, "It weighs eighteen pounds."

The gentleman took the rope, paid for it, and went away. The man present remarked, "I thought you just bought that rope for twelve pounds."

"Well — I must have made some mistake, then."

This was the secret of Job's success; swindling whenever and from whom he could.

Sometimes Dobson would collect a variety of things

and carry them to Boston to dispose of to more advantage, and if he could purchase any thing there very cheap, would return laden for this market. It was said he once sent a quantity of old junk away, and to make it weigh heavy, occasionally threw into the bag a shovelful of mud. If he did not do it, it was through fear of being detected and punished; for of law he was exceedingly fearful, since he had the difficulty with the sailor. When in Boston, Job would contrive to pay his passage, or rather make the visit cost him nothing, by purloining trifling things wherever he purchased. Having large pockets to his coat, he could slip in a half-pound of silk, a few papers of needles, or three or four fine handkerchiefs, when he was unnoticed. It was said he usually pursued this course, which made him purchase goods in Boston oftener than he otherwise would, and remain there for a longer time. ·

Dobson grew wealthy rapidly, but with all his riches he was an extremely ignorant man. He could scarcely read; his penmanship was on a par with his reading, and his knowledge of figures extremely limited. Sell him a few articles, and he would be longer in coming to their value than a schoolboy eight years old, but he never made a mistake, excepting in his own favor. He would add up and subtract and divide a dozen times, if he were not perfectly satisfied that he should not be the loser.

When Dobson purchased his house, he began to look about for a wife. His habits were so coarse, and his manners so unrefined, that few females would have any thing to say to him, and those who did were partial to his money. His looks were any thing but agreeable. Meanness — meanness — meanness — was stamped on every part of him, from the crown of his head to the sole of his foot; and it was conspicuous in all he said, in all he did. And females — to their credit be it said — can overlook nearly every fault in a man but this one, which is so despicable that few will give it the least countenance. Well, after inviting one and another without success, to accompany him on a party of pleasure, or to attend some concert, when it would not cost him more than a shilling, he finally succeeded in obtaining the consent of Miss Dolly Daton to accompany him to the Bowery. They were as happy as their dispositions would allow them to be; but when Dobson learned that the dinner would cost them a shilling apiece, he was in a world of trouble. He sat down and thought. After rising from his brown study, he told Dolly that his business was urgent in town, and he should not be able to stop to dinner. The horse was harnessed, and, after beating down old Davis from twenty-five cents to a shilling, Dobson and his girl started for home. Dolly was rejoiced when she arrived at her door, and declared to herself that it was the last time she would ever be seen in company with a mean man, and ever after would not speak to Job when she met him. It was more than six months ere Dobson ceased to be troubled at the expense occasioned by his visit to the Cape.

Finally Job got a wife, and was married at the minister's. She was from the country, and a stranger in the place, or she would never have consented to be chained to such a man as Dobson. He would allow but just so much in his house at a time, and be grumbling eternally about the waste of flour and meal. To save expense, he would permit but a certain quantity of wood to be consumed daily, entertained no company, eat but

little butter, dispensed with milk, and sweetened his
tea in the pot.   Occasionally, he had milk, when he
could buy it by the gallon, and pay for it from the store,
with some article on which he made two hundred per
cent.   It is unnecessary to say that Job and his wife
lived miserably unhappy.   She had a kind heart, and
was inclined to be generous, but she was cramped in
all she attempted to do, and never expended a cent
without letting her husband know what she bought.
Girls sometimes think they are made for this life if they
secure wealthy husbands; but, when too late, they find
their mistake.   So found the wife of Dobson, but she
made the best of it, and never told her deprivations and
sorrows to others.

Job would seldom permit his wife to go shopping
alone, for fear she would pay too high for her articles.
Once she purchased some calico for twelve and a half cents
per yard to make her a dress.   After an examination,
Job declared that it was worth but twelve cents at the
most, and insisted that his wife should return it.   In
vain did she plead, but her husband was inexorable, and
the poor woman was obliged to carry the calico back.
The shopkeeper refused to take it; but, according to
instructions, she left it on the counter.   Dobson, in a
great rage, went down to the merchant and demanded
his money.   But he insisted in vain, denounced the
shopkeeper as a cheat, declaring he would never purchase of him again, and came off, muttering and swearing as he went along with the calico.   His poor wife
never heard the last of the bargain, and never again
ventured to buy without special instructions from Job.

Dobson took a newspaper one year, and paid for it
in his way; but when the carrier boy, who had been

faithful to leave his paper every week, in storm and sunshine, heat and cold, handed him an address on New Year's day, Job looked daggers at him. "What does this mean, boy?"

"The New Year's Address, sir," said the lad.

"You give it to me, I suppose."

"No, sir; we expect a little change for it."

"Then I don't want the stuff," said Job, as he threw it in the little fellow's face. "I pay for the paper, and that is enough without your sponging in this way."

"Very well," said the boy, as he walked off, whistling to himself. But he ever after marked Job as a mean and contemptible wretch.

Once Dobson let two chambers of his house to a poor widow, and as regularly as the quarter-day arrived, he was at the door for his pay. Once it was not ready, and he threatened to turn her out of doors, and it was only by a great deal of persuasion, and the promise that he should receive a trifle for his indulgence, that she was permitted to remain.

Whenever a hand was employed about Job's house, in repairing or painting it, he was always present to oversee the work, and notice if the mechanic was idle for a moment. He would purchase materials and pay out of the shop, as was his invariable custom. Dobson never, to our knowledge, bought a single article or employed a single man, unless he settled for the whole in goods, without expending a dollar in cash. Seldom did he employ a mechanic who left him without having a dispute. He would never hold to his agreement, but endeavor to pay as little as he could for the work done. For all that he could possibly do for himself, he was careful not to pay another. He sawed his own wood, wheeled home his own flour, and did his own menial work, unless he could contrive to pay out of his shop in such articles as yielded him a great profit ; then, and not otherwise, would he employ poor laborers.

When Dobson wished to make a good trade, and could not succeed with the merchant, or trader, he would endeavor to connive with his clerks. Many a time has he gone into stores when he knew the owners were at their meals, endeavoring to trade with the boys, in the mean time, filling his pockets with nuts or apples, or eating his fill from the raisin-cask, the cheese-case, or the sugar-box. So in the market he would go round from cart to cart, not wishing to buy, but try the apples, the berries, the butter, the cheese. or whatever the farmers had, and often in this way has Job made out a good dinner, without it costing him a farthing.

Dobson liked to make a good appearance, and to be thought much of by the people ; he accordingly hired part of a pew in one of our churches, and went regularly to meeting, excepting on those days when it was given out that a contribution would be taken up ; then he was always absent.

The collector of the parish had much difficulty in obtaining the amount of Job's tax, and often said, "He was more trouble to him than all the rest of the parish." For such debts must be paid in money ; but Dobson declared, time and again, that he would quit the church unless he could pay for preaching out of his shop. There was never a bill presented to him that he did not either dispute, or neglect to pay, till the trouble of sending it was worth nearly as much as the bill amounted to.

By pursuing such a course, Dobson grew rich rapidly and was worth a considerable amount of property. His wife, who had been a faithful slave to him, became sick, and without proper treatment — for Job would not employ a physician or nurse, if he could possibly avoid it — she lingered a few weeks, and then died. It left no impression on Dobson's mind, save the expense he should incur. After his wife had been buried, and her friends had borne the expense, he refused to pay them. He even declared that the bill for rough boards that contained her mortal part, should not be paid by him, as he did not order them. Every one said the poor woman was better off, that she was kindly released from a world of sorrow by One who took pity upon her.

The character of Dobson had become so well known, that his name was associated with all that was low, mean, and grovelling in human nature. His meanness, his avarice, his ignorance, his cheating, all went to make up a character that everybody detested. As he passed the street, the very boys turned aside with fear, and looked on him as an inhabitant of a darker world. Men would exclaim, when an act of meanness was committed, "You are as bad as old Dobson," while the females turned away from his presence, and laughed at the "old fool." Since the death of his wife, Dobson has endeavored to find another companion; he is too well known. With all his money, he is now shunned, and looked upon by females as a creature too grovelling to claim affinity to humanity. Long since he gave up trade, and lives on the income of his property and the interest of his money. His looks, his acts, now proclaim him the victim of despair. In the midst of wealth, he is pining away in sorrow and want. With all the comforts, with all the blessings of life within reach, he refuses to secure them, and is drinking the

29

bitter dregs of poverty. Still adding to his thousands, he is fearful that he shall come to want, that his immense riches will be wrested from him by some means or another, and that want will be his inevitable doom.

Such is the folly, such the madness of men. They will chase a phantom through life, but never grasp it, and are constantly miserable. To be mean and to be happy, is impossible. The kind and benevolent enjoy life, make friends, and pass their days in peace, amid sunshine and flowers.

Everybody, by pursuing a course like the hero of our story, can become rich, but he must forego the blessing of life, and be the victim of sorrow and despair. To court wealth is to court misery, to secure the ill-will and the hatred of mankind, and to pass through life a detested thing, whose presence will contaminate, whose friendship will destroy. Be contented with virtuous poverty; pursue the even tenor of your ways, as your means will allow, and as opportunities present, and you will secure the love and esteem of man, the approbation of God, and finally die lamented by a world which you have made better and happier by your generous deeds, your consistent life, and your blessed example.

THE REVENGE.

How few who speak a bitter word
    Can tell the pang it gives !
What angry feelings it hath stirred !
    What malice it revives !
Like a barbed arrow, sure and deep,
    It sinketh in the breast,
And though for years it seems to sleep,
    'Tis an unquiet guest.

" No, I cannot learn a trade," said Clara to her mother,
sobbing; " I cannot do it.   What will people say, when
they hear that one of the Howels has gone into a tailor's
shop, or a mantuamaker's to work ?   Oh, I can't do it;
I can't learn a trade."

" You do not realize, my child," said her mother,
" that I am unable to support you and the other children, now your father is dead, and that something must
be done, or we shall soon be in want of the necessaries
of life.   Would you not rather learn a trade than to
have it said that we were supported by charity ? "

" You can get along, mother, without thinking about
my working in a shop.   We have never wanted for any
thing."

" The little your father left me is almost gone ; by
the utmost care and prudence it will not last over a
twelvemonth longer, and then we shall be sadly off with-

out any income. You must learn a trade, Clara; and you may as well consent to it first as last."

"No—no—I cannot," said the proud girl, sobbing still louder, "I cannot do it. What would the girls say to see me go to a milliner's shop? They would all laugh at me. O mother, I don't see how you can expect me to do it. I would willingly take in nice sewing, do a little lace work, or teach painting, or keep a school, if I was competent, but I cannot, I cannot learn a trade."

"My child, you talk very foolish indeed. Who would laugh at you for working? Not one of your acquaintances. They would commend you for it. Now, it is frequently thrown in my teeth, that I support two or three girls in idleness, who are able to earn their own living—that I wish to bring them up as ladies, to the ruin of them and myself. There is a great deal of truth, I confess in what they say, and I feel ashamed of it. If I were rich, and able to furnish you with suitable clothing, I would not make this request of you, —but as it is, you must do something soon, and you better make up your mind to do it cheerfully."

"Well, I can't learn a trade," said the daughter, still crying, "I will do any thing else."

"You must do it, or be compelled to live on the charities of others."

"If three or four of my acquaintances would go to work in a shop with me, I should not hesitate to go."

"But the parents of most of your acquaintances are rich, and there is not so much necessity of their learning a trade. Your schoolmate, Jane Carlton, has just gone into a shop, and I understand it was by her particular request."

"Jane Carlton is nobody; she never was thought much of, and she has always been used to such kind of work. I hope you do not put her on an equal with me."

"Certainly, Clara, she is your equal. I am no better off than her mother. She is poor and so am I; and if it was not too humiliating for Jane to learn a trade, certainly it will not be for you."

"How you talk, mother. When father was alive, we were well off, and had every thing we needed; but Jane's mother has always been poor, and she has always associated with a low set of girls."

"Who do you call low, Clara?"

"Why, the Hodge children, and the Nortons, and some others."

"They are poor, I know, but certainly they are far from being despised, and all of them are honorable and industrious girls. With all their poverty, so long as they are virtuous and behave themselves, they will command respect. Now, my child, you must give up your false notions, and conclude to do something to gain a support."

"I can't learn a trade, and there is an end of it," said Clara, and she left the room a little angry with her judicious mother.

Mrs. Howel had been a widow some eight or ten years. Her husband was a mechanic, and made a good living by his trade. He even laid up a few hundred dollars, which had supported his wife and three children, with what little sewing Mrs. Howel did, for the few past years. Clara was the oldest child, and, as the family grew up, and needed more clothing, her mother had been talking with her of the importance of learning a trade, for it was now impossible for her with her own hands to earn

29*

enough to support them all. Clara knew the situation of the family, and yet was too proud to work in a shop and endeavor in this way to assist her poor mother. She had hoped to continue in her present easy circumstances until something should occur which would place her in a situation where she would not be obliged to go out and work; she might have some property left her by her relations, who were wealthy, or she might get married. But any thing was preferable to learning a trade.

Month after month passed away, and still Clara would not give her consent to work in a shop, when one day her mother said to her, " My child, I have come to the conclusion to have you learn a trade. My friends have wondered at my keeping you at home doing nothing, while I have to work so hard to support you and the other children; they say I must never expect any assistance from them while I permit you to live in such idle habits. I am ashamed when they speak to me about it, for I am sensible of the correctness of what they say, and that you ought to earn your own living. You must make up your mind before another week to go to a trade."

Now came a flood of tears to Clara's eyes, as she said, " I cannot do it. It would be a disgrace to the name of Howel if I should attempt it."

" You must do it, Clara, and there is an end of it."

" No; I will starve first, mother! I will not go into a shop to work; any light sewing I will do with pleasure; but as to learning a trade, I will never consent to do it."

In vain did her mother advise and entreat her; but she persisted in her determination not to obey her and work. The consequence of her course was laid before her. Perhaps she would be left alone in the world for her younger sisters to look up to, and in that case, if she had no means of support, the poorhouse must bring her up at last. But Clara did not care; her friends would not let her come to want; she should be provided for. What little sewing her mother could obtain for Clara, which the proud girl thought respectable, and without daring to lisp it to any one, she would do; but it was a trifle indeed that she earned.

Mrs. Howel had become quite poor; but her daughter to appear respectable and carry out her foolish caprices and whims, would often stint her food to clothe her back, and make what she considered a decent appearance in society. As Clara was quite pretty and appeared well, she was waited upon by two or three young men, but they were not altogether to her fancy. They were children of mechanics, who had been brought up to some laborious pursuits, and their hands were too rough, or their countenances too sunburnt, or their prospects were too slim. There was one young man in particular who was strongly attached to Clara. His name was Henry Watson, a steady and industrious youth. He offered himself to her.

"What!" said the proud girl, "do you think I would have a miserable tool of a mechanic? Do you mean to insult me?" and her temper was kindled to its highest pitch as she told him to leave the house. Henry was ill prepared for such treatment from one he had always esteemed, and whom he tenderly loved.

"Clara," said he, as he left the house, "you will regret the manner in which you have treated me. Remember what I say, you will regret it," but she would not hear another word, and the young mechanic went away, resolved to be diligent in business, and secure a partner more worthy of himself; which we are happy to say he soon found, and never had occasion to regret his choice. He removed from the town to a larger place, where his business increased, and he became independent in his circumstances.

Clara had set her cap for a gentleman, a law student, a minister, or a merchant, she was not very particular which, so long as he dressed well, talked fashionably about the splendid parties, the beautiful girls, and the respectability of his business. But Clara was doomed to be disappointed. Her mother had become so reduced in her circumstances, that she had by degrees sold off her furniture, so that but very little remained in the house. Her other children, not having the same notion which was so unfortunate in Clara, had just gone to trades, one to a milliner, the other to a mantuamaker. It would be many months before they would earn any thing for themselves, and it was as much as the mother could do to support the family. At this period she told Clara that she was fearful of being obliged to call on the parish for help, and that unless she would consent to do something, her friends would never help her. But the haughty Clara still persisted in having her own way, and even censured her mother for permitting her younger sisters to learn trades.

In a day or two after this conversation Mrs. Howel was taken sick, and, as her neighbors called in, they were surprised at her destitute circumstances. They did not permit her to suffer for any thing she needed for her comfort, and Clara was as attentive as possible to her mother. She appeared to grow worse day by day. A relation of her husband kindly consented to take her two daughters, who were at trades, saying they should be welcome to their board till their trades were completed. This was a great relief to the poor woman, who seemed to get no better, although she received the best of attendance. After lingering a few months, Mrs. Howel died. Her last advice to Clara was to learn some trade, that she might earn her own living.

"You cannot expect to find such a friend as your mother," said she; "and in the world you will have much to encounter. If you still indulge in your foolish pride, it will eventually prove your ruin; but if you look upon yourself as you are, a poor, dependent girl, and endeavor to do what is right, you will gain friends, and succeed in what you undertake. Above all, be humbled at the feet of your Saviour, and learn meekness of him, and do what he commands you, and at last you will meet me in heaven."

Clara was deeply affected at the death of her mother, as were also her sisters. They followed her to the narrow house appointed for all living, and came away with sad hearts. Clara went to the chamber recently occupied by her mother, and sat down in her loneliness and wept. Now she thought of the advice of her excellent parent, and how little she had regarded it, what sorrow she had brought upon her, and the anxiety she caused her during her sickness. "Oh, that I had been more obedient, and appreciated her worth!" she exclaimed in an agony of feeling; and she retired to rest to lose her sorrow in the arms of sleep.

Clara occupied the house in which her mother died some few months, occasionally doing some fine sewing. When her sisters had completed their trades, they all kept house, and lived comfortably. Time passed on, and the young women with trades had worked hard and laid by a little money. Their habits were noticed by two brothers who were in business for themselves, and had accumulated a little property by industry and economy, and they offered themselves to the young women, who accepted, and the girls became the happy wives of virtuous and kind-hearted men.

Clara now went to reside with one of her sisters, and was obliged to do most of her work in the kitchen, for the wife continued to do something at her trade, whenever a friend brought in a garment. She thus materially assisted her husband; and while they both exerted themselves it could not be otherwise than they should prosper.

Though her sister did all she could for her, Clara seemed to be unhappy. She probably felt she had done wrong in not going to a trade when her mother so urgently requested her. Indeed, she expressed her regret to her sister. If she had been less proud and more obedient, she might have been as pleasantly situated herself. She felt that she had thought too much of her name and what people would say, especially those young women who now did not care a fig for her, or, if she were in the utmost need, would not raise a finger, or go a rod, to render her assistance. She might have been the happy partner of a young man who had once solicited her hand, but who, on being rejected, doubtless blessed his stars, and found a devoted wife and an agreeable companion in the person of Jane Carlton, the young woman once so lightly esteemed by Clara, but a pattern of industry and moral worth, though in humble circumstances. To see her sisters and some of her companions she once passed with scorn, become so pleasantly and happily situated in life, was calculated to leave no pleas-

ant reflection on the mind of Clara. She saw and she
realized what she had lost by her proud spirit, and it
was not to be wondered at that she was unhappy, that
she was sour and morose in her disposition, and that
all the little children ran from her trembling with fear.

Clara had now arrived at the age of thirty-five ; but by
the disposition which she had nurtured, and the unpleasant feelings in which she had indulged, she appeared a
great deal older. It was the thought of her former conduct and the course she had pursued in her early years,
when she was too proud to learn a trade, when requested
by one of the best of parents, that preyed so deeply on her
spirits. She had rejected, too, the attentions of two or
three young men who were then starting in life with a
small income, but who were now in good circumstances,
making a handsome living, and were blessed with kind
and happy companions. To realize that all the blessings
of life had once been within her reach and that she had
rejected them, was no agreeable subject to reflect upon.
And she was growing old, and the prospect was that she
would become what she had always despised, and what
she once was certain she should never become — an old
maid. As she thought over the matter day by day, and
saw how rapidly her face was wrinkling, her hair turning gray, her teeth decaying, and the color departing
from her cheeks, she came to the conclusion, if ever her
hand should be solicited in marriage again, to accept of
the very first offer. Any husband would be better than
none, and then the disgrace of dying an old maid would
be destroyed. Clara had so often put on her best dress,
and trimmed up as spruce as possible for the last few
years, if haply she might entrap a beau, that she had
wellnigh despaired of accomplishing her object. But,

"Never despair while there is life," was her motto, and she persevered in her endeavors to obtain the desideratum. Failing in all her efforts, and the years going rapidly by, she at last turned another corner in her life — she reached the age of forty years. During the past fifteen or twenty years, she had resided with her sisters, doing the house-work, and assisting them in various ways, while they supported her. Clara, or, as we ought to call her now, Miss Howel, had become so soured in her disposition and temper, that she would scold the children for some trifling thing, if not give them a slap, and even speak unkindly to her sisters and friends. She had become so disagreeable that very few indeed had any love or sym-pathy for her; and when she went to visit a friend, she generally left in a miff, or gave some one present a se-vere reprimand for some supposed misbehavior. She was a stanch old maid, and had become the butt of rid-icule in the neighborhood, so that a thousand jokes were perpetrated upon her by those who knew her disposi-tion and conduct.

As the years flew by, and the prospect became more slim for her to change her situation and secure a com-panion, the more strenuous were her efforts to appear agreeable to strangers. Whenever she heard of a wid-ower that she could visit, or a gentleman who had passed the meridian of life unmarried, she would contrive to be introduced, or to cross his track with her best appear-ance, so as to attract attention; but all in vain; no one seemed to notice poor Miss Howel, or to care a copper farthing for her.

Time cannot be stayed in its flight, otherwise Clara would never have passed her twenty-fifth birthday; but the tide rolled on, and she was now in her forty-fifth year, and not married; but still she hoped; trimmed her dress; consulted her glass, and endeavored to walk as spry as ever. But Miss Howel was an old maid, and everybody knew it.

One day in her favorite walks she met a gentleman who appeared to be about her own age, who inquired where a neighbor of hers resided. She informed him, while he kindly thanked her, smiled, and went on. "Who knows," thought Clara, "but he is in search of a wife, and merely asked that question as a kind of introduction to me? He is a splendid gentleman! What an eye! What a manly brow! But I will ascertain of Mrs. Foster to-night." In her pleasant reverie, Miss Howel passed on, dreaming of pleasure yet to come.

That night found Clara anxiously inquiring of her neighbor respecting the stranger. Mrs. Foster, who knew her peculiarities, joked her so seriously about getting a husband, that Miss Howel was quite offended, and rose to go out in a pet at the moment the stranger entered the door. He was introduced to Clara as Mr. Jameson, a distant relative of hers. Clara was now full of smiles; she sat down and conversed as rapidly as she was accustomed to, for upwards of an hour, and then departed, after strongly inviting Mr. Jameson to call and see her. The stranger was said to be a single man and quite wealthy. He had travelled much, and been conversant with all classes and conditions of men. He had studied human nature, and could read Clara through and through.

In a day or two he called on Clara, and was free and sociable. She returned his visit; and the story soon spread around the neighborhood that Miss Howel was engaged. The story pleased her not a little; for the

30

anxiety she manifested to have it so, almost made her believe that she had at last found a beau. The glass was consulted every hour, the curling tongs were seldom cold, and pink saucers were in great demand. No stone was left unturned, no time was thought to be lost, when spent in adorning her person and heightening her charms. What is more foolish and contemptible than for women of a certain age to pursue such a course? And yet such cases are not rare. Age seems to give new vigor to their desire for display.

Mr. Jameson appeared to have serious intentions in visiting and receiving the visits of Clara; and when he saw the neighborhood really on tiptoe about it, he did not deny that it was actually so, and that even the wedding-day was appointed. Although Clara had no such intimations from him to that effect, she readily believed what her neighbors said, and actually undertook to make preparations for the ceremony. Mr. Jameson was a little astonished one day, when Miss Howel remarked, "Had we better make any display at the wedding?" But he replied, "Oh, no; we may as well have but a small number present."

"As you think best, my dear," said Clara; "but I should like to disappoint some of our neighbors, who are so inquisitive, and not let them know a lisp about the time. It will be in season for them to know after the ceremony is performed."

The day for the marriage of Miss Howel was appointed. A number of guests had been invited, and the minister had arrived, and every thing was in readiness for the performance of the ceremony but the presence of the bridegroom. Mr. Jameson had left town that afternoon on very urgent business, and was expected to arrive at dusk; but he still lingered. An hour passed and they were fearful lest some accident had befallen him, when presently a young man in great haste appeared at the door, inquiring for Miss Howell. He presented her a letter, and hurried away. She opened it trembling, and began to read its contents, when she gave a shriek, fell, and was hurried to her chamber. In the midst of the confusion, the clergyman took the letter, and, after the excitement had in some measure subsided, read its contents to the company, as follows:

" MISS HOWELL, — Do you recollect some twenty-five or thirty years ago, your hand was solicited in marriage by a young mechanic, and that you ordered him from the house? Do you remember his language to you, that at some future day you would bitterly regret that step? You do remember it, and now I have my revenge. I ask no more. HENRY WATSON."

The assembly were dumb with astonishment. They dispersed, each to his abode, conversing on the strange affair. Some pitied Clara, others condemned, while they all pronounced the revenge a just but a cruel one.

Miss Howell kept her room for a few days; but after that she was seldom seen in company. She lived to the age of about sixty, and died an old maid.

Those who despise work, and turn with disgust from industry, must not expect to prosper. Though they may flourish for a season, the time must come when they will regret their course, and mourn bitterly over their follies. Many a girl has lived in misery and died in poverty, destitute of sympathizing friends, who might have been happy, had numerous friends, and died on the bosom of love and friendship, had she not turned from her young men of worth and industry, because they were poor, and clothed in a coarse exterior. To be sure of success in life, be industrious, let your smiles and your approbation fall as often on the poor as the rich, the humble as the distinguished, and you will gain friends, be respected, and pass your days in peace and happiness.

AN ADVENTURE.

CHAPTER I.

Ye who are tempted to depart
From Virtue's heavenly way,
To whom is held the maddening cup
To lead your hearts astray,
Resolve, as long as reason holds
Her empire in your soul,
You will not touch or look upon
The false and damning bowl.

I WAS riding through the pleasant town of Gorham, in company with a friend, several years since, on a delightful day in autumn. When we had passed the village, and were perhaps a mile beyond, a young woman came rushing into the road from a small dwelling, exclaiming to us — "Stop, sirs, stop." Without uttering another word, she ran back. We instantly stopped our horse, jumped from the chaise, and entered the house. The first scene presented to us was a man with a knife in his hand, swearing vengeance upon a half-frantic woman, who was endeavoring to prevent him from stabbing her, as he was attempting to do. Two or three young children were screaming, while the little furniture was scattered all about the room. Soon as the man saw us, he exclaimed with an oath, "Enter this door, and you are dead men! Be off, or I will run you

30*

through!" Fearing every moment the madman, as he appeared to be, would stab the poor woman to the heart, we made a rush towards him, and before he had an opportunity to carry his threat into execution, we had him secure. The instrument we snatched from his hand, and with the assistance of the young lady, secured him with a rope. Never did a man use more threatening language than he, while we were laboring to prevent him from doing an injury to the woman and ourselves. It was some time after we had secured the wretch, before the lady recovered herself sufficiently to relate the cause of the affair.

Mr. Sentese was her husband, to whom she had been married eighteen or twenty years. For the first few years of her wedded life he had treated her with the utmost kindness, and they had prospered on their little farm. About a dozen years before he commenced the use of ardent spirit, and from that time he was an altered man. The habit of intemperance had been growing upon him, so that it was no uncommon thing to receive abuse from him. He had now been constantly drunk for about a week, and without any provocation, attempted to take the life of his wife. Had not Ellen, her daughter, seen and hailed us as we were passing, she continued, "I have no doubt my life would have been sacrificed."

After hearing the tale of wrong from the lips of the wife and mother, we could not but feel a deep interest in her welfare, and sympathize with the more than fatherless children. What course to pursue, we were not long in deciding. My friend, whom I shall call Mr. T——, went to the village for an officer to arrest the monster, while I remained in the farmhouse.

But very little furniture was found in the rooms, yet every thing looked neat and tidy about the house, which spoke well for Mrs. Sentese. She had managed to keep her children from rags, and also to give them better instruction than could have been expected. Her eldest daughter, Ellen, was quite a pretty miss of some sixteen years, and her behavior on this occasion bespoke an excellent mind. In our communication with her, we found her quite intelligent, but she felt deeply the wound that had been inflicted on the family by the intemperance of her father, as the occasional tears testified.

In the course of an hour Mr. T—— returned with an officer, and the depraved and wretched husband and parent was carried away. We stopped for a short time only, and as we departed from the house, we received the thanks of the mother and all the children. " We will never forget your kindness," said Ellen ; " and if you ever come this way, we shall be happy to have you call and see us."

" Depend upon it, we shall," we replied, and started on our journey, while the mother and children watched us from the door till we had driven out of sight.

It was about two years after the circumstance just related, that Mr. T—— and myself were returning from Standish, when he remarked, " Let us call at the house we stopped at some time since, where they had the trouble with the intemperate husband. As I have never seen or heard from them since, I feel a curiosity to know what has become of them."

" Agreed," said I ; and in a short time our horse was hitched at the door.

We knocked, and presently Ellen appeared. She rec-

ognized us at once, and, after a hearty shake of the hand,
we were politely invited to walk in. The old lady was
as glad as her daughter to see us. They had often wondered why we did not call upon them; "and we have
glorious news to tell you." remarked the mother.
" Since that dreadful affair, Mr. Sentese has become a reformed man. For two years past, I believe, not a drop
of spirit has entered his lips. When he came to himself, and knew what he had done, he could hardly believe it, and from that time he resolved never to touch
another glass of rum, and he has sacredly kept his resolution. He has been one of the best of husbands and
fathers ever since. He works hard every day, and now
we have all the necessaries of life. Perhaps you have
noticed the difference in the appearance of our rooms.
We do not look so poverty-stricken as we did two years
ago. O gentlemen, we cannot feel too thankful for
your timely assistance! Had you not come in as you
did, how differently might the affair have terminated!"

Just at this time, Mr. Sentese entered the room. When
we were introduced to him, with tears in his eyes, he regretted the course he formerly pursued, and thanked
God that he had become another man. Together we
remained more than an hour, and were about taking
our departure, fearing we should not return home till
late, when he strongly urged us to remain for the night.
We refused at first, but when Ellen and her mother
seemed so anxious for us to stop with them, we finally
concluded to let Mr. Sentese put up our horse. We
never passed a more agreeable time, and in no strange
house were we ever so much at home.

As we retired for the night, Mr. T—— said to me,

"What a beautiful girl Ellen has become! So free and easy in her manners: so artless, and yet so dignified!" To which I could not but assent.

In the morning, Ellen arose early and prepared breakfast, of which we heartily partook, at the same time engaging in pleasant conversation. It was two or three hours after breakfast before we were ready to start, and then my friend and Ellen did not seem to get half through with what they had to say.

Riding slowly along, I found Mr. T—— often in a brown study. He confessed that he had been peculiarly struck with the appearance of the young lady.

"But this wont do," said I, "for you are engaged to Miss ——."

"I know it, but how can I help it? She appears so amiable, besides being so beautiful. I must confess I love her."

"You will soon forget her."

"Perhaps not. She has made a deep impression on my mind, there is no dispute about it."

Thus conversing, we jogged along, enjoying the varied scenery in the wood, till we arrived at Portland.

Not many months passed before my friend T—— was married to Miss ——, and in a short time after, he left his native city to do business in another place.

CHAPTER II.

At home — abroad — thy constant love,
  With influence divine,
Like to a flame from heaven above
  Will all around me shine :
And should a cloud of sorrow rise,
  To shade life's blissful day,
Thy love will brighten all the skies,
  And drive the storm away.

PROUT'S NECK! who has not visited this delightful place ? A dozen miles from Portland, through one of the pleasantest woods in the world, this neck is a retreat for all the lovers of the grand and the beautiful in nature. The huge rocks and sandy beaches, with the sea stretching far away in the distance, present a scene that no admirer of God's works can gaze upon and not feel emotions of pleasure. We love to visit Prout's Neck — ask the Libbys and old Prout himself if we don't — for there we spend many a pleasant and profitable hour. Beckett and myself, when wearied with editorial and city life, often take our guns or our lines, and direct our course to the Neck, feeling all the better for the jaunt.

One beautiful day last summer, as we were riding leisurely along, towards the residence of old Prout, our guns in the chaise, loaded and capped, ready for execution should we see any thing worth firing at, we discovered a large bird on an out-building. Seizing my gun, I jumped from the chaise and hastened towards the creature. When within gunshot, I discharged my piece, and down fell the bird. A woman who lived in the first house came out and inquired what I had shot. As I showed her the bird, she looked up smiling, and said, "Have I not seen you before?"

"I cannot say. Your countenance looks familiar to me."

"Isn't your name Mr. ——?"

"That is my name."

"Why, sir, how glad I am to see you. Don't you know me?"

"I'm sure I do not."

"My name was Ellen Sentese before I was married."

At once I recognized her. Five years had altered her a little, but she had the same sweet voice and pleasant look. Requesting friend Beckett to wait a few moments, I stepped into the house, when Ellen informed me that she had been married about three years. "I lived in Gorham," said she, "with my parents, until I removed with my husband to Bath, three years ago, where he was in business. He thought that he should prefer a farm, and that it would be better for his health than to remain longer in trade, accordingly, about four months since, he quit his place, and but recently removed here."

"Are you pleased with your new situation?" I inquired.

"Very much. I can have a view of the salt water from our back window, and that is always pleasant to me; and you see we are pretty well supplied with delightful trees. This is a beautiful situation."

"So I think. But how are your parents?"

"Quite well. Mother's health has not been remarkably good for the last year or two; but she keeps about; and father is as healthy as ever, and in good spirits, too. Ever since he left off drinking, he has been another man. He is as kind a father as one could wish to have. Yes-

terday father and mother were here and spent the day.
It was the first time they have been here since we removed from Bath.   They are delighted with the place."

"But your husband I don't know; where is he?"

"He has gone over to Mr. Libby's, and will return
very soon.   I think you have seen him."

"I have no doubt you have a good husband."

"There never was a better one.   He was a widower
when I married him.   That little girl sitting in the
rocking-chair is a child by his first wife, and a beautiful
thing she is.   I don't see but I love her as well as I do
my own child.   Mary, go and see the gentleman.   Go,
don't be bashful, dear."

The little thing came slowly along.   I took up the
child, which was indeed a fine one.

"What is your name?" I inquired.

"Mary T——," said she.

"Mary T——, did I understand her?"

"Yes," said Ellen.

"Is your husband any relation to my old friend, Mr.
T——?"

"It is the same."

At that moment Mr. T—— made his appearance,
and never was I more pleased to see an individual.   I
had not seen him before for several years, and knew not
till then that his former wife was not living.   He
briefly related to me the incidents of his life since we
parted five years before.   He lived with his first wife
but about two years, when consumption, that disease so
prevalent in this climate, carried her off.   She was
every thing a woman could be, and Mr. T—— loved her
tenderly and affectionately.   To repair his loss, he knew
not where to look, excepting to Miss Sentese — as much

like his wife as two beings could be. For this purpose, he paid a visit to Gorham, was kindly received, his request granted, and he again became a happy man. Tired of mercantile life, he purchased a farm, where he hoped to enjoy himself with his family. After spending half an hour in pleasant conversation with these friends, I left them, assuring them that I should often call at their house — it being directly on the road to Prout's Neck, my favorite resort.

No wonder Beckett exclaimed, as I jumped into the chaise, " I thought you had concluded to spend the day in the house ! Who in the world did you find there that you were acquainted with ? "

The whole story was immediately told him, as we proceeded to the Neck. We enjoyed ourselves in gunning and fishing, and returned at night, with better spirits, to engage in the turmoils of business.

It is seldom I go to Prout's Neck when I do not call at the house of Mr. T——. I always find Ellen the same cheerful and agreeable woman.

31

THE TWO APPRENTICES.

Temptations thicken as we yield,
  And seem less fatal too;
And every step in uice we take,
  'Tis easier to pursue.
Once past the bounds of virtuous life,
  Our feet will swiftly glide,
Till we are borne with rapid force
  Down, down destruction's tide.

"I SHALL have as many favors as you, Bill, and get along as comfortably, if I do occasionally provoke the old man."

"No, Dick, I think not. Mr. Porter is a man who says but little, yet he knows when we are faithful to him and perform our duty as we ought, and will remember it when we ask him a favor."

"That's what you always say; but I know better. Do you suppose he knew that I took a half-day when he was absent? or that he thinks more highly of you for sticking to your work?"

"Whether he knows or not, I know I did my duty, and if he ever finds it out, I shall not be censured. I shall always endeavor to perform my duty."

"And a big fool you are, Bill, for that. I intend to enjoy myself as often as I can; but I don't think there is any wrong in taking an hour's time, working as hard as we do; and as often as I get an opportunity, I shall go away."

"I shall not, but will endeavor to discharge my duty, and then no fault can be found."

"I tell you what you are after, Bill; it is to curry favor with the old man in hopes to be benefited by it; but I tell you you are deceiving yourself, and so you will find out in the end. You will succeed no better than I shall."

"You wrong me, Dick. I wish to do only what is right—what I promised to do when Mr. Porter took me to learn the cabinet-maker's trade. You know I do no more than my duty."

"Your same old story, Bill. But I don't want to hear such stuff. I will have a scrape, now and then, and the old man shall be no wiser for it."

Richard Jackson and William Leighton were the apprentices of Mr. Porter. They were nearly of the same age, and had been in the employ of Mr. Porter for about two years, learning the trade of a cabinet-maker. Richard was a headstrong, unprincipled boy, who was determined to be under no restraint. Whenever he was checked in any wrong course, or his errors were pointed out to him by his master, instead of being sorry for the past, and striving to do better for the future, he would make some unkind reply, or grumble a long while to himself. If he should be reproved for using a profane word, he would say, just loud enough for his companion to hear, "I will swear as much as I please," or, "It is none of your business what I do," and the like. Having lost his father at an early age, he had been brought up by a too indulgent mother, who had but little if any government over her boy, and so he was suffered to go on unrestrained in evil paths, contracting bad habits, until his mother had obtained for him a situation with Mr. Porter.

William was a kind-hearted, obedient lad. It was not often that he was reproved by his master; but sometimes, when influenced by his companion, he would forget his duty and do a wrong act. But when he was checked in his course, he would manifest his sorrow by his looks, and sometimes the tear would fall from his eye, while he told Richard that he would not be guilty of such a thing again. It was his general endeavor to give satisfaction to his master, and to do nothing behind his back which he would not approve if he were presnt. Although he was frequently sneered at by his fellow-apprentice, and called a simpleton and a fool, he heeded it not, but made the interest of his master his study. William had been brought up in a good family. His parents spared no pains to train him to virtue, leaving on his mind the impression that truth and integrity will finally triumph over vice and error. And this was the doctrine he endeavored to teach his companion, who derided and laughed at him for his folly.

One day when Mr. Porter was absent from town, a gentleman called at the shop, stating that he had a little job which he wished to have done immediately, as he must leave the place that night.

"We can't do it ourselves," said Richard; "and Mr. Porter is away."

"Oh, yes, we can, Mr." said William; "I know we can do it."

"We cannot, sir," said the other; "they'll do it for you in the shop below;" and then he turned to William, saying in a whisper, "What a fool you are! Let the man go. I aint going to work myself to death for nothing."

The gentleman had started for the door, when William ran to him and said, "If you will leave your job, it shall be done, I assure you."

"I must have it to-night," said the man.

"Walk in and tell me just what you want; I will assure you of its being done, and to your satisfaction."

The gentleman gave the direction to the apprentice, and left the shop. He had no sooner gone than Richard let loose his temper on his companion. "I shall not help you," said he, "for you had no business to engage the job. I never saw so big a simpleton in all my life. To-day we might have had some fine sport, and no one would have been the wiser for it, and now you have taken in a plaguy job."

"But Mr. Porter would have taken in the work had he been at home," said William, "and I feel bound to look out for his interest, and I always shall. Whether you help me or not, as I have promised, the work shall be done to-night."

So William took hold of the job; he kept close to his bench, spending but a few minutes to his dinner, and just before dark he had the work completed. When the gentleman called, he appeared well pleased with the workmanship, praised the lad for fulfilling his promise, and paid him two dollars for the job.

"I like industry and punctuality in a boy," said the stranger, "and, as these traits appear to be in you I know you will succeed."

As a mark of his esteem, he handed him twenty-five cents for his own use, and departed. He had no sooner

31

gone, than Richard said, "Let us keep the two dollars for spending money. The old man will never know any thing about it."

"By no means," replied William; "I did the job myself in the time belonging to Mr. Porter, and the money is his and he shall have it."

"But he wont thank you for it. If you are not a fool you will keep it."

"It would be the same as stealing if I should take it; and that sin I will never be guilty of."

"No, it would not. Sometimes the old man has sent me to buy articles for him, and I have kept part of the change, a few cents, perhaps, to buy apples or nuts with, and I will do the same again. As long as I buy things to eat with his money, it is not wrong."

"Most certainly it is, Richard, unless you can get his consent. It is something I would never do."

As Mr. Porter would not return till the next day, William folded the two dollars in a piece of paper and put it in one corner of his pocket, so that he might be sure and not lose it. He and Richard retired together but as William had worked hard, he soon fell asleep. His companion, as soon as he discovered this, slid easily from the bed and took the money from the pocket of the faithful boy and hid it in the crevice of the chimney, and then as softly went to his bed again.

The next day, as soon as they were dressed, William felt in his pocket for the two dollars, and discovered that the money was gone. With tears in his eyes, he accused Richard of taking it, "for," said he, "the last thing I did before going to bed was to look at the money, and no one has been here but you."

"You are a liar," said Richard, with an oath; "I have not seen your money; you have probably misplaced it, and now you accuse me of stealing!"

William felt in each of his pockets, turned them inside out, felt again, and then turned over his clothes in his trunk, looked about the floor, and everywhere he could think of, but without success. "Now tell me, Dick, have you not got that money?"

"Have I not told you once or twice? Yet you accuse me of stealing. It is more than likely you have spent it yourself, and the old man ought to know it."

"I shall tell him myself, when he comes home."

"But he wont believe you. He'll give you a jawing, and more than likely turn you away. I would rather keep it a secret."

William went to work with a sad heart. He had earned two dollars for his master, by working hard, and it was lost. The thought would sometimes enter his mind that he had better conceal it from his master; but then he would say to himself that it was his duty to let him know about it.

When Mr. Porter came home, the faithful lad related the whole affair, but he was not censured. "Perhaps you may yet find the money," said his master; "but if you should not, don't let it trouble you."

William did not tell Mr. Porter that he suspected that his companion had stolen it, although he had no doubt in his own mind that such was the case.

A year or more had passed away since the two dollars were taken, when one night Richard said to his companion, "Bill, what do you suppose I am going to do to-morrow?"

"I'm sure I cannot tell; but I hope nothing wrong."

"I'm going to leave the old man. I am tired of working in the shop. I can get better wages in Boston or New York, and I am determined to go to one place or the other."

"A foolish idea, Dick; you had better remain where you are. Here you have friends, and if you are sick or destitute you know where to go; but if you leave, you will be among strangers; and if you are successful and get business, you may not turn out well. You certainly cannot get a better place, or find a better master."

"I shall go to-morrow, Bill, and you are a fool for staying here. I can get double the wages in Boston, and can be my own man."

"But you will be a runaway boy, and will always be ashamed to come home and see your friends, even if you should succeed and prosper."

"I'm tired of this place, and shall never care about returning. But don't tell the old man where I am gone, for he might take a notion to send after me." ·

William advised him, with all the arguments in his power, not to think of leaving his place, but it was of no avail. The next day came, and Richard had left his place. Mr. Porter simply remarked, "I am sorry for the boy; he will not find such good friends away; and he may get into bad company, and be ruined."

That week, on reckoning up what he had received and paid away, Mr. Porter missed six or eight dollars, and how to account for it he did not know, unless Richard had been dishonest and taken it away. But, as he had no proof, and did not know but he might have lost it himself, he said nothing about it. The place of Richard was immediately supplied by another youth, and the change was not regretted by William or any member of the family.

As the years passed away, William continued faithful to his employer, passing his leisure hours in reading or writing, and thus improving his mind. Young Leighton became one-and-twenty, the age when all apprentices are free from their masters, and are at liberty to go where they please, and to work for whom they feel disposed. As Mr. Porter had become attached to William he made a proposition to enter into full copartnership, and carry on business together. This he was pleased to do; but his passion for study had so increased, that after a few month's work, he relinquished his business, and gave his whole attention to study. A friend of Leighton, an able lawyer, persuaded him to study in his office, which he consented to do. He possessed a fine, discriminating mind, and improved rapidly in his studies. In a year or two, he was admitted to the bar, and was pronounced by good judges a man of talents, well versed in his profession. As a pleader or a counsellor, few were his superiors, and his business rapidly increased.

Leighton had practised at the bar some five or six years, when he was put up as a candidate for representative to Congress. He met with a little opposition, but was elected by a large majority. In the House of Representatives, he did honor to himself and to the district whose united voice had sent him there. Few spoke better or more to the purpose; yet he was modest and unassuming. He knew when to speak, and how to address the assembly, and thus won laurels to which hundreds aspired, yet died without winning.

During a congressional session, a gentleman stopped at the boarding-house of Mr. Leighton, and informed him that a man who was in prison was very anxious to see him, and urgently requested that he might call. The first leisure hour he had, the stranger accompanied him to the cell, where, haggard and dirty, was chained a human being.

"Sir," said the prisoner, "I learn that you reside in S——. That is my native place. I am now under sentence of death for highway robbery. It is right that I should suffer; but I am among strangers; no one knows me, no one cares for me. Soon I shall receive the just deserts of a life of crime. But I had a mother once in S——, and also a friend. My object in sending for you is this: if my mother is living, and has heard of my life of crime, I want her to know that I died a penitent; that her counsels and admonitions are remembered in my last hours. But I pray she may never know the end to which I come. Pray, sir, keep this a secret. My mother's name is Jackson. Do you know of such a woman?"

"What, widow Mary Jackson?"

"Yes, sir; do you know her?"

"And are you her son Richard?"

"I am indeed, sir."

"My dear man," said Leighton, grasping the prisoner by the hand and weeping; "can it be possible? Is this Richard Jackson?" and the tears fell fast.

"Sir, you astonish me," said the prisoner. "Have you seen me before? Have I robbed you? O sir, tell me!"

"I was your early friend, your fellow-apprentice, William Leighton."

"O God! am I dreaming? Can it be?" and the poor man clasped him, weeping like a child.

After a few moments, Jackson exclaimed, "Have I come to this? have I come to this?" and he wept still more. "Oh, that I had taken your excellent advice, when you besought me to look out for my master's interest when I was a boy. Would to Heaven I had never left my excellent place!" continued he, still weeping; and it was a long time before he could restrain his tears. At last, Jackson briefly stated his career of vice. When he left his master, he went to Boston, where he worked for a few weeks, spending his money with idle and vicious companions as fast as he earned it. Thence he started for New York. Here he commenced work again, with the determination to keep aloof from bad company, but he had a vicious propensity; he contracted bad habits; became intemperate, and was dishonest. He had been in jail two or three times for petty theft, and afterwards served two or three years in the state prison. He had now become hardened in sin and lived by fraud and plunder. From one degree of crime to another he passed, stealing whenever he found an opportunity, till at last, he took to the highways, and was finally apprehended, had his trial, and was condemned to suffer for his crime on the gallows. He confessed that he stole the two dollars from Leighton's pocket when he was asleep, and also took from eight to ten dollars from Mr. Porter before he ran away. "Such has been my course," said he; "but I can censure none but myself. You gave me good advice; you set an excellent example before me; but I heeded it not, and now I receive the just deserts of my folly. My poor mother! how she will grieve when she hears of the death of her erring son! but may God sustain her."

Mr. Leighton did little else but weep as his early friend

related his course of vice, his deeds of darkness ; he could now only point him to his God, and bid him seek that forgiveness from above of which he now stood in so much need.

Till the day of his execution, Mr. Leighton was a constant visitor to the cell of the prisoner. He never conversed with him, when he did not regret his vicious practices, his spurning good advice, and leaving his kind employer. During the last hour of his life, by Jackson's particular request, Mr. Leighton was with him. He addressed a few words to the spectators, besought them to live a virtuous life, and while young not to take a farthing that belonged to another, and never, on any consideration, to leave a good place and a good master. "This," said he, "and I wish all the young men in the land could hear me, — this has been my ruin. Had I listened to good advice, had I obeyed my master, I should never have come to this ignominious end."

He bid adieu to his friend, thanked him for his kindnesses, invoked the blessing of Heaven upon him and his aged mother, spent a few moments in prayer, rose, and was launched into eternity.

Young men, for no trifling cause, should leave their employers. The hope of doing better and becoming their own masters is a trifling excuse. Where one succeeds better in the end, hundreds are lost. Bad habits are indulged, injurious connections are formed, and a thousand evils contracted which eventually prove their ruin. Seek your master's interest, obey his just commands, and you will never regret this course to the latest period of life.

DON'T BE DISCOURAGED.

In sorrow yield not to despair,
　Or be in grief depressed,
Nor let the plants of anguish bear
　Their fruit within your breast.
Look up in doubt, look up in fear —
　Joy gathers in the sky;
And when Misfortune's storms are near,
　You'll see a blessing nigh.

EDWARD HARRIS had been in business for himself several years. For the first twelvemonth and more, he succeeded better than he had anticipated, and was able to pay his creditors, and obtain a larger amount of goods. When Edward started in business for himself, he had no other capital than an honest heart and a virtuous life, yet he found no difficulty in obtaining what stock he needed. What young Harris made the first year, he lost by bad debts the second, and when his notes became due, it was with difficulty that he met them promptly. He was often obliged to hire money of the brokers, paying a large premium, so as to preserve his credit and meet his demands. In this way Edward went behind-hand, and every month his affairs were in a worse condition, till at last he was obliged to have his notes protested. It was a severe stroke to the young man, and it lay heavy upon his mind. Sometimes it was with dif-

32

ficulty that he closed his eyes at night. Having a young
family dependent upon him, he felt his situation more
keenly; but he had the satisfaction of knowing that he
had done the best in his power to succeed in business.
When his creditors found their notes against him had
been protested, some of them wrote him unfeeling letters, saying he might have known his situation before
purchasing goods, and that he should have managed his
affairs so as to secure them.   He wrote in reply, that he
should still exert himself in their behalf, and if they
would wait patiently and not put him to unnecessary
trouble and expense, he would endeavor to pay them
every cent. A few of his creditors believed him to be an
honest but an unfortunate young man, and they agreed
not to trouble him, but wait until he was able to deal
justly by them.   Other creditors were not so kind; they
censured him severely, and demanded immediate payment, and to secure themselves they sent their demands
to lawyers, instructing them to attach whatever property
they could get at.   Edward was exceedingly annoyed
by the sheriffs, constables, and lawyers, who picked up
every dollar's worth of property they could lay their
hands upon, charging him with costs, after selling it for
half its value.

When Edward failed, he was owing a broker several
hundred dollars, for which he was paying at the rate
of from thirty to forty per cent.   None of his creditors
were more alarmed than this man.   Every few days he
called upon young Harris, to inquire if he could do
any thing for him; he would take twenty dollars, five
dollars, or any thing that he could spare, and endorse
it on his duebill. "You know I have always accommodated you," said he, "and let you have money when you

wanted it; and money, you know, is not like goods on which you make a profit; and you must not let me lose. Haven't you some security that you can give me?"

Edward assured the broker that he should not lose by him in the end, if he would be patient; but as for security, he had none to give. But the moneyed man was not satisfied; week after week he called upon him, till at last the young merchant was obliged to tell him, that unless he would be patient he could never pay him a cent. As soon as he was able to do any thing for him, he would not be backward, he assured him, but pay him a little at a time. The broker murmured, spoke of it as being a hard case, when he had been so very accommodating, but still was not disposed to let the poor fellow alone, but must needs torment him by reminding him of his debt every time he had an opportunity. He seemed fearful lest Edward should forget the obligation he was under to him, for his unparalleled kindness and generosity in loaning him money from time to time, at the rate of thirty or forty per cent. .

What course now to pursue, it was difficult for Edward to determine. If he had a friend to assist him, he might do well; but his credit was gone, and he could not purchase goods. While settling up his affairs, as a relief to his mind, he would take a walk out of the city into the woods, and listen to the singing of the birds, or watch the little stream that murmured along. For a while he would forget his situation in viewing the beauties of nature.

Although Edward was in such low circumstances, he did not suffer himself wholly to despair. At times he would look to the future, and fancy he saw it pregnant with blessings. To yield to discouraging circumstances he had ever been taught was not the policy of true wisdom. If he were alone in the world, he often said, he could bear his misfortunes with more fortitude; but a wife and one or two children were dependent upon him and must necessarily suffer with him.

One day, as Edward was taking his accustomed walk in the woods, he strayed further than usual. Being weary, he sat upon an old stump beside a beautiful stream. It was a delightful spot; birds were twittering around him; winds were sighing through the trees, and the pleasant stream was running at his feet. For a long time he sat listening to the birds, or watching the little squirrels that ran about the trees, when his attention was called to an aged oak. Its size and venerable appearance attracted his attention. He walked towards it, and at that moment saw a squirrel run into its nest at the foot of the tree. Taking his cane, he ran it into the hole and pried up some of the dirt. The stick struck against what he thought to be a small flat stone, which he endeavored to pry up. He thus amused himself in digging, when, to his astonishment, what he concluded to be a rock, proved to be a small iron box, very much corroded by age. In a short time, he dug it up. By its weight he thought it must contain something valuable. With a large rock, he easily broke it open, and lo! out rolled a multitude of gold and silver coins of various sizes; besides, there was a piece of silver plate on which was rudely carved these words; "2d house in —— Street, east side — west corner of cellar: 1743." Recovering from his surprise, Edward collected the contents of the box in his handkerchief, and walked towards home. He said nothing about the treasure he had found, which on being counted amounted to about three hundred dollars. It was very acceptable to him at this time. Having but recently failed, he had not money sufficient to carry him through the winter; now he concluded he had enough to supply him with the necessaries of life until he should find some employment whereby he could gain a livelihood. Besides, what was he to understand by the inscription on the silver plate? The street he well knew, though it had taken another name within a half-century; but how could he distinguish the "second house" from the numerous dwellings in the street? From the oldest citizens he inquired as to the age of the several houses in the street, and was pointed to one on the east side that was as old as any house in the place. That must be the one alluded to, thought Edward, and in the cellar of that house he did not doubt treasures were hidden. The owner of the building was a gentleman in moderate circumstances, who had no desire to sell it, he learned, unless he received all it was worth and a little more. But Edward was not in a condition to purchase. He had but little money, was insolvent, and out of business. To mention what he knew to another would be to lose the treasure, if indeed it was there. Upon this course he resolved, as soon as it should be expedient, and he could arrange his matters, to enter into business again, be prudent and industrious, and at some future time purchase the house.

With energy, who ever was a drone in the world? With a determination to do something, who ever has groped his way along in dust and shadows? Energy is every thing to a man in this life. It is a much better capital than dollars, and in the end is more profitable. With all his discouragements, with a debt of a thousand dollars and more on his hands, with harsh treatment from creditors, lawyers, sheriffs, and constables, Edward did not yield to discouragement, did not lie trembling on his back. He went forth to battle with Discouragement and Prejudice, and nobly did he conquer. With a capital of less than a hundred dollars, he commenced business again, but not in his old stand; for his former landlord had lost thirty or forty dollars by him before, and he swore he should never have another store of him. He commenced business — and what was the result? In a year or two, he settled off with his creditors — the brokers and all — sheriffs' fees and constables' fees into the bargain. He had again established his credit, and was rapidly collecting property. In a few years more, he was in hopes to be able to purchase the house in ―― Street, on which his eye had been placed since his good fortune. In the fall of another year, he had purchased a large stock of goods for the winter trade, which had the appearance of being brisk and profitable. Edward had returned to town but a few days, when one night he was aroused from his slumbers by the cry of fire. When he arrived at the scene of destruction, it proved to be his own store in flames. Mr. Harris was as cool and collected as one could be under these circumstances; for but a portion of his stock was insured. Not a hundred dollars' worth was saved from his store, and the building was wholly consumed. It was a severe blow to Edward, more especially when he ascertained that his policy of insurance had expired but a day or two previously, and that he was not worth a dollar in the world. This was the second time he had been reduced and lost all; but his noble spirit did not leave him. He still looked to the future, and commenced business again, just as soon as he could obtain a store. To be sure he had but little to trade upon, and was largely in debt. Unlike many in such circumstances, he did not ask the sympathy of others, or whine about his irreparable loss. He felt he had something left yet, and when he started again he was as cheerful as ever. His creditors, to whom he made known his loss and his inability to meet his notes as he expected, generously wrote him that he might suit his own convenience, about paying them. In doing business again, Edward was prudent as could he be, making the most of the money he received. For the first few months after his loss by fire, he did as well as one could reasonably expect, and was regaining rapidly the amount of property destroyed. One afternoon as he was trading with a customer, he was waited upon by a sheriff, who informed him that he had instructions to attach his stock, at the same time showing him the writ. Edward was thunderstruck, and could hardly believe the officer, when he was informed that his property had been attached by the instruction of one of his creditors, one, too, who had promised to wait for his debt in consideration of his serious loss by fire. To see his property consumed to ashes, was nothing in comparison with this unfeeling act. He could not pay the debt at present, so he informed the officer; but the latter gentleman was only performing his duty, he said, and must, therefore, take charge of his stock. When a man is reduced, friends are scarce; and when Mr. Harris asked one or two of his neighbors for a little assistance, to keep his goods from being sacrificed, they all had too much on their hands already to grant him a favor. Seeing he could not prevent the goods from being sacrificed he let the officer do his duty, who put a keeper into the store. In a few days the goods were advertised for sale, the handbill stating they were taken on execution. Under the hammer of the auctioneer the articles were sold, one by one, to the highest bidder, bringing at most one-third less than they were worth. The consquence was, the mean and wicked creditor received his pay in full for his debt, while Edward was again thrown out of employment, and his honorable creditors had not received a farthing.

What could Mr. Harris do now? Three times had he started in business, and lost all he had accumulated. Should he try again? " Yes," said his stout heart, as he looked upon his wife and children ; " I will try again and keep trying, till I die. Never will I sit down in discouragement so long as I can move a limb, and stir about." Following up his good resolution, for the fourth time, our young merchant commenced business, and in a smaller way than he had ever begun before. He could not muster together ten dollars when he started, but still his capital did not consist in silver and gold. He commenced with this trifle, and, by prudence, he continued to maintain his family and hold his own for the first year. He had made a living, and that was all. At this rate, Edward thought he should never collect money together sufficient to purchase the house in —— Street, providing it could be bought ; but " Perseverance conquers all things," being his motto, he went forward, still trying to do better, and not at all dampened in his zeal at his trifling success. Two more years passed away, and Edward had made a little headway. He had settled most of his debts, and was worth clear of the world at least fifty dollars, and his credit was tolerably good. About this time he noticed that the house on which he had had his eye for several years past, was advertised for sale or to let. Losing not a moment, he sought the advertiser and bargained with him for the use of the house one year, with the understanding that he should have an opportunity of purchasing it after that time if he should be able and was pleased with the house. Within one week Edward had removed into the old house —the house to which his eye had been turned for so long a period. No one but himself had seen the plate that he found in the woods, which he now examined again and read as before, " 2nd house in —— Street, east side —west corner of cellar: 1743."

In a few days Edward commenced his search, but he found nothing that appeared to indicate the treasure he supposed to be buried there. He had dug over all the western side of the cellar, and gave it up as a useless task, when the thought struck him that in the wall something might be hidden, and the more he looked the more he was convinced that he was right in his conjectures. He succeeded in removing a large stone, behind which was a cavity, and there he soon discovered the treasure. Something like two thousand dollars in gold and silver were brought to light, having been buried three-quarters of a century at least. Edward made inquiries for a long time to ascertain to whom this money properly belonged, for he did not feel like making use of it himself until he had left no effort untried to find the owner. Not being successful, he appropriated the money and purchased the old house. As his business had increased, and no further drawbacks had been experienced, he was in comfortable circumstances, and in a fair way to become wealthy.

Who that has failed, or been burnt out, and lost all, will fold his hands and cease his efforts?

THE YOUNG MERCHANT.

Striving ever, you will gain
 Wisdom, virtue, and renown,
And an excellence attain,
 Better than a kingly crown.
It will keep you by the side
 Of the noble and the wise,
And your life will be a guide,
 Leading thousands to the skies.

" What do you think about accommodating this young man?" said Mr. Pelby, a bank director, to his associates, on discount day. "He appears to be sound, and the amount is but trifling."

"I don't know," replied Mr. Barrow, a small, gray-eyed man, who looked as if he were born to skin flints and make money by the operation, "I don't know about it. We have lost so much in years past, that I think we better not discount it. The interest on a hundred dollars is but trifling. What do you say, Mr. Ormard?"

"'Tisn't worth talking about — so small a sum. I wouldn't be bothered with it."

"Perhaps," said Pelby, "it may be of great assistance to the young man at this time, if he could have the money."

"Let him go to the broker's, then," said Mr. Jameson, a fat man, who had made his money by grinding the poor and shaving notes; "let him go to the broker's, if he wants the money so much. You know we have sufficient funds there and we shall realize four times as much."

"For my part," said Barrow, "I don't think it worth while to be troubled with small notes; they are of but very little consequence, even if they should be promptly paid."

"True," replied Pelby; "but Mr. Somers spoke to me about the note, and wished I might say a word in his favor; but, on the whole, I think we may as well not accept it. Here, Mr. Jake," addressing the cashier, and handing him the note, "tell Mr. Somers we are short of money to-day and cannot discount."

Mr. Somers was a young man of sterling integrity. He had recently commenced business for himself, with but little capital, and therefore felt the need of some assistance. He had no father or rich relatives to draw upon, or exert themselves in his behalf; and when an opportunity presented for the safe investment of a little · money, he made strong efforts to obtain it through the banks, but was seldom accommodated. It is exceedingly difficult for a person with no capital to succeed well in business, especially with no wealthy friends to render him assistance. So Somers knew by experience; but he was industrious and persevering, and determined to do something. He saw a chance to make money by investing about a hundred dollars, and it was on this occasion that he had spoken to Mr. Pelby, and dropped his note in the bank. He was fearful of the result, and when the cashier informed him that his note was not accepted he turned away with feelings rather indignant towards the directors, but determined that he would obtain the money. He called at the broker's, paid three or four per cent a month, took the amount, and made the purchase. In a few weeks the broker was paid, but the interest accumulated so fast, that his profits were not so great as he had anticipated. Still Somers was not discouraged. He found it exceedingly difficult at times to raise the money that was absolutely necessary for the payment of his notes, but, by prudence and economy, and occasionally calling on the broker, he worried through the first year of his mercantile life. In taking an account of his stock, he found that he had actually made a little besides his living and the few losses he had sustained by bad debts. He commenced again with renewed zeal, determined still to persevere, with the hope that before another twelvemonth he should be free from all embarrassment.

Once more Somers concluded that he would make an attempt to get a note discounted. He called upon Mr. Pelby, told him his situation, and asked him to use his influence in his behalf at the bank on the next day.

"I will do all I can, Mr. Somers," said the director. "Will the note be paid promptly?"

"Certainly, sir."

"Have you a good name on the note?"

"I think I have."

"Perhaps we can accommodate you."

Somers also called upon Mr. Barrow, who promised to use his influence, and thought there was no doubt but he could obtain the money.

The directors had assembled in the bank, and, among others, Somers' note was produced.

"We had better accept this small note from a worthy young man," said Pelby to his associates.

"Plague on those little notes," said Jameson; "we are eternally bothered by them. Why don't our young men who want a few dollars call upon the brokers? It is their business to accommodate them, not ours."

" So I say," replied Ormand; " we did not open the bank to accommodate every man to a few dollars who may want the amount. We should have nothing else to do."

" Oh, let the young man be accommodated this once," said Pelby; " he is good for the amount, and is working hard to get along."

" Perhaps it may be as well," said Barrow, " but I shall have nothing to say about it."

" 'Tis of no use. Here, cashier; tell the man that it was not possible for us to do any thing for him to-day," said Jameson, handing Mr. Jake the note.

Mr. Somers was disappointed on learning that he could not be accommodated; more especially as he had conversed with two of the directors of the bank, who seemed to be favorably disposed towards him; but he said nothing and went his way, resolving to be diligent in business and surmount all the difficulties in his path, hoping before many months to be relieved from the necessity of asking accommodation at the banks. Somers prospered beyond his expectations. Attentive to his business, and economical in his habits, he won the confidence of others, and received a large share of patronage.

During his second year of business, on taking account of his stock, he ascertained that his profits were larger than on the previous year, and he had found less difficulty in meeting his payments.

From this time, Somers began to prosper; his business increased, and every thing went on smoothly with him; he had no occasion to solicit favors at the bank, and it was

33

easy for him to meet his payments. With his little capital he made safe investments, took advantage of the market, and had quick returns. A great many schemes were presented for his countenance, where large profits were anticipated, but he rejected them all, and preferred to trade in his own certain business than to trust to that which was visionary. Here he was right. While many of his friends failed in business, Somers prospered, and in a few years was considered a safe and substantial merchant.

A pleasant day in summer, as Somers was busy in his store, in stepped Pelby, the old bank director. "I am glad to hear of your prosperity," said he. "I always knew you would succeed in business."

"I have made out thus far better than I had reason to expect. When I started, you know, it was with difficulty that I made my payments; but, persevering and exerting myself, I have prospered."

"If you should ever be in want of money to carry on your business, we should be glad to accommodate you at our bank. We will discount your paper for any amount you may need."

Mr. Somers thanked the director for his offer, and remarked, "When I needed accommodation, you would not oblige me, you remember, although I earnestly solicited it. Now, as I do not stand in need of assistance, you offer it to me."

"It was not my fault; the other directors did not know you, and they seldom discount for strangers. We should be very happy now to do any thing for you."

"There is young Mr. P——, who has just started in business, who, I know, is in need of a little help. Suppose you make him the offer."

"Oh, we don't know any thing about him. He may be one of the most worthy of men, but he is unknown to the directors;" and wishing Mr. Somers good-morning, Pelby walked down the street.

Not a month went by, when passing along one day, Mr. Somers met Mr. Barrow, another bank director, who took him by the hand and smilingly inquired for his health.

"Well, sir, how do you get along these times?" said Mr. Barrow.

"Pretty well, sir."

"Do you need more capital in your business?"

"Oh, no; my credit is good, but I prefer to make cash purchases."

"If you should be in want of money any time, we would be ready to discount your note at the bank. We like to oblige when we know it is safe."

"I don't know as I am in want of accommodation at present."

"Perhaps you will find it to your advantage to invest more capital in your business. We will discount for you any reasonable amount, and should be happy to do so."

Somers thanked him for the offer, but as he passed along could not but reflect on the change that a few years had produced. When poor he had never received a smile or a kind look from Barrow, now he was pleasant and sociable. Once he would not exert himself to render him assistance; now he would do all in his power to help him. Somers had become rich, and, as is the custom of mankind, friends began to flock around him, but he treated them all with respect and kindness.

One morning, Ormand came into his store and purchased a few articles, and freely entered into conversation with Somers. In years past, this gentleman was stiff and taciturn, but now he was talkative, and appeared to feel a deep interest in the welfare of Somers.

"I am glad to hear of your prosperity," said he; "I always knew you would do well from the time you started in business, and have often spoken in your favor. I suppose you have capital enough at present?"

"Yes, as much as I can safely invest."

"If you should be in need of more at any time, you can readily be assisted by calling at our bank. We are always ready to accommodate."

"If I should want to be accommodated I will call, but at present I have as much capital in my business as I need."

After bidding Somers good-morning, the director left.

The young merchant continued to prosper, and his store was the most frequent resort of the bank directors, who, when they ascertained his standing, and knew him to be accumulating property did what they could to help him along. They purchased of him themselves, and often directed customers to his store.

Somers is now one of our most active and wealthy citizens. He does an extensive business, and employs a number of hands. His losses have been small. From an humble beginning, he has risen to his present standing, and is an example of persevering industry to all young men. He was always punctual in his payments, industrious in his habits, and strictly attentive to his business. Let his example be imitated by all youth, and like him they will prosper. From a poor boy, he has become a wealthy man, and now exerts a good influence on all around him. He is kind-hearted and liberal, and yearly distributes of his property to assist those who are poor and needy.

How difficult it is for a young man just starting in business to obtain assistance! If he attempts to obtain help from the bank, not once in a dozen times is he successful. The directors, being men of property, in many cases do not sympathize with him, and will not exert themselves to render him necessary help. So he struggles on for the first few years of his life, and if he happens to fail, as there seems nothing to prevent him, the directors rejoice at their good luck in not having lost by him, when, if they had accommodated him, he would have succeeded and overcome all his troubles. If, in spite of the obstacles thrown in his path, he succeeds and accumulates property, they quickly make his acquaintance, and are ready to do all in their power for him. Such is the way of the world.

33*

A COMMON ERROR.

The shade and the valley,
  Why should they be thine,
Where birds never linger,
  And suns never shine?
Up! forth to the hillside,
  Where buttercups bloom,
And dandelions scatter
  Their gold and perfume,
And blossoms are floating
  Like butterflies' wings,
And the sweetest of songsters
  Right merrily sings.

Do you see yon poor, decrepit old lady, as she slowly
wends her way, the very picture of poverty and misery?
Her home is the almshouse, of which she has been an inmate for more than twenty years. She has but few acquaintances and fewer friends. She answers to the
name of "Old Suke." Her time is spent in knitting or
mending, and occasionally she has permission of absence
from the house for part of a day, when she walks in the
most secluded parts of the town, visits the graveyard,
and then returns to her home and her task. From the
appearance of Old Suke, one would suppose that she had
been born in poverty and obscurity; that kind friends
and acquaintances she never knew; that her life had
been an unbroken series of disappointments and sorrows.
But it was not so. Susan Elder was the only child of

a respectable merchant; her father, fifty years ago, was considered one of the wealthiest men of the town; he was respected and beloved, a man of honor, and exerted a wide influence. Her mother was kind and indulgent, was benevolent to the poor, and took pleasure in visiting the sick and the needy. Their only daughter was a bright and active girl, gay, buoyant, and cheerful. Her infant years were passed in a round of pleasure; indulgent parents bestowed upon her all that the heart could desire, and no wish of hers was ever ungratified. But as Susan grew older, and youthful bloom and gayety were fast verging into maiden comeliness and decision, she became the reverse of what she was in early life; instead of that open, pleasant demeanor, which won so many admirers, she betrayed a proud and haughty spirit. Her father was rich, and this lifted her up so that she looked upon those who had been her companions in childhood, but who were in lower circumstance, as far beneath her. The young men who had attended school with her, played with her, and had been intimate at her father's house, were not her chosen companions now. There was one, Henry Simpson, who had loved Susan from her infancy. They had been associates through life; together they tripped the fields, plucked the flowers, and chased the golden butterfly. The parents of Henry were poor, but worthy and industrious people. Their son had been early put to a trade, and was a good-hearted, kind, and affectionate lad; his conduct secured the approbation of all who knew him.

When Susan first assumed her foolish airs, tossed her head in pride, and denounced the hard-fisted mechanic and brown-faced farmer, Henry would laugh at her folly and occasionally mimic her actions, thinking that by this

course she would be induced to change her disposition,
and again become the pleasant friend, the kind companion, and the cheerful associate.   But vain was his hope.
By degrees, her conduct became insufferable, even to
him, who loved her purely and affectionately.   Opportunities were now sought by Susan to say something to
irritate his feelings and pain his heart.   " Before I would
marry a mechanic or a farmer," she would repeat, " I
would spend my days in a convent.   If ever I marry,
it shall be a man of wealth, noble and high-spirited."
Though Henry loved her ardently, he did not hesitate
to tell her what he thought would be the consequence
of indulging in foolish pride, and her unkind treatment
to him and her friends — to her parents even, who respected and highly esteemed their young friend, and
nothing would have pleased them more than for him to
become their son-in-law.   This was Henry's sole ambition, although he had never divulged it; it was this that
encouraged him in his trade, and made him happy during all his working hours — the hope of some future day
taking Susan to be his own.   From childhood Susan
was his companion by day and his dream by night; and
when he saw the sad change in her, he was miserably
unhappy.   The more he conversed with her, and set
before her the consequences of the course she was pursuing, she seemed the more indifferent to him, and more
inclined to avoid his presence.   It was a foolish idea of
the silly girl, when she neglected and despised such worth
as was ever exhibited in the devoted young man, and
imaged out to herself a lover dressed in gold and lace,
with thousands at his command.   But the idea, even at
that early period, was becoming fashionable, that to labor was not respectable, unless one had a fortune, and

did not depend upon his hands for a support. Such an
opinion has been the ruin of many a female, and is now
working sad havoc among the would-be ladies of our
country. Every day they speak contemptuously of labor,
and by their example and influence endeavor to bring reproach upon those who work for a support. It is seen
in every fashionable party, in almost every merchant's
house, and even by the fireside of some independent mechanics. Hundreds, like the foolish Susan, are pursuing
the same course, and like her will ere long reap the bitter fruits of their folly.

Young Simpson was still a visitor at the house of Mr.
Elder, who, with his wife, always welcomed him. They
loved him as a son, and they could never think of the
treatment of their daughter to him without sorrow and
regret; but they still hoped that she would change in
her character and disposition as time passed away. But
their hopes were never realized. When Susan was about
twenty years of age, a young officer appeared in the
neighborhood, dressed in the extreme of fashion, and
made quite a parade. The moment Susan saw him, she
determined in her own mind that he should become her
husband, if it were possible. She would take particular
pains to see and be seen by him; and entertaining two
or three evening parties, the fine young gentleman was
a favored guest. Such efforts on the part of Susan were
not unavailing; they had their desired effect. It was
not long before the officer became a constant visitor at
the house of Mr. Elder, and the foolish girl was daily
seen hanging on his arm, perambulating the public
streets. Such airs as they assumed, dressed in the extreme of fashion, made many of the staid inhabitants of
the town look on them with wonder and astonishment;

and the old ladies, as usual, prophesied that no good would come of the affair. The young officer had plenty of money, was reputed to be the son of a very wealthy gentleman, who would probably at his decease leave him his whole estate. But to the more sober and intelligent of the people, he appeared to be exceedingly illiterate and coarse in his manners; but Susan was so deeply smitten with his dress, and what she considered his gentility, that she thought of but little else.

Without recording the preliminaries of the affair, it is sufficient to state that the day was appointed for the marriage of Susan to the captain. Although Susan's parents had been bitterly opposed to the match, they finally gave their consent, and every thing seemed to move on prosperously and harmoniously. The day that was to complete the happiness of Susan arrived, the hour had come, and the assembly was together, and they were married. Henry was present on the occasion; but, as he was a man in every sense of the word, and had generous feelings, and possessed a noble heart, he did not faint away, nor, on the occasion, exclaim, "My early love is lost; there now is no happiness for me!" No; but, like a true philosopher, who looks on the sorrows and the disappointments of life with a correct eye, he thought it was all for the best, and would not, if he could, change the scene before him. Unlike hundreds in a similar case, he did not treat with contempt the companion of Susan. Although the captain was not a favorite with him, having no partiality to the airs he put on, or to the trappings of dress, he treated him with due respect. So much, however, could not be said of the captain.

The day of the wedding passed off pleasantly, and the

next, when there was a rumor circulated through the place that Captain Henley was not in truth the officer he represented himself to be ; for the report was, that a poor pauper had arrived in town, who had boldly declared that the reputed captain was his own son. Curiosity was on tiptoe to ascertain the truth of what the old gentleman said ; and not a few who had seen and despised the conduct of Susan, and who had been shunned on account of their industrious habits, we have no doubt, wished it might prove as the old man stated. But the report was not fully believed, till the pauper was seen wending his way to the dwelling of Mr. Elder. On his rapping at the door, who should appear but Susan herself, who, vexed that such a creature should not enter by the back way, instantly ordered him there, and shut the door in his face.

"O Charles," said she to her husband, "what a dirty, miserable vagabond I have just driven from the door ! What do you suppose the ugly wretch wants ? I do wish you would send him from the backdoor."

"Certainly," said the captain ; but who can tell his surprise and chagrin when he beheld before him his poor old father, who sprang to embrace a long-lost son. What could he do ? where fly ? what say ? His deception, his fraud, all that he had done, rushed at once into his mind, and he wished for annihilation. He pushed the old man from him, exclaiming, "Begone ; I know you not."

"You are my son Dick. You villain, you rascal, to treat your father in this manner ! You know you stole a large amount when you ran away !" exclaimed the old man.

The noise brought Susan and her parents to the door,

and such a scene as ensued, we have not language to
describe. The coarse old father was belaboring his son
Dick, while the captain was motionless, not knowing
where to turn, or what to do, and the proud Susan
screaming and fainting, while her father and mother
were dumb with astonishment. The neighbors gathered round, and such a scene of confusion, of mortifica-
tion, was seldom witnessed. Some one throwing the
old man a few coppers, he waddled off, while Susan was
carried to her room in a state of insensibility. In the
confusion of the moment, the captain was not thought
of, and, on inquiry, it was ascertained that he was last
seen walking rapidly down the street. He had a large
amount of money in his possession, which he had bor-
rowed that very day from Mr. Elder. Besides this, Mr.
Elder had become responsible for him in various places,
which he was obliged to pay. It was ascertianed that
the captain had ever been an unprincipled and thiev-
ish character; that he had even stolen the dress which
so captivated the foolish Susan, and won her heart. His
parents were miserable beings, intemperate and filthy,
and had long been supported in the poorhouse, and their
son was brought up in ignorance and sin, and never
had a quarter's schooling in his life. It was never known
to a certainty whither he went, or what finally became
of him, but it was currently reported that Dick had been
detected and was punished for some highly criminal offence, and finally came to a miserable end in the state's
prison.

It was many months before the foolish Susan could
be induced to see company; the affair had so mortified
her pride and broken down her spirits that she seemed
another being. It was the town's talk; and no one

pitied the haughty girl. It was a just punishment for her folly. She had despised the laboring man and the mechanic, to become the wife of the son of a wretched pauper, who was a thief and a scoundrel, who had wronged her father, and ruined herself.

Henry Simpson, as was his custom, continued to call on his friends, the parents of Susan. It was some time after the affair before the haughty girl would see the mechanic, who once loved her and had hoped to make her his bride. The circumstance of her folly was never mentioned by Henry in her presence, and he treated her with the utmost kindness. Every opportunity Susan could get, she would express the warmest attachment to her early friend. She made him presents; did little favors unsolicited, and really seemed to be strongly attached to the youth. But it was too late now to hope for any thing but friendship. Henry had secured the affections of the daughter of a neighbor, and expected soon to be united to her. Still Susan hoped it would be otherwise, that Henry would yet recall his early love, and become her partner. She never relinquished this hope entirely until the day that Henry was married. Then she yielded almost to despair. She felt that she could censure none but herself; that she alone was the author of her misfortunes. It was her own folly that destroyed her. Once she was surrounded by every thing desirable in life, the cup of happiness was within her reach; but alas! alas, for human pride and folly, she cast it away, and wrought her own destruction.

While her parents lived, Susan was in comfortable circumstances, and she lacked for no care or attention; but when they died, the little property that was left was soon lost by mismanagement, and finally, without any

34

means of support, poor Susan was compelled to go to the almshouse, where she has been for many a long year. Few remember the time of her prosperity, but everybody has heard the tale of her woes and the fall of her pride. Old Susan has nearly reached the age of fourscore years, and, according to the course of nature, cannot long survive. When she goes hence, who will mourn her departure? Who will shed a tear over her grave?

From the story of Susan many a female can learn an instructive and useful lesson. In our cities and large towns there are hundreds walking in the same course, and who, unless they learn from the fate of others, and abjure pride and folly in all their ramifications, will come to an end as miserable. If your parents are wealthy, this is no excuse for you to hold high your heads, and cast contempt upon those who labor for a support. You have yet to learn that riches may take to themselves wings and fly away, while industry, worth, and integrity, will rise and go far beyond your standard of refinement and respectability. It is often the case with those who make the most show and parade, that when their debts are paid, they have not a sixpence left to help themselves with. If you would not learn by dear-bought experience, we pray you to discard your notions of true worth and merit, and understand that the seat of true virtue lies in the heart and not in exterior grace, high-sounding titles, or fashionable dresses. Despise not, neither look with contempt upon, an honest and worthy man, no matter what may be his employment, or who may be his parents. If he is virtuous, industrious, and intelligent, he will make a good companion, a kind friend, or an affectionate husband. He is really worth double the man who has nothing to bring you but what you see before you, and thirty thousand dollars when his father dies. All know that wealth is desirable in such a world as this; but our peace and happiness should never be sacrificed at its shrine. A pleasant exterior and winning manners are not to be discarded; but when these alone make a man, or at least take the place of the real man, we should avoid them, and unite rather our destiny with honest rags. There is great danger, when a man is brought up to live upon others, without ever earning a copper himself, that he will turn out a vagabond or a pauper. But if property has been left him, and he has squandered it away, there is no hope that he will retrieve it again by his industry. But, on the other hand, if a young man has been early taught to earn his own living, and to depend upon himself, the presumption is that he will accumulate property, and become independent. Let females, then, govern themselves accordingly, when their hands are solicited in marriage. Where intelligence and moral worth appear to be equal in the rich and the poor man, by all means choose the latter. If you have a few thousands to bring to your husband, be sure the latter will retain it and add to it, while the former may squander it away. If you are poor, and have nothing but modesty and culinary habits to present your lover — which indeed are more valuable than gold — be sure to take the poor man, and you will never see the day that you regret your choice.

In thus doing you will find it for your interest and happiness; make idleness and titles unfashionable, while you elevate all that is worth elevating — all that is ennobling in human nature.

THE BARKEEPER.

Intemperance! the imp that first
From the arch demon came;
That every glorious thing has scathed
With his sharp tongue of flame.

"When will father come home?" inquired Sarah Johnson of her mother, just as the old wooden clock had told the hour of ten.

"I cannot tell, my child," replied her mother. "I expect him every moment."

"But where has he gone that he should stay so late, when he told me he would return in less than an hour with my medicine?"

"I am afraid, Sarah, that he stopped into old Sanborn's, and has been persuaded to drink; but I hope not."

"I cannot think that father would drink to-night, when he knows that I am suffering for the medicine."

"I trust it is not so; but when a man is accustomed to drink, he forgets his obligations to his family and does not realize the sorrow he brings upon them."

Mrs. Johnson was a hard-working woman; her husband for some years had been in the habit of using spirituous liquors, and for a few months past she noticed that the habit grew stronger and stronger, so that not unfrequently he came home intoxicated. In the village where they resided, there was but one individual who would so degrade himself as to retail rum, and that was " Old Sanborn," as he was called, a man about sixty years of age, who had amassed a handsome property from the income of his bar. Although the wives of the intemperate and the friends of the moderate drinkers had often laid before him the evils of his course, and endeavored to persuade him to relinquish his traffic, he seemed perfectly calloused to reason and humanity.

" It is in the line of my business to retail spirit," he would remark, " and so I shall continue to do as long as I have purchasers."

" But you are destroying the health of our friends, and ruining their families," the neighbors remarked, " and we cannot suffer this state of things without a word to you -- without entreating you to pull down your bar, and retail spirit no longer."

" That I will never do. It is no one's business what I sell. In this way I get a living and am able to support my family."

All that was said to old Sanborn had no effect upon him; he had grown gray in the business, and seemed determined to persist in his unholy traffic, regardless of the entreaties and remonstrances of his neighbors.

Sarah Johnson, a girl of about twelve years, had long been confined to the house by sickness, and on the night in question was more ill than usual. A physician had prescribed some medicine, and after supper her father had gone to obtain it. But hour after hour went by, and he came not, although the girl was suffering for the articles. The clock struck eleven, when the little girl said, as she raised herself in bed, " I am afraid father

has met with some accident. I wish we had some one
to send and see what has become of him."

"I think he will be here soon," said the anxious
mother. "I am fearful he has stopped at Sanborn's,
and that he is passing his time with those miserable
men who meet there night after night to drink and tell
foolish stories."

Mrs. Johnson had hardly spoken, before the door
opened, and in came her husband. His looks told plainly
that the intoxicating cup had been no stranger to him.

"O father! where have you been all this time?" said
Sarah; "I have waited and waited for you, and thought
some accident must have happened to you to keep you
so long. Where have you been?"

"I stopped a moment or two in Sanborn's shop, that's
all," said he, as he staggered to a chair.

Sarah burst into tears when she saw the condition of
her father, while her poor mother could hardly refrain
from weeping; nor could she learn from her husband
any thing about the medicine he had gone to purchase.
After considerable effort, he was safe in bed.

The next morning, Mrs. Johnson ascertained that
the money she had given her husband to buy medicine
for the sick daughter had been expended for rum at
Sanborn's. It was all the money she had in the world,
and this she earned by spinning. Where to obtain the
means to purchase the articles for the child she did not
know. A little change would be due her from a neighbor in a few days, but she was fearful that before then
her daughter would experience severe illness in waiting for the medicine. When Mr. Johnson was expos-
tulated with by his wife for his conduct, he did not
manifest any sorrow, neither did he exert himself to

assist his sick child. Rum had calloused his affections, and home and wife and child had no attractions for him. He merely went to his house for his meals and lodging, and cared not for the sorrows and the sufferings he had brought upon them. Once it was not so; he was the best of husbands and fathers; he loved his home, and exerted himself to promote the happiness and welfare of his family. But within a few months how changed! The spirit of love and kindness had given place to indifference and neglect.

The next day, Sarah appeared to be more unwell. " I am sorry," said she, " father did not buy the medicine for me;" and, seeing her mother shedding tears, she said, "I can get along without it. I hope I shall be better soon, and then I can assist you."

" I trust you will, my child. If you were only well, I might sometimes go out to work, and could earn enough to support us well, even if your father persisted in his present course."

"And I could do a great deal myself. I know I could earn something."

In a day or two, Mrs. Johnson was able to purchase the medicine for her child, but it seemed to produce but little effect. Sarah was still feeble, could eat but a trifle, and her strength was exhausted. Some days she would not rise from her bed, while at other times she appeared quite smart. She had been complaining for some months, and doubtless grew weaker day by day.

Mr. Johnson persisted in his intemperate course ; he earned but little, and this he expended foolishly, without assisting in the least his suffering family.

One morning Mrs. Johnson saw old Sanborn passing the house. She went to the door and invited him in.

"Sir," said she, after he was seated, "I have asked you in to beg of you one favor, that is, not to let my husband have any spirit from your shop."

"Why, madam," said the old fellow, "as to that, I can't refuse gentlemen who call at my bar. I keep shop to accommodate the people of the village, and am bound to let them have what they call for, providing they pay me for it. Your next-door neighbor may call me in and request me not to let her husband have any more coffee or tea, because she don't like it."

"You know the effects of rum, Mr. Sanborn, as well as I; but you know not, and I pray you never may, the sorrow it has brought upon me. Look at that child," pointing to her sick daughter in bed, "her sufferings have been more than I can describe, caused by the intemperance of her father. She has been deprived of medicine, and sometimes of the necessaries of life, when the money has gone into your pocket, which should have been expended for our family. Can you censure me for feeling as I do, and entreating you not to furnish my husband with the means of intoxication?"

"O sir!" said Sarah, looking the old man in the face, "could you realize how much my poor mother suffers, I know you would not have a heart to sell rum to my father. I am sick, and can say but little, but I do wish you would not let my father have any more rum."

"I think you are all foolish, talking as you do, as if I was to blame because Mr. Johnson drinks. 'Tisn't my fault, and no blame should be attached to me."

"Yes, sir, you are to blame," said the mother. "Suppose you did not keep rum for sale; there is no other store in the village where it can be purchased, and consequently, we should have no drunkards in town."

"If I should give up my bar, it would not be long before somebody else would open a store and sell spirit, and I should lose the best part of my custom."

"I do not think any one else in the place would sell it; but if you will refuse to let my husband have spirit, you will not be the loser in the end, I assure you."

"No, I can't do it, and what is more, I sha'n't," said old Sanborn, and, seizing his hat in a pet, he left the house, muttering to himself till he had reached the street.

"What I can do I know not," said Mrs. Johnson to Sarah; "there is no hope that Sanborn will give up the sale of spirit, and as long as he keeps it I am afraid your father will drink."

"Mother, we must bear it as well as we can, and perhaps something may yet take place, and we again be happy."

A few days after this conversation, Mrs. Johnson, on looking from the window, observed a team going by with a hogshead upon it. It struck her at once that it was new rum for old Sanborn. Nor did she mistake; it went directly to his shop and was rolled in. "It is abominable," thought she. "There is enough spirit there to ruin the whole village, and something must be done or we shall all come to want."

With such feelings, she called upon her nearest neighbor and told her what she had seen.

"It appears that Sanborn is determined to ruin us all," said she, "and it is high time that the traffic in ardent spirits in our village should come to an end. A great deal has been done in other places, as I understand, and hundreds of inebriates have been reclaimed. What can we do?"

"I feel that something should be done immediately," said her neighbor, "for I have a family of sons growing up, and they are just as likely to be enticed into the grog-shop as the children of my neighbors. I will do any thing I can to prevent the sale of spirits."

Mrs. Johnson called on several neighbors, and found they all entertained but one opinion, and this was, that Sanborn's shop was a nuisance to the village, and that he ought to be prohibited from selling rum. She went home encouraged, and a thought struck her at once. "Mr. Sanborn must give up the sale of spirit. If he will not do it willingly, I will see what I can do. He has almost ruined my family."

It was a cold day in November. About four o'clock in the afternoon, Mrs. Johnson put on her cloak and bonnet and walked down to old Sanborn's. As she went in, she saw her husband just put down a glass, the contents of which he had drank, and several other men were in the act of drinking. Calling Sanborn aside, she said, "I wish to speak to my husband. Will you call your friends into the next room, and let me speak a word to him?"

"Oh, yes, yes," said he, and turning to his friends, he requested them to step into the adjoining room. They all obeyed him.

"Husband," said Mrs. Johnson, "I wish you would go home immediately."

Feeling ashamed, he passed out the door. No sooner was the room clear, than Mrs. Johnson turned every rum-faucet in the shop. Gin, brandy, and new rum mingled with the dirt on the floor, while she followed her husband home.

In fifteen or twenty minutes, Old Sanborn entered the shop, and to his surprise found the floor covered with spirit and every cask empty.

With an oath, he contemplated what had been done, breathing out vengeance on the poor woman he had driven to perpetrate such an act. His friends did not open their mouths, but passed into the street. "I'm glad of it!" they each and all exclaimed. Although they had patronized the old retailer, in their hearts they felt that he was wrong, and now their indignation was kindled against him. "I never felt so rejoiced at any thing in my life," one of them remarked to the rest. "Nor I," said another. "Nor I," said a third. "We should have a day set apart to rejoice over what Mrs. Johnson has done," said they all. As they separated to go to their several homes, they each concluded never to patronize a rumseller again.

When Mrs. Johnson reached her home, she told her husband what she had done, but he, instead of reproving her, said, "It is good enough for the old rascal. I hope the lesson will be a useful one, and that he will never attempt to keep another bar and continue to get away money from the poor."

"I am glad to hear you talk so," said his wife; "and why will you not resolve to drink no more from this time? It would be a happy season for me, for our poor child, and for yourself."

"I will drink no more."

"O father, how happy we shall be!" said the child. "We shall enjoy what we used to when you brought things home for us, and always looked so pleasant, and spoke kindly to me."

The wife and the daughter wept for joy, while the husband himself could not restrain his tears.

From that day Mr. Johnson was an altered man. He really felt that his past conduct had been a source of great grief to his family, and he strove with all his might to live as become those who see the error of their ways and repent as in dust and ashes. In a day or two he obtained work, and all his earnings were carried into his family. His daughter, after several weeks, was restored to health. Peace and contentment reigned in their dwelling. The gloom that for months had settled over their heads gave place to sunshine and warmth. They are now contented and happy, and have found that enjoyment which for a long time was denied them.

Old Sanborn was exceedingly wroth at the loss of his liquor, swore vengeance on the head of her he had made worse than a widow, and declared he would again fill his shop with spirit, and supply the whole neighborhood. Immediately he sent for a cask of new rum, and a quantity of other spirits. After a few days it came, and in rolling the hogshead into his shop, the plank broke and it fell; the head was stove in, and all its contents soaked into the earth. The old fellow was so angry, that he threw his brandy and gin glasses on the ground, exclaiming, "The curse of God is on me. I will never sell another glass of spirits." Old Sanborn kept good his word; he became perfectly temperate, forsook all his bad habits, and the last we heard of him, he had been appointed to deliver a lecture on temperance on the anniversary of the society in his village.

www.ingramcontent.com/pod-product-compliance
Lightning Source LLC
Chambersburg PA
CBHW020240110726

47898CB00004B/1340